I0554322

# THE BOX
PUPPETS AND PUPPETEERS

C.C. Monö

Black Chair Publishing

STOCKHOLM, SWEDEN

Black Chair Publishing
Stockholm, Sweden

Publisher's Note: This is a work of fiction. Names, characters, places, and incidents are a product of the author's imagination. Locales and public names are sometimes used for atmospheric purposes. Any resemblance to actual people, living or dead, or to businesses, companies, events, institutions, or locales is completely coincidental.

THE BOX/ C.C. Monö – 1st ed.
ISBN 978-91-983963-8-6

To Cindy, Zoey and Emmy with love.

Twenty-two-year-old Axel Hallman is admitted to the highly esteemed Eagle King's Academy as one of twelve students. Flown to Brussels, he's catapulted into a world filled with luxury, gruelling trainings, and dark secrets. In this world built on lies, ambition and egotism, he's primed to become one of the most influential and powerful leaders of his time. The only problem is – Axel never wanted to become a ruler.

Soon it's clear that Axel isn't the only one at odds with The Academy. A network called The Box lurks in the shadows. They know a great deal about Axel's hatred for The EKA, but their agenda remains unknown.

Summer arrives and the students face their midterm exams. Axel gets the lowest score of all students. Frustrated and disappointed he makes a decision. He's going to quit.

When the management assistant, Nicole Swan, finds out about his plans, she decides to intervene. She knows what happened to a former student who decided to quit, Sarah Wangai. The Academy killed her.

"The measure of a man is what he does with power."
*Plato*

## CHAPTER 1

Good God! What have I done?

The thought echoed through Nicole's mind as her high heels struck the marble floor, shattering the stillness of the night. What have I done?

In the dimmed light of the crystal chandeliers, she passed a gold statue of vast proportions. The crowned eagle peered out over the grand foyer, its wings spread wide as if ready to attack. With the exception of the armed guards hiding among the shadows, the reception area was deserted for the night. Well, almost deserted. A tall man was waiting for her by the elevators, standing next to a gigantic pillar.

"Ms Swan," he said in his thick Irish accent.

His piercing blue eyes fell upon her chest for a second, but it was a second too long. Nicole gave the man a dimpled smile and bowed. "Good evening, Professor Jackson," she chirped. "Taking a break from the party?"

"Not willingly," he replied with an indifferent expression. Still, the sharpness of his tone tickled her fear. "You didn't answer your phone?"

Nicole looked down at her beautiful 1970s vintage gown, sparkling in rose-gold. "I didn't know where to put it, sir."

The man's nostrils flared. "Watch it," he snarled. When she didn't reply, he stepped away from the pillar and made a half-hearted nod towards the elevators. "Come. Let's go."

"I'm sorry, sir, but I was requested to the principal's office."

Professor Jackson glared at her. Although his face was calm, she guessed he was struggling with his emotions. Nicole had worked long enough with the man to know he wanted to be the principal of The Academy, not the *assistant* principal. Anything that reminded him that he wasn't at the very top tended to annoy him.

"I said you're coming with me," he declared. "We're going to the Lounge."

Without a sound two guards appeared behind Nicole, their faces stern and attentive.

"I see," she replied, struggling to maintain her smile as worry spread through her heart.

The Lounge was situated between the fourth and fifth floors. To be specific, it hung along the top, western wall of the restaurant, also known as the great hall. Regular employees, including Nicole who was the management assistant, weren't allowed to enter the Lounge uninvited. It was a place where teachers and management went to relax.

Nicole glanced at Professor Jackson as they took the elevator. As always, he was groomed to perfection. In honour of the End of Term Dinner, he wore an exquisite tuxedo. His shoes were polished into mirrors, and his bow tie threatened to flap its wings in pride. He was a despicable man but no one would question his loyalty to The EKA.

When the golden wing-shaped doors slid aside, the professor stepped out and placed his palm against a panel by a wooden door. It swung open; a sweet, smoky fragrance swept out and bid them welcome. "Stay here," he ordered the guards.

The Lounge had a colonial style to it with dark mahogany furniture, thick rugs and leather armchairs, all of it bathing in cosy lights.

Nicole glanced at the bar and felt her skin prickle with fear. The place was unattended. No one else was here.

Professor Jackson walked over to the two-way mirror overlooking the great hall. With his hands behind his back, he gazed out over the students and staff below. "I'm a man who observes things," he stated. "Small, important things. Like Mr

Hallman leaving the party and you following him a few minutes later."

He turned and walked towards her in a slow, calculating manner that made her skin crawl. "You met him in the foyer, at the relaxation area. Why?"

His sharp cologne forced itself on her, grabbing and groping every inch of her body. It made her feel violated, and the air around her grew thick as soup.

"I…"

At that moment, the door to the Lounge opened. A short gentleman in his sixties strode in, his round spectacles trembling upon the tip of his nose. The Academy's legendary Principal Cunningham smiled. "Ah, you're here," he declared and unbuttoned his tuxedo jacket.

Nicole had often reflected upon the fact that the headmaster and his assistant principal were different in almost every aspect. Principal Cunningham was short, had a double chin and a barren scalp. Unlike his subordinate, he was neither moody, aggressive, nor self-absorbed. While Nicole felt as though Professor Jackson had to struggle to uphold an air of aristocracy, Principal Cunningham exerted a natural poise of dignity and grace. He had mesmerised the entire world with his calm confidence. He was the leader of leaders, powerful beyond words, yet he radiated a gentleness that Nicole, and many with her, admired.

Professor Jackson cleared his throat, snapping Nicole out of her thoughts. "Ms Swan was about to explain herself," he said, his words sharp and poisonous.

The principal raised a bushy brow and eyed Nicole with interest. "Go on, Ms Swan. I'm listening."

Nicole turned her body away from Professor Jackson as if he didn't exist, knowing it would annoy the hell out of him. "Well, sir, I was at the party when Mr Hallman left. I could tell he was upset. He's had a rough time, and I thought he needed someone to talk to."

"You know you can't meddle with Mr Hallman's training," Principal Cunningham said in his calm voice. "He needs to find his own path, or he'll never be the leader he's expected to be."

Nicole nodded and looked down at her feet. Guilt clawed itself through her heart. She had betrayed The Academy.

* * *

Professor Jackson clamped his jaw shut. Nicole had turned her back to him in the most arrogant manner. The woman was like a thorn in the arse; a constant pain that wouldn't go away. While annoying students graduated and left, irritating staff members lingered on and on. At least until he could find a way to get rid of them.

Over by the two-way mirror, Principal Cunningham stood silent for a moment, his eyes drilling deep into Nicole's. "Of all places, why did you meet Mr Hallman by the pond?"

"Well, sir, I thought Mr Hallman would be more open and honest if we spoke without being monitored."

"Honest?" Professor Jackson huffed. "With you? A management assistant?"

"I was willing to give it a try, sir."

"What did he say?" Principal Cunningham asked.

Nicole's expression turned grim. "We were interrupted before he could say much." She glanced at Professor Jackson as if to say, 'and that is your fault.'

The nerve of that woman!

"Still," she continued, "he did tell me something alarming. He said he's going to quit."

A horrific silence fell over the Lounge. Professor Jackson's mind reeled back to a very disappointing moment twelve years ago when a student named Sarah Wangai had decided to quit her studies. Despite her potential, she hadn't had the heart to become a ruler. In the end, they'd been forced to neutralise her. It wouldn't do to have a student who thought The Academy wasn't good enough for them. It would've ruined their reputation. Everyone knew that The EKA never failed.

"What did you say?" the principal asked, eyes locked on Nicole.

"I told him it was a bad idea."

"Did you now?" Professor Jackson glowered at her. "Did you tell him *why* it's a bad idea?"

"You mean did I tell him it would kill him?" Nicole gave him an innocent smile. "Of course not."

"Very well." Principal Cunningham withdrew a handkerchief from his pocket and rubbed his nose. "I appreciate the information, Ms Swan. Please keep a close eye on Mr Hallman during the students' end of term holiday in Italy. Should he approach you regarding his situation or his feelings, stop him at once and call me. Do not speak to him. Understood?"

"Yes, sir," Nicole replied and curtsied.

"Splendid. Then you may leave."

Once Nicole had left, Professor Jackson turned to his boss. "I hope you realise she needs to be punished, sir. We must set an example. If we turn a blind eye to this unacceptable behaviour, what will she do next?"

"You still don't understand, do you?" the principal said with an amused tone. Stepping up to the two-way mirror, he looked out at the students below. "We've failed with wild-cards before, because you assume they think and act like regular students. They don't."

"Sir!"

The principal raised a finger in warning. "No. I don't want to hear your excuses. Unacceptable or not, Ms Swan did the right thing to check up on him. After all, you didn't do it."

May the devil take the man and shove a pitchfork up his wrinkled arse! Professor Jackson felt himself get pulled towards the flames of anger. "We're not running a day-care centre, sir. I saw him leave, but treating him like a child won't help him evolve. Even wild-cards must adapt to the world outside."

"That's where you're wrong, Professor. Wild-cards do not adapt to the world. They change it."

"Bah! Let's not argue about semantics. To change the world, one must first understand it. That means learning how to adapt and conform. We can't send Mr Hallman into the world with his doubts and uncertainty. If he doesn't toughen up, he'll be eaten alive. Besides, The Seven will never accept a student who can't be controlled."

"Indeed, Professor, but we must control him without killing his instincts."

"What instincts?" Professor Jackson barked. "Questioning the importance of what we do here? Running away like a baby when he gets a bad grade? Where is that power you and the analysts keep promising? The determination? I sure as hell haven't seen it! Have you?"

At last, the principal's smile vanished. It was almost a relief until the man seemed to grow a foot taller and he began to speak.

"I advise you to be very careful, Professor Jackson. Like you, I am disappointed with Mr Hallman's lack of development, but I don't blame him. It's *your* job to ensure our students evolve according to plan." The principal paused and raised his left brow. "Tell me, who do you think I'll get rid of first? The prodigy who hasn't progressed, or the professor who is unable to teach him?"

CHAPTER 2

The candles flickered, and the young man leaned over to grab his cup of coffee. "Are, we certain about the location?"

"Yes." Cat pushed her empty plate aside and spread out a map on the table. "Falcon sent me the coordinates this morning." She squinted and leaned closer. "Right...there." She jabbed a slender finger at a point on the printed satellite map. "We've been keeping the place under surveillance for about eight months."

The young man turned his attention to a set of photos scattered next to the map. "What a pigsty."

"I guess that's why they chose it. It's our job to come up with a plan to infiltrate the place. It shouldn't be difficult to access. Doing it unnoticed is a different matter."

Leaning forward, the young man observed the map with great focus, but behind his composed façade bubbled a shameful excitement. This was his and Cat's chance to impress the senior members; to prove they had what it took to be a central part of The Box.

Cat looked at him and blew aside a strand of copper blonde hair. "I've made a few calls this morning. Pixie is up to her neck in work. She and her agents are helping Thor to organise everything for the next few weeks.

"As to Falcon, he and his hackers are also swamped with work. They'll provide us with any necessary documents or IT support we need, but that's it. As to our fathers, they're focusing on Axel."

The young man scratched his chin. He could feel Cat watching him in the golden light of the candles. "In other words, it's up to us?"

"Indeed it is."

"Well?" He smiled. "Where do we begin?"

Cat leaned in and gave him a warm kiss, her soft lips tasting of wine. "We start from the beginning," she declared. "We create a set of plans depending on the most likely outcomes. Then we'll let the seniors choose. We have six months to get it all done."

CHAPTER 3

Large cypress trees lined the final stretch of the road. At the top of the hill, the two eight-seat Cadillacs passed through a pair of wide gates, guarded by armed women in red uniforms. Axel glanced at Nicole Swan who was sitting in the front of the bus. He needed to speak with her. Alone.

He was considering what he would say, when Thabo leaned over him, blocking his view.

"Nice," the man said in a placid voice as he peered out at the magnificent, illuminated mansion. "Not bad at all."

Axel gave a stiff smile. Of all the students at The Academy, Thabo was the only one resembling a friend. He was kind, even helpful at times, and not many people within The Academy were. Nicole being the exception, of course.

His eyes returned to the beautiful woman at the front of the bus. He really needed to talk to her.

The sun had said its goodnight and vanished behind the Tuscan horizon. Still, a warm breeze swept over Axel as he followed Thabo out the vehicles, greeted by the crickets' monotonous song.

A wrinkled old woman appeared at the double doors to the mansion, drying her hands on an apron. Following her were three young men who hurried over to unload the students' bags with superb efficiency. The woman's eyes found Nicole's and she brightened. *"Benvenuta, Signorina Swan."*

Axel watched Nicole as she replied in rapid Italian, making the other woman laugh. She's one hell of an assistant, he thought. Confident, skilled, beautiful—

"Leaders," Nicole called, interrupting his thoughts as well as the merry conversations around her. "Welcome to La Villa Rossa, or the Red Villa. Some believe the name originates from the mid-eighteenth century, when a band of robbers murdered a young merchant and his wife at this very location. Although it's an amusing tale, the name probably comes from the spectacular rose garden at the back, which is more than a hundred years old.

"As to the building itself, it's used as summerhouse by a former student of ours. This person has been kind enough to let us use the premises for the next two weeks."

"Summerhouse?" Dalilah whispered to Thabo. "It looks like a bloody castle."

Pointing towards a sea of light shimmering atop a nearby hill, Nicole continued, "Over there is Volterra, a charming little town with old buildings and tiny alleyways. We shall visit it together. Oh, that reminds me. If you want to leave the premises, you'll need approval from Mr Nakata and his security team. You may not leave the grounds by yourself. Smaller groups of three or more are fine, but you'll need to inform me first so we can organise with the security clearance."

For a brief moment, Nicole's eyes met Axel's. "I believe that's it," she said with a jovial tone. "All that's left for me to do, is to show you your rooms. Shall we?"

* * *

They stepped into a large vestibule with red-tiled flooring and yellow painted walls. It was exactly as she remembered it, jam-packed with fantastic Italian arts and artefacts.

Nicole took the students up a wide staircase curving up along the right wall.

"Who's the owner of this place?" Axel's voice cut through the chatter, and all of a sudden, he was walking next to her, his aftershave nibbling at her senses.

"Someone who wants to remain unknown, Mr Hallman," she said with a little wink.

The sound of his laughter warmed her heart.

"Why would a former student want to remain unknown to *us*?" With a choleric expression glued on her chiselled face, Izabella Martins squeezed herself between Axel and Nicole. In the process, she brushed her chest against Axel.

The young woman moved, not with grace but with determination. It was in her blood. Izabella came from a wealthy family. She'd started a marketing and advertising agency at the age of fifteen. Two years later she sold it and became a millionaire.

"Well?" the young Brazilian demanded, staring at Nicole.

"I wouldn't know, Ms Martins," Nicole replied in a gentle tone and continued up the stairs. "I only follow orders."

She didn't like Izabella very much, although she couldn't say why. There was something about the woman that made her uneasy. And, if she was completely honest, it bothered her that Izabella had a thing for Axel. He deserved someone better.

As soon as the thought entered her mind, she pushed it away. She had no right to think such thoughts. She was an assistant, nothing more.

They reached the top of the stairs and stood between two long corridors that ran in opposite directions. "The left wing is private and off limits," Nicole explained. "Come. Your rooms are in the right wing. Let me show you."

She had placed Axel at the end of the corridor, in the largest of all the guest rooms. Not that it was very big; only twenty or so square metres. It had cream-coloured walls, Italian artwork and a king-sized bed so inviting it had to be illegal.

"Do you like it, sir?" she asked.

He ran a hand over the old wooden desk, before peering into a small restroom. "It's nice," he concluded.

It was hard to tell what he was feeling. Just as Axel could display warmth and sincerity, he could put on a mask of complete blankness.

"Do you know what I miss the most about my old life?" he

wondered aloud.

"No, sir."

"Privacy." He was standing in front of a built-in bookshelf, looking at titles resting upon the shelves.

"Oh." Nicole found her smile stiffen a little. "I understand. You must be exhausted. I'll see you at dinner."

She turned to leave and heard him laugh. "No, Ms Swan. I wasn't referring to your company." His unusual grey eyes glistened. "I'm tired, that's all. Tired of always being watched and evaluated."

"Oh," she said again, this time with a disgraceful sense of relief. "Well, there are no cameras or microphones here. This is a private residence and you are here on holiday, not to be monitored."

A frown rippled across his face followed by apparent confusion. "I don't want to be rude, Ms Swan, but I'm finding that hard to believe."

"I understand your scepticism, sir," Nicole laughed. "But you're not under surveillance here."

She fell silent as a short man knocked on the open door. "Good evening, sir," he said at a near whisper and bowed. "I'm here with your bag."

"You can put it over there." Axel nodded towards the wardrobe.

"Shall I unpack, sir?"

"Not right now. Can you do it during dinner?"

"Certainly, sir." The servant bowed.

When they were alone again, Axel looked at Nicole with an apprehensive glimmer in his eyes. "We need to talk."

"Indeed we do," she replied, "but dinner is in thirty minutes. We'll talk tonight."

CHAPTER 4

FOUR YEARS EARLIER

He was, as someone would put it, between the devil and the deep blue sea. Hayato Sano had made an awful mistake. Three actually. First, he'd let himself be drawn into a game of power he couldn't control. Second, he'd disobeyed The Box. Third...well...he hadn't done the third yet, but he would. Tonight. It too would be a mistake, but what choice did he have? No matter what he did, he'd suffer.

Running a hand over his slim jaw, Hayato glanced down at the map of Sri Lanka. On the surface he had it all. He was twenty-five years old, an EKA graduate and the CEO of Francis Security, a global security company.

Since a few months back, the world knew him as the whiz kid who saved Francis Security from bankruptcy. He'd turned it into one of the most advanced and successful security companies in the world. It was quite a feat. Already, less than twenty-four hours after graduating, people were saying he was the best leader The Academy had ever produced.

*Produced.* What a disgusting word. It was true, but disgusting nonetheless.

The private jet made a slight turn to the right. Hayato looked away from the map and out over the ocean below. It was June 16. They'd left Tokyo seven hours ago. Since then they'd had a break from the hysteria that had engulfed the entire world. People gave more attention to an EKA graduation than an Olympic opening ceremony. It was absurd; absolutely outrageous.

"I can't believe it was only yesterday you graduated," Jerome said, shuffling through a thick pile of papers. "In fact, I still can't believe you were an EKA student." He pushed back his glasses and frowned. "Did you sign the contract with K-Trix?"

"Yes."

"I can't find it. Are you sure?"

"Positive."

Hayato had signed the contract three hours before the graduation ceremony had begun. He remembered this because The Box's little communication device had delivered the final message. *You know what you must do.* A simple statement, but *so* much weight to it.

*Yes,* he'd replied, but in the end, he hadn't done it. He'd been too afraid.

"Ah. Found it." Jerome's boyish face lit up and his eyes scanned the document. "Fantastic. I can't believe you pulled it off. We're now twice the size from yesterday. Shall I inform the communication department that we're ready to meet the press?"

"Not yet. I want to wait until after tonight."

"As you wish, sir." Jerome looked at the document again. "I can't believe you did it."

Hayato smiled. Jerome was not part of The Academy and had little knowledge of how things worked. Sometimes that was refreshing. As his personal assistant, Jerome was brilliant, hardworking, bright and curious. He was twice the age of Hayato, though you could hardly tell by the looks of him.

"We arrive in Colombo at three, local time," Jerome continued, now looking at his computer. "You have six interviews before your dinner with Mr Ramanayake. We'll eat at the hotel restaurant to save time. Here's the agreement, by the way." Jerome handed Hayato a thick folder. "The meeting should be a mere formality, but Mr Ramanayake is known to be a bit whimsical. We have to be careful. Once he's signed the agreement, we can relax. Tomorrow we'll visit TechSec's headquarters to inform the staff. If all goes well, I'll give the communication department a heads up tonight, after the contract has been signed."

"Mhm."

"One more thing." Jerome scratched his freckled nose. "You also have an interview *after* dinner, at ten tonight."

"I know, Jerome, you told me a few hours ago."

"Sorry, sir. Better safe than sorry."

"So they say." Hayato unbuckled his seatbelt and got to his feet. The bodyguard provided by The Academy looked up from his book. Hayato gave the man a crooked smile. "Relax. I need to stretch my legs, but I promise not to leave the plane until we land."

Jerome laughed, but the bodyguard seemed unimpressed and turned back to his book.

After a few stretching exercises, Hayato slipped into the toilet. There, in the cramped space, he pulled out a note with a hand-drawn map of a hotel suite. Only a few hours left.

CHAPTER 5

# PRESENT DAY

It was after midnight and the air conditioner made such a racket, Izabella couldn't sleep. To make matters worse, the damn thing wouldn't cool the air properly. She turned it off and opened the windows. That brought in the mosquitos. Now she had the air conditioner off and the windows closed, which left her itchy with bites, sticky with sweat, and angry. Very angry.

She slapped her cheek as something bit her. A second later, the buzzing returned. She'd missed the little sucker, or maybe it was another one.

Cursing, she got out of bed and was about to turn on the lights when she heard something that made her stop, hand on the switch. The floorboards outside her door creaked. Someone else was up and about. She tiptoed over to her door and placed her ear against it. She could hear footsteps continue down the corridor. Careful not to make a sound, she turned the knob and eased the door open a fraction.

A graceful figure was moving through the low-lit corridor. Holding a pair of high heels in her right hand, she advanced on light feet. If it hadn't been for the soft moan of the floorboards, she might as well have hovered.

In a few steps, Nicole reached Axel's door. There she stopped and glanced back the way she'd come. Izabella held her breath. For a second she thought Nicole was looking right at her. Then the woman turned back and put on her shoes. After adjusting her black suit jacket, she gave Axel's door a gentle tap.

Izabella could feel her neck redden in rage as the door opened. One look at Axel's face and she knew; he had expected this visit.

* * *

"Hi," Nicole whispered with a little smile. "I'm sorry I couldn't come sooner. Is it too late?"

Damn, she was beautiful. She had everything; the high cheekbones, the full lips, the perfect nose…Axel caught himself staring at her. "No. Come on in."

After a quick glance down the corridor, she entered his room with that composed confidence he found so enthralling. He wanted to reach out and pull her close.

"I didn't mean for it to get this late," she explained. "I got stuck in a meeting."

"At this hour?"

"Unfortunately, it's not uncommon." Nicole strode over to the window and pulled the curtains shut with a quick tug. "It wouldn't do for anyone to see us now," she murmured. Then, to Axel's surprise, she stilled, one hand still clasping the edge of the soft fabric. "I…" Her voice faltered. Silence fell over the room as delicate as a silk shawl on a feathered bed.

"What's wrong?" he asked.

"You can't quit. They'll never allow it. It would ruin their reputation, and they'll rather have you dead than admit failure." Her posture lost some of its poise. "I mean that literally. They *will* kill you."

Without warning, a brutal weariness overcame Axel. It struck him so hard, he stepped back and dropped into an armchair, positioned in one corner.

Nicole turned. "You can't quit, yet nor can you continue as you have."

"Meaning?"

"Meaning that some of the teachers feel that you're questioning

The Academy. They say it's like 'having a priest questioning the existence of his God'. It's unacceptable."

Jesus. Axel rubbed his hands over his face. What was he to make of this? Was he facing another Academy test, or was Nicole trying to help him?

"You realise how absurd this is, don't you?" he said, choosing to neither reject nor accept Nicole's claims.

She was watching him with her lips parted a fraction, her long hair falling in waves over her shoulders. "Absurd or not, the management doesn't trust you," she replied. "That's why they push you harder than any other student. It's a matter of testing your willingness to be here."

"And if I quit, they'll kill me?"

"Yes." She crossed the floor and took a seat on the edge of the bed. "It's the most certain thing I know. They can't have a student who, by free will, chooses to leave. As the saying goes; 'The Academy never fails'."

"What do you suggest I do?" he asked after a brief pause.

His question seemed to surprise her. Perhaps she wasn't used to having people ask for her opinion. She bit the corner of her lip and was silent for a long time. "Well," she said at last, releasing the word as if it was a white dove. The corner of her eyes crinkled as she smiled. "Swimming away from the coast won't bring you closer to land."

"What does that mean?"

"It means that if you want things to change, you should stop questioning your teachers. I know it's easier said than done, but I think you need to find a way to impress the management."

To do that, I'll need to swallow my pride, Axel thought and felt a foul taste in the back of his throat. But if Nicole is right, what choice do I have?

He gave her a nod and realised he trusted her far more than he should. "I'll think about it."

Nicole wasn't happy with his answer, he could see that, but she nodded nonetheless. "Please do," she said and stood, her fingers playing with a gold bracelet around her wrist. "But I beg you; don't think too long. The Academy is not known for its patience."

That night, Axel lay awake for a long time, contemplating his precarious situation and considering his alternatives. He stared at the ceiling for hours. When the knock came at five o'clock in the morning, he felt as though he hadn't slept at all.

Thinking, or rather *hoping* it was Nicole, he swung his legs over the bed and grabbed his robe, but when he opened the door, no one was there. Peering into the dark corridor, he saw someone disappearing around the corner towards the stairs.

He considered following, when something caught his attention on the floor. Squatting, he found it was a small note with his name on it. With a frown, he unfolded it. *The Secret Garden of La Villa Rossa,* said the title, and beneath it was a detailed map.

* * *

Falcon stood erect, watching the distant sea as he enjoyed his coffee. It was a few hours until sundown, but the sky was already dark as night. Rain hammered against the massive windows. Soon, black clouds, filled with thunderous anger, would fall upon Borneo with purpose.

"Sir? I think we have a problem."

Falcon turned as Nelly came jogging up the stairs. "What kind of a problem?"

"We did a check to see if the list of guests had been published and noted a change in the code. The system has been upgraded." Nelly's eyebrows twitched with worry. "I had a chat with the ladies and they agree. We might not be able to hack into the system in time. You should come."

Following Nelly, Falcon steered his steps toward the workroom below. "When was the upgrade done?"

"Must have been an hour ago. Two tops."

"Explain the situation please. In terms I'll understand."

"They've changed their tracking system. Once an individual enters the party, we'll have no way to track their movements."

"We won't be able to see Axel?"

"We won't be able to see anyone."

"I see."

They entered a small and cramped basement. Nelly stepped over a box and rounded a bike. She reached for a pair of boots standing in a dusty corner. As she flipped the left one to its side, a section of the wall slid open. Together they entered the heart and soul of the bungalow; the workroom.

Although there were no windows, the place felt light and cosy. Expensive rugs covered the wooden floor. Over by the kitchenette, a kettle rumbled with its belly full of boiling water. None of the hackers paid them any attention. A frenetic tapping on keyboards filled Falcon's ears and drowned out the low music.

Falcon eyed the massive screen on the wall in front of him, watching the strings of code as they appeared.

"See?" Nelly asked and pointed.

"Can't say I do." Falcon smiled and glanced at a wall-mounted clock. "Five days, six hours and forty-two minutes left."

"We'll have it solved by then," one of the hackers promised, staring at her monitors. "Don't worry."

"When someone tells me not to worry, I worry."

"I mean that if we can't crack it, we'll have to find another way, that's all. This won't stop us."

Falcon picked up his phone. "Even so, we should inform Thor."

CHAPTER 6

The morning sun had already warmed the rose-scented winds as they swept over La Villa Rossa. Axel walked at a slow pace, heading away from the mansion. The premises held a myriad of narrow paths and secluded sub-gardens, all filled with nooks and crannies. He passed a gardener watering an orange tree and another trimming the hedge. They both bowed as he walked by.

Following the map, he crossed a lily pond over a red Japanese-inspired bridge. He made a left and continued through several topiary gardens, past impressive fountains and colourful flowerbeds, until he reached a rather gloomy place, enclosed by a thick wall of greenery.

In the centre of this strange place was a round flowerbed with nothing more than a single white rose. It stood in the dappled shade of a large canopy belonging to a great oak growing on the other side of the hedge.

Looking up from the map, he spotted a concrete bench. He made his way over and began searching behind it until he found a tiny gap in the otherwise impenetrable hedge. With a little laugh of surprise, Axel squeezed through. It was a tight fit, but soon the bushes gave way and he stepped out on a small grass terrace overlooking the valley below. He'd found the secret garden.

After shoving the map into his pocket, he looked around, not sure what to do next. There were no gazebos or large statues, no remarkable fountains or enigmatic ponds. It was no more than a few bushes and the large oak, under which stood another wooden bench. This one was white and a lot more detailed. It had a small gold sign attached to it. 'In memory of S.W.', it read. Axel considered the sign for a while, wondering what S.W. stood for.

His attention shifted as he spotted a metal railing sticking up behind a few bushes. Curiosity lured him over and he found a staircase made of stone leading down to a dirt trail. The students weren't supposed to leave the premises, but who'd know if he took a little stroll?

On quick feet he started to descend. The path coiled its way amid wild knee-high grass and old olive trees. When he reached the bottom of the valley, the trail sprung upon a small stream where old trees bent over the water as if thirsty. Insects fled his path as Axel followed the track through wide meadows and small patches of woodlands.

After about forty-five minutes he reached an old stone bridge. Here he came to a dead stop. Under a gnarled tree, by the edge of the river, sat a man watching the slow-moving water. Having no desire for conversation, Axel began to retreat.

"Hello, Axel," the man said with a calm and husky voice. "Found the secret garden, did you?" He had a slight accent that was difficult to place; American, mixed with something else.

Axel stood nailed to the ground. No EKA employee would ever address him by his first name.

The stranger turned and, in an instant, he was on his feet. "What would The Academy say if they knew you were out here on your own?" Wiping his hands on the worn jeans, the man advanced. He was tall, about the same height as Axel, but not as broad across his shoulders. He moved like a man who had nothing to fear, and such men were best avoided.

"You're very quiet," the stranger observed. He had a thick, blond beard, wore a bright red cap and large sunglasses.

"Who are you?"

The man smiled. "You can call me Thor."

Axel waited for more. Professor Jackson always said that 'a great leader never begs for information. He's given it'.

Thor scratched the bridge of his crooked nose. Axel observed the casual movement, noting the long fingers, the trimmed nails and the small cut on one of the knuckles.

"No offence, young man," Thor said, "but at this point, a sane person in your shoes would ask me why I'm here."

"No offence taken." Axel scowled. "After all, a sane person in *your* shoes would *tell* me why they're here." They would also, he added to himself, show an Academy leader some respect.

Thor adjusted his sunglasses "I guess you've got a point," he said. "I thought perhaps you were following one of Professor Jackson's idiotic instructions, the one about leaders demand information, not ask for it."

Axel felt a surge of embarrassment wash through him, but Thor didn't seem to notice. He laughed and shook his head. "The stupidity of The EKA never ceases to amaze me. Anyway, back to the question you never asked; why am I here? Well, there are two answers to that question; purpose and location. Regarding the purpose, I wanted to introduce myself. As to the location, I chose it because it's secluded. The road here is seldom used, and we're far enough from La Villa Rossa to avoid any unnecessary risks. You got the map, I assume."

"It was you?"

"Not really. I had one of Lorena De Paz's servants deliver it for me. Not everyone is fond of her, you know."

"De Paz?" Axel knitted his brows. The name rang a bell.

"She's the owner of La Villa Rossa. You remember her, don't you? A former EKA student. Participated in the killing of Sarah Wangai. That last part is unofficial, of course. The Academy threw Sarah off a roof, something you would've figured out, had you only bothered to do a little more research. You accepted Dr Vella's answers without much of a fight."

Oh, crap. Axel felt the hairs on his neck stand to attention. Thor watched him with an amused expression on his face. "Yeah, you got it. I'm part of the network that's behind the voice you heard in the Chamber a few months ago, the effects you saw in your

Speechomat, and the one who told you about the murder of Sarah Wangai."

Axel opened his mouth, closed it, then paused. Despite a desperate attempt to find something rational to say, he found there was only one word worth uttering.

"Why?" he asked.

"A fair question." Thor looked up at the cloudless sky. For a moment he seemed to ponder something. "Banal as it may sound, we want this world to be a better place. We've had enough of politicians bickering about power and billionaires refusing to pay taxes because they think it's 'unfair'. We're tired of crime, murder, war, terrorism and selfishness. It's exhausting. We humans are supposed to be better than this.

"Every day we choose our behaviour, which means that every day we have a chance to start over; to do good instead of bad, to give instead of take, to love instead of hate. It's absurd that *we're* the biggest threat to this planet and ourselves. We, who choose our behaviour, are choosing *not* to change."

Axel was quiet. He wasn't sure if he should be frightened or fascinated by the man's ranting.

"At the heart of the problem, we find The Academy," Thor continued. "Or rather, their glorification of leadership." He glanced at his watch. "Come, you need to return to the mansion before people start wondering where you are. I'll try to explain it as we go."

They made their way back, treading along the river as the sun rose upon the sky. "We've been observing you for years," Thor said with a quiet voice. "If The Academy finds out half the things we know about you, you're a dead man."

"Fantastic," Axel muttered with unhidden sarcasm. It seemed that as of late, he was collecting threats like others collected stamps.

"It shouldn't come as a surprise. The Academy is spending a ridiculous amount of money on you, and you don't even want to become a leader."

"How do you know so much about me?"

"The global network I'm part of is called The Box. We intend to destroy The Academy and start a revolution. And you"—he paused—"you will be at its centre."

CHAPTER 7

Axel stopped and stared at Thor. For a second, he was lost for words. "You can't destroy The Academy!"

"Why not?"

"Because it's the bloody Academy!"

Thor pulled at his beard. "Your point being?"

"For starters it's impossible!"

"Not at all. You know, some of history's finest achievements began as crazy ideas." He started down the path again.

"This is nuts."

"On the contrary. It's the sanest thing you've heard in a long time, only you don't realise it...yet."

Jesus! Axel drew a deep breath and held back his frustration. "I still don't understand. Why me?"

"Because you're what The Academy refers to as a 'wild-card'."

Axel's mind whirled. A few months earlier he'd overheard Professor Jackson use the term 'wild-card', but he still didn't know what it meant.

"What's a wild-card?" he asked.

Thor yanked free a piece of grass and looped it around his finger. "A wild-card is a person who's drawn towards two extremes. One is good and the other is bad. The Academy uses the term to describe a rare individual who has a complex psychological mind-set that can either turn them into a splendid leader, or a complete failure."

A complete failure? Without thinking, Axel took a step back. Of course. All of a sudden, it all made sense. If The Academy deemed him a wild-card, then they had to be terrified that he'd end up a massive disappointment to them. No wonder they feared his questions. They thought it was a sign of failure.

"Is that why you're approaching me?" he asked, his mouth suddenly dry. "You want me to fail?"

"Hell no!" Thor shook his head. "We want you to graduate."

"Then I'm not following."

"That's because I haven't told you everything yet."

The arrogance was astonishing. To hide his anger, Axel bent down and picked up a stone from the dirt path. He rolled it back and forth in his hand a few times, then flung it into the river. "All right, tell me."

"Like I said, wild-cards are drawn towards two extremes. Due to the law of nature, they'll eventually pick a side, either by choice or necessity. This tends to occur before their twenty-eighth birthday. Once they've picked their path, there's no turning back. They'll follow what they consider their destiny, no matter what.

"A part of you wants to do good. You started Talk Thirteen when you were a child, wanting children your own age to collaborate. On the other hand, you have a personality that suggests you could become a brutal ruler. You're intelligent and charismatic, but also manipulative, selfish…"

"Wait a minute! I'm not manipulative."

"Really?" Thor didn't hide his amusement. "Let me see. When you were eight, you told Philip Cote he didn't have the guts to pour his soup over Big Hal, knowing that Philip never backed down from a bet. When you were ten, you persuaded Trent Reed to slice the tyres of your teacher's car, and he never once ratted on you, even when he got suspended."

Axel managed rather well to maintain his composure. "How do you know these things?"

Thor shrugged. "My point is that from an early age, you realised you could manipulate people. I have plenty of stories where you stood in the shadows, pulling strings."

"You make me sound like an arsehole."

"I'm stating the facts. If you think that makes you look like an arsehole, then that's your problem, not mine. The point is this; at the moment you can go either way. You can do great good in this world, or great evil. You can rule people or encourage cooperation. That makes you perfect for our task."

"And what the hell is your task?"

"I told you; to prevent The Academy from enslaving the world."

"Jesus! You *are* nuts."

Thor laughed. "Hear me out. The idea of the Eagle King's Academy first saw light about twenty years ago. As you know, the official version states that a group of secret business owners, individuals who wanted to make the world a better place, set up The EKA. Although it sounds great, it's a load of crap.

"Here's what *really* happened. Twenty-nine years ago, five billionaires met on a luxurious yacht, just outside the coast of Monaco. They were all business owners and investors who knew how to turn a single dollar into a fortune. It'd be wrong to call them friends. Rather, they were business partners, who over the years had grown to respect one another's skills.

"They met in secret, for they had an idea, one that would take their collaboration to a whole new level. If it succeeded, they'd be able to divide the world amongst themselves, gaining riches and powers beyond imagination.

"You have to understand that since the mid-1900s, interest in leadership has exploded. It's a gigantic industry, and the five billionaires wanted to take control of, and dominate, that market. Doing so would increase their wealth substantially, but remember, they were already billionaires. It wasn't money that inspired them to collaborate. It was the dream of power."

Thor waved off a bothersome fly and turned to the river. "Most companies and organisations are hierarchically structured. That makes them easy to manipulate."

"How?"

Thor shook his head. "Think about it. Control the person at the top and you'll control the entire organisation."

"What kind of control mechanisms are we talking about?" Axel asked. "Bribes? Threats? Trickeries?"

"Loyalty. Genuine loyalty works far better than any threat or bribery. This is where The Academy comes into play. The EKA picks their students with great care. They choose individuals who are intelligent, smart, and charismatic, people who look good, come across as authoritative, and love power and the limelight that follows. More than anything, they choose individuals they can control.

"Once their loyalty has been proven, the students are sent out into the world like Trojan horses. With each graduating student, the five billionaires get access to new organisations, governments and companies." Thor tapped the side of his head. "It's brilliant. They can control all kinds of institutions and businesses without owning them. All they need is Academy graduates."

A brief silence emerged as Axel worked through the information. "In theory it sounds plausible," he said after a while, "but a CEO or chairman of a board, can't simply do what he or she pleases. There are laws and regulations that determine what can and cannot be done."

"True, but these laws are monitored by organisations and authorities who are as hierarchically structured as most business. Why do you think The EKA places many of their leaders in charge of law enforcement agencies and government institutions?"

"To control the laws," Axel mumbled. He almost smiled. If this was true, it was indeed a brilliant plan.

"The Seven are using people's obsession with leadership as means of gaining power. Unless we stop them, they'll enslave the world, and people won't even realise it."

Axel looked up. "The Seven?"

CHAPTER 8

FOUR YEARS EARLIER

Noise, exotic smells and heat filled the small airport. Several security guards pushed through the wall of journalists, trying to create a pathway to the waiting car. Hayato's bodyguard did his task with fierce determination, shoving people out of Hayato's way.

"What business brings you to Sri Lanka?" someone shouted.

"The business kind," Hayato replied, and laughter erupted around him.

"What will happen to Francis Security now that you've graduated?"

Hayato pretended not to hear the question. When an EKA student graduated, it was custom for Principal Cunningham to announce the student's new employer in his public speech. Yesterday, he'd only stated that Hayato Sano would continue as CEO for Francis Security a little while longer.

The speculations had exploded.

"Are the rumours true?" another journalist shouted. "Will Principal Cunningham step aside? Are you taking over as headmaster of The EKA?" The question came from a middle-aged woman who had somehow managed to shove a microphone under his nose.

As it turned out, Hayato didn't have to answer the question. His bodyguard gave the woman a good shove and she disappeared into the crowd, taking her microphone with her.

"This is absurd," came Jerome's voice from behind. "How can

we do any business with this kind of spectacle?"

"It will pass."

They reached their car. Luxurious as it was, it had a nauseating smell of warm plastic and sticky leather. Hayato checked his watch. Seven hours left. Then it would all be over.

A few minutes later, the car snaked its way through Colombo's heavy traffic, followed by blood-sucking journalists. Jerome kept working, feeding Hayato with important documents. They had kept the potential acquisition of TechSec a secret for months. If it went through tonight, it'd make Francis Security one of the fastest growing companies in the world.

All of this was a waste of time of course, at least from Hayato's perspective. Still, he flipped through the papers with fabricated interest, while his mind went over the plan.

They arrived at the Cinnamon Lakeside hotel at twenty minutes past four. The hotel security kept the journalists away from the premises as a tired Hayato stepped out of the car. Jerome, on the other hand, seemed excited. While he checked them in, a government representative ushered Hayato straight to a small but cosy room near the restaurant. Then followed three hours of mind-numbing interviews.

Afterwards, Hayato went to his suite, accompanied by his bodyguard and Jerome. While changing his suit for dinner, his assistant fretted over Mr Ramanayake.

"He's expressed some concern," Jerome professed.

"About what?"

"About you being an Academy leader. They feel cheated, he says."

Hayato smiled as he buttoned his shirt. "It's a bluff. If they felt cheated, they wouldn't meet us."

"I don't know, sir. He sounds quite serious."

"I'm sure he does."

Jerome made a face and looked at Hayato's bodyguard as if

begging for help. The large man remained impassive and Jerome sighed. "Sir, they're threatening to pull out unless we can ensure them that their staff will be protected."

"Come on. Mr Ramanayake doesn't care about his employees. If he did, he'd pay them a lot more, and he'd give them fair benefits, like health insurance."

"But he—"

"It's a bluff, Jerome. The man's curious, that's all. Like everyone else, he wants to know my plans." Hayato pulled on his suit jacket. "Well?" he asked and held out his hands. "Am I presentable enough?"

"Your calmness is making me nervous," Jerome complained.
Hayato smiled, but the calmness was an illusion. He was terrified of what was to come.

Mr Ramanayake and his entourage waited for them at a secluded table in a corner of the restaurant. The CEO of TechSec was a heavy-set man who smelled of lemon and old wine. Mud-coloured eyes watched Hayato with a mixture of intelligence and amusement. For the first half hour, the man rambled on about his concerns. Hayato listened with patience, watching the man's goatee wobble with each word. The fellow was a toothless pussycat who dreamt of being a lion. The best way to handle such men was to let them think you feared their bite. Such attention pacified them into submission, although they seldom realised it.

Halfway through dinner, the older man leaned back in his chair, no more empty threats to deliver and still no wiser as to what Hayato had in store for the future. "Mr Sano," he said and wiped his mouth with the linen serviette, "I guess we have an understanding."

Hayato nodded. "I believe we do. Shall we sign the agreement?"
"Now?"

"Why not? What is there to wait for?"

Mr Ramanayake let loose a thunderous laughter that filled the restaurant with unashamed arrogance. "Yes, why not?"

Once the signatures were in place, the little group enjoyed the rest of their dinner. Perhaps *enjoyed* was an overstatement. Hayato endured it until quarter to ten when he excused himself. "I do apologise, but I have another interview. We'll meet again tomorrow as planned."

Mr Ramanayake stood, swaying a fraction as his alcohol-drenched brain tried to find its balance. His colourful tie hung like a dead parrot around his neck. "It's been a pleasure doing business with you, Mr Sano." He grinned. "Perhaps I can invite you and Mr Stewart to my humble home for dinner tomorrow."

"A generous offer indeed. Unfortunately, I'm heading for Mumbai tomorrow evening. We're setting up our new office there."

"You're what?" Mr Ramanayake stiffened. "You didn't tell me that."

"I didn't? Must have slipped my mind." Out of the corner of his eye, Hayato could see his bodyguard take a step forward, ready to act. "It's a matter of efficiency. We have to streamline our business now that we've acquired both TechSec and K-Trix."

"You're buying K-Trix?" Mr Ramanayake's dark voice drew curious eyes from the surrounding tables.

"We are. They have the best antivirus on the market."

"*We* have the best antivirus."

Hayato folded his napkin and threw it on the table. "If by 'we' you mean TechSec, I should remind you that it's no longer yours. It's mine. And no, TechSec does not have the best antivirus on the market. K-Trix does. TechSec has the best anti-spyware. We're picking the best of both companies and selling the rest. Don't worry, the employees we intend to keep will be shipped to Mumbai and given an employment package they cannot refuse."

"They'll never do it!" Mr Ramanayake bellowed. "They're loyal to me!"

"Again, I'm sorry to say you're wrong. We've already signed binding contracts with key personnel. It was…a precautionary move, in case our negotiations collapsed, you see. We wanted the brains behind your product, even if we couldn't get the product itself." Hayato held up his copy of the agreement. "Must say, I'm happy though. Now I have the product too. Saves us several months." He patted a stunned man on the shoulder and walked away.

The conversation had rendered Hayato five minutes late to his interview. Not that the reporter seemed to mind. She was very excited to meet him. The interview was dull and unimaginative, but even so Hayato did his best to appear joyful and relaxed. This would be the last interview he'd ever do, and he wanted it to be memorable.

Afterwards, Hayato bid Jerome goodnight, thanked him for a job well done, and made his way back to the Presidential Suite. His bodyguard followed him to the door. "What time tomorrow, sir?" the man asked.

"Six-thirty."

"Very good, sir. Have a nice evening."

When Hayato closed the door behind him, he stood unmoving for a few seconds, letting out a slow, nervous breath.

It was time.

CHAPTER 9

PRESENT DAY

Axel gave Thor a blank look. "The Seven?"

"Silly isn't it? Five billionaires who call themselves 'The Seven'." Thor laughed and pulled down his bright cap a little further. "It's ridiculous, but don't be fooled. The number seven is the most significant number across cultures. It's often associated with magic, wisdom, luck, or power, ingrained in people's subconscious, thereby influencing their way of thinking. It's a good name to use. If I tell you that The Seven owns The Academy, you're bound to think of them as more powerful than if I refer to them as The Five."

Axel considered this for a moment and, with childish disappointment, accepted that Thor had a point. It would've been nice to object, but the reality was 'The Seven' sounded better than 'The Five'.

"It's a cliché," he mumbled for the sake of saying something.

"Sure is. The Seven are masters at playing with people's subconscious. They've taken it to the extreme, using stereotypes and clichés to manipulate people's thoughts and behaviours. Why do you think it's called the *Eagle King's* Academy? I'll tell you why, because 'Eagle' and 'King' are both deep-rooted words. They signal strength and power. It may seem like nothing, but they influence the way we perceive The Academy."

"I always thought the name was a bit silly," Axel murmured.

"I agree, but then you have the secrecy. The EKA is veiled in mysteries that have people entranced. The changing of locations, the confidentiality, the unknown; it's all creating an air of mystery that lures people into a subdued state of mind."

"I'm not following."

"I mean, it's a matter of shifting people's focus from one thing to another. This is common practice in both politics and business. You create or boost one topic to draw attention away from another. The EKA is using people's obsession with leadership, in combination with mysteries, secrecy, and luxury, to gain the public's fascination and admiration. They've done it so well, people glorify this institution without considering its true power."

A small, colourless butterfly crossed their path and Thor watched it with apparent affection. "They only choose butterflies with colour," he said.

"Sorry?"

Thor gave Axel a smile. "Just thinking aloud. The point here is, The Academy wants to appear perfect in every aspect, from the people they hire to the unfailing success of every graduate. Do you think it's a coincidence that you and the other students are physically attractive and mature looking?"

"Never thought about it."

"Yet you know, as well as I do, that people believe good-looking individuals are more intelligent and friendlier than those with a mundane face. And, if you have a mature appearance, you come across as more competent. Again, it's a matter of The Academy manipulating people's perception of The EKA."

Axel grimaced. "Do you know of two students called Paul and Dalilah?"

"Yes."

"Have you seen them?"

"I've seen photos of them. What's your point?"

"The two of them look like beer kegs with arms."

Thor frowned. "That's rude."

Axel shrugged, feeling a little embarrassed. "Those are

Federico's words, not mine."

"If you take them in your mouth, they're yours," Thor said unimpressed. "Plus, you're forgetting something. The world you live in right now is not representative of the world in general. Paul and Dalilah may not be as attractive as the rest of you, but they're not *unattractive*. The difference is vital. They are neither better nor worse than most people on this planet, and what they lack in beauty, they make up for with their mature appearance."

Axel pondered this and had to admit there was a certain logic to it.

Thor fished out an envelope from his back pocket and handed it to Axel. "Time is running out and we must proceed. In there is a list with important information. This may sound a bit odd, but we want you to study that list and memorise it within a day or two. Okay? And before you ask; no, I won't tell you what it's for. Not now."

* * *

Thor watched Axel disappear behind the trees. The young man had so much to learn and so little patience. Life within The Academy had already begun to change him, but Thor tried to be positive. The Box had failed with Sarah Wangai. They had failed with Hayato Sano. They would *not* fail with Axel.

Considering the circumstances, everything had gone well. The Swede had been upset, worried, confused and agitated, but he had listened, and that made all the difference.

Thor peered up into the blue sky and gave a little wave. "Did you get that?" he asked.

"Yes," replied a soft voice in his left ear. "We got it all."

"Oh, hi, Nelly. How are you?"

"Very well, thank you. As are you, I see."

Thor laughed and began treading back towards the old bridge where he'd parked the car. As he walked he grabbed the edge of his beard and with a wince, he pulled it off. "What's the weather like on your side of the world?" he asked.

"Stop flirting with the members of my team," came Falcon's unruffled voice. "You're distracting them."

"Am I?" Thor asked and looked up at the sky again.

"You are. And wipe that smug smile off your face."

"Come on," Thor said, peeling off the fake latex nose he'd been wearing. "I'm happy. It went rather well, don't you think?"

"We shall see, but I think we can prepare the next step."

"I agree," said Thor. "I'll speak with the others tonight, but go ahead and start your preparations."

"Very well. We're pulling back the drone now. Talk to you soon."

\* \* \*

Izabella sat under the gigantic oak, scratching one of the previous night's mosquito bites as she waited. She'd seen Nicole sneak into Axel's room after midnight, but the woman hadn't stayed long. Maybe Axel wasn't sleeping with her after all, but if not, why had the two of them met under such secrecy?

The question had kept her up for hours. That and the heat. Izabella yawned and moved her manicured fingers to another itchy bite. Of course, the heat had one advantage; tossing and turning had kept her subconscious alert. She'd heard Axel leave early that morning. The way he'd moved indicated he'd been trying to be quiet, but in comparison to Nicole, he'd sounded like Chinese military parade on speed.

Naturally, she'd followed him. He'd led her out into the garden, stopping every now and again to look down at a piece of paper, a map, before moving on. After about twenty minutes, he'd led her to a hidden sub-garden behind a seemingly impenetrable hedge. To her great dismay, she'd found that she hadn't been able to trail him down the slope without being noticed. Since then, she'd been sitting, waiting. How undignified!

A movement caught her eye and she ripped herself free from

her thoughts. Way down the slope, Axel stepped out of an olive grove, making his way towards her. Izabella got to her feet. Peering down, she saw Axel holding something. It looked like a large envelope.

She moved closer to the edge, staying out of sight behind a group of bushes. Axel stopped and slid the envelope into his waistline, under his shirt.

I knew it, she thought, and began backing away as he started up the hill again. I knew it!

A sardonic smile made its way onto Izabella's lips. She felt a wonderful, malicious excitement grow in her chest. It was the sense of an approaching revenge. Axel had rejected and humiliated her in front of the others. Now it was payback time.

CHAPTER 10

The young man pulled Cat towards him in a warm embrace. "Love you," he whispered and gave her a delicate kiss.

"You better," she teased as they pulled apart. When he reached for his bag in the back seat, she grew serious. "I'll inform the others of our progress."

"Okay," he said. "I'll check with Thor to see if there's any update on the California Project."

"Sounds good." She gave him another kiss. "Sometimes I wonder what the hell we're doing," she laughed.

He smiled. "Wasn't it Mahatma Gandhi who said, 'You may never know what results come of your actions, but if you do nothing, there will be no results'?"

"Could be."

The young man slung the bag over his shoulder. "All right, got to go. I'll call you when I get home."

It was always difficult to leave Cat. Due to the circumstances, they could seldom meet in person. He jogged over to Amersham underground station. Before disappearing through the doors, he turned and gave her a last wave. She smiled and made a shooing gesture.

When he arrived at Heathrow, he had enough time to enjoy a cappuccino and scone at a small café. Watching travellers rush by, he thought about The Box and something his father had said many years ago. 'Regular people far outnumber those with power and wealth, yet there's only strength in numbers if the numbers can organise themselves.'

But can we do it? The young man took a bite of his scone. Can we really enlighten and organise people, or are we merely creating chaos?

* * *

The Academy Watcher, Paavo Nurmi, chewed on a protein bar as he watched the old man fidget with his phone. The plane from London was twenty minutes late.

Some of the younger Watchers found this type of fieldwork tedious. They wanted to be where the action was. Their youthful hearts filled them with arrogance, and life had yet to teach them that success came to those who analysed rather than observed their surroundings.

Paavo hadn't expected his target's father to appear at the airport. After all, the old man and his son lived in different parts of the city.

Then again, Paavo thought and wiped his hands on a small tissue, perhaps he shouldn't be surprised. The Master of Watchers, Ms Brown, had claimed that Paavo's target was displaying behavioural patterns that didn't fit with The Academy's expectations. Maybe that included the father somehow?

He watched the old man and contemplated his presence some more until his target arrived. When the young man stepped out from baggage claim, he appeared weary but in a good mood. He did not seem surprised to see his father, but embraced him with a loving hug. Then the two of them strolled off, heads close and whispering to one another.

Before following, Paavo picked up his phone and sent a quick text to the on-duty coordinator.

*4-42 – Target identified.*

* * *

Mr Nakata received a short text message from Ms Brown. Mr Nurmi had identified his target. Nodding to himself, he pocketed his phone and knocked on the door.

"Come in," barked a voice on the other side.

Professor Jackson was sitting behind his desk, shuffling papers. "Oh, it's you," he said, but didn't sound very annoyed. "What do you want?"

Mr Nakata bowed. "A few months ago, Mr Hallman said he read article mentioning Ms Wangai. You ask me to find this article."

"Aye. And?"

"Two of my best hunters have looked. They find nothing. There is no article."

He could tell the news annoyed Professor Jackson to his core. The man let out a little growl and his lips vanished in a tight line.

"Dammit! Mr Hallman lied?"

"So it seems."

"Well, can't say I'm surprised," Professor Jackson muttered after a moment's silence. "I've never trusted the man. Of course, bad news is bad news no matter how prepared one is." The professor started tapping a pen against a pile of papers. "But how in God's name did he find out about Ms Wangai? Did he read about it somewhere else, or did someone tell him?"

"I think someone tell him," Mr Nakata replied, and then decided it was time to say what he'd come to say. "This is not good. We should inform principal."

As if stunned by the stupidity of the suggestion, Professor Jackson looked up and made a face. "Why?" he snorted. "*I* am informed."

"Mr Hallman should not have known about Ms Wangai."

"I agree, but we're not telling the principal. Not now."

"Why not?"

"Because I bloody well say so," the professor snapped, his left eye twitching as it sometimes did when he tried to control his fury. His fingers found the perfect knot of his tie and began the process of adjusting it. "We shall investigate this further before approaching the principal. Until then, you'll keep this to yourself."

Mr Nakata didn't appreciate the order, but he trusted the tall man in front of him, and thus inclined his head in agreement.

The assistant principal gave a nod of appreciation. "You know," he said and picked up his pen again, "I've been meaning to talk to you. I have another delicate task for you."

Raising a brow, Mr Nakata listened as Professor Jackson described his request. When he was done, the Head of Security shook his head. This he could not agree to.

"It's against the rules," he declared.

"No one needs to know. All I'm asking is that you give me a copy of his file. That's it."

Mr Nakata frowned. "Files are protected. If I open, it will be logged."

"But it's *your* system. You can eradicate any signs, can't you?"

"Why you want the file?"

The assistant principal's face darkened. "What's wrong with you? I'm your superior. What I need the file for is none of your goddamn concern."

"Ah, but you ask me to break security rule. I am Head of Security."

"Why are you making this complicated?" Professor Jackson snarled. "You know damn well that I wouldn't ask you unless it was in the best interest of The Academy."

This was true enough. Mr Nakata had no doubt that the assistant principal had good reason for his request, but he *also* knew that if things went sour, he'd be the one who'd have to face the consequences of his actions. He stood up and gave a little bow. "I will think about it," he said and left.

CHAPTER 11

During the next few days, Axel got up an hour early every morning to study Thor's list. The content made little sense, but he memorised it nonetheless. Thor himself was a mystery. The man hadn't offered any information about himself and that bothered Axel. He wanted to know with whom he was dealing. Besides, there was something about the man that felt familiar.

Unfortunately, there wasn't much time to contemplate Thor and his background. The following days were filled with activities ranging from white water rafting to whole day excursions in cities like Florence and Rome. On the sixth day, right before lunch, Nicole gathered the students on the patio under a pergola roofed by a flowering vine. "Has anyone heard of the Diamond Ball?" she asked when they were all seated around a large table.

No one replied.

"Then let me tell you a story."

For half an hour, Nicole told a strange tale about a seamstress named Cassia, who lived in Rome during the height of the Roman Empire. She fell in love and married a wealthy noble. A year later, he was murdered, and to find the killer, she organised a masquerade ball.

While the guests danced, played exhilarating games and stuffed themselves with exquisite foods, Cassia moved among her guests, listening to their conversations. Some she spoke to, asking a few simple questions. If she liked their answers, she gave them a little gift, a beautiful necklace with a white diamond.

As the night drew on, the guests grew intoxicated on expensive wines. Hidden behind their masks, some felt safe enough to share a few secrets, in return for a necklace. Bit by bit, Cassia pieced together information about her husband's murderer. When dawn arrived, she knew who he was. A day later, one of her husband's former business partners was found butchered in his home. Around his neck was a chain with a black diamond, and in his right hand, a note admitting several atrocities.

When Nicole was done, she looked around at the students and when her eyes met Axel's, she gave him one of her dimpled smiles. "That's the story of how the Diamond Ball came to be."

"Why are you telling us this?" Cordelia asked with an acid smile.

"Because for the past twenty-three years, there's been a secret masquerade in Venice," Nicole explained. "It's called the Diamond Ball, and only the most influential people in the world are invited. This year, you're on that list."

Axel's grandmother had once said that 'silences come in many shapes and forms'. This particular one came with half suspicion, half bewilderment.

"Who's hosting this Diamond Ball?" Dalilah asked with unconcealed scepticism.

"Her identity is unknown," Nicole replied, "but she's referred to as The Hostess. Whoever she is, she's very powerful, and the ball will be a perfect opportunity for you to test your skills."

"Ah," Thabo sighed. "Could you elaborate on that, please?"

"Of course, Mr Zulu. The Diamond Ball is not merely a lavish feast. More than anything, it's a game. Each guest will dress up in a grand outfit to mask their identity, just like in the story of Cassia. They'll make up an alter ego, a story of who they are and what they do for a living in case someone starts asking questions.

"When you arrive tomorrow, a servant will place a chain around your neck. He or she will ask you to choose a small box from a tray. Do not open it until The Hostess says you can. Inside is a diamond. A servant will attach it to your necklace. Most diamonds are white, but five people will find themselves with a black rock. They're in trouble, for the object of the game is to gather as many white diamonds as possible and never ever get stuck with a black one."

"How does that work?" Ava asked. "I mean, how do I gather diamonds?"

"You win them from other players by beating them in a game."

"And if one gets a black rock?" Cordelia pondered out loud. "What then?"

"Same principle, Ms Campbell. You get rid of them by beating another player. It's a bit like the card game *Old maid*. There are only five black rocks in play. If you end up without a white diamond, that's fine. Most guests will leave the party with an empty chain. It's the black rocks you must avoid."

Dalilah, who sat next to Axel, spun her phone in her hand. "What kind of games are we talking about?"

"Oh, I'd say almost anything goes. There are only three rules you need to observe. First, never challenge The Hostess to play. She will be very offended if you do. She's not part of the game and will rarely speak or interact with the guests. Respect that. If by any chance you *do* speak to her, be sure to address her as 'My Lady'.

"Second, *always* obey the Gamers. They are the ones who approve, observe and judge the games played. They can command guests to challenge each other, or punish those who break a rule. Their word is law. If they say you lost a game, you lost it. If they say you cheated, you cheated. Don't give them a reason to dislike you. Also, only the Gamers can move diamonds from one necklace to another.

"Third, you can use anyone but The Hostess as pawns in a game, as long as it's accepted by a Gamer. As a matter of fact, many challenges involve tricking or manipulating others. You can gain a fair bit of respect by proving yourself skilled in this area. That said, be careful. If you fail to trick a player, or your inexperience is observed, chances are more senior players will target you.

"At the end of the evening, and this is important, those with a black diamond will be forced to reveal their true identity in front of everyone. It is the beginning of their Year of Shame."

"Year of Shame?" Julie asked, fidgeting with one of her earrings.

"Yes, it's their punishment for failing. For one year, the other guests will torment the losers. They'll use their influence and power to ruin businesses, careers, reputations, even destroying families. It can be quite a witch-hunt. I'm sure you've heard of talented actors with glorious careers, suddenly struggling to get casted for something as trivial as a TV commercial. Or entrepreneurs who have their businesses ruined in a matter of months. I know of politicians who ended up with a black diamond and soon found themselves in the middle of devastating scandals.

"Many players come solely for the thrill of the games or for the grand party that starts after the games are over. Nevertheless, I'd say most come for personal reasons, hoping to put a black rock on the chain of a rival. You'll do well to remember that. Behind the polished surface, there are political and business battles taking place. Those exposed to the Year of Shame will seldom recover from it, and suicide is not uncommon."

Nicole released her smile and let it vanish with the wind. With grave eyes, she looked around the table. "Now, whatever you do, you mustn't end up with a black diamond. If you do, or if anyone discovers your true identity, The Academy will have no choice but to expel you."

Silence settled over the patio. The students watched her with unruffled expressions, but the signs of uneasiness were there; small things, like Edward pulling at his lower lip, and Layla, tearing at the cuticle of her left thumb.

"It's a test?" Axel asked with a quiet voice.

Izabella leaned back in her chair and flicked her hair sideways, out of her face. "Is that why you brought us to Italy? To test us?"

"No, Ms Martins. You're here on vacation."

"If we're here to be tested, then you can't call it a vacation," Paul objected.

"Does one thing have to exclude the other? It's true the Diamond Ball will test your skills, and yes, if you fail the principal will expel you. But the objective of this trip is to give you a couple of weeks to recharge your batteries. As to the ball, I'm sure you'll enjoy yourselves. It's quite an experience."

"When's the ball?"

"Tomorrow evening, Mr Harris."

"I wonder what I'll do with all my diamonds!" Edward smirked.

A scatter of laughter followed but Axel did not join in. Nicole's smile had vanished and he wondered what she was thinking as she bent over and picked up a leather briefcase from under her chair.

"To be admitted to the ball, you need a formal invitation," she said, handing out black envelopes, sealed with gold wax. "These are your tickets. It's quite a procedure to get in, and if you don't get it right the first time, you'll be sent away."

CHAPTER 12

Warm rain hammered against the bungalow as Falcon descended the stairs towards the hidden workroom. As he stepped in, one of the hackers gave him a broad smile. "We've got it! They've posted the list."

Falcon turned to the large screen displaying a long list of names. "It's about time," he said in a calm voice. "Have we solved the tracking system yet?"

"Not really, but we've got an idea," said Nelly, and a sneaky smile blossomed in the young woman's face as everyone turned to look at her. "If we can get an earpiece past the scanners, then we can establish a one-way communication."

"How?"

"It's the inside tracking system they've changed, not the registering." Nelly reached for her cup of coffee and began to explain the hackers' idea.

When she was done, Falcon rubbed his slim jaw. "It might work. Can one of you show me the flowchart again? The one presenting the security process?"

\* \* \*

"Ten minutes to landing," one of the pilots declared.

The students had spent the morning going over the complicated process of entering the ball, as well as the rules inside. After lunch, Nicole had divided them into groups of three. They'd had a couple of hours of rest after that, until a helicopter had arrived to pick up the first group.

"Venice!" Dalilah exclaimed and pointed. Then, as if thinking her excitement could be considered un-leader-like, she dropped her voice a notch, adding, "I wonder where they'll drop us off."

The floating city with its red-tiled rooftops, canals and four hundred bridges seemed to bask itself in the evening light. The helicopter thundered its way out over the Venetian Lagoon, then banked hard to the right, flashing its belly to the setting sun. For a terrifying moment, Axel saw nothing but green water and a few boats whizzing by in a blur.

The throbbing of the rotor blades pressed hard against their ears. At a gradual descent, the chopper turned its back on Venice, and half a minute later, it touched down on an impressive yacht resting at ease in the dark water.

"Well, boys," said Dalilah as the rotor blades began to slow. "Now it's everyone for themselves."

The beginning of a smile twitched Thabo's lips. "Isn't it always so?"


"Your cabin, sir." The servant stepped aside, allowing Axel to enter. "They'll pick you up somewhere between seven and eight." He had a nasal voice, but a charming French accent that fitted him as perfectly as the butler uniform he was wearing. "I'm sorry, but what's your number, sir?"

"Sixteen, forty-five," Axel responded without hesitation as he strode into a sumptuous room.

"Very good, sir. Your things will be delivered to you shortly." The man pointed at a direct-dial phone. "Should you need anything, press zero." With a tiny bow, he withdrew.

Axel looked around his cabin. It was more of an admiral suite than anything else. The spacious and well-furnished living room had a partitioned living/dining area. An en-suite master bedroom offered a king-sized bed, wide closets and access to a grand bathroom. Through large windows, the silhouette of Venice stood dark against the golden sky. Axel pulled the curtains shut.

Shortly thereafter, a young man arrived with a suitcase, two briefcases, and a red robe so dark it was almost black. Axel started with one of the briefcases.

There was no zipper or buckles, no way to open it unless one knew how to do it. He pressed his right thumb against a spot under the handle. There was faint buzz as his fingerprint was scanned, followed by a click as the lid opened.

What the hell?

Protected by thick black foam, lay a mask made out of gold and black metal. The detail was astonishing, beautiful even, but the mask itself was the most grotesque thing Axel had ever seen. It looked like a demon warthog after a night of heavy drinking.

Axel pulled out the mask. It stared at him with mad, eyeless sockets and a monstrous grin. Two sharp tusks, made of gold, stuck out on either side of the wrinkled snout. The more he stared at the mask, the more hideous it grew.

"Assholes!" he spat, feeling his cheeks burn from fury and shame. He'd been made a fool. He threw the mask into the briefcase. Next, he scanned his fingerprint on the suitcase. It contained a flamboyant black and gold coat made of silk, a matching waistcoat, and breeches. There was also a white shirt, stockings, and gloves, plus a pair of gold shoes that glimmered in the warm light of the cabin.

Stockings? They wanted him to walk around like an intoxicated warthog in stockings?

At the bottom of the bag, Axel found a pair of clean underwear and a toiletry bag.

The second briefcase held a black wig, a make-up kit and a pair of red lenses, all with detailed instructions.

After a hot shower that washed away some of his foul mood, Axel began the painstaking process of getting dressed. While wrestling on the stockings, he heard the sound of another helicopter landing on the yacht before taking off again a few minutes later. As darkness fell over the lagoon, Axel worked in front of the bathroom mirror. He attached the wig with a bit of difficulty and painted black around his eyes, mouth and jaw. The hardest part was inserting the red lenses. That took nearly twenty minutes and hurt like hell.

All done, he tried on the mask. It fitted him perfectly. The openings around his eyes were wide enough so he could see the world without interference. Although the ugly snout hid most of his mouth, he could talk, eat and drink without hindrance. Any skin exposed was coloured black, even his lips. He would be impossible to recognise, but oh, the humiliation.

He spent the rest of the time in an armchair, going through the details of his alter ego; the history, strengths and weaknesses of his character. Twenty-three minutes to eight, there was a knock on the door.

"Sir?" came the nasal, French voice. "It's time."

## CHAPTER 13

---

## FOUR YEARS EARLIER

The Presidential Suite had a wide terrace overlooking Beira Lake. Hayato Sano stood by the railing, gazing out at the million lights pressing against the black water from all directions. Leaning over, he peered down at the terrace below. It stuck out a couple of metres, as did the terrace below that. "It's like a pyramid," his friend had said while they'd done their planning. "That's why it's perfect."

Hayato tightened his grip around the paper bag. He could feel the weight of the money. Eight stacks of hundred-dollar bills, plus around sixty thousand Sri Lankan rupees. It was the only thing he'd bring from his old life. His phone, watch and wallet were on the bedside table. The computer sat on a desk, and he had left his clothes folded inside his bag. If all went well, the police would assume that something or someone had forced him to leave in a hurry.

Here it goes, Hayato thought trying to shake free the nervousness. After a quick glance in all directions, he swung his leg over the railing. A gust of wind caught his tie and yanked it loose from the tiepin. A rush of adrenaline pumped through his veins and he almost laughed. He'd made two major life-changing mistakes so far. This would be his third.

Perhaps it was wrong to call it a mistake. The only real mistake he'd ever made was joining The Academy. After that, it had been a matter of dealing with the consequences. He pushed the thoughts aside and focused on the task at hand.

Thick beams, a foot apart, ran horizontal below the edge. Hayato stepped out on the first one, then the next. Letting go of the railing behind him, he moved forward. Once he reached the last beam, he hesitated despite himself.

This was it, he thought, then jumped.

With a heavy thump, he landed flat on his feet and fell forward. Pain shot through his knees as they struck against the tiled floor. Light fell upon him where he lay. He scuttled over to a large potted plant. There, in the shadows, he pulled out the crumpled note from his back pocket. *Second door to the right.*

Hayato got to his feet, hurried over to the door in question and gave it a light push. It swung open without sound. After a quick glance at his note again, he stepped into the darkness.

The spotlights on the terrace gave off enough light to guide him past the furniture towards the bed. As instructed, he found the backpack under it.

For the next ten minutes he worked fast. He stripped clean of his tailored suit before pulling on a pair of knee-long shorts and a white t-shirt. There was also a pair of butt-ugly sneakers and a black cap. Once he was done, he shoved a few thousand Rupees into his pocket and left the remaining cash in the rucksack, along with his suit pants, tie, shirt, and expensive shoes. Then he slung the backpack over his shoulder. It was time to leave.

Giving himself no chance to think, he opened the door and stepped into the corridor as if it was the most natural thing in the world. With an uncharacteristic gait, he strolled over to the elevators, counting one step per second to maintain a composed appearance.

A middle-aged couple stood by the elevators in silence. Hayato thought his heart would stop when the two of them turned and threw him a fleeting glance. The man gave him a polite nod and turned away, but the woman watched him with a hint of curiosity.

On their way down, Hayato kept his back to the couple. He tried to ignore the compact silence that engulfed the trio. His heart was beating fast. It was difficult to stand still, pretending to be relaxed when he could feel the woman's eyes upon him.

After what seemed ages, they reached the foyer. The woman threw him a last glance, then gave her head a tiny shake, as if coming to some sort of conclusion. Her companion said something and the two of them strode over to the reception. With a sigh of relief, Hayato pulled his cap even further down and slipped out of the entrance.

Outside, the noise from the traffic was deafening. Hayato jogged over to *Sir Chittampalam A Gardiner Mawatha* and, with a wave of his hand, he stopped a tuk-tuk. He was taking a seat when a familiar voice crushed his plans.

"Sir?" Jerome's childish, and at the moment very flummoxed face, appeared. "What are you doing?" he panted. Then, with a grimace, he looked down. "And what in the world are you wearing?"

CHAPTER 14

## PRESENT DAY

At a slow pace, the boatman navigated the wooden vessel through the narrow canals. They were entering the less visited parts of the city. Nicole sat hidden under the wooden coach roof while they slid past gondolas and small boats. She took in the world around her, studying the charming buildings and watching their lights dance across the calm surface of the black water. A calm breeze brought with it the salty smell of sea, blended with whiffs of spices. Behind her, the pleasant chatter of joyful tourists faded to a quiet murmur.

Their destination was a closed door, only a footstep from the surface. The boatman jumped out and gave the door a hard double-knock after which he helped Nicole out the vessel. She gave him a nod, and, with a slight hesitation, as if surprised she'd noticed him, the man returned it.

The door opened a fraction. "Code?"

"Fifteen, thirty-two."

A short pause, followed by, "Welcome."

Nicole entered a short, dark corridor, lit by thick candles. A man stepped aside. Everything about him was black, from his suit, shirt and tie, to his gloved hands and full-covering mask. Further on, embedded in the wooden walls were polished metal panels, twinkling in the faint light. Nicole knew what they were. The Academy had them at every entrance. These custom-made body scanners could identify both weapons and bugging devices of all sorts. They were splendid machines, but came with a price tag even

The EKA found absurd.

"Good stranger."

Nicole shifted her gaze towards the inner doors. There stood two men in tailcoats, their entire faces covered by white, smiling masks; simple but well made. As she approached them, they both gave her a deep, elaborate bow, their movements synchronised with ridiculous precision.

The man on her right held out his hand. From a pocket in the robe, Nicole pulled the invitation card. As he accepted it, the man on her left leaned forward and spoke with a low voice. "A seamstress she was; a judge she became. Tell me, good stranger; what was her name?"

"Cassia," Nicole whispered.

"The Hostess bids you welcome," both men said in sync, and pushed open the beautiful arched doors.

Soft light spilled into the corridor. Nicole stepped into a big room, lit by crystal chandeliers. Rose petals drifted from the ceiling and fell upon the guests, all hidden behind their red robes. Although no one spoke, one could taste the excitement in the air.

There were a few other entrances to the room and every minute a new guest would arrive. Heads turned, and under the hoods, curious eyes scanned the newcomer. Who was it? Where had he or she come from? Was it a newbie or an experienced player?

Careful not to trample on anyone's robe, Nicole swept towards the centre of the room, taking in the surroundings. Along one of the walls were five gold elevators. Above each was a monster's head. Whenever the eyes lit up in one of them, the doors would open below and a servant in a white mask and olive-coloured suit picked a guest at random to enter.

Nicole didn't have to wait long. Less than ten minutes after her arrival, she was ushered into the second elevator on her right. It brought her to a small but bright room where a little girl in a white mask was waiting for her.

"Welcome," the child said with a merry voice, holding out the sides of her olive-coloured dress as she curtsied. "Please, let us get you prepared." Her clear British accent was as perfect as her appearance.

Having done this before, Nicole knew what to do, and pulled back her hood. "Thank you, my dear," she said as a wave of cool air washed over her feathered mask. Next, she took off her robe and handed it to the girl who threw it down a laundry chute.

"You're beautiful," the child sighed. "Your mask is fabulous and your dress extraordinary!"

"You like it?" Nicole spun around and the long white gown billowed out around her.

"Oh, indeed! You'll be the prettiest one out there."

Nicole laughed and spun again. She knew the girl was lying. It was part of her job to compliment the guests, but it felt good to play along.

The little girl giggled. "Your necklace, miss," she said and held out a black metal chain, thin like a piece of yarn but strong as the thickest iron. "Let me fasten it for you." She reached for a stool that stood pushed against the wall.

"No need for that." Nicole went down on one knee, her dress spilling out around her. She felt the girl's delicate fingers brush against her neck as she fastened the chain. There was a faint hiss as the ends of the necklace merged and locked.

\* \* \*

"There you go, sir." The little girl, perhaps seven or eight years old, tugged at Axel's chain before jumping off the stool. "Let me take a look." She came around, placing her small hands on her hips like a miniature adult. "It's a fantastic outfit, sir. You'll be the finest dressed guest out there."

"I doubt it," Axel muttered. "Unless everyone else comes as ham."

"Ham, sir?"

Axel pulled on his gold gloves and pointed at his mask. "The only way this can be considered 'fine', is if everyone else comes dressed as a pig's arse."

With a giggle, the little girl hurried over to a giltwood table and grabbed a braided basket filled with black ring boxes. Axel picked one and felt a tingle of nervousness spider its way up his neck. He slipped it into his pocket and squared his shoulders. This was it. Time to play.

CHAPTER 15

Axel stepped out on a wide balcony. It ran around a fantastic ballroom hall, held up by majestic, arched pillars. He adjusted his mask, giving himself a moment to set his bearings. Then, with pretended dispassion, he walked up to the balustrade and looked down at the wonders below.

Wow.

The thought almost escaped his lips. His eyes fell upon a circular dance floor where the parquet made up a map of the world. Guests in stunning outfits swept over the countries in a waltz. It was quite a sight.

On his left, the orchestra sat on a gilded stage, suspended three metres up in the air. Thick gold chains, attached to a painted ceiling as grand as the one in the Sistine Chapel, held the whole thing in place. Beneath the stage was a pool of fire, breathing odd-coloured flames that kissed the underside of the remarkable platform.

"Champagne, sir?"

A waitress held out a tray. She was un-masked but covered from head to toe in extravagant body paint. Stunned, Axel's eyes travelled over the woman's naked breasts and down. She was a leopard and even had a long tail. How the hell had she attached that?

Axel had never liked the taste of alcohol but he accepted a glass nonetheless. The Academy had taught him that a true leader was expected to drink in social gatherings.

His attention returned to the Grand Hall and a moon-shaped platform near the dance floor. On it stood a divan made of black metal, shaped as a scorpion and stuffed with soft, off-white cushions.

"Care for some Beluga caviar, sir?"

A waiter appeared. Axel struggled not to stare. The man looked like a walking Vincent Van Gogh painting. The *Wheatfield with Cypresses*, to be specific.

"Why not?" Axel mumbled. He accepted a small toast from the man's tray and looked down at the black roe. Beluga caviar cost several thousands of dollars per kilo, and was illegal in many countries due to the sturgeon being an endangered species.

Popping the toast in his mouth, Axel set off towards the marble staircase. It was an impressive thing that started off as two separate entities, then joined into one massive staircase.

There were no windows as far as Axel could see. Instead, crystal chandeliers and wall-mounted lamps filled the Grand Hall with light. Above the orchestra, a hologram countdown timer ticked zero hours, forty-two minutes and twelve seconds…eleven seconds…ten seconds.

Axel was so engrossed in everything, he hadn't noticed the gold cage until he stood right next to it.

"Oh." He stopped. The object dangled over the edge of the balcony. Inside, there was a man on a swing, dressed as a bird.

"Quite a sight, huh?"

Axel spun around. The owner of the voice wore a black hooded cape and stood leaning against a wide pillar with a nonchalant stance. He spoke with an odd, cockney-like accent, swallowing half of the syllables as he did. "A chap on a swing, dressed as a chicken. Bonkers, ain't it?"

"He's no more chicken than you." Axel smiled and pointed at the man's mask. "A crow, is it?"

The stranger touched the beak of his elegant mask. Beneath it, the black-painted lips curved into a smile. "Yup. And you're a pig, huh?"

What a schmuck. "A warthog."

After a quick glance towards the entrance, the man tugged at his hood and approached Axel with a conspiratorial smirk. "Well, let me give you some advice, Warthog. Don't gawk at small stuff. You know, like a man in a gold cage. It'll tip people off. They'll know you're a greenhorn and they'll use it against you."

"I see." Axel laughed and began strolling along the balustrade again, forcing himself to sip his drink. "You assume that everyone staring at a swinging bird is a newbie, is that it?"

"Are you saying you're not?" The Crow asked.

"I'm saying you won't know."

The Crow gave Axel a doubtful look. "Nah. I'll wager a fair sum you're a newbie."

They had to push through a group of men and women, conversing next to a life-size sculpture made of fruit.

As Axel walked by, he heard a flirtatious, "Ooo," and from out of nowhere, a strong hand grabbed him by the wrist. "A warthog!" Yanked to the side, Axel came face to face with a voluptuous woman in a Barbie mask and a tight, pink gown from which her large bosom screamed to be released. In fact, they were already halfway over the edge, threatening to pop out like a Champagne cork at New Year's Eve.

Her fingers swept over his mask. "Such handicraft. I *love* it!"

"Ahem." The Crow stepped forward, snatching the woman's left hand and kissing it under his beak. "Do you have a name, my lovely?"

The woman giggled, but was quick to wrench her hand from The Crow's grip. "I'm Mona Lisa, a good friend of Mr Da Vinci. Perhaps you've heard of him?"

"What a coincidence," said a short, portly man in a lemur mask. "I saw Mr Da Vinci only minutes ago. He was talking to a mermaid whom I swear was Gloria Withwood."

A few of the others laughed. The woman clasped her hands in a theatrical display of excitement and pressed them against her bulging chest. Or perhaps it was the other way around; her chest pressing against her arms. It was hard to tell.

"Withwood? The singer?" she effused.

"I'm not a fan of Withwood," said a tall man with an abstract mask and top-hat, "but I'll tell you this; I overheard one of the guests say she'd seen Principal Cunningham here."

There was a brief pause among the listeners, the kind of attentive silence that falls upon a group who've just heard something that's out of place. Top-Hat looked around the group. It was hard to read his emotions behind his mask, but the way he massaged his left thumb, Axel suspected he was confused at the lack of reaction he was getting.

The Crow gave Axel a discreet tug. "Come," he whispered.

No one seemed to note their departure. Everyone was preoccupied with Top-Hat.

"What do you think?" The Crow asked as they strode off. "Was it an act, or is Top-Hat a greenhorn?"

"Why would I tell you?" Axel asked. "Are you asking for help or testing my skills?"

The Crow laughed. "Good. You're learning."

"Learning would suggest I'm new to the game." Axel raised his glass in a flirtatious cheer to two passing women.

"Ha!" The Crow exclaimed. "I thought I'd get you with that one." He glanced over his shoulder again towards the entrance. "All right," he continued. "I pick up an accent. Where you from?"

"Europe. I won't be more specific than that."

"Fair enough."

"What about you?" Axel asked. "You speak with a British accent, but twice you've strayed away from it. I believe your true accent is a blend between American and something else."

The Crow shook his head. "Nice try, mate, but you're wrong."

"No, I'm not. I've been trained by the best."

Hearing this, the stranger stopped. He stared at Axel. "Is that so?"

"Yes, but why do you pretend to be surprised?"

"Shit, man, I wasn't expecting you to offer me such valuable information. At least not for free."

"Please." Axel let out a mocked sigh of annoyance. He grabbed an hors d'oeuvre offered by a passing waitress, ignoring her stunning body paint. "What can I possibly tell you that you don't already know?"

The Crow tilted his head. "Listen, mate, I'm not sure I understand."

"Of course you do. You know *exactly* who I am."

CHAPTER 16

"Please enter your six-digit code," the automatic, female voice demanded. Paavo lowered the phone and punched in his code. Once he was done, the voice continued. "ID?"

"Agent four forty-two," he replied.

"Case?"

"MA-23."

"Password?"

"Yujin."

There was brief pause. "Access granted."

"Good evening, Mr Nurmi," came the kind but efficient voice of the on-duty coordinator. "You're twenty hours late."

"I've been busy."

"Everyone's busy. What's your status?"

Paavo cleared his throat. He was a good agent, one of the best, which was why Ms Brown overlooked his laidback attitude towards daily updates. She knew he would report when he had something to convey.

"No major developments so far, but I request permission for a wiretap, level one."

"Reason?"

"I think it's possible that the target is hiding something."

There was a smattering of fingers against a keyboard as the coordinator documented his request.

"Also, I'd like any information we have on his father."

"Reason?"

"No other reason but curiosity."

"Very well, I'll pass your request on to Ms Brown."

* * *

Eight hundred and forty kilometres away, Axel and The Crow found a secluded spot under an arched pillar. They had walked past the staircase to the balcony on other side of the Grand Hall. From here, they had good view over the main entrances and the arriving guests.

"The female is Fortuna, goddess of fortune and luck." The Crow pointed at one of two gigantic statues, standing on either side of the staircase. "And that's Mercury; the god of trade, merchants and thieves. He's easy to identify with the winged sandals." The Crow paused and looked over to the entrances.

"How did you get in?" Axel asked, caring little for the statues and their meaning. "Were you invited?"

The Crow shifted his gaze, first to Axel and then to the spectacle below. "I'm confused. Who do you think I am?"

"Give it a rest. I know who you are."

The Crow grinned. "What tipped you off?"

"A few things. Claiming I was a greenhorn was the first. It admitted your own experience. That could've been a strategy of some kind, but when Top-Hat exposed his inexperience, you showed no interest in him. He'd be an easier target than me, but still you focused on *moi*."

"Okay, how did he expose his inexperience?"

"Come on, that's easy. The most influential people in the world are at this party. Of course Principal Cunningham is here. Only a rookie would consider that news."

"You didn't, and you're a rookie."

Axel smiled. "Yeah, but I'm special." He pointed at Thor's chin. "The beard was also a giveaway, even if you've coloured it black. And that scab on your knuckle, it was a fresh cut last time we met."

The Crow looked down at his hand, and at last, he dropped his accent. "Good. You did better than I expected."

Axel ignored Thor's compliment. He didn't trust the man. How could he? He knew nothing about him.

"How did you get in?" Axel asked, hoping to lure some information out of the man.

Thor didn't take the bait. He shook his head and turned to stairs where three women in marvellous outfits, descended towards the Grand Hall.

"Believe it or not, The Box has a few powerful friends," he said. "That's all you need to know."

"All right," Axel replied as annoyance bubbled up within him. "Then why are you here?"

Below the large beak, Thor's black-painted lips curved into a tired grin. "You've managed to piss off enough Academy professors to put yourself at risk, not to mention threatening our entire operation. My task is to help you impress The EKA tonight."

"Hence the list," Axel mused and settled both hands on the balustrade. "They're guests, right?"

"*Potential* guests, but about sixty per cent of them have arrived already. I know who they are, and thanks to our list, you know their strengths and weaknesses." Thor pointed at the hologram countdown timer rotating above the orchestra. "In thirty-four minutes, the games will begin. You'll have four hours to gather as many white diamonds as possible. Using the information we've given you, you should be able to gather at least four to six diamonds."

"Only six?"

"Trust me. Six is an impressive number. Get more than that and you'll attract the wrong kind of attention."

Axel watched as a tall woman entered the ball. "How do you know who's who?" he asked.

"An excellent question." Thor leaned forward, resting his lower arms on the balustrade. "As you know, each invitation comes with a robe. The robe is marked with a little chip containing a unique ID. Before entering the party, the guest hands the robe to a young servant who throws it into the laundry chute. Here, scanners read the chip and send all its information to the chain placed around the guest's neck. *Voilà.* You're marked, and The Hostess can track you wherever you go."

"How do you know this?" Axel asked with unhidden suspicion. Thor's familiarity with both The Academy and the Diamond Ball bothered him. The man knew too much.

A thought struck him. "Do you work for The Hostess?"

"God no. You have to be mental to work for her. No, we figured this out years ago. *How*, is none of your business. We had hoped to hack the actual tracking system, but that failed. Instead we're monitoring the scanning process." Thor pointed at his ear and added with a cheerful whisper, "I hear voices. Whenever a guest on our list arrives, I'm informed. You see the woman in the ugly green dress? That's Melissa Riggs."

Axel watched the woman as his mind went through Thor's list. Melissa Riggs. "An Australian actress. Strength; a superb memory. Weakness; terrified of cats. She's also a dyslexic."

"Excellent. The man on her right is the German Chancellor."

"A quick thinker. Analytical. Has got a stiff shoulder and can't move his left arm above his head."

"Correct. Stay away from him if you can. He hates losing. Now the woman behind him, the one in the silver dress, that's Ms Morin, the Director of the IMF…"

The rest of that sentence was lost to Axel. He spotted Nicole out on the dance floor. She was dancing with a tall man in a simple black suit and hideous laughing mask. Axel knew it was her, for she had told the students what she'd look like in case they needed her. Now he watched her long dress billowing out around her as she spun with the waltz. She moved with such grace it was a pleasure to watch.

A soft "ahem" made Axel turn. "What are you looking at?" Thor asked, and there was amusement in his voice.

"Who's the guy dancing with the woman dressed as a swan?"

Thor's lips twitched into a smile. "I'm not sure. We've only kept track of those who were on your list. He was not."

They both stood silent, watching Nicole as she danced.

"Shall we continue?" Thor asked after a minute or so. His husky voice broke whatever spell they'd been under.

Reluctantly, Axel turned away from Nicole. "Sure."

"Good. As I was saying, the woman over there is the Director of the IMF…"

It became something of a game. Thor pointed out individuals among the guests and Axel played along, proving that he knew their strengths and weaknesses. He might not trust Thor, but if the man was willing to help him impress the Academy, then what did Axel have to lose?

They kept going until the lights in the Grand Hall dimmed.

"And so it begins," Thor said, pulling back from the balustrade. "Time to play. Remember what the Roman poet Virgil said, 'Fortune sides with him who dares'."

CHAPTER 17

"Ladies and Gentlemen!" The hourglass figured woman up on stage spoke in a singsong voice. She held a vintage-styled microphone close to her lips, as if she was about to kiss it. "Welcome to the Diamond Ball!"

Cheers filled the Grand Hall.

"Is that The Hostess?" Axel asked in a whisper.

Thor shook his head. "No. That's the Chief Gamer." He pulled at his black hood and leaned in. "I think I better go. From now on, we should avoid one another. Good luck."

"Yeah, thanks."

On stage, the Chief Gamer moved her wide hips. Her olive-green gown swayed with the movements. She made it seem instinctual, yet under the edge of her angel-like mask, her mouth bore a measured smile.

"Two rules I need to mention," she trilled. "First, always obey the Gamers, for in here, they are the law." Spotlights swept over the excited crowd. "Second, you cannot leave the premises until the games have been completed. Once the party starts, you may leave if you wish. Remember, you can donate your diamonds to charity on your way out. This year's categories are; medical research, art and culture, and animal welfare. More information will be found at the exit."

Animal welfare? Axel wrinkled his nose and thought of the Beluga caviar. Unbelievable.

"Well folks, that's enough of the chitchat," the Chief Gamer twittered. "You all received a little black box when you entered. I want you to get them out now." A thrilled murmur rippled through the crowd. Axel turned the box in his hand and tried to open it. It wouldn't budge. "My Gamers will now attach the diamonds to your chains. Please remain where you are."

As the last word faded, the Grand Hall blackened.

Axel stood, hearing the quietness beat against his eardrums. He dared not breathe or move. Seconds passed, and like everyone else, he waited.

Something twinkled under the ceiling. Looking up, Axel saw tiny lights drift towards the floor without a sound. They came through the darkness like shimmering snowflakes. They looked soft, almost magical as they fell, but when he caught one, it proved to be nothing more than a hard, technological gadget.

As the little light flickered and died in his hand, a soft hint of orchestra strings began. On the stage, through the falling lights, Axel saw the contours of the Chief Gamer behind her microphone.

The music rose over the Grand Hall. Gentle at first, then gaining in strength like a bear awakening from a long slumber. Behind the crowd, a choir had gathered on the marble stairs, their humming voices mingling with the music.

A moment later, the woman on stage sang out with the most beautiful voice.

*"Let the games commence;*
*with secrets, lies, pretence.*
*Keep yourself unknown;*
*or we'll cast you off your throne.*
*The black rock you must fear;*
*stay away from it, stay clear.*
*Protect your given name;*
*or you'll face the Year of Shame."*

Drums rang out and the falling lights ceased, replaced by a spectacular light show. A hatch dropped in the ceiling, and out of it tumbled a young woman. Her gold dress flapped around her in desperation as she plunged towards the floor.

Out of nowhere, a man swept in on a trapeze. The woman stretched out her arms. He grabbed her, and with a jolt, threw her upwards. Another acrobat appeared, seizing the woman's arms.

Step by step, the acrobats raised the petite figure towards the ceiling. When she reached the top, the music died. The last acrobat released his grip and the crowd saw the woman stretch out to her full length. As she did, her dress unfolded, displaying an array of deep red, yellow, and orange colours.

Plummeting towards the floor, the fabric of her dress twirled and flapped, creating the illusion of a dancing flame. An impressed "Ooh" rose from the crowd.

A split second before she vanished behind the orchestra, a wall of fire rose under the suspended stage, and when it settled, the woman was gone.

Music erupted once more. The floor trembled and the Grand Hall exploded in hologram fireworks.

Before Axel could react, the box was out of his hand. A Gamer looked up at him with a half-smiling, half-weeping mask. She held his box, making sure he could see it. Then she placed a small metal device against its side. The box opened and Axel peered down at a gold ring with spokes like a wheel. In the centre sat a white diamond.

Relief washed over him. The Gamer took out the ornament and, with the use of her device, fastened the ring to Axel's necklace. She gave it a tug and threw the empty box into a sack on her back. With a quick bow she moved on to the next guest.

* * *

At the other end of the Grand Hall, Nicole's heart pounded with exhilaration as the Gamer held up her white diamond. "I'm glad," she mouthed and patted him on the arm. The Gamer bowed and attached the rock to her chain.

The music and spectacular light show around them had

increased in intensity, until now, all of a sudden, it came to an abrupt end. The lights went out. Nothing but a soft whisper of strings filled the void around them.

Nicole felt the tension grow. A single beam of light appeared, aimed at a spot behind the stage. At first there was nothing. Then the woman who had fallen a few minutes earlier reappeared. She wore a different dress this time, a white one that glowed and sparkled like a diamond. Applause broke out while invisible lines hoisted the thin figure towards the ceiling.

"Welcome!" an amplified voice declared.

As one, the guests turned to the scorpion-shaped divan. Bathing in pillows and golden light, lay a woman in a crimson-coloured gown and an exquisite butterfly mask. Next to her stood two guards, dressed in black.

The Hostess looked out over her guests. "Shall we begin?" she asked.

"Yes!" the guests roared.

"Very well." Above the stage, the hologram countdown timer appeared once more. "You have four hours, starting...now!"

## CHAPTER 18

Mikael sat on his sofa, surrounded by chaos. Three weeks had passed since he'd moved in to his new apartment and still most of his things were in boxes.

He was lost in a great Stephen King novel when the doorbell rang. The piercing sound scared the hell out of him, and it made him drop his pizza slice. Unbelievable! Cursing, he threw the book aside and picked up the greasy mess in his lap. After a second's hesitation, he stuffed it in his mouth and walked over to the door.

"Hi," he said with his mouth full. "Working on a Saturday?"

"Good evening, Mr Andersson." The woman, who was about his own age, gave him a white-toothed smile. She came to him twice a month but refused to tell him her name. As always, she wore plain clothes, this time a pair of jeans, a striped cardigan and a soaked summer-jacket. She had the kind of charmless, plastic appearance that was too symmetrical and perfect.

"How's your new apartment?" she asked with the kind of politeness that said she didn't care.

"I love it."

"Still unpacking, I see."

"Uh-huh." Mikael scratched his thin moustache, wishing the woman would simply leave. "Well, I'd invited you in, but…" He looked down at her sodden sneakers. "You're all wet."

"Don't worry about it, sir. I'm only here to deliver the script."

"I know. I was just being polite."

"So was I."

They exchanged a glance before Mikael wiped his hand on his trousers and accepted the thick envelope. He knew what it contained.

Since entering The EKA, The Academy had controlled Axel's social media accounts. They posted comments and photos in his name, keeping up the appearance that he was travelling the world, doing various kinds of humanitarian work. Although none of it was true, no one seemed to doubt the authenticity of it all. Everyone knew Axel had started Talk Thirteen.

Every second week, The Academy provided Mikael with detailed but fabricated accounts of Axel's latest whereabouts and doings. This was meant to simplify Mikael's life. After all, people expected him to know what his best friend was up to.

"Anything we should know about?" the woman asked.

It was the same damn question she always asked, and Mikael gave her the same damn answer. "No, everyone's too busy with their own lives to care about Axel's."

The woman smiled. "That will change the day he graduates."

Mikael smiled back. "True." He looked down at the envelope and suddenly felt a great sense of loss. His friendship with Axel would never be what it once had been, and all of a sudden, he missed his best friend.

"Is he doing okay?" he asked. "I've left several messages for him, but he hasn't called me back."

"I don't know his current status," the woman replied with a toneless voice and began pulling up the zipper of her jacket. "But I'm sure he's doing swell."

\* \* \*

"You look lost." A soft arm slipped around Axel's. "Never look lost at the Diamond Ball. It attracts vultures." The woman wore an extravagant peacock feather dress with matching shoes in the boldest blues and greens. She gave Axel's arm a little tug. "Come. Walk with me."

More dragged than led, Axel followed the woman away from the dance floor. He'd been standing there observing people, trying to decide what to do. Now, all of a sudden, he walked arm-in-arm with Ms Emerson, an influential reporter.

"And who might you be?" he inquired, feeling the need to say something.

"No, no, no." Ms Peacock laughed. "That's not how you do it." Her gold mask covered only the top half of her face. Her mouth, she hid behind a shimmering green, handheld fan. "A straightforward question like that is considered rude. Only a beginner is that direct. An experienced player will ask you for a name, and a *gifted* player will comment on your outfit first." She turned to Axel, and a glimmer of a smiled peaked through her fan. "I love your mask, by the way. A warthog, that's ingenious."

Sensing he was losing control of the situation, Axel peered up at the statue of Fortuna, bathing in warm light. Beside him, Ms Peacock laughed again.

"Come on, young man. You can't simply ignore my comment. That would be rude."

"Very well. Thank you."

"Thank you, is a polite answer, but consider my statement again. I said your mask was '*ingenious*'. Thus, I'm hinting that I see a deeper meaning in your outfit. In other words, I'm asking you a question. To play like a pro, you have to respond with a bit of information. In my case, for example, the peacock can symbolise integrity and beauty, immortality and resurrection, or the all-seeing eye. If you were to say that my outfit was 'ingenious', I'd give you a hint as to which interpretation I considered the most important for my character."

Axel pressed his lips shut. He hadn't chosen his costume and had no idea what a warthog might symbolise. Perhaps stupidity, or maybe ugliness.

"You're silent," Ms Peacock observed. "Does that mean you have no idea why you're wearing that mask? No, no. Don't tell me. Let me guess. Either someone chose the outfit for you, or…" She tilted her head and gave her fan a little flick. "Or you picked it because you thought it looked cool."

Before he could stop himself, Axel snorted and the woman laughed. "Aha, you *don't* like it. That means someone else chose it for you." She squeezed Axel's arm in a friendly manner. "Don't worry, I won't tell anyone."

They were strolling beside linen-draped tables, arranged alongside an entire wall of the Grand Hall. The amount of food offered was ridiculous, all of it presented in the most creative ways. There were exquisite hors d'oeuvres served on golden rose petals, wine pouring out of crystal fountains, an oyster bar inside a vast ice statue and a miniature forest made of fruit and vegetables. Over by the desserts, stood chocolate and strawberry volcanoes, cupcakes covered in edible gold and pastries in all shapes and forms.

Among the more absurd displays, were the men and women who sat with their bodies hidden under the tables, red apples clenched between their teeth.

Axel glanced at one of them, an ugly chap who looked so uncomfortable, it was hard not to laugh.

"The boar is a brave creature," Ms Peacock said, reclaiming Axel's attention. "If I remember it right, the Celts consider it a symbol of fearlessness and strength. Don't be embarrassed about your costume, be proud. It's a formable piece of art."

She pulled Axel to a stop in front of a fruit statue, imitating Auguste Rodin's famous sculpture, 'The Thinker'. "Hm," she said, inspecting the fruits. "Someone told me they have Ruby Roman grapes this year. I still haven't found one." She poked around a bit and then looked up at the sculpture's face. "Are you hiding them somewhere?"

When the sculpture didn't move, she leaned forward and pointed a finger at its face. "I'm warning you," she snapped. "I've been to enough of these balls to know how things work. Come on, now. Where are they?"

To Axel's astonishment, the sculpture stirred, then twisted his body to his left. "They're at the back, Madame."

"That's just sneaky," Ms Peacock declared and yanked a bunch of grapes from the man's spine.

Axel saw the man cringe.

"These cost about two hundred and fifty dollars each," she said and handed Axel a grape the size of a Ping-Pong ball. She took a bite of her fruit and nodded towards two enormous doors behind the stairs, guarded by men with black suits and masks. "Come, let me show you the Game Quarters."

CHAPTER 19

FOUR YEARS EARLIER

Jerome stared at his boss, who quite clearly wasn't happy to see him. Most people would take that as a subtle sign to withdraw. Jerome did not. He was Hayato Sano's personal assistant, and whatever his boss did, Jerome would do too.

He pushed back his glasses and squeezed into the tuk-tuk. "So?" he said to his tight-lipped boss. "Where are we going?"

"I didn't know *we* were going anywhere," Hayato countered.

"Nor did I, sir." Jerome smiled. "Yet here we are."

The two of them stared at each other. They did it long enough to annoy the driver, who muttered something in Sinhalese and gestured at the traffic. "Where?" he snapped.

"Sky Lounge," Hayato ordered with repressed calm.

Jerome wrinkled his nose. "Sky Lounge? What's that?"

"A place," Hayato grumbled and turned away.

What a sourpuss.

The tuk-tuk driver manoeuvred them out into the wild Sri Lankan traffic. Soon, Jerome held on for dear life, trying not to breathe in the overwhelming stink of fumes. Their driver must have been suicidal, for he was crisscrossing the small tin can through the traffic like there was no tomorrow.

"What are you up to, sir?" Jerome asked after a while, desperate to focus his attention on something other than the traffic.

Hayato stared out his side of the tuk-tuk for a moment. His shoulders rose, then dropped with a heavy sigh. "Can we talk about this tomorrow? I'm not in the mood right now."

At that moment, the tuk-tuk swerved hard to the left. "I'm not sure there will be a tomorrow," Jerome squeaked, gripping the metal bar in front of him. "Slow down, man," he barked at the driver, "and will you please stick to one lane? No! Don't look at me. Focus on the road! The road!"

The driver gave him a confused frown. "Huh?"

"Never mind. Just don't get us killed. And for God's sake, keep your eyes on the *road!*" Jerome rolled his eyes and sat back. "Anyway," he continued after a brief pause, "why are we going to the Sky Lounge?"

"Has anyone told you, you're like a little terrier?"

"I believe you've mentioned it before, sir."

"Then it's worth mentioning again."

"Noted, sir. Tell me; why the Sky Lounge?"

Hayato pulled down his cap a little further and glanced out at the outrageous traffic. "I graduated yesterday and we've signed a massive deal tonight. I wanted to celebrate."

"I see," Jerome said, but truth be told, he couldn't see it at all. It would be an exaggeration to call Hayato his friend, but over the past year they'd done pretty much everything together. Such was the life of a busy CEO and his assistant. Needless to say, during this time, Hayato had never celebrated anything, not even his birthday. Or Jerome's for that matter. The idea that his boss was sneaking out to party seemed…improbable. "And what's with the backpack and the ugly shoes?"

"A disguise."

"From who, if I may ask?"

Hayato shrugged and held on as the driver made a sharp U-turn. "You and everyone else."

"It's not a very good disguise, you know. I was sitting in the foyer when I saw you come out of the elevators. Spotted you at once."

"What were you doing in the foyer?"

"Reading. I like having people around me. All this travelling and sitting in silent hotel rooms, it bores me after a while."

Hayato didn't ask anything else after that. The two of them sat in silence until the tuk-tuk came to a stop in front of the Kingsbury hotel.

"This is the Sky Lounge?" Jerome asked and stepped out. "I must say, it's not what I'd expected."

"Do you have any cash?" his boss wondered.

Jerome grimaced. "Why would I have cash when we live in a world that takes credit cards?"

"I don't think tuk-tuk drivers take plastic." Hayato turned to the driver. "Can you wait a second? My friend will get some money."

"Excuse me?"

"Come on, Jerome. You might as well make yourself useful. Run to the reception and see if you can withdraw some cash."

A tingle of warning tickled Jerome's gut. "Are you trying to get rid of me, sir?"

His boss smiled and held out his hands. "I believe you've proven that's an impossible task." He laughed and started getting out of the tuk-tuk. "I won't leave, I promise. I'll even stand here where you can see me at all times."

Five minutes later, Jerome was in the middle of explaining their peculiar situation to a pretty receptionist, when a noise made him turn. Looking over his shoulder, he saw the red tuk-tuk and his boss disappear into the traffic.

"The son of a…!"

CHAPTER 20

# PRESENT DAY

"You can win your diamonds in one of three ways," Ms Peacock explained over the buzz and music of the Grand Hall. "The most common way is to challenge another guest at a particular game. As you will see, there are several rooms in the Quarters, each with a number of games. To play, you pick a room, choose an opponent and then negotiate the game to play. Simple.

"In fact, for some of the more experienced players, it's too simple. They prefer betting. You can bet on anything, and you can do it anywhere, not only within the Quarters. All you need is an opponent, something to bet on, and the acceptance of a Gamer."

They had reached a pair of double doors, guarded by two men in black suits and masks. Like statues, they stood unmoving, one on each side of the open doors.

"Whatever you do, don't provoke the guards," Ms Peacock whispered as they passed the men. "I've heard disturbing rumours of their brutality."

What kind of rumours, Axel wondered, and what did the guards consider provocative? Of course, he didn't ask. That would've proven his inexperience. Therefore, he simply smiled and gave away nothing of his thoughts.

Ms Peacock glanced at him over the edge of her fan. The woman unnerved him. He saw the calm amusement in her eyes and heard the friendliness in her voice. Yet there was something else hiding in her manner. Something that worried him. Willpower perhaps, or…eagerness. Yes. Eagerness.

Arm in arm, the two of them walked through the doors and reached a short flight of stairs with waterfalls on either side.

"Now this is the Quarters," Ms Peacock explained as they descended onto a long bridge made of white stone. There was water, black as oil and sprinkled with rose petals, that fell on either side from the painted ceiling.

From the main walkway, smaller arched bridges curved out like legs on a centipede, each leading to a door. The place was well trafficked by Gamers and merry guests. The latter chatted, laughed and gestured as they moved between doors with obvious ease.

Ms Peacock walked on, her glimmering stilettos muffled by a red carpet. "Come. It gets less crowded the further we get from the entrance."

Axel obeyed without comment. The more he spoke, the more he risked saying something that would display his inexperience. At the same time, he could almost hear Professor Jackson warn him. "No one is kind for the sake of being kind. What is she after?"

To hide his unease, he turned his head to the jugglers, fire eaters and sword swallowers performing on small platforms in the water.

"There's a system you should know," Ms Peacock started. "As you can see, each door has a symbol painted on it." She pointed her fan at a door with a half-smiling, half-weeping face painted on it. "A theatre mask like that, shows it's a game room. The figure three beneath it, indicates that this is Game Room Three." She pointed at another door on their right. "The Rabbit indicates it's a naughty chamber. They tend to fill up later on in the evening, when alcohol has loosened people's morality. There's also a symbol with a hummingbird inside a barbed wire circle. You'll find it further down the corridor. Those are safe havens. No one can challenge you in there, but you can't stay too long. The Gamers will throw you out if you do. We're here to play, not hide."

Ms Peacock came to a stop and peered over her shoulder. "This will do. Most of the commotion is right by the entrance since the further down the corridor you get, the harsher the games." She paused and nodded at a passing couple, their costumes shimmering in the nervous light from a nearby torch. "As a beginner, you should stay close to the Grand Hall. I recommend you going no further than Game Room Two."

She walked up to the stone railing and peered down into the water. Axel followed her, keeping his face blank. He positioned himself on her right-hand side. When he looked at her, he could see the stone bridge disappear into the dimmed light behind her. A shiver of unease crawled up his back.

"You know, keeping silent can also be a giveaway." Ms Peacock smiled. "In your case for example, I'd say your silence is a sign of fear. You're afraid of exposing your inexperience."

Inside his gloves, Axel's palms were getting sweaty. "I wouldn't say that," he lied and returned her smile. "I'm merely curious to see what you're up to."

"Good answer." Ms Peacock laughed, using her fan to move a strand of her deep auburn hair from her eyes. "A lie, but still a good answer." She glanced over his shoulder towards the entrance, then lowered her voice. "Most of the guests have been to the Diamond Ball before. Some of them are business or political rivals; others come from countries at war with one another. There are alliances and battles taking place that are difficult, if not impossible, to recognise. Experienced players often use newcomers as pawns in these games of power. Some of them prowl the Grand Hall and the Quarters in search of rookies to target. They are particularly active during the first hour, so be careful. Should anyone approach you, try to act like a pro. If done correctly, it'll keep some of the vultures away."

The woman stood back from the railing, waving her handheld fan as she did. A dreadful twinkle of satisfaction gleamed in her teal-lensed eyes.

"One more tip before I go. Always make sure that you can see what colour diamond a player has. If they hide their necklace, you should run. Chances are they're stuck with a black rock and have plans on making it yours."

Axel's eyes dropped to the woman's ivory neck. In a graceful manner, she slid her fan to the side. A large, black diamond appeared, glittering in outmost spitefulness.

For a moment, the diamond was all he could see.

"You have a lot to learn, young man," Ms Peacock said with a laugh. "But don't worry, we've all started somewhere."

She reached out and grabbed his chin between her thumb and index finger. "This time you need not worry. This rock has already been called for. As a payment. You see, the third way to win diamonds is to sell favours or information to other players. It doesn't happen very often, for the price tends to be steeper than anyone is willing to pay. That said, if an agreement has been made between two parties, the Gamers seldom interfere."

Ms Peacock nodded towards the entrance. Axel turned and saw a tall Gamer observing them from the stairs. He stared at them with the kind of intensity you sometimes see in the face of a boxing referee; head pushed forward and the eyes unblinking. Yet Axel's attention slipped. What he saw was the glimpse of a white-feathered dress, slipping through the large doors towards the Grand Hall. The sight of it made Axel's heart stop. Nicole.

"Someone wants to help you." Ms Peacock smiled. "More than you know, I think."

\* \* \*

From a secluded part of the balcony, Nicole saw Axel step out from the Quarters. He scanned the Grand Hall, looking for her, no doubt.

"How did he do?" Nicole asked.

"He did all right," Ms Peacock replied behind her fan, "but a senior player would've noted his inexperience within a minute."

"And now?"

Ms Peacock's eyes shone with amusement. "My dear, your

friend is a rookie. Even with my help, I doubt he'll make it through the evening without losing his diamond. As you know, most players go home empty-handed."

Nicole didn't respond to that. If Axel were to impress the management, he'd have to perform better than the other students. He would have to gain a second diamond.

She turned to the Gamer. "Can you confirm that she did her part?"

The man nodded.

"And you will monitor Ms Peacock as agreed?"

The man nodded again.

"I will not break our deal," Ms Peacock huffed.

"I believe you," Nicole said. "Nevertheless, I need to protect my interests. If you tell anyone about my friend, this deal is annulled."

"I know."

"Then let's do it." Nicole turned to the Gamer, and without any emotional involvement, he swapped their diamonds.

When he was done, Ms Peacock reached out and placed a hand on Nicole's arm. "I've been to the Diamond Ball many times," she said gravely. "I have never seen anyone take a black rock for someone else. I hope your friend is worth it."

Nicole looked away. "He is."

"Then I wish you well, Lady Swan. Now go out and make sure you lose that black rock."

When Ms Peacock had left, trailed by the silent Gamer, Nicole closed her eyes for a moment. Her hands trembled as she fingered the black diamond on her chain. God. What have I done? She was supposed to obey and serve, not meddle with things that weren't her business. Certainly not matters concerning the students.

"Those who believe themselves immune to fire, will one day be scorched by the flames." The words were uttered by a soft voice that bespoke an expensive education.

Startled, Nicole turned as a man in a grey suit and hippopotamus mask stepped up to the balustrade. He was short and his outfit lacked any extravagance. Still, he positioned himself with his hands wide apart on the railing, like a king inspecting his grounds. "Those were my wife's words. She had a knack for saying clever things."

Silence coiled itself around Nicole. She tried to think of something smart to say, but a terrified mind is an empty mind, and so she remained quiet and unmoving.

"Failure to recognise one's own limitations is a dangerous thing, Ms Swan. Wouldn't you agree?" Principal Cunningham looked at her with his dark, unnerving eyes. There was wisdom there, as well as brutal determination.

Nicole loved the old principal for reasons few would ever know or understand, but she also feared him. Or rather, she feared his disappointment, not his wrath.

"Yes, sir," she whispered.

He surprised her by turning back to the Grand Hall with a short-lived laughter. "We can teach our students everything they need to know, but we can't teach them experience. That they must learn on their own. Now they're strutting about down there, thinking themselves invincible. I fear their egos will be bruised and battered by morning."

"That has been the case before, sir."

The principal nodded, more to himself than anything else. He was a clever and unpredictable man in a sophisticated way. It made him both lovable and dangerous at the same time. Nicole knew he liked her, but she also knew he'd never let his feelings interfere with business. Never.

"You wear the black," he said.

Nicole's hand moved up to her necklace. "I had a bit of bad luck this evening."

"Ah."

"I will not carry this rock for long, sir. I'll pass it on soon enough."

"Ah," the principal repeated. Then he stood back from the balustrade. "I hope you know your limitations, Ms Swan."

"Yes, sir."

Leaning in, he whispered, "Be careful."

She saw the worry in his eyes before he strolled off. For a moment she stood there, feeling naked, vulnerable and scared. How in the world would she get rid of the black rock?

CHAPTER 21

Everywhere he turned there were things to see; trees of gold, stools made of elephant feet, white tigers lead by body-painted servants. The list was endless. Axel steered his steps towards the scorpion divan, moving slowly between mingling and dancing guests. Looking up, he noted Ms Peacock, observing him from the balcony. She seemed displeased, perhaps at his gawking at everything around him.

Thor was nowhere to be seen, and Axel made no serious effort to find him. He was more concerned about Nicole. He had to talk to her. Why would she take a black diamond for his sake?

According to the hologram timer, thirty minutes had passed. The notion awoke butterflies in his gut. He had to get started. His eyes shifted to the scorpion divan. The Hostess lay on her side, watching the guests while scratching a tiger behind its ear. Her hair had been coloured gold and her butterfly mask glittered in various coloured diamonds.

"She is a remarkable lady, don't you agree?" A gaunt man in a superb black and gold fire mask appeared at his side. Thor had identified him as Mr Ganesh, a fifty-three-year-old tech magnet from India. Brilliant, but something of an oddball.

"Yes," Axel replied shaking his hand.

Mr Fire bobbed his head with enthusiasm. "I like your costume," he said. "A good and powerful choice, Mr Hog."

"Thank you. As is yours," Axel declared and heard his voice tremble a little.

The man behind the fire mask bowed deep. "Mr Flame is my name, and I'm on my way to the Quarters. Would you like to join me?"

"No thank you. I'm…waiting for someone."

Axel turned as if to leave when the little man grabbed his elbow with a bony hand. His eyes shone. "The one you're looking for is awaiting you at Game Room Three," he whispered. "I am to take you there."

Game Room Three was a peculiar place, made up like a winter landscape. Real snow drifted down from a high, sky-painted ceiling. Guests trotted around in borrowed fur coats. Along the walls stood small, snow-covered booths, similar to those found at a winter carnival. Buzzing noises and roaring laughter mingled with cheerful music and colourful blinking lights. A thick scent of perfume and mulled wine hung in the air.

"Hurry up," the scrawny man called over his shoulder, pushing through the lively crowd.

"Where are we going?" Axel asked.

The man laughed. "Don't worry, son. I'll show you." They passed an ice statue carved like a polar bear, and Mr Flame's steps slowed. "Let's see," he pondered aloud, leading Axel down the line of games.

There was ring toss, shooting challenges, frog flingers, duck fishing, dart games, etcetera. Juvenile as the games were, people stood clustered around some of the booths, bundled up in their fur coats, cheering on as guests competed against one another in the cold.

"Son of a whore!" someone bellowed. A figure pushed through the crowd. "Get out of my way, piggy!"

The man gave Axel a forcible shove, sending him sprawling to the floor. Around them, laughter erupted. In a blink of an eye, two servants had pulled Axel onto his feet.

"Such a sore loser," Mr Flame sighed. "There are plenty of sore losers around here. I hope you're not one of them." As he uttered the words, his eyes hardened. "Game!" he barked and snapped his fingers.

From out of nowhere, a Gamer appeared. "We want to play," Mr Flame professed, and as if by magic, his heavy Indian accent changed to one of British. "I'm challenging this young man to a game of Connect Five."

"What!" Axel stared at the man. "You tricked me!"

"How observant of you." Mr Flame brushed some snow off his shoulders. "I say we play a game of Connect Five, Diamond version. Any objections?"

The Gamer turned to Axel. Within the Quarters, one couldn't oppose a challenge, but one had the right to negotiate which game to play.

"Well, yes…or…" Axel turned and scanned the room. "Ah shit," he growled. "I guess it doesn't matter. All right, as you wish."

The Gamer nodded and led the two men to an empty booth where digital Connect Four game boards lined the shelves. She picked one and placed it on a high table, with two chairs on either side.

Axel took a seat and the screen in front of him flickered to life. A large game grid appeared, but instead of the normal seven-column Connect Four grid, this one had nineteen. Below it was a yellow disc, made to look like an animated smile. It gave Axel the finger when he looked at it.

"This is how it works." Mr Flame grinned, showing a set of non-bleached teeth. "It's similar to a traditional Connect Four but with a few modifications. You have ten seconds to drop your disc, and you need five in a row to win. Every now and again, a random disc will move from one position to another. Connected discs move as one. Understood."

Asshole, Axel thought and nodded.

"Great. We'll play with black and white discs." The man pulled out his necklace behind a high collar. Three white diamonds dangled from the chain. "You didn't see this, did you, Mr Hog? Don't worry. It'll soon be over."

This brought laughter from some of the onlookers gathering behind them.

Axel let out a long, relaxing breath. "I thought you were a vibrant man with a vibrant taste," he said, replacing his weak, anxious tone with one of confidence. "Why black and white?"

A flash of surprise dashed across Mr Flame's watery eyes. "I like black," he stated.

"Come on. You chose the game, let me choose the colours of the discs."

"No."

"What? You refuse me such a simple wish?" Behind Axel, the crowd grew in number, drawn by the prospect of a potential conflict. Axel turned and looked at them with mocked confusion. "Odd, isn't it? Makes me wonder what he's hiding."

Mr Flame's eyes darkened. "Fine. We'll play with yellow and blue."

Axel shook his head. "No. *I* choose the colours."

"Yeah," someone yelled, "let The Hog pick!"

Mr Flame glared at the onlookers, knowing he was being analysed. "All right. Just pick the damn colours so we can get this over and done with," he growled.

Taking his time, Axel flipped through the colour alternatives on the game boards. "I want…that one," he said at last, choosing green and red discs.

The Gamer nodded and Mr Flame's grin vanished at once.

"I…" he began, his eyes flickering between Axel and the crowd. Poor man. He knew he'd lose.

Being colour blind had to suck, Axel thought as he scurried back to the Grand Hall a few minutes later. It was time to fish for another idiot.

On his way over the long bridge, he passed Ms Peacock. She looked down at his necklace where two white diamonds dangled. Laughter lines gathered in the corner of her teal eyes as she smiled behind her fan.

"Impressed?" Axel whispered when they were side by side. He didn't look at her, and she didn't reply, but as he left, he thought he heard a suppressed giggle.

## CHAPTER 22

In the main building of the Central Station, Paavo Nurmi waited for the courier. He stood near the large wall-mounted information board, reading a Time magazine. When the woman arrived, she was fifteen minutes late.

"Finally!" she exclaimed and threw herself in his arms. As they embraced, she placed her lips to his ear. "Yujin," she whispered.

"No not at all." He laughed and kissed her cheek. "It's fantastic to see you again." Reaching out, he took her carry-on like a true gentleman. "Let me help you with that. I've got the car outside."

It had stopped raining and, in spite of the hour, the city centre pulsated with life. The courier kept talking and laughing, holding her young arm in his as they strolled over to the parking lot. Once she got into the car, her facade faded.

"You're late," Paavo growled, closing the door behind him.

"And you're being followed," she snapped back, staring into the right wing mirror.

"What?" He stared at her as she leaned forward, chewing the side of her lower lip.

"There," she said in a calm voice. "You see the woman in the grey jacket, carrying a book?"

Paavo turned and looked over his shoulder. "The ugly one?"

"She's not ugly. Perhaps not EKA material, but not ugly. And yeah, that's the one. She was watching you."

"Bullshit!" Paavo had been an agent long before this little brat was born, first with Supo, the Finnish Security Intelligence Service, then with Interpol, and now at The Academy. "I would've known."

The courier looked at him with obvious disgust. "Your job is to *observe* people. *My* job is to be unnoticed. I know what I'm talking about; you're being watched." She settled back. "Now, can you drop me where I'll be able to get a cab? I need to get back to the airport."

\* \* \*

"You need to change tactics, my dear."

Axel turned from the buffet tables. "I beg your pardon."

He was staring into an elegant falcon mask. His mind spun. Oh yes, Ms Boyce, the film producer.

Tucking a strand of blonde hair behind her ear, she tipped her crystal glass in the direction of his necklace. "Anyone hiding four diamonds underneath his collar, is hardly considered an easy target."

Axel opened his mouth, but she shook her head. "Don't waste your time trying to convince me otherwise. I'm here with a proposition. If you're interested, join me. If not, have a nice evening."

She turned and walked away, her dress swaying as she moved. It was a modest, white dress with a medieval design. There were speckles of brown spots on it, like old coffee stains. What a peculiar choice for such a grand mask.

He watched her go with an irresistible urge to follow. I better not, he thought and saw her vanish behind a group of men. I better not.

In an attempt to quench the tingling in his stomach, he drew a deep breath. It didn't help at all.

Oh, what the hell! Fortune sides with him who dares, right? Placing his empty glass on the nearest table, Axel set off after her.

"I will not insult your intelligence by pretending I'm new to the game," the woman said when he caught up with her at the entrance of the Quarters. Lifting the front of her dress, she descended the stairs as she spoke. "I've played for several years and must admit I'm rather good at it. You, on the other hand, are something of a mystery. I can't make up my mind whether you are a novice or not. Somehow, you come across as neither and both at the same time."

"Your proposition?" Axel asked, thinking it best not to get himself sucked into a discussion he couldn't control.

"There you go." Ms Boyce smiled. "Would a novice pose his question like that? Would an experienced player? I'm not sure."

They both fell silent as they stepped out onto the white bridge, pushing their way through the hordes of people moving about outside Game Room One. Once they'd passed Game Room Two, they could again walk side by side.

"What about the proposition?" Axel repeated, ignoring the sense of unease that spread through his veins.

"I'll tell you, but not here," the woman declared. "We'll meet a friend of mine first. After that, we'll tell you our proposition."

Behind his mask, Axel allowed himself a nervous smile. Maybe the woman wasn't lying. Perhaps there *was* a proposition, but more likely, he was stepping into a potential trap. Of course, stepping into traps had been his strategy from the start. When people think they're fooling someone, they're less likely to focus on their own defences. It makes them weak. It makes them a perfect target.

The lights grew dimmer as they left the entrance behind them. After Game Room Six, there were no more entertainers out in the water and far fewer guests. A sense of looming danger filled Axel, and his feet were less eager to move on.

When they reached Game Room Nine, Ms Boyce stepped off the main bridge and pulled open a thick door resting upon oiled hinges. "Here we are," she said, holding open the door.

To enter, Axel had to push through a thick, black curtain. He found himself in a tiny, dark room. Ms Boyce followed, and as she closed the door behind them, a deep roar shattered the silence. An enormous hologram tiger materialised and flung itself over Axel.

"Holy shit!" he barked and stumbled back, slamming into the woman behind him.

She laughed. "Ah. Scared you, did it?"

Before he could reply, the wall in front of them slid open.

Game Room Nine was dark, save for the ultraviolet panels, whose light gave life to animated colours on the walls, ceiling and floor. It was a bit like entering a fluorescent Picasso painting. A waitress passed Axel, carrying a silver tray with smoking drinks. Her naked body was lit up in a complex pattern of glowing paint.

"Follow me," Ms Boyce ordered, and pushed past him.

As she did, Axel froze in astonishment. The woman's dress had lit up in an explosion of fluorescence colours. It looked as if she'd wrapped herself in molten gold, only the patterns of her dress created the impression of folded wings.

"It had better be the dress you're staring at," Ms Boyce warned.

"What else would I look at?" Axel countered with a grin and hurried after her.

He received no more than a smile for an answer. She led him past a series of circular cubicles. They were extraordinary things, enclosed by digital drapes that functioned as large, movable screens. She stepped into one where the drapes showed a video of a deciduous forest. The digital beads rattled against each other as Axel followed her. It was the first time he'd walked through a screen, he mused.

"That was fast," said a tall woman, waiting for them on a black sofa curved like a half-moon.

"It wasn't very hard," Ms Boyce replied. "He's got a curious soul."

"We knew that already," the woman said and turned to Axel, "but I didn't expect it to be that easy."

She wore a short, silver-coloured dress with gleaming pink and purple threads woven into the fabric. For a terrifying moment, Axel couldn't remember who she was. Thor had pointed her out, but...

Then it came to him. Ms Dobrin. She was a former British MP who'd started a prominent global charity in London. Her mask looked like the face of a Roman goddess, while her hair vanished under the hood of a long, silvery cape.

Holding a glass of Champagne, she pointed at a beautiful bow and arrow beside her crafted from white wood. "You can call me The Huntress," she said. "And you're The Hog, I believe?"

"Only if it pleases you," Axel replied and bowed at the waist.

The women laughed. It was a polite, non-humorous laugh, and it made him feel both foolish and humiliated.

To regain some sort of dignity, he dropped into the couch and leaned back as if he owned the place. "Well then. What can I do for you?"

"He's got the right attitude," Ms Dobrin approved, tapping the side of her glass with a long, white nail.

"Perhaps, but I caught him off guard at the entrance. He wasn't expecting the tiger."

"Ah. A rookie, then."

Axel swallowed his displeasure and looked up at the flickering curtains around him. He wouldn't let himself be provoked. "What about that proposition?" he asked, keeping his voice flat.

"I don't think it's his skills we should worry about." Ms Boyce pondered aloud. "It's his temper."

Ms Dobrin guided her glass to her lips and gave him a shrewd smile. "Is that true, Mr Hog? Do you have a bad temper?"

"Only when it serves my purposes."

"Ah! Excellent answer. You've got an eye for the game, I'll give you that. A bit rough around the edges, but you've got the hunger for it. The passion."

"Really?"

"Indeed. We've been watching you tonight, and that glimmer in your eyes...I've seen it before. It's not merely the thrill of a challenge or the fear of ending up with a black rock that drives you. No, I think you see beauty in complex trickery and manipulation. I bet you appreciate it, as some appreciate great wine. It's the game you love, not the prize."

To his surprise, Axel realised she might be right. There was something irresistible about setting up a trap and luring a target into it. And he seemed to have a knack for it. Realising the seconds were ticking, he pushed the thought aside and let out an exaggerated sigh. "Shall I come back another time?"

The two women exchanged a glance, and in that moment of silence, Axel knew they'd come to an agreement of some sort. It was Ms Boyce who spoke first. "Have you heard of Section Two?"

"Maybe."

"Then you haven't." She settled back. "Section Two is like a VIP room. The stakes are higher here, but so are the rewards. To get in, you need at least four diamonds and an invitation. The diamonds are not a problem. You already have four. It's getting invited that's difficult."

"Let me guess," Axel said, scratching the back of his neck with a finger. "To get invited, someone has to like me."

"Rather, you have to be…useful."

"Ah. You need me."

"There's a player we want you to destroy. If you succeed, you'll gain every diamond we have, plus whatever you collect along the way." Ms Boyce held up her chain. "We have eight together and they're yours, *if* you leave our target with a black rock on his chain."

Axel pursed his lips. A black rock. That made things a bit more complicated. "What has this person done to piss you off?"

"That's none of your concern. You'll either accept the challenge or not."

This was folly. Axel already had four diamonds, which was enough to impress The Academy.

"Who is he?" he heard himself ask.

"We'll tell you his name if you accept. But know this, the man is a *very* good player."

A tingle of excitement slithered up Axel's spine, giving him goosebumps. "Okay. I'm in."

* * *

At the bar stood a short woman, dressed in a magnificent midnight blue gown and sparkling mask. She smiled. His size and shape matched, as did his movements, although he'd added a slight arrogance to his walk. Now that she'd picked up fragments of his voice, she knew; the Warthog was Axel.

This conclusion was both impressive and bewildering. For the past hour, she'd seen Axel trick and manipulate people as if he knew their every weakness. He was brilliant, and that could only mean one thing. He was cheating.

Izabella emptied her glass and snapped her fingers at the bartender to refill it. While she waited, her fingers played with the long strands of her midnight-blue hair. There were still so many questions. For example, how did Nicole fit into all of this? The woman had taken a black rock to help Axel. At least, that's how Izabella had interpreted the situation. What in the hell were the two of them up to?

CHAPTER 23

Christopher Bell, teacher in Leadership Etiquette, had taught his students to always lead with their chests. "That's how you signal confidence," he'd said, "by keeping your backs straight and your chests up."

Axel took the advice to heart as he stepped off the main bridge and walked up to a black metal door. Laughter and music echoed between the walls, but the bridge itself was set in darkness, save for a single torch burning next to the door.

Without hesitation, he knocked.

"Yes," came a voice above him.

As Ms Boyce had instructed him, Axel refrained from looking up. "It's a test," she had explained. "Only a novice will look up, and novices aren't allowed at Section Two, no matter how many diamonds they have."

"*Gloria virtutis umbra*," Axel whispered. *Glory is the shadow of virtue.*

With no more than a faint whisper, the door opened and gold light spilled out, accompanied by soft music. Stepping over the threshold, Axel found himself in a room, much like an Irish country pub, with a low ceiling and crooked oak beams.

The scene vanished in front of him, replaced by a black suit jacket belonging to a very large man.

"Yes?" the guard rumbled.

Axel kept his eyes level with the man's chest. "Night-wasp," he replied. The man grunted and stepped aside. "Welcome."

A waiter approached with an empty tray. His body was a work of art, painted as a mahogany jigsaw puzzle, with a few pieces missing, showing hints of organs behind them. "Would you like something to drink, sir?" he asked.

"A beer," Axel said, for he knew it wouldn't do to drink sparkling water in a place like this.

"What kind, sir?"

Pulling off his gloves, Axel glanced in the direction of a large fireplace. Next to it sat a young woman on a stool. She sang a gentle tune while her fingers danced over the tensed strings of her guitar.

"*Crown Ambassador*," Axel stated, and followed the waiter to the bar.

He made a quick count of the guests. There were twenty-one altogether; fifteen men and six women, all wearing costumes that signalled strength or viciousness.

Three of the guests were lounging in leather sofas near the log fire. At the bar stood a woman, waiting for her drink; the rest sat scattered around the room. They sat at rustic tables with monitors built into the polished surface. Among them, Axel spotted his target.

The fellow in question wore a bull mask. Perhaps it was a sign of the power he felt at heart but lacked in figure. He was a short and skinny man, who seemed no wider around his waist than an oversized lamppost.

His true name was Mr Luca Gallo, a forty-seven-year-old bachelor, born in Uruguay but now a Spanish citizen. According to The Box's list, he was an ambitious businessman with a murky background.

"Avoid him," Thor had said when they'd seen him earlier that evening. "He's a greedy and sneaky bastard with a bad temper and powerful friends. A terrible combination."

Didn't look like much, though, Axel thought and took a seat at the bar. He gave the woman next to him a little smile but she ignored him.

For the next twenty minutes, Axel sipped his beer in complete silence, pretending to enjoy the music while in fact he observed the guests. He watched them play their games, studied their movements and gestures, searched for tension between players and analysed their behaviours. Thanks to Thor, he recognised all but a few. They were business owners from all corners of the world, billionaires, a few politicians, a Hollywood star, a famous scientist, and a prince.

"Sir. You may begin." The modulated voice came from a lone waitress behind the counter. She flickered a glance into the shadows where two figures sat at a secluded table. Both of them were very careful not to look at him.

All right, Axel thought and stood up. Time to play.

* * *

Izabella pounded the door with as much confidence as Axel had had.

"Yes," came a voice above her. She looked up at the monstrous face made of stone.

"I'm Lady Blue, and I want to enter," she declared.

"No," the voice replied.

That took her by surprise. "But…I'm Lady Blue."

"Yes?"

"I'm a distinguished guest!"

"It's still no."

Izabella folded her lips and glanced back towards the Grand Hall entrance. "Look, I was asked to come here," she said, adding annoyance to her voice. "You have to let me in."

"No."

"Don't be ridiculous…"

"You cannot enter. Have a nice evening."

The flaming light in the stone figure's eyes died. Damn it!

CHAPTER 24

"Who wants to lose first?" Axel threw his gold gloves on the table. The Gamer at the table looked up for a brief moment, but the four players kept their eyes on their screens.

"Piss off!" said one of them. He wore an impressive dragon mask in all shades of blue. Beneath it was the edge of his thick, blue beard. It stuck out like the bristles of a broom.

His name was Mr Martel Louvet, a French billionaire with powerful connections. Another man best avoided according to Thor.

"I'll leave when your rocks hang around my neck," Axel replied.

Nearby, someone laughed. The Dragon kept his eyes on the screen. "You've got four petty rocks, but an ego the size of my dick," he said in a gruff voice. "Return to Game Room One before you get hurt."

"Come on, you shouldn't use such foul language in front of a lady."

The only woman at the table gave Axel a glare. "Go to hell," she snapped.

There was more laughter.

"Cute." Axel grinned and turned back to The Dragon. According to Ms Dobrin, the rules were a bit different in Section Two. One couldn't just challenge an unwilling player. All games had to be agreed upon. "Let me see if I've understood this, I've got four diamonds, you've got a small penis, and somehow that makes you unwilling to challenge me?"

The Dragon pushed back his chair and got to his feet with the air of a man who was about to do something stupid. Then, from out of nowhere, he bellowed out a laugh and pointed at an empty chair next to his. "*Bon*, Piggy. But *I* choose the game. *Oui?*"

Axel shrugged. "As you wish."

The man turned to the silent Gamer. "Has our agreement been noted?"

He got a nod in reply.

"*Bon*," The Dragon repeated and sat down. "Let us get this over and done with."

Axel turned his attention to the table screen in front of him. Ms Boyce had tried to explain how they worked. Hidden cameras monitored both the Quarters and the Grand Hall. In Section Two, players had access to many of them.

"N2:45," The Dragon said after a while. Axel tapped in the camera code and found himself staring at a room glowing in pink light. There were thick cushions on the floor. In the corner of the screen, Axel saw a couple having sex, yet The Dragon's interest was on a man and woman kneeling at a low table.

"For three rocks," his opponent said with a smirk in his voice. "What will the woman order when the waiter arrives? Wine, beer, or something stronger?"

Axel looked down at his screen. A peculiar calm filled him. He didn't recognise the woman, but the man was Eryk Sokal, an adored photographer who worked with the rich and famous. He had a weakness for sex and cocaine, and according to Thor's list, he also enjoyed dominating women. Often with his fists, although that part hadn't reached the public yet.

"She won't order anything," Axel said after a while. "It will be the man who makes the order."

The Dragon's eyes narrowed. "What makes you say that?"

Axel laughed and tapped the side of his head. "It's a hog's secret, Monsieur. Now your turn."

"*Bon*. She'll have wine!"

The Gamer tapped a knuckle against the table. They had made their bets.

## CHAPTER 25

"Let me order," said the man on Axel's screen. "A bottle of white, and bring us a plate of snow." He laughed like a neighing horse and gave the painted waitress a good whack on her naked behind. "Be quick about it."

The Dragon raised his head and made a sound halfway between a laugh and an exhalation. "*Ce n'est pas possible!* How did you know?"

Axel grinned and sipped his beer. The thrill was indescribable. "Want a re-match?"

"Of course!" The Dragon cracked his knuckles and turned back to the screen.

During the next twenty minutes, Axel felt like a God. It was so easy. Unlike other games that required various skills, betting was nothing more than a matter of reading and understanding people.

Axel found that his Academy training together with Thor's list, gave him an edge that made all the difference. He knew who had a bad knee, which players were uncreative, and who lost focus when someone invaded their personal space. At the same time he analysed players for signs of lies, fear and lack of confidence. When he combined these factors, he got enough information to make sensible bets.

"*Merde!*" The Dragon bolted out of his chair and threw his glass into the fireplace. It shattered into a million pieces. "You're cheating!" he bellowed with his thick, French accent.

"Impossible," the woman at their table said. "*You* are the one picking the games."

"Shut up!"

The Gamer raised a finger of warning. In an instant, the large guard from the door approached. The Frenchman didn't see him as he stared at Axel with flaming hate. "You're cheating," he growled again.

Axel laughed. "Don't be such a baby."

It was a stupid thing to say, but he was high from adrenaline and bloated with self-confidence. The man flew forward. He was quick, but not quick enough. A large hand grabbed him by the neck, and with a loud whack his face connected with the table.

"The Gamer says it's fair," the guard rumbled. "It's time to pay your dues." He held the squirming Frenchman while the Gamer removed six rocks from the man's necklace. Then the guard hauled him out of Section Two.

Suppressing the desire to whoop and pump his fist in the air, Axel turned to the amused faces in the room. "Who's next?" he asked. "You?" He pointed a long finger at Mr Luca Gallo, as if picking the man at random.

The thick lips of his target curved into a smile. "I think that's a bad idea," he replied with a slight lisp and an unnerving, childlike voice.

"Very well." Axel stood up. "If none of you have the guts to face a hog, then so be it. I'll have to find my luck elsewhere."

"I'll play you," came a silvery voice from the other end of the room. In the warm light of burning candles, Ms Boyce stood up. "It'll be a pleasure to take those rocks from you. Beating The Dragon means nothing. He is, after all, a man."

Ms Dobrin laughed. "No. You can take half of The Hog's rocks. The other half belongs to me."

A light chuckle made Axel turn back to Mr Gallo.

"What's so funny?"

"Women," the target replied, as if that would explain everything.

"Yes. Braver than most men it seems," Axel said.

The chuckling stopped. "You will play *me*," Mr Gallo declared.

Twenty minutes later, Axel stared at his screen, elbows on the table and forehead hanging heavy against the palm of his hands. Next to him, Mr Gallo brushed a hand over his black suit jacket. It was a beautiful thing, made of the finest fabric and gold stitches. "What do you say, Piglet? Again?"

Axel closed his eyes and cursed under his breath. "Perhaps later," he managed. "It seems I've run into some bad luck."

"Luck has nothing to do with it."

"Either way, unlike The Dragon I know when to stop."

With an ivory toothpick, Mr Gallo picked up an olive from a crystal bowl. Settling back in his chair, he popped it into his mouth and flashed a row of small teeth. "A wise decision, young man," he lisped with a scornful tone. "Give me what's mine and bugger off."

When Axel stepped out on the bridge four minutes later, the sound of laughter still rang in his ears. Without a word, he walked over and grasped the railing. Staring into the black water, he took a few seconds to steady his galloping heart. Once his breathing was under control, he set off to Game Room Six.

On his way, he passed a woman in an impressive blue gown and mask. She curtsied when their eyes met, and he bowed back. Something about the way she watched him made Axel look over his shoulder. When he did, he found she was looking at him, but when their eyes met, she turned and walked away.

Game Room Six was buzzing with excitement. In the middle of the open space stood a glass box. It was big enough to fit two players and a Gamer as well as a second but smaller see-through cage. Axel entered in time to see a Gamer release a white rabbit into the inner box. The animal scurried off to one corner. Blindfolded, the players held a gun each, aimed into the cage at random through narrow slits. Axel looked away. He'd seen the game played on the monitors in Section Two. It never ended well for the rabbit.

Ms Peacock was at the bar, chatting with a few other guests.

"I need to talk to you," he declared as he stepped up beside her, careful not to tread on the plumed train of her peacock dress.

When she saw who it was, she lit up. "Wow!" she whispered. "Five rocks. I'm impressed."

There was a muffled pang, followed by a disappointed "Aww" from the crowd around the cage. Axel leaned close to her ear. "They're yours for a little favour."

She stared at him for a heartbeat, then took him by the arm. "I think we should find us a quiet place to talk."

\* \* \*

Nicole stood with a glass of wine and a smile on her face. She was watching an elderly woman in an iron mask challenge Aseem in a memory game. The two players were still at a point where Aseem clearly thought he was fooling the woman and not the other way around. Nicole had been to the Diamond Ball several times and had seen the Iron Lady trick many young men over the years.

Her thoughts dispersed when a familiar fragrance tickled her senses. Bergamot, lemon and lime.

"Ms Peacock," she said, eyes still on Aseem.

The woman appeared by her side, a handheld fan covering her mouth. "How did you know it was me?"

"A talent, I guess." Nicole turned and gave the woman a smile. They weren't friends. One didn't have friends at the Diamond Ball. Still, they had collaborated on a few occasions, and in some unexplainable way, Nicole felt as though she could trust the woman.

"You still have the black, I see," Ms Peacock said.

"Yes. It's not an easy thing to get rid of. People keep their distance when they see it."

"Then you're in luck, my feathered friend."

"Why?"

"I want it back."

"Excuse me?"

"I want you to give me your black rock in return for my single white." The woman snapped her fingers and their Gamer appeared.

"Let it be noted that I'll relieve Lady Swan of her black rock, in return for a white. I won't demand anything else and I will not break our previous agreement. This is not a favour, and she won't owe me anything."

The Gamer gave her a clear nod and turned to Nicole who frowned.

"Why?"

"That's my business, Lady Swan."

"Are you saying you'll take my black rock and demand nothing in return?"

"Correct."

A sense of hope was beginning to well up inside Nicole. "Really?"

"Yes."

"Well, in that case I'll accept your offer." Nicole laughed.

"I would've been very disappointed if you hadn't," Ms Peacock replied.

As the Gamer swapped their diamonds, Ms Peacock leaned close and whispered, "You worried in vain, my dear. The man you care for, your *friend*, he's a very capable player. In fact, if this is his first ball, then he was born to do this."

CHAPTER 26

The guard held out a massive hand as if ready to stop an approaching freight train. "You only have one rock."

"I'm well aware of that, but it's black! I can't have more than one if it's black, can I?"

The guard shook his big head and began to close the door. "You only have one."

"Wait! I need to speak with one of the players. The Bull. Can you at least get him for me?"

"No."

"Can you pass on a message?"

"Do I look like a messenger?" the guard growled.

"Please. I have some information to sell…"

"Go away," the guard said and closed the door.

Axel cursed aloud and almost kicked the stairs. Then he remembered his uncomfortable shoes and marched back to the main bridge instead. He leaned against its railing and stared into the water. Now what would he do?

"All right, what's your message?"

Axel turned at the sound of the voice. The guard had returned and was standing by the door with his arms crossed over his large chest.

Confused, Axel walked over to the man. "Have you changed your mind?" he asked.

"Tell me the message or I might change my mind again."

"Fair enough," Axel said with a smile. "Tell The Bull that I've got some information to sell."

"What kind of information?"

"Tell him I've identified an enemy of his and I have a proposition that will interest him."

The guard let out a bored sigh. "As you wish." He walked back into Section Two and shut the door behind him.

Axel returned to the main bridge. He stood with his back against the railing, staring at the closed door as if pondering its place in the universe. He was still standing there five minutes later, when Mr Gallo sauntered out.

"You've got information for me," said the little man as he crossed the connecting bridge.

"I do."

Mr Gallo chuckled as he came closer. "It seems your bad luck hasn't changed, Mr Hog."

"I wouldn't say that. You shouldn't believe everything you see."

"Are you telling me it's *not* a black rock I see on your chain?" Mr Gallo grinned as his words slithered out of his mouth.

"What makes you think it's there because of bad luck?"

When hearing this, Mr Gallo burst out into a fit of laughter. "You like the colour? Is that it?"

"Nah. They say grey is my thing."

The thin man reached the railing. With a shake of his head, he stared down at the rose petals floating by in the black water. "You're a very strange man, Mr Hog. I can't decide if you're brave or dumb as a bag of beans."

"Bag of beans? Did you just make that up?"

Mr Gallo's eyes grew cold. "You are playing a dangerous game, Mr Hog."

"Aren't we all?" And with that, Axel patted the man on his shoulder. "Game."

"Huh?"

"I'm challenging you to a game."

"You can't…" Mr Gallo fell silent and stood paralyzed for a moment. Axel watched as it dawned on him that he'd left Section Two. This was the Quarters where regular rules governed. Out here, he couldn't decline a challenge.

"You piece of shit," he cried. "You set me up!"

Axel held out his hands. "What can I say? Your curiosity got the better of you."

Behind them, a Gamer appeared from the dark. She tapped her knuckle against the railing, a sign that she approved the challenge, making it binding.

"You have no idea who I am or what I am capable of." Mr Gallo trembled as he spoke. "You're a dead man. Do you hear me? I will kill you until you're deader than dead, until you're a pool of nothingness that even Death himself will reject."

Axel began to laugh. "Be careful, little man," he said and leaned forward, before breathing his next few words into his target's ear. "I can ruin you in a matter of minutes, Mr Gallo."

A mayhem of emotions flickered in the little man's eyes. Then, in the dancing light of the torch, Mr Gallo sprang forward. Clutching Axel by the throat, he dug his fingers deep into the flesh. "I will kill you!" he bellowed.

* * *

Standing alone outside Game Room Twelve, a short distance from the commotion, Izabella watched as Axel struggled to pry the attacker's hands open. What the hell was going on?

She'd seen Axel speak to the peacock lady. The woman had then met with Nicole and reclaimed the same black rock she'd given Nicole in the beginning of the games. After that, Ms Peacock went back to Axel and gave *him* the black diamond. And now Axel was being beaten up by a thin man half his size.

Izabella's eyes shifted as the black metal door she'd knocked on earlier, flung open. A massive guard stepped out on the connecting bridge. He marched over and wrenched The Bull from Axel, but as he did, the little man threw a perfect kick. It caught Axel right in the groin.

"Ouch. That must have hurt."

Izabella spun and found a fleshy gentleman step up beside her. He wore an upside-down mask that didn't impress her.

"Yeah, must have," she agreed and turned back to watch Axel who was now on the ground. "And for your information, there's no use in you challenging me. I'm already engaged in a game."

"You're involved in that?" The stranger made a little nod towards the hullabaloo further down the bridge.

"I don't want to be rude or anything, but I need to focus here."

The stranger laughed. "Of course. My apologies for the intrusion, and I bid you good luck."

As the man strode away, Izabella experienced a brief moment of hesitation. Was she being unwise? While the other students focused on gaining diamonds, she was here, focusing on Axel.

Then her senses came back to her. Yes it was a risk, but if she could prove that Axel was up to no good, then the rewards would be far greater than if she collected a few diamonds. Of that, she was certain.

\* \* \*

God it hurt. Axel sat on his knees, trying to breathe. The guard looked down at him behind his black mask, waiting for an explanation.

"I've challenged this man to a game," Axel wheezed. "He can't refuse. We're outside Section Two."

The guard turned, first to the Gamer who nodded, then to Mr Gallo who stood with his arms crossed and hatred burning in his eyes. "If the Gamer says yes, it's yes," the guard concluded. "You *will* play."

The little man took a step forward, pointing a bony finger at Axel. "When I've beaten you, you'll tell me your real name, Piggy. After that I'll decide what to do with you."

The Gamer guided them into a dark theatre room, accessed via Section Two. Axel and Mr Gallo were given a touch-pad each and then motioned to sit down in comfortable armchairs, facing a wide screen. Behind them a crowd gathered, among them Ms Boyce and Ms Dobrin.

Axel had to give it to the man. Unlike most people, Mr Gallo's attention didn't seem to suffer when he was angry. He made no hasty decisions, nor did he let himself be stressed by the whispering crowd. On the contrary, he seemed to grow more focused, and it took forever before he and Axel could agree on a bet.

"What about her?" Mr Gallo pressed a button on his touch-pad and on the large screen a man and woman appeared. The man was challenging the woman to complete a complex jigsaw puzzle in less than two minutes. "She will not succeed," Mr Gallo declared. He looked at Axel, waiting for an answer.

The woman on the screen was Ms Emily Brugger, the chairman of the governing board of the Swiss National Bank. According to The Box's list, she had a vicious IQ and superb analytical skills. It ought to make her perfect for this challenge, but was she good enough?

"Well?" Mr Gallo pressed.

"Make the damn bet, will you?" someone yelled at the back, drawing laughter from the crowd.

"I bet she will do it," Axel said.

The Gamer knocked his knuckles against the table and silence entered the room. On the screen, the woman began to sort out her pieces. She worked with extraordinary speed. Axel watched as she did the corners first, followed by the sides. After a minute she was more than half way through. After ninety-four seconds she was done.

Behind Axel, the crowd remained quiet, but this time there was a different kind of silence. A tense, worried kind.

"I guess that's it," Axel said, fighting to keep his excitement in check. "You lost."

Mr Gallo stared at the screen and said nothing. On his chain twinkled somewhere between eight to ten diamonds. Axel tried to count them as the Gamer unhooked the black diamond from his own chain.

Mr Gallo got to his feet. With his chin held high, he adjusted his suit jacket. "Show me your face," he whispered, still staring at the now black screen.

"You've lost. Let it go," Axel replied.

"I said, show me your face."

Axel laughed. He couldn't stop himself. "No."

The Gamer approached Mr Gallo, her steps slow but fearless.

"Do not touch me," he warned her.

She didn't pay him any attention. This was her job. She reached out towards him. That's when he struck her. His closed fist slammed into the half-smiling and half-weeping mask. Something cracked and crunched beneath it. The Gamer fell back, already unconscious. Her head struck the floor in front of Axel's feet with a sickening thump.

For a heartbeat, nothing happened. Then all hell broke loose. Two guards flew forward. Mr Gallo got the first one with his knee, sending the man to the ground with a cry.

"Let's go," someone said, grabbing Axel by the arm. It was Ms Boyce. Her eyes were wide behind the falcon mask. "Now! You don't want to be here when the guards come."

Behind her, guests were scurrying back to Section Two. Mr Gallo was on the floor, wrestling the guard with remarkable fury. Axel's eyes fell upon the unconscious Gamer. Blood seeped out from underneath the cracked mask.

"I want my rocks," he said.

"We'll deal with it later," Ms Dobrin yelled from over by the door.

Axel took a step forward but Ms Boyce held him back. "We'll give you ours. Isn't that enough?"

A section of the wall began to open. The fingers around Axel's arm vanished. "You really should run," Ms Boyce said, and then she was gone.

Axel gawked as a troop of black-masked guards rushed in,

heading straight for Mr Gallo. Axel was so engrossed in the moment that he failed to see the guards approaching him from behind.

CHAPTER 27

FOUR YEARS EARLIER

Hayato had no illusion that his getaway would fool The Academy. Even if Jerome hadn't seen him, it would only be a matter of days before they figured out he'd run. It would shock and bewilder them. Well, most of them. They'd never understand why an Academy student would go through the pain of graduating and then flee two days later.

Now, because of Jerome, Hayato had perhaps two, maybe three, hours before they'd be on his tail. After that, it wouldn't take long before The Box would know too.

Hayato headed north. The plan was to draw his pursuers in that direction before slipping off to the east and then south.

Despite his fear and exhaustion, Hayato smiled. Poor Jerome. He must be furious, but better furious than dead.

From Fort Railway Station, Hayato had taken a taxi to Negombo, a modest beach town north of Colombo. There he'd changed to a different cab, heading to the city of Kurunegala, about an hour and a half away. Following his friend's instructions, he'd asked the driver to drop him off at the Puwakgas junction.

It was after three in the morning when he arrived. As promised, an old Peugeot stood parked outside a yellow building complex. Hayato crossed the street at a light jog. When he approached the waiting vehicle, a young man stepped out.

"Mr Black?" he asked.

"Yes."

The man opened the door to the back seat. "Welcome," he said as Hayato slid in.

He sat up and blinked. They had stopped. The driver looked at him through the rear-view mirror. "This is Wariyapola," he declared.

It wasn't much to see. The car's headlights braved the darkness around them, throwing a pale light upon the empty road in front of them. Hayato could see a few makeshift kiosks further on. All deserted for the night.

Something caught his eye. A figure by the side of the road. It was an old woman, the shape of her visible thanks to a tiny lantern at her feet. She stood in front of a low, metal gate, leaning on a simple cane.

"Thank you," Hayato croaked to the driver and reached for the door.

"Good luck," the man replied.

Hayato grabbed his bag. Yes, he needed luck. Lots of it.

"Thank you," he repeated and stepped out.

With a grumble, the car disappeared into the foreboding dark. When its taillights had vanished, Hayato slung his rucksack over his shoulder and drew a breath that smelled of dust and hot asphalt.

He crossed the night-drenched street, slapping at something buzzing near his ear. The old lady greeted him with a toothless grin, holding up the lantern so she could look at him. She had a pockmarked and wrinkled face, much like a peach pit. As the lantern swayed in the warm wind, attracting bugs big and small, she stared at him, trying to read his soul.

*If grandma doesn't like you, then you're in trouble*, his friend had written. Now Hayato stood here, waiting for a verdict.

"Mhm," the old lady said with a throaty voice, lowering the lantern. With no other words or gestures, she swung around and hobbled towards a bungalow, nestled in among the trees.

Not knowing what else to do, Hayato followed her a few steps behind. She guided him to a guestroom behind the small building.

It was a tiny place with a separate entrance and an abundance of insects. They buzzed, fluttered, hopped and skittered around him in the most unsettling way.

There was one window, without glass or mosquito netting. The woman placed her lantern on a wobbly table and pointed at two bottles of water by the bed.

"Thanks. You're very kind," Hayato said, taking in the surroundings.

For some reason this made the woman laugh, and she walked out into the blackness with no apparent worry for what might hide in the dark.

Hayato threw his bag on the floor. There was a towel on the bed but he was too tired to wash up. He was almost too tired to go to bed but knew he needed to rest. After blowing out the candle in the lantern, he dropped into the hard bed.

As he closed his eyes, he felt something crawl over his leg. With a yelp, he jumped out, only to realise he was standing in complete darkness with no way to light the lantern or find out what was sharing his bed.

The absurdity of it all threw him into a fit of laughter. Only a few hours had passed and already his life was like nothing it ever had been. The thought thrilled and terrified him.

He was free.

Pulling the bed sheets loose, he shook them with vigour. Something hit the concrete floor. It sounded like a beetle. Or cockroach. Whatever it was, he heard it scurry off. A shudder ran through his body and he sprung back into bed. There he rolled himself in the sheets like a cocoon and fell asleep before his head hit the pillow.

Hayato woke to the sound of a knock and realised he hadn't moved at all. For a moment he lay there, feeling the thin fabric against his sticky skin. It took a few seconds for his mind to drag itself out of the foggy remnants of worried sleep.

The knock came again. This time, with a bit of effort, he unwrapped himself from the sheets and peered at the direction of the sound. Outside, the wakening sky gave contours to the room.

With his hair plastered to his sweaty scalp, he heaved himself out of bed, trying not to think of what might be running about on the floor.

Another knock. He found his shorts and gave them a good shake before pulling them on. The last thing he wanted right now was a poisonous spider inside his drawers. But as he approached the crooked door, he realised spiders were the least of his worries. This notion came with a faint smell of a familiar cologne.

Pushing the door open, he stared at the boyish face.

"I believe you owe me an apology sir," it said.

CHAPTER 28

PRESENT DAY

Axel sat on the ledge of an open window, looking out over rooftops below. He could see a small section of a narrow canal where the green, tranquil water reflected the world like a mirror.

With a moan Axel leaned back against the window frame. His ribs hurt. As did his leg, neck and right eye. His feet were also in pain, but that was because his new shoes were giving him blisters. Hell, his whole body ached, but he didn't care. He had bigger problems to worry about.

Axel touched the black rock on his chain. More than an hour had passed since the guards had locked him into this room. Axel's initial anger had now turned into fear. His plan had failed. There was no way out and no one to help him. Neither Nicole nor Thor knew where he was.

A soft creaking of the door made him turn, and there she stood with a glass of wine in her hand. The Hostess.

"Good evening," she said with a near perfect high-class British accent.

Baffled, Axel stared at her without uttering a word. He had never expected to see her here. The Hostess had a party going on. Why bother to see him in person? Why not send her guards to deal with him?

The woman strode towards him, her remarkable crimson-coloured dress flapping around her. "You've been waiting a long time," she said. "I hope you haven't been uncomfortable."

Regaining some composure, Axel straightened his back and lifted his chin. "I've been beaten, locked up, and had my mask ripped off my face." Then, remembering Nicole's instructions, he added, "My Lady."

"Is that all?" The woman tittered, raising her glass in a little toast. "Goodness gracious. You ought to be honoured. By the sound of it, my men respect you."

Axel had come to the conclusion that there were different kinds of confidence. People like Professor Jackson had a self-assurance that seemed to balance on a knife's edge, as if it required a lot of effort to maintain it. The Hostess on the other hand, had her confidence moulded into her DNA. Axel saw it as clearly as he saw the paleness of her skin and the sparkling gold painted over her short hair.

"May I ask why I'm here?" he began. "It was my opponent who attacked the Gamer, not me." Axel held up the black diamond. "The man should be wearing this. I've done nothing wrong."

The Hostess cocked her head and looked at him in an unexpected, kind-hearted way. Like him, she wore coloured lenses, only hers glimmered in gold, not red. "Let me tell you, Mr Hallman. I don't mind people who cheat. After all, we call it 'survival of the fittest', not 'survival of the most honourable one'." She giggled. "Truth be told, I've cheated a fair bit myself over the years, but what I can't stand, are *wannabes*. I absolutely loathe people who try to play in the big league when they don't belong there. It's…humiliating."

Was she testing him, or trying to provoke a response? Meeting her gaze dead on, he gave her a grin that could mean anything. "True," he replied. Pathetic, isn't it? Anyway, how do you know my name?"

The woman laughed, and let her golden eyes travel to the window and the night outside. "Let's just say that your principal and I have an understanding. The nature of this understanding is irrelevant. What I want to know is this; Mr Bull claims that you know his identity. Is this true?"

Axel let his fingers trail the soreness of his neck as the cogwheels in his head spun. The thing about lying, he thought, is that you can't hide it completely. There are always signs, a glance down to your right, decreased blinking rate, or dilated pupils. These are small things you're not aware of, or can't control.

As he stood there, feeling her eyes upon him, Axel realised why The Hostess had had his mask taken. She wanted to read his face. Not that it worried him too much. His time at The Academy had proven him a good liar. What concerned him was how The Hostess would judge his word against Mr Gallo's. If he denied his knowledge of Mr Gallo's identity, would she believe him?

"Yes, My Lady," he replied, not daring to take the chance. "I know who he is."

"Interesting. Tell me how."

"I came to an agreement with two of your guests. If I could place a black rock on Mr Gallo's chain, I'd win all of their diamonds, plus anything I took from Mr Gallo himself. When we discussed the terms of the challenge, they told me his real name."

"Hm." The Hostess looked into her glass for a moment, her mouth serious. "I'll accept your answer for now. I know of Ms Falcon and Ms Huntress from before. Both of them are experienced players. They might have figured out his identity over the course of their participation."

Axel should have known The Hostess would figure out his agreement with Ms Boyce and Ms Dobrin, after all, this was her ball, her guards and her Gamers. Even so, he was taken a bit by surprise.

"What I don't understand," The Hostess continued, "is why they would ask *you* to take on this challenge?"

"Oh," said Axel and grinned. "They chose me because I'm good at reading people, My Lady."

"Are you now?" The Hostess laughed. "At least there's nothing wrong with your confidence." She shook her head. "Well, my security advisor tells me you're either bloody brilliant or a cheater."

Axel felt a sting of worry. "Have you been keeping an eye on me," he said with a false cheerfulness.

"Certainly. What did you expect? You and your fellow students are on the road to becoming very powerful people. I believe it's in my interest to keep an eye on you." She leaned in, her face beaming like the sun. "Why do you think the guard at Section Two changed his mind and brought your message to Mr Gallo? Because I told him to, of course. I wanted to know what you were up to."

Axel managed to maintain his smile. "I take your interest in me as a compliment, My Lady."

"Take it any way you like," the woman giggled. "I still haven't made up my mind about you." With a graceful motion, she reached out and grabbed his chin, pressing her fingers hard against his skin. "Your professor in communications thinks highly of you, yet I've received no information indicating that you could beat the most experienced players at my ball. I'm certain Principal Cunningham would've told me if he thought that was the case."

Holding him in a firm grip, The Hostess leaned in until her lips almost touched his. "Either you're lying to me, Mr Hallman, or your principal has no idea how talented you are. We're about to find out the truth."

* * *

Principal Cunningham stood among a group of guests when Nicole slid past and gave him a little but noticeable shove.

"Oh, pardon me," she said before making her way over to the buffet tables. She picked a few things at random and then headed over to a secluded corner, far away from the dance floor.

He followed her after a few minutes, strolling with one hand in his pocket and the other holding a glass of whiskey. "I'm glad to see you've lost your black rock," he observed with a smile.

"Yes." She threw a quick glance around them. "Sir, I fear Mr Hallman has gotten himself into some serious trouble!"

CHAPTER 29

Pixie, The Box's Security coordinator, got the call ten minutes before midnight. "Go on," she said as she walked out of the living room, leaving her half-sleeping husband on the sofa, watching a film. It had been years since he'd last questioned her odd working hours.

On the other end of the line, the agent was breathing hard. "I believe Mr Nurmi met with a courier today. Either that, or he has an adult daughter we don't know about."

"He has no family," said Pixie. "Do you have any idea what was delivered?"

"No, but it was small enough to fit in a carry-on."

"Where is Mr Nurmi now?"

"I'm sorry, I don't know. He drove off with the courier before I could get to the car. Seemed to be in a hurry."

"Do you think he saw you?"

"No."

Pixie entered her small home office, closing the door behind her. For a moment she stood motionless, thinking. Then she ran a hand over her braided hair and walked over to her computer.

"All right. What are your thoughts on the matter? After all, you're the one in the field."

"My guess is that he's planning on wiring Mikael Andersson's apartment. I'm on my way there now."

\* \* \*

The large owl let out an ominous call where it sat on the neighbour's chimney. Paavo looked at it, and then continued to circle the large villa.

He had dropped the courier off at Odenplan before heading to the island of Lidingö where his target, Mikael Andersson's father, Walter Andersson, lived.

Peering up at the façade he saw two open windows on the top floor, but they were out of reach. He decided that his best choice was to enter via the basement door on the back of the house.

With the owl watching, he picked the lock in under a minute and stepped in. He spent another minute looking for any sign of an alarm system. Satisfied there weren't any, he ascended up an old, creaking staircase.

Most agents followed their instructions without question. Paavo did not. He knew that to identify a rotten apple, one had to think outside the famous box. It was how he'd become one of the most successful agents within The EKA.

After reading The Academy's profile on Mikael Andersson, Paavo had concluded that if the young man had something to hide, he wouldn't be stupid enough to talk about it in his own home. He was Axel's best friend and had to know The Academy watched him.

This had made Paavo turn his attention to Mikael's father. The old man had paid for all of his son's peculiar travels over the past two years. It could be a simple act of kindness, yet Paavo didn't think so. His gut told him the two men were up to something.

Reaching the ground floor, Paavo un-shouldered his backpack and got to work. On light feet, he moved around the dark rooms, installing the tiny microphones with great efficiency. When he reached the living room, he worked to the sound of an old grandfather clock, ticking with unconcerned loudness.

Once the living room was completed, Paavo moved on to what he suspected was the old man's office. With a gentle nudge, he opened the door. It let out a little whining screech.

The sound brought Paavo to a dead halt. He held his breath and stared into the room with growing dismay. As expected, he was in the old man's office, but it wasn't empty. By the wide windows, near an old desk that seemed to drown under a flood of papers and books, stood a worn armchair. In it sat the old man.

The old man sat slumped forward, eyes closed and with a thick book resting in his lap. In the hazy orange glow from an antique desk lamp, he looked at ease. His breathing was calm and steady, chin resting against his chest.

Paavo released his breath, cursing to himself. *Saatana perkele.* Was he losing his touch? A small surprise like this shouldn't bother him. He rolled his shoulders to get the adrenaline out of his system. Bloody hell, he was getting old.

Careful not to touch the door, he slipped into the room. It seemed that every damn floorboard creaked under his feet. With his eyes locked on the sleeping man, he moved towards the desk, one step at the time. The room smelled of stale air and old leather. On one wall hung a large map, full of colourful pins. A sign of a well-travelled man perhaps, or maybe the pins represented something else.

Another floorboard groaned, and the old man stirred in his chair. Paavo stopped. His fingers slid under the jacket behind his back and pulled out a long dagger. With a flick of his wrist, the knife spun in his hand until he held it in a reversed grip.

The old man stirred again, moving his head to the side. Paavo shifted his weight onto his right foot, eyes locked on the hollow of the old man's neck. Seconds passed. Nothing happened. When a minute or so had elapsed, Paavo moved towards the desk. He was anxious to get out. The last thing he wanted was to explain a murder to Ms Brown. With his knife in his mouth, he resumed his work.

## CHAPTER 30

Trailed by two armed guards, The Hostess led Axel down a long spiral staircase, draped in red fabric. Remarkable paintings covered the walls, but Axel was unable to pay them much attention. His mind was lost in a heap of worries. He had no idea where they were heading, and the guards suggested he was now more of a prisoner than a guest.

They reached the end of the stairs and faced a long, rather gloomy corridor. One of the guards pushed past Axel and opened a strange ornate door made of black mahogany and ivory. As he did, a muffled cry came from somewhere down the corridor.

"Fancy a cup of tea?" The Hostess asked, ignoring the noise.

"Sure." Axel pretended not to notice the second guard hurrying off in the direction of the sound. "Do you own this building?"

With a snicker, the woman placed a hand on his arm. "Here's a bit of advice, young man. Every year there's at least one brickhead who tries to uncover my identity. It's a waste of their time, and mine, as I end up having to punish them for their stupidity. So, before you do yourself any harm, leave my identity out of this."

She gave his arm a gentle pat and stepped through the door. He followed her, letting a thick, Persian carpet greet his feet. "No offence, My Lady," he began, and then stopped as he beheld the chamber they'd entered. It was small, extravagant and stank of incense. Art covered the walls and in one corner stood a beautiful enclosure made of ivory and glass, filled with butterflies of all colours and sizes.

"You were saying?" The Hostess asked, opening a hatch in the enclosure.

"I…" Axel stared as butterflies spilled out into the room. "I'm not interested in your identity," he replied somewhat distracted. "I merely wanted to know the size of this place. It seems endless."

"Even the tiniest space can seem infinite if you don't see its end," the woman retorted, letting a butterfly land on her hand. "It's the same with humans, you know. If you hide your limitations, you appear limitless. That's how you build heroes, although I'm sure you know that already."

She blew the butterfly away and turned to a masked servant standing in the shadows by the wall. "Tea for my guest. And tell Jacob I'm ready."

The servant curtsied and disappeared through an opening in the wall.

"Have a seat, Mr Hallman." The Hostess pointed at two wide leather armchairs, standing side by side in the middle of the room. In front of them hung a large piece of glass in gold chains. "We're going to test your skills, young man. If you're as good as you say you are, I'll let you go. If I find out you've been lying to me, I shall be disappointed."

The way she said it, suggested she wasn't very good with disappointments. Without a word, Axel sat down in one of the chairs, trying to ignore his thundering heart. A moment later, the young servant appeared with a cup of steaming tea. As she held out the tray, he looked up at her and recoiled in shock. The woman wasn't wearing a mask. Ugly burn-scars covered her face, and the red skin stretched over her skull like molten plastic. He winced, and she responded by looking away.

Axel regained his composure and accepted his cup. The servant bowed and went down on all fours in front of him. He stared at her. "What are you doing?"

"You're supposed to put your feet up," The Hostess explained. She clapped her hands twice and a middle-aged man appeared. He had a face as destroyed as the young woman's. Without hesitation, he dropped on all fours in front of The Hostess and she placed her feet upon him.

Axel threw a quick glance over his shoulder, ignoring a butterfly that had settled on his chair. Along the walls stood several servants, all of them watching him with impassive eyes behind burned-scarred faces. It made Axel sick and he shivered despite the warmth of the nearby fire.

Again, The Hostess clapped her hands. From an adjacent door came a gloved guard holding a syringe. He made his way around Axel's chair and took position behind him, pointing the needle against his neck.

"Batrachotoxin," The Hostess said, pointing a finger at the syringe. "A thousand times more poisonous than cyanide. It brings death to a man in less than ten minutes." She sniggered as the lights began to dim. "Shall we begin?"

Axel found it hard to pull his eyes from the syringe.

"Pay attention now," The Hostess warned. There was a flicker on the large piece of glass. It was some kind of TV.

A woman in her mid-thirties was sitting in front of a metal table in a small, dark cell. She was crying.

Next to her stood a heavy-set man with a bald, egg-shaped head. "Well?" he said and licked his thin lips. "What's it going to be?"

A second man came into view. "Or maybe you prefer both?" he laughed. He was smaller than his companion and had a pair of wild, mutton chop sideburns.

"She owes that man some money," The Hostess explained. "For two months, she's failed to pay her debt. Now, the creditor must punish her. A good beating or spreading her legs for the men you see. Those are the two choices she has. What will she choose? You have fifty seconds to come up with your answer. Fifty seconds to prove your skills."

This was insane. Axel was about to object when something in The Hostess' eyes stopped him. Her mouth had curved into a smile, yet her eyes were cold, calculating and unforgiving.

The guard stepped forward, placing a strong hand on Axel's shoulder and aiming the syringe needle against Axel's neck.

"As you wish, My Lady," Axel replied, his tongue as dry as a bone.

Doing his best to ignore the needle, he turned his attention back to the screen. The woman was sobbing loudly now, but he had to ignore it. To survive this, he must focus.

The woman wore frameless glasses, silver earrings and a simple cardigan. Her bleached hair was short and straight. She had a ring on her left hand, suggesting she was married.

"Forty seconds," The Hostess informed.

Axel felt sweat forming on his brow. How could he possibly know which of the two alternatives the woman would choose? There were hundreds of unknown factors that would affect her decision; how she'd been raised, her attitude towards sex, her relationship with her husband, and how she dealt with physical pain etcetera.

"Thirty seconds."

The hand on Axel's shoulder twitched ever so slightly. On the screen, the bald man grinned and licked his lips again. His eyes were filled with eagerness as they darted from the woman to the man with the sideburns and back.

Wait a minute. Axel frowned.

"Twenty seconds, Mr Hallman."

The men were excited. The sick bastards probably got a kick out of beating and raping helpless women, but there was more to it than that. The way the men kept sharing amused glances, and looking into the camera...

"Ten seconds. I need an answer, Mr Hallman."

The grip on Axel's shoulder hardened.

"It doesn't matter what she chooses," Axel said in a low voice. "She never had a choice. Those men will beat and rape her no matter what she chooses. I can see it in their eyes."

The Hostess clasped her hands in front of her as if praying.

"Oh, bravo, Mr Hallman," she exclaimed. "*Bravo!*" She laughed, shaking her head. "I must say I'm impressed. I didn't think you'd figure that out. Tell you what; let's try another challenge."

CHAPTER 31

Axel felt the acidic fumes of vomit at the back of his throat. The things he'd had to see and analyse. The cruelty. It wasn't right. To sit and watch people get punished and not be able to do anything. It was horrible, and he could feel something dark and evil spread through his soul.

The one thing that would haunt him the most was a young man who'd been caught stealing. Axel had no idea what the fellow had stolen, but it had to be something of great value, for the interrogator had given the man a choice; suicide or forever be in the service of The Hostess. The man had chosen the latter, thinking it was a simple choice.

"As you wish," the interrogator had said, and to Axel's horror, guards had tied the man to a chair and thrown some kind of acid in his face. At the sound of the screaming man, the servant under Axel's feet had stiffened. Did she recall the day it had happened to her?

"You think I'm harsh?" The Hostess asked. Her gentle voice snapped Axel out of his thoughts.

"No, My Lady," he lied. "Not at all."

The woman wasn't harsh. She was bloody insane.

"I'm pleased to hear that," The Hostess said. "Power is like a house of cards. All it takes is one mistake and you'll lose it all. One can't govern without rules, and rules are nothing if not maintained. It's the same with consequences. Fail me and I'll punish you. I can't be lenient, for then I lose it all."

"The man," Axel began, careful not to touch the needle aimed at his neck. "The one who chose to be in your service? What will happen to him now?"

"Oh." The Hostess smoothed out a wrinkle in her fabulous dress. "That young man chose life. He's marked as mine now, and I will train him to become a member of my staff. It won't be the life he'd expected but it *is* a life. Also, by living, the man will remind others what might happen if they don't respect me. In that sense, his life will have a purpose."

She gave Axel a look that couldn't be interpreted in any other way but a warning. "You haven't touched your tea, Mr Hallman."

Axel smiled, pointing his thumb at the guard behind him. "I'm trying not to move, My Lady."

"Of course." The woman giggled and gave the man behind Axel a quick glance. He immediately withdrew. "I think we're done here," she continued and took her feet off the manservant in front of her. She gave him a little kick. The man scurried off towards the bar. As Axel stood up, his servant remained on all fours until he gave her a light tap with his foot. Only then did she move.

"Come on, Mr Hallman," The Hostess twittered. "We haven't got all day."

Followed by two guards and a Gamer, they left the room and made their way down the long corridor. There were metal doors on either side. Passing one of them, it opened. A man with a familiar face stepped out. He scratched one of his sideburns and gave Axel a fleeting smile.

Behind him, Axel could see the woman from his first game with The Hostess, the one who hadn't paid her debt. She lay naked and still on the table, her frameless glasses broken beside her. Next to her the bald man was pulling up his trousers.

"Did you enjoy yourself, Mr Sweeny," The Hostess asked without looking back at the man exiting the room.

"Yes, My Lady."

"Then I expect that contract signed by morning."

"It will be, My Lady," the man said. "I'm a man of my word."

Mr Gallo sat hunched forward, hands tied behind his back, and chin resting against his naked chest. He looked up when the little procession entered the cell, his face swollen and discoloured from where he'd taken a beating.

When he saw Axel without a mask he laughed. "Now you're a dead man," he slurred. "I never forget a face."

The Hostess rolled her eyes. "Oh, the drama." She sighed and looked down at Mr Gallo. "Listen," she said, her voice suddenly sharp and dangerous. "I've tested this young man. Although I can't rule out some elaborate flimflam, I've concluded that it's quite possible you were beaten fair and square."

"Bullshit!"

"Ugh. I detest foul language." The woman sighed again and seemed to ponder her alternatives. After a moment she turned to Axel and picked a piece of hair from his shoulder. "Young man, I've decided to give you a choice. If you want, I will negotiate a truce between you and Mr Gallo. You will take back the black rock and let him keep his white stones. The both of you will forget this ever happened and move on."

"The hell I will!" Mr Gallo barked.

Before anyone had a chance to react, one of the guards stepped forward and gave him a mammoth blow with the back of his hand.

"Don't worry, young man. He *will* forget," The Hostess assured Axel.

Axel looked down at Mr Gallo who was licking blood from the corner of his mouth. This was wrong. So very, very wrong, yet he pushed on. He couldn't keep the black rock. It would ruin his life.

"What if I demand my right?" he asked with a low voice. "What if I want the diamonds I won?"

"Then things become complicated," The Hostess chirped. "Enemies are inevitable in our line of business, but it's important to remember that one can't fight an entire world by oneself. If you take what you claim is yours, then you must also deal with the consequences. I should remind you that some men, and women for that matter, value pride higher than wisdom. Mr Gallo is one of them."

The man on the chair kept his silence this time, but his eyes cried vengeance.

"He assaulted a member of my staff," The Hostess continued. "I had my plans for him, but I'll let you decide his fate."

Mr Gallo's head flew up. "What?"

His outburst was met with another hard blow. Afterwards, a long silence entered the room. Everyone stared at Axel who felt as though his soul hurt.

"I'm honoured," he said at last, knowing he was still being evaluated.

The Hostess stuck her arm under his. "Good. But before you make your choice, remember what I told you; rules are nothing if they're not maintained."

"Yes, My Lady."

"A great leader must be firm and just. It's what the followers expect. It's what they *need*!"

"I understand, My Lady."

"Excellent. Now I'm curious to know; what is your choice?"

Axel steeled himself, knowing what he had to do. He pointed at the line of white diamonds clinging to Mr Gallo's necklace. "Those rocks are *mine*."

"As you wish," The Hostess said.

At once, the guard stepped forward and grabbed Mr Gallo's head, pulling it back with force. The thin man struggled against his ropes, screaming and cursing while the Gamer removed his diamonds.

Once the rocks dangled on Axel's chain, The Hostess considered the man on the chair. "What about the consequences?" she asked.

Axel exhaled. A sudden calmness fell over him, the kind that comes from accepting that you only have one choice. His muscles relaxed. With his feet planted firmly on the ground, he felt the darkness well up inside him. It was the same darkness he'd been battling for the past few hours. It came with force, and with it, came a ruthlessness he hadn't known he possessed.

"The choice," he whispered.

"I'm sorry?"

"I said, give him the choice. Suicide or a life in your service."

The Hostess clasped her hands over her chest. "A gift? Oh, how sweet of you, Mr Hallman. I shall accept. At least until you've completed your studies. After that, he's yours. You've earned him. You really have."

"Hallman? Studies?" Mr Gallo looked confused. "What do you mean suicide?"

The Hostess wasn't listening. She was giggling.

CHAPTER 32

The wiring of the old man's office took forever. Paavo had to move with care, stopping every time something creaked or squeaked. A few times the old man shifted in his seat, but other than that, he slept through the whole process. Lucky for him.

Paavo itched to get out of there, but still he kept his calm and completed his task. Once he was done, he made his way to the first floor.

The wiring upstairs proceeded without problems, although Paavo found it frustrating the way the house popped and creaked. It made him uneasy. Thus it was with some relief when he flung the rucksack on his back and began descending the staircase. He placed his feet near the wall where the steps were less likely to complain.

When he reached the lower steps, he threw an instinctive glance towards the office. Soft light fell through the open door, braving the shadows that ruled the rest of the house. He saw the stacks of paper on the desk, the antique lamp and the wide armchair.

That's when he froze. The chair was empty.

\* \* \*

The very end of the Quarters was set in darkness, save for a single candle burning on the stone railing. Axel stood motionless, listening to distant laughter and the lapping of water against the bridge. He tried to decide what he was feeling and came up with nothing. Nothing but a vast emptiness. As if he'd lost his soul.

"It won't do for us to be seen together," The Hostess had explained before sending him away. "But don't worry, I shall see to it that all the administration concerning Mr Gallo and his business is taken care of."

"Administration?"

"Indeed!" She'd laughed. "One can't simply steal a man without organising everything around it. I'll keep you posted."

Axel wished she hadn't said that. He never wanted to see, or hear from, the woman again.

Cold fingers nudged his elbow.

"Yes. I'm ready," he sighed and adjusted his mask. Without thinking, his fingers slipped down and brushed against the heavy chain. So many diamonds. The Academy would be proud.

The silent person prodded him again and together they made their way back to Section Two. This time the door opened before Axel had a chance to knock, and the guard stepped aside with a respectful nod.

Ms Boyce and Ms Dobrin sat at their table among the shadows. When they saw him enter, their bodies stiffened in unison.

"Good evening, ladies," he said and dropped into a chair in front of them. "I've now fulfilled my part of the agreement. The Bull has a black rock on his chain."

Ms Boyce glanced at Ms Dobrin. "She let you go?"

"She did."

"And where is the Bull?"

Axel forced a smile, blocking out all images that came to mind. "Let's just say he called it a day."

Ms Dobrin picked up a glass with something pink and bubbly. She gave it a look, and when it seemed to hiss at her, she drained it in one go.

"If the Bull is gone," she said, "will he then suffer the Year of Shame?"

"I don't know," Axel admitted. He hadn't given that any thought. "Not that I see why it matters. We agreed that if a black rock hung around the man's chain, I'd get your diamonds."

"Of course." Ms Dobrin picked up a napkin and dabbed it against her mouth. "We only have one problem; neither The Bull, nor our Gamer is here. How do we know you're telling us the truth?"

Axel snapped his fingers. From the shadows came a tall Gamer. "I understand your concern. Thankfully, The Hostess has been kind enough to offer us another Gamer. This one can confirm that The Bull has a black rock on his chain."

The Gamer tapped his knuckle against the table in confirmation.

Stunned, the two women exchanged another glance.

"Don't you want to know why?" Ms Boyce asked.

"I don't care why," Axel replied. All he wanted was to go home.

"He likes to abuse women," Ms Dobrin said. "Many lives have been destroyed to satisfy his pleasures. It had to stop."

Axel looked away. "I doubt he'll hurt anyone else," he mumbled.

He could sense the new darkness within him. It had infected his soul and was sucking the energy right out of him. He needed to leave. Now!

"What are you waiting for?" he asked the silent Gamer. "Give me their diamonds."

\* \* \*

Thor stood on the bridge, halfway between Section Two and the Grand Hall entrance. He stared at a fire-breather spitting flames in the dim light.

Axel frightened him. The man was unpredictable. Wild-cards were supposed to be unpredictable, but this was different. How, Thor couldn't say. It was just something about the young Swede that gave him the creeps.

He let go of his thoughts and waited a beat before he spun around, clasping a surprised Axel by the wrist. The man pulled back by sheer instinct, but Thor's grip was brutal.

"Mr Hog," he said with a smile and placed a firm hand on Axel's shoulder. That's when he saw the diamonds. They hung in row around the young man's neck.

"Holy shit!" Thor blurted before he could stop himself.

For a fleeting moment, he noted clouded confusion in Axel's posture, as if someone had yanked the young man out of a deep sleep.

"You," Axel began with a hint of a slur. "You're still here?"

"What the hell have you done?" Thor growled between his teeth, pulling Axel towards the railing. "How many rocks have you got there?"

"Seventeen."

"Seventeen! Are you mad? I told you; no more than *six*."

"You told me to impress The Academy."

"Jesus! Six would've been more than enough. Thabo's got two. The others have one or none!" He paused and glanced at the fire-breather. "Where have you been? Section Two?"

Axel met his glare like the devil himself. "I've been with The Hostess."

It took a few long seconds before Thor could reply. "You what?"

Axel rattled his heavy chain. "'Fortune sides with him who dares', right?"

Thor's fingers closed into a fist. "You dumb son of a…" He swallowed the rest of the sentence. "You're in way over your head. You're putting us all in jeopardy here."

"I was told to play the game, and that's what I've been doing."

"Shit!" Thor trembled with fury. "You don't get it, do you? If you want to survive this, you do as *I* tell you."

"Why? Because you say so?"

"Yes!"

Axel shook his head. "I know nothing about you. Why should I trust you when all you've given me is your name?"

"What are your alternatives? Huh? You're caught between a rock and a hard place, and I'm the only one who can guide you through it. You listen to me. You have no idea how dangerous that woman is."

Hearing this, Axel let out a low, dark laugh. He lowered his voice and leaned forward. "Oh, I know who she is. The way she spoke of Principal Cunningham as if she owned him. I figured it out, all by myself. She's one of The Seven."

CHAPTER 33

An acrobat swung across the bridge, blocking her view for an instant. She was about to curse at him when a pudgy hand fell upon her shoulder.

"Game!"

Izabella pulled her eyes from Axel and frowned at the man with The Upside-Down mask. "You again. Didn't I tell you I'm already occupied in a game?"

"You did," the man laughed, "but I have reason to believe it's not true. I've checked, you see." A Gamer stepped up beside him and bowed.

"But…I'm busy."

"Yes, you are. You're playing with me." The man offered her his arm.

She stared at it then glanced back at Axel. For hours he'd been gone, then out of the blue, there he was, talking to a man dressed as a crow. By the looks of it, the two men knew each other, but they were not pleased to see each other.

"I can tell you something about The Hog," The Upside-Down man said, his voice carrying a touch of humour. "Seeing as you're so interested in him, I mean."

She started to object but he cut her off, "Don't worry. I'll give it to you for free."

"Really?"

"Yes."

"What is it then?"

"Well, I heard from a trustworthy source, that The Hog beat one of the best players at the ball."

Izabella gave a scornful laugh. "Your *reliable* source isn't very reliable. The Hog's not that good."

"I'm afraid I must disagree. Besides, didn't you see the line of rocks on his chain?"

Hearing this, Izabella turned once more and looked in the direction of Axel, but she was too far away to see his necklace.

"No."

"Ah." He looked at her and she could smell curry and wine on his breath. "You know," he continued, "for your single diamond, I will tell you everything that happened in Section Two. I was there, you know."

\* \* \*

Over the years, Principal Cunningham had grown tired of games. After all, being the principal of the world's greatest leadership academy meant playing games on a daily basis. Nevertheless, the Diamond Ball was an enjoyable event. There was something refreshing about hiding behind a mask. He could move among people without being recognised and harassed with questions.

Strolling along the edge of the balcony, he looked down at the dance floor, contemplating the situation. Axel appeared to have bitten off a tad more than he could chew. The guards seldom interfered at the ball, but when they did, it often meant The Hostess was infuriated. She was not the worst of The Seven, but she was bad enough.

"Sir."

He turned and found himself staring into the red eyes of the man in question. "Yes?" he asked, keeping relief hidden from his voice.

"Don't," Axel warned. "You know who I am."

There was a slight sway in his posture, as if he'd had a drink too many. Of course, Principal Cunningham knew the boy didn't drink, so this was something else, maybe deep exhaustion or stress.

"Excuse my curiosity, young man, but how do you know *my*

identity?"

"I figured it out."

"I'd love to know how you did that."

Axel snorted and stepped forward so close their masks almost touched. "You see the diamonds on my chain?"

Unable to look down without headbutting his student, the principal shook his head. "Not at the moment, no."

"There are seventeen of them. Seventeen white rocks. I've won them."

"Very impressive, young man. Would you like me to applaud you?"

Axel's jaw tensed and his shoulders rose. "It *is* impressive."

"Yes, I believe that's what I said."

"Don't make fun of me. You all assume I'm a failure, but these rocks prove I'm great."

"Yet, didn't you get the lowest score on the midterm exams?"

The young man's eyes widened as if slapped. "That wasn't my fault!"

Principal Cunningham took a sudden step forward, forcing Axel back. It was time to remind the young man who was in charge here. "Listen, Mr Hallman," he whispered with a calm and gentle voice. "If I had doubted your ability to become a leader, I'd have gotten rid of you already. I don't doubt your abilities, but skill is one thing, attitude and willingness another. Until you've made up your mind whether you want to become a leader or not, the number of diamonds you've collected is irrelevant to me."

The principal stepped back and raised his glass in a salute. "Now have a lovely evening," he said and walked away.

\* \* \*

Nicole was standing by the dance floor, moving her hips to the music and waiving off admirers wishing to dance. All of a sudden, Axel was at her side. He leaned forward, shoulders up as if about to charge.

"Get me out of here," he whispered.

She looked down at his diamonds. "My God. How many…"

"I want to leave."

Nicole reached out and placed a hand on his arm. He was trembling.

"What's wrong?" she asked.

"Get me out!"

"You know we can't leave. Not until the game is over."

Axel closed his eyes and swayed a little. "Please," he begged.

"I don't understand. Are you in pain?"

Axel shook his head. Someone bumped into them from behind. The Grand Hall was filling up with people. In fifteen minutes, the games would end, and the Year of Shame Ceremony would begin. Those stuck with a black rock would find their lives forever changed.

"You!" A tall man in a blue dragon mask pushed Nicole aside. He stepped up, grabbing Axel by the neck, but Nicole was fast, pressing her body between Axel and the man, forcing him to let go. "We were just leaving."

The man's eyes narrowed. He pointed at Axel, his finger trembling as he spoke. "That bastard is a cheat!"

As if saying the words fuelled his wrath, The Dragon lurched forward. Nicole reacted on instinct and with the palm of her hand, struck the man's Adam's apple. It wasn't hard, but it drove him back, stumbling and gasping for air. He crashed into a group of guests and someone cursed.

"Come." Nicole turned Axel around and began pushing him through the crowd. On the balcony, behind the arched pillars, were divans where Axel could rest through the remaining ceremony. As soon as the games were over and the party started, they could leave.

She didn't get far. People poured in from the Quarters. In the disarray, a strong hand grabbed her hair from behind.

"Go up the stairs," Nicole yelled before The Dragon pulled her back. Gripping the man's fist, she spun around and slipped under his arm. In one smooth movement, she came up on his side, pressing his elbow forward. A little pressure on his joints and he went down on his knees with a grunt.

"You are being rude," she said. Then, looking up at the bewildered guests around her, she smiled. "I think he's had a little too much to drink." She applied additional pressure, forcing the man to throw himself forward. "Oops. Let me get you some water," she said and released her grip.

Nicole caught up with Axel who was walking rather than running. Taking his hand again, she more or less dragged him up the stairs.

Once up on the balcony, she guided him to a soft divan, not too far from the exit. Guests stood packed along the railing, waiting for the Year of Shame Ceremony to begin.

"We'll wait here," she said. "Once the ceremony is over, we'll leave."

"The hell you are!" snapped an angry voice. They both turned and saw The Dragon come stomping towards them. This time he had company, two companions in exquisite costumes. "You're not leaving till I have your name."

"Piss off," Axel muttered, but there was no power in his words.

"I'm going to snap your ugly head off, you little bastard."

"That's enough, sir," Nicole warned and stepped out to block the stranger's path. He was a head taller than she was, and with his two friends at his side, he showed no fear. Men could be so stupid.

"Step away, birdie," said The Dragon, his words twisted by his French tonality. "This is none of your damn business."

"As a matter of fact, it *is* my business, monsieur. You should leave before you end up in trouble."

"*Non!* I want his name."

Several of the nearby guests had turned and were now watching the confrontation with amusement. Nicole sighed and turned to The Dragon's companions. "Could you please remove your friend? I really don't want to hurt him."

Someone giggled, and The Dragon's face darkened. "Get out of my way, bitch," he hissed and stepped forward to push her aside. He had to be a complete moron; one of those men who still thought size mattered. Hadn't he figured out she knew how to defend herself?

Nicole sidestepped his attack, exposing the hidden slits in her dress as she bent down and swept his feet from under him. He fell with a satisfying yelp.

The nearby guests broke out in spontaneous applause.

"You go, girl!" someone yelled.

One of The Dragon's companions, a beefy man in a silver costume, bolted forward and threw a quick but untrained punch. Nicole blocked it with ease, snapped the back of her hand against his forehead. As his head arched back, she double-punched him in the solar plexus. The large man dropped to his knees with a pained huff, gasping for air.

Meanwhile, the second companion, wearing a golden skull, was already moving forward. Nicole saw him in the corner of her eye and threw a rapid side-kick. Her left leg came to a dead stop with the heel of her white shoe pressing hard against the hollow of his neck. She could actually feel him gulp.

"Sweet!" someone exclaimed, and more applause broke out.

"Easy now," the man mumbled and took a step back.

Nicole retracted her leg and turned her attention back to The Dragon. "Listen, monsieur. There are times when the wisest decision is to accept failure and move on."

"This has nothing to do with failure," The Dragon fumed, getting to his feet. "He cheated! I don't know how he did it, but no one is that good."

Around them, interested eyes turned to Axel. She could hear the crowd whisper, picking up words of admiration, but also suspicion. What pained her the most was that a tiny part of her was just as sceptical. Hayato Sano had managed to gather seven rocks, and that had been the beginning of his legendary status. Axel had close to twenty.

"You're wrong," Nicole replied, stopping herself from further thought. "My master *is* that good."

"Bah! Your *master* made predictions that were impossible."

"He knows the identity of the guests," the gold-skulled man agreed. "I was there. I saw it too."

A murmur of concern rippled through the crowd. They didn't like the sound of that.

"Don't be ridiculous." Nicole laughed. "How would that even be possible?"

The silver man stood, pressing a hand against his solar plexus. "That's what we intend to find out, you arrogant bitch," he wheezed. It looked like he was about to say something else, but as he opened his mouth, his face connected with Nicole's foot. He was unconscious before he struck the floor.

"Oh, sorry about that," she said, looking down at the man sprawled on the floor. "My leg spasms at the word 'bitch'."

She looked up in time to see The Dragon and the gold-skulled man, yanked back by a group of masked guards. As if on cue, the crowd dispersed. Nicole watched as the guards dragged her three attackers into an opening in the wall. As the wall closed behind them, she turned and looked at Axel. He sat with his head in his hands as if he hadn't noticed a thing.

* * *

The Hostess stood with her mask in her hands, watching the screen with a smile. She was in her private den, a cosy and quiet place with direct access to the Grand Hall.

"That Ms Swan is a feisty one, isn't she?"

"Yes, My Lady."

"Maybe I should ask her to work for me."

The security advisor, Lorena De Paz kept her eyes on the monitors. "I hear Principal Cunningham is very fond of her," she said.

"Perhaps, but I own the principal." The Hostess scratched the tip of her sharp nose and frowned. "Remind The Dragon and his friends that this is *my* party. Once you're certain they've understood, strip them of their rocks and send them home."

"As you wish, My Lady. And Ms Swan?"

"Let her be. I think Mr Hallman needs someone to look after him tonight. He's had a tough evening."

De Paz pressed her lips together into a thin line and gave her underlings their orders. The Hostess tittered. "How many rocks did you gather the first time you and your class were here?" she asked, scratching Vulgar behind her ear. The female tiger gave a low hiss, her pale blue eyes gleaming with warning and unpredictability; a wonderful combination.

"I'm not envious, My Lady, if that's what you're insinuating," the security advisor replied. "I'm sceptical, and that's what you pay me to be. The Dragon is right. Mr Hallman was *too* good."

"You keep saying, yet he passed our tests. *Your* tests to be specific."

"There's no doubt he's brilliant at reading people, but…"

"But?"

"I can't put my finger on it. Something's bothering me."

Giggling, The Hostess put on her mask. "Inform Principal Cunningham that I want to speak with him after the Year of Shame Ceremony is over. Bring him here."

CHAPTER 34

Paavo waited and listened. He couldn't hear a sound apart from the damn grandfather clock ticking in the living room. It was time to get out. Inching his foot forward, he stepped off the staircase and held his breath as the floor whined beneath his feet. Still, nothing happened.

Staying close to the wall, he slid around the corner, moving towards the basement door. He tried to steady his body. His rapid breathing was making it hard to hear anything.

Out of the blue, he smiled. This was what he loved the most about his job. The unexpected tension. The adrenaline. It made him feel alive.

As he reached the main entrance, he peered around the corner to the hallway. It was empty. Spinning the knife in his hand, he let out an excited breath and moved on.

When he reached the guest toilet, he noted a thin beam of light stretching out from under the door. Ah, there you are, Paavo thought and felt more at ease. For a brief moment, he felt an urge to pound on the door, just to scare the hell out of the man. When he'd been younger, he might have done so. He'd been more unpredictable then.

On quick feet, he hurried past the kitchen and reached the basement door. After a final glance towards the living room, he opened it and let out a gasp. The old man stood right in front of him with a wide smile upon his lips.

"Well hello," he said in a cheerful tone before breaking a bottle over Paavo's forehead.

\* \* \*

Axel rocked with the motion of a motorboat. Beside him, Nicole looked out over the black water, the hood of her red robe hiding her face. Maybe she understood that her presence was all he needed, for she'd been silent ever since they'd left the ball.

Somewhere in his clouded mind, he knew Nicole's handling of The Dragon and his shithole friends had been impressive. At the moment, he couldn't remember what she'd done to them, but it *had* been extraordinary.

He also had vague memories of seeing Mr Gallo carried onto stage in an open litter. There had been four other guests with him, and they all had been terrified. Well, not Mr Gallo. He had seemed drunk, hadn't he? Axel wasn't sure. He couldn't remember much. Guards had removed the masks of the black rock wearers as their names had appeared on a gigantic screen. All the while, the crowd had laughed and cheered.

Axel stared at his feet. His thoughts were thick as syrup and every time he closed his eyes, images of scorched faces and abused people appeared. It made him want to retch, which was why he stared at his gold shoes, too exhausted to even hate the damn things for pinching his heels and toes.

Once back at the yacht, Nicole followed Axel to his cabin. The sun still had a few hours of sleep before morning. Someone had made his bed and lit a single light to keep the darkness at bay.

"You shouldn't sleep with the lenses in," Nicole said to him.

She helped him out of his robe and then his jacket. With trembling fingers, Axel dug the lenses out of his eyes. After that, Nicole used a wet towel to clean the paint off his face. She traced her fingers along the side of his bruised neck.

"What have you done?" she asked with a voice so gentle it stung his heart. She held his face and stroked his cheeks with her thumbs. Only then did he realise he was crying.

\* \* \*

Axel's face remained blank, but tears trickled down his cheeks.

Something had broken inside him. One didn't have to be a psychiatrist to see that.

Nicole had no idea what had happened. Nor did she know what to do. She stood there, wiping the tears from his face, wondering if tomorrow he would hate her for it. Crying was a sign of weakness in the eyes of the powerful, which made no sense whatsoever. All humans carry strengths and weaknesses within them. Why wouldn't leaders?

"Do you want to talk about it?" she asked.

He shook his head.

"Then you should try to sleep." With her hand in his, she led him to bed.

A sigh escaped his lips as he crawled in under the thick covers, his back towards her.

"You did well tonight," she said and dimmed the lights. "No other student has gathered that many diamonds. I'm proud of you." When he didn't answer, she turned to leave. "I'll see you tomorrow."

"Don't go," he whispered, his voice thick and hollow.

"You know I can't stay, Axel. I've interfered too much already."

"Please. Don't go."

For the longest time, Nicole stood torn between feelings and reason. He needed her, yet there was no doubt in her mind what the right choice was.

"Please…"

In the hazy light, Nicole nodded. Her fingers undid her mask and she placed it on the bedside table. She hung her robe over a chair and sat down on the edge of the bed. "I'll stay a little while. You'll feel better tomorrow."

Silence stretched. Then came his voice again. "So much evil."

It was all he said. Not a word more. Somehow she knew his tears were falling again. What in the world had happened to him?

Nicole lay down, and very gently placed her arm around him. He took her hand and pulled her close. She could feel his heart beat, and at that moment she knew – Axel had changed.

* * *

Izabella was furious. She'd given up her only diamond for information about Axel, but now she could find neither him nor Ms Swan. There were rumours, though. A guest dressed as a white swan had kicked the living daylights out of three guests. Then, after the ceremony, the woman had left the ball with a man dressed as a hog. Izabella stood on the balcony, looking out over the Grand Hall turned nightclub. She needed a plan.

## CHAPTER 35

Mikael's father was a man who enjoyed sleeping in, therefore, when he knocked on his son's door at half-past five in the morning, Mikael knew something was wrong.

"Get your jacket, son. We need to talk."

The two of them set off into the nearby Nacka Nature Reserve. It was too early for most people to be out and about. The summer sun had been up for a while, but in the shade, it was still cool. Birds sang and squabbled among the trees, and somewhere in the distance, a woodpecker hammered with fury after unsuspecting insects.

The two men spoke little and of nothing important until they'd made a right at Brotorp, onto a wide path leading into the forest.

"I had a visitor last night," the old man said in a hushed tone. "The Academy agent sent to watch you. The one called Nurmi. Stuffed my house full of microphones, he did."

Mikael stopped walking. "What?"

"It's true. I was in my office last night when I got a call from Pixie. A courier had delivered a bag to Nurmi. She thought he was going to wire your apartment, so we were discussing various alternatives when all of a sudden, the hidden alarm goes off." The old man started to walk again. "Imagine my surprise when I see the man we were discussing, heading up the basement stairs. Pixie told me to get out of there, but there was no way I could do that without getting caught."

"Are you serious?" Mikael exclaimed.

"I most certainly am."

"Holy shit!"

"Mind your tongue, son."

Mikael stared at his father and frowned. "Why do I get the feeling you're not upset about the whole thing?"

Mr Walter Andersson smiled. "I suppose I should be."

Mikael ran his thumb and index finger over his moustache. "Dad. What have you done?"

The old man rubbed his nose the way he did when he was proud of himself. "Well, since I couldn't get out of there, I did the only thing I could think of. I pretended I'd fallen asleep in my chair. After a few minutes, Mr Nurmi came in. I think my being there rattled him a bit. Not that it stopped him from bugging my office. When he was done, he went up to the second floor. That's when I snuck out. I hid behind the door to the basement and called the police."

"You called the cops?"

"Yes, I did. I thought it'd be fun to get the man in a bit of trouble, but he worked faster than I'd expected. Before the police arrived, he was done. I'm standing there in the dark when all of a sudden, he opens the door and stares at me."

"Oh shit!"

Once more, Mikael's feet came to a dead halt. He and his father were on the middle of a small wooden bridge, crossing a narrow river. Around them birds trilled and a gentle breeze swept over the forest.

"What did you do?" he asked, emphasising every word.

His father grinned. "I hit him over the head with a bottle. It's the first proper fight I've been in since I was a kid."

"God." Mikael placed his hands on his head and moaned. "You didn't kill him, did you?"

"Don't be silly. That would've gotten *me* in trouble. No, I just knocked him out a little. Told the police I thought he was a thief and feared for my life. Now he's at the police station."

"Argh!"

"Come on, son. It's not that bad. I've been sitting behind a desk, strategizing for years. It felt great with a little adventure. I know he'll be out before lunch, but at least the whole thing will create a bit of work for The Academy, and that's good enough for me."

\* \* \*

Ms Brown stepped into Principal Cunningham's office, knowing it wouldn't be a pleasant conversation. The Belgian sun flowed through the large windows, filling the room with light.

"Good morning," the principal said, sounding like a man who'd rather say something else. He had arrived only hours ago, but was already sitting behind his desk, a bit red-eyed but alert. Next to him stood Mr Nakata with his customary, straight-faced expression.

"I apologise," she said.

But he waved her silent. "I'm curious, Ms Brown. Why are we spending money overseeing an old man?"

The principal spoke with an unsettling calmness, holding her gaze until it prickled her skin. Was he angry or merely annoyed?

"I don't know, sir. The agent in question, Mr Nurmi, was supposed to monitor Mikael Andersson, not his father."

"Why Mikael?"

"He's been travelling a lot."

"The young man wants to see the world. How's that an issue?"

"That's the thing, sir. I don't think he's travelling to see the world. Most of the time he goes to London, and his father pays for the trips. As of yet, we don't know what he's doing there. It might be nothing, but there's something about this that doesn't feel right, which is why I sent Mr Nurmi to Stockholm. He was supposed to monitor Mikael."

Principal Cunningham took off his round glasses and pinched the root of his large nose. "Has Mr Nurmi found anything of interest?"

"Not yet, sir, but bearing in mind last night's events, it appears his attention has turned to Mikael's father."

With a little shrug, the principal returned his glasses to their regular position on his nose. "I shall see to it that he's released within the hour. I know Mr Nurmi has proven himself before, but I expect you to give him an official warning nonetheless. We can't have Watchers doing whatever they please."

"Yes, sir."

"Other than that, go ahead with your investigation. Keep me updated on the progress."

"I will, sir."

"Good, then the two of you are excused."

On their way back to the elevators, Mr Nakata walked with his eyes on the floor and a slight frown upon his face. Two servants tending a few potted plants, stood up and bowed. Ms Brown gave them a tired nod.

"I'm sorry about this," she said. "Once Mr Nurmi is released, I'll have him exchanged for someone else. The man's great at uncovering things, but the older he gets, the more wilful he becomes."

"No." Mr Nakata clasped his hands behind his back. "Let him continue. Send me file on Mikael and father. And Mr Nurmi's reports from now on."

Taken by surprise, Ms Brown nodded. "As you wish, sir. May I ask why?"

"No, you may not."

* * *

Axel woke to the sound of curtains being pulled aside. Bright light penetrated his eyelids.

"Good morning, Axel. How are you feeling?"

It took a second before he remembered where he was. Then the images from the previous night flashed through his mind and he wished he could go back to sleep.

"What time is it?" he mumbled.

"Seven-thirty."

"Ugh. That's early."

He felt the edge of his bed move as Nicole took a seat beside him. He pried an eye open and found her watching him with a tiny smile. Her hair was blonde again, pulled up in a simple bun. She wore the usual black suit, and a gold chain with a pendant shaped like a dolphin.

A smile broke across Axel's face, and for a moment, the nightmares from the night before vanished.

"They want you back at The Academy."

Her voice broke the spell. Axel blinked and felt his smile fade. "Excuse me?"

"Principal Cunningham wants you in Brussels. We have a private jet waiting for you at Venice airport."

"They're calling me back? Why?"

Nicole reached out and touched his hand. "I wish I knew."

CHAPTER 36

## FOUR YEARS EARLIER

Dawn threw its purple light over the sky. Some of it trickled down through the branches. Hayato watched as it struck Jerome's tired face.

"I'm disappointed, sir," the man said.

There it was. The finalisation of his third mistake. If The Academy didn't kill him now, The Box would. It was a surreal feeling. Standing there, knowing his life was slipping through his fingers.

"You're not the only one," Hayato said. "I'm sorry I left you, but I—"

"No," Jerome snorted. "I meant I'm disappointed you're not smarter than this. Where are your shoes?"

"My shoes?" Hayato stared at his assistant. Well, *former* assistant if one had to be technical. "What are you talking about?"

"Your shoes! I followed your shoes. Do you remember the new security system that your bodyguard requested several months ago? The one for your office?"

"Yes."

"It included a high-tech tracking system. By injecting a microscopic chip inside the soles of your shoes, he can keep an eye on you via GPS."

"Wait a minute. Who authorised that?"

"You did, sir. Sort of. You gave the man permission to buy the system."

"I did *not* authorise him to stalk me, and by the way, how did *you* get your hands on the system?"

A sly smile cracked Jerome's youthful face. "When I heard about the new system, I demanded access to it. After all, I'm your assistant. If anyone needs to keep track of you, it's me."

Hayato felt his energy escape him. "Now what? You want me to return to Colombo?"

"It's up to you, sir. Where you go, I follow."

"Listen, Jerome, you don't understand. I'm leaving for good. If I return, I die."

His assistant stood there, staring at him with a bewildered expression. Then he seemed to make up his mind and raised his chin. "Wherever you go, I go."

They spent a while arguing like an old couple. In the end, Jerome crossed his arms over his chest and declared that he'd rather live a short and exciting life than a long and boring one.

"So speaks a man who doesn't understand the danger he's in," Hayato moaned.

"Perhaps, but do you want to stand here discussing the matter until the police arrive?"

The police were the least of Hayato's problems. It was The Academy and The Box that frightened him.

Taking charge, Jerome pushed past Hayato into the small room. "Lord, what a rat-hole!" he said from the dark. "Come on, let's get out of here."

For a moment, Hayato looked up at the purple sky. Then the corner of his mouth twitched with an unwilling smile and he followed Jerome into the room.

"Where are your shoes?" Jerome demanded. "And I don't mean those ugly monsters." He nodded towards the blue sneakers next to the door. "I mean your *real* shoes."

"They're in my bag."

"Splendid. Let's bring them. I have an idea." He took Hayato's backpack and headed for the door. "We'll sort things out along the way, but first we run."

Hayato left a one hundred dollar bill under the lantern and followed his assistant. What other choice did he have?

An old Mercedes awaited them at the street, the engine running. "Hatton National Bank in Kurunegala," Jerome said as he jumped into the back, followed by Hayato. "This guy brought me here from Colombo," he whispered as the driver made a U-turn and started back towards the city. "We need to ditch him before the media finds out you've disappeared."

Hayato nodded and turned to the window. He needed to think.

"So?" Jerome asked as they stood outside the Hatton National Bank, watching the taxi disappear around a corner.

The sky was almost blue, with only a hint of orange on the horizon. The city's early birds were out and about, many of them throwing peculiar glances at the odd pair; one dressed in a pinstriped suit and the other in shorts and ugly sneakers.

"So, what?" Hayato asked.

"Where are we heading?"

"I thought you were leading the way." Hayato smiled.

"I do have a plan on how to avoid getting caught, but you're the one running away, sir. So where are we heading?"

"I think I'll keep that to myself for the time being."

Jerome looked at his watch then at the building behind them. "As you wish, sir, but seeing as your bodyguard will soon know we're here, may I suggest we withdraw some money?"

It was a good suggestion. There were a couple of ATMs in the near vicinity, and the two men spent several valuable minutes, withdrawing as much money as they could.

When they were done, Jerome looked at his watch again. "I think it's time we find us a tuk-tuk," he declared.

Finding a tuk-tuk in Sri Lanka was about as difficult as finding water in the ocean. Before they'd even crossed the street, a man pulled up and offered to take them wherever they wanted. He was the third man to do so since they had stepped out of the taxi.

"To the post office," Jerome said pushing Hayato into the small vehicle.

Hayato raised a brow. "The post office?"

"Yes. We're getting rid of any pursuers."

As the driver pulled out onto the road, Jerome took out Hayato's shoes from the backpack, and in a discreet motion, dropped them behind their seat. "Now that will keep the police busy for a while," he said, his voice almost lost in the chugging sound of the engine.

"You've watched too many movies." Hayato laughed, but it wasn't a bad idea.

They got off at the post office and Hayato found a wastebasket where he threw away his old suit. He didn't want to risk that any other chips had been planted on him.

Jerome got rid of his own watch, suit jacket and his phone. He discarded the battery and SIM card in a different bin a few hundred metres away.

"I need to get rid of my shoes," he said when he was done. "It wouldn't surprise me if there's a hidden chip in one of the soles."

"Where are you going to get a pair of shoes?" Hayato asked. "Everything is closed."

Jerome scanned the surroundings and spotted an elderly man some twenty metres away. The old fellow was sitting in the shade of a magnificent tree, watching the world go by.

"Tell you what," Jerome said and nodded towards the man. "I'll trade my shoes for his."

Before Hayato could reply, Jerome was off, crossing the street at a light jog. Hayato kept his distance, watching as his assistant engaged in a lively conversation with the old man.

Although Hayato couldn't hear a single word of what was being said, he soon realised that the old man was rather sceptical to Jerome's generous offer. And for good reason. Who in their right mind would want to trade Gucci loafers for a pair of worn sandals?

The negotiation went on for almost ten minutes before Jerome, looking rather flustered, took off his shoes and handed them to the old man along with a number of dollar bills.

"What happened?" Hayato asked when Jerome returned.

"I've been robbed, that's what happened. I had to pay the old fart fifty dollars. Fifty bucks and a pair of nine hundred dollar loafers in return for these." Jerome looked down at the worn sandals on his feet.

"At least he let you keep the socks." Hayato grinned.

Jerome muttered something inaudible and looked over his shoulder at the old man. "Come on," he said and started down the street towards the nearest tuk-tuk. "If we stay any longer, I fear I'll end up paying the old bugger to steal my pants as well."

Hayato laughed. "All right, let's go. Next stop is Maho."

Maho was a small village north of Kurunegala. From Hayato's perspective, it was no more than an intersection with a few local kiosks. After stocking up on some bananas, a packet of cookies and some water, they took another tuk-tuk. This time they went east to Madagalla. And on they went, going from village to village, changing to a new tuk-tuk or taxi at each stop.

Hayato made sure they never went in a straight line, stopping only at towns or villages with two or more alternative routes in and out. Sometimes they turned back west, or even south, but the overall direction was north-east.

In Kekirawa they stopped for a lunch of chicken noodles with curry. They ate in silence, giving Hayato time to consider the situation. Jerome had no idea what he'd gotten himself into, but he wouldn't turn away now. That was not Jerome's style. If he'd made up his mind about something, he seldom changed it.

It was almost dark when they arrived at the city of Dambulla. They were tired, dirty and hungry, but the red Toyota was waiting for them at Mirisgonioya Junction, as planned.

CHAPTER 37

PRESENT DAY

Thor turned off the engine and let the boat come to a stop. He was close enough to see the airport, but not so close that anyone would be able to hear him. After manoeuvring to the bow, he sat down in the warm sun, plugged in his earphones and made the call. It took thirty seconds of entering codes and voice recognition tests before he could enter the meeting.

"Thor here," he declared and undid the top buttons of his shirt.

"Good," came Falcon's quiet voice. "Then we can begin. I believe I'm the chair today. Shall we start with you, Thor? We're all dying to know how it went yesterday."

Leaning back, Thor adjusted his sunglasses. "Well, it was a bit chaotic…"

He spent the next twenty minutes going over the previous night's events. No one interrupted or asked any questions. When he was done, there was a long, brooding silence.

Security coordinator, Pixie, was the first to speak when he was done. "Seventeen diamonds. Is he out of his mind?"

"He's a wild-card," Smooth said. "But what worries me is, we don't know what happened between him and The Hostess. If she gets involved, things will become very complicated."

"As if they weren't complicated enough as it is," Thor observed.

"He might have told on us already," Walter Andersson said. "Maybe she let him go in return for information."

"It's possible," Cat agreed.

Thor looked up at the blue sky, watching a seagull play upon the warm winds. "I say we continue as planned, but with greater caution."

"Which leads us to our next predicament," Walter grumbled. "It appears Mikael and I have become targets."

As the boat rocked with the motion of the waves, Thor listened as the old man and Pixie told the others of the events in Stockholm the previous night.

"The problem is that Cat and I aren't done with our assignment yet," Mikael added when his father was done. "I guess we can do some of the work by phone, but sooner or later, we have to meet."

"Certainly," Smooth said. "Besides, now that you're a target, it'll be harder for you to find a secure place to call from."

"Where are you now, Mikael?" Falcon wondered.

"In a meeting room at the Stockholm University library. It was the best I could do in such short notice."

"Can't we send someone to check for bugs," Cat asked.

"We've talked about it," Pixie said, "but if we remove any wires, then The Academy will know that Mikael is more than just Axel's best friend. It'll blow his cover. At the moment it's best to pretend like we don't know they exist."

Thor looked at his watch and sat up. "Sorry, guys, I've got to go. My plane to LA leaves in little over an hour."

"Which reminds me," Pixie said. "Juan will pick you up at the LAX. We have booked you a room near Hermosa Beach."

"Thanks. I'll be back in Brussels in no more than two, three days at the most."

"What about the device?" Smooth asked.

Falcon cleared his throat. "Everything has been prepared. It will be done today."

* * *

The EKA resided in a remarkable Art Nouveau-inspired building, set on the prestigious *Avenue Louise* in Brussels. Making his way towards the main entrance, Axel peered up. Although the building dwarfed all others on the street, it didn't feel out of place or intrusive. On the contrary, it blended in with the charming surroundings, and passers-by seldom gave it a second glance.

Once he'd cleared the security checkpoint, Axel stepped through the thick inner doors, entering the fairylike world of The EKA.

The extravagant foyer greeted him with pleasurable scents of flowers, grass and strawberries. It brought forth fond summer memories from his childhood.

"Welcome home, Mr Hallman!" A silver-tongued voice cut through the harmonious birdsong, piercing Axel's bubble of reminiscences. The EKA concierge manager, Mr Milton, approached with a broad smile plastered on his sneaky face. "I hope you've had a wonderful time in Tuscany."

"It was shorter than I'd expected," Axel declared.

Behind him, his suitcase swapped hands between Julien, the driver, and Mr Milton.

"I am to let you know they're waiting for you on the twelfth floor," Mr Milton said, hurrying after him with the bag swinging in his grip. "Do you want me to order you breakfast?"

"No, I ate on the plane."

"Ah." Being experienced enough to register and adapt to a student's foul mood, Mr Milton kept his mouth shut until they'd reached the reception. There he handed the suitcase to Ms Lise Davis, a junior receptionist with a freckled face that seemed frozen in a constant expression of anguish. She was a tiny woman, about the same age as Axel but appeared younger somehow.

"Make sure Mr Hallman's bag is brought to his apartment at once."

Hearing Mr Milton bark out the order, Axel came to think about something his grandmother used to say. 'Never trust a man who faces his superiors with a purr and his subordinates with a growl. Such men are neither cats nor wolfs. They're weasels.'

This particular weasel remained quiet while they took the elevator up to the twelfth floor. On nimble feet, he led Axel to a small conference room where a grim-faced Professor Jackson awaited him.

"Hello, Mr Hallman," the professor said with his smooth, Irish accent. "Our apologies for shortening your vacation." He didn't sound sorry at all as he, with a flick of a hand, sent Mr Milton away. "Follow me. We've been waiting for you."

A panel of men and women sat at a long table. Only two of the individuals were unknown to Axel. In the middle sat Principal Cunningham. The bags under his eyes spoke of a long and weary night. Still he exuded the kind of confidence that comes with experience and age. He gestured towards a single chair opposite the panel.

"Nice to see you, Mr Hallman. Have a seat. You already know your professors and Mr Nakata, but I don't think you've had the pleasure of meeting Dr Young, our Chief Analyst."

A heavy-set man in his late fifties bobbed his head. With his battered old suit and thick glasses, he looked out of place among the well-dressed professors.

"Next to Dr Young is one of his spectacular assistants, Dr Miwa." The young woman gave Axel a nervous nod.

"Why am I here, sir?" Axel asked, desperate to get this over and done with.

The panel sat with their backs against the window, making their faces harder to read. One of the oldest tricks in the book when it came to dominating others.

"We're here to decide on your future," Principal Cunningham said.

Axel smiled. Stay calm. It's just another game, he reminded himself. Just another test. "I'm listening."

The principal cocked his head. Dr Young and Dr Miwa exchanged a glance before typing something on their computers.

"I've told the panel that you put on quite a show yesterday," the principal said. "Was it sixteen diamonds you collected?"

Everyone in the panel stiffened.

"It was seventeen, sir." With great pleasure, Axel stood up and pulled out a small gilded sack from his pocket. He emptied the contents on the table and dropped back into his chair with a satisfied sigh. Seventeen white diamonds, each in a golden ring, spilled out with a loud clatter.

Nicole had donated her rocks to animal welfare when she and Axel had left the ball. He'd considered doing the same, now he was happy he hadn't.

The entire room stared at his diamonds with open bafflement.

"I'll be damned." A frown had settled on Professor Plouffe's rounded face, and his double chins quavered. "How in the world did you do that?"

Professor Jackson tapped his pen against the table. "Aye, Mr Hallman. How *did* you do that?"

No 'congratulations' or 'well done', nothing but plain scepticism. Axel slid back in his chair. He hoped no one saw the trembling in his legs. Whether they shook out of fear or anger, he couldn't tell. "I analysed and tricked people," he said with a steady voice, as if it was the most obvious thing in the world.

"Seventeen is a substantial number," the principal observed. "I think I'd like to hear your story from the beginning. In detail."

CHAPTER 38

Falcon stood in the middle of the workroom, staring at the large screen. He could feel the others watching him. The seconds ticked and the screen remained black. The mole was late.

A few more minutes passed before the screen flickered and a unified sigh filled the room when the long-awaited message arrived.

*Sorry I'm late. Still haven't cracked the surveillance system. Having issues with the code. Can't freeze screen without risk of exposure. I should have it solved within a few weeks, but for now, I'll have to proceed without it.*

"Okay," Falcon said, feeling the tension rise in the room. "Ask him about the risks."

Nelly's fingers flashed across her keyboard.

It took a moment, then the screen flickered again and a new message arrived under the first. *Risk level is acceptable. Guards are focusing on Axel and professors.*

Falcon turned to the hacker closest to him. "Good. Wish him luck."

\* \* \*

The mole was wearing the black sweatshirt and sweatpants The Box had given him. It looked identical to those of The Academy, but for some reason, The Box wanted him to wear this particular one.

He started to ascend the stairs at a light jog. It proved to be a foolish thing to do. By the time he reached the second floor, he was already breathing hard, feeling as though he might vomit. He was neither overweight nor ill, only out of shape. That's what happened when you spent hours and hours in front of a computer.

Panting and moaning, he dragged himself up, keeping his face aimed at his feet. The only cameras within the stairwell were those connected to the smoke detectors. Unless the alarm went off, they remained unused. Still, better safe than sorry, as his great aunt used to say.

By the time he reached the ninth floor, he was sweating like a pig. He clung to the metal railing for a couple of seconds, afraid his thunderous heart would burst if he took another step.

Shaking with exhaustion and dread, he drew his black mask from the waistline under his sweatshirt. Once it was in place, he pulled the hood over his head and pushed open a crack in the door. The small hallway was empty, save for a marble statue of a lion bowing to the King of Eagles. Under it was a sign, 'Our Future; Our Hope'.

The mole held back a shiver and stepped in. Against his better judgment, he glanced up at the cameras staring down at him. Dear God, please don't let them see me, he thought and hurried over to Axel's door. Pressing the key-card against the lock, the door swung open and he was in.

Moving as quickly as he could, he made his way through the long, dark corridor toward the bedroom. If the guards were monitoring Axel's apartment at the moment, it would all be over.

He reached the bedroom. Axel, or maybe the maid, had pulled the curtains aside. The room was filled with light. It made him feel vulnerable. Reaching the bedside table, he activated the device one last time, and wrote; *I'm in. Will now return card.*

*For freedom*, came the reply.

"For Freedom," the mole echoed and sucked in a breath of courage. He snatched the card from the device and opened the drawer. He found the wallet where he'd left it a few months ago. His fingers fumbled as he opened it. The replica was still there. Thank God.

Once he had replaced the fake card with the real one, he returned the wallet and headed back to the corridor. He was one, maybe two metres from the living room when he saw the housekeeping cart. It rolled into view as if in slow motion.

Mother of pearl!

Without thinking, the mole threw himself into the nearest room; the small kitchen. For a split second, he had no idea where to hide. As a result, he ended up sliding in behind the door. It was a terrible hiding place, yet he stood there, trying his best not to breathe.

Pressed against the wall, peering through the thin crack between the door and the wall, he saw the cart appear. It stopped. There was a moment's silence before the maid walked into the kitchen. The mole saw her as she strode over to the kitchen sink. Bending forward, the woman opened the lower cupboard and emptied the rubbish. Then she checked the dishwasher.

She moved like a darn sloth, but there was little for her to do in the kitchen. After what seemed forever, she turned and walked out, never once looking in his direction. He caught a glimpse of her face as she moved on towards the bedroom.

Knees shaking, the mole stepped out from behind the door. He wanted to vomit. Daring a careful glance into the corridor, he saw the cleaning cart outside Axel's office. Argh. After a deep breath, he left the kitchen and hurried down the corridor towards the front door. Before turning the corner, he glanced over his shoulder. The cart remained where it had. He was safe.

Pulling off his mask, the mole wiped his sweaty forehead with the back of his hand. With the mask tucked into his waistline, he left the apartment and jogged over to the door to the stairwell and yanked it open. He froze.

Mr Milton had been on his way up the stairs. Now he stared at the mole, surprise imprinted in his face.

"By golly, you scared me," the mole said and tried to smile.

Mr Milton's eyes narrowed. "Wrong floor?" he asked.

"What?" the mole asked, turning his good ear towards the man.

Mr Milton pointed at the number painted above the door and raised his voice. "This is Mr Reed's and Mr Hallman's floor. What are you doing here?"

The mole's smile faded. "We had an issue with Mr Reed's Speechomat. I tried to update it before lunch but couldn't get any access from the office. Turned out the power cord had been wrenched out of the wall. Probably the maid when she cleaned behind the machine."

Mr Milton's frown deepened. "Why aren't you wearing your suit?"

"I'm sorry?"

"Your suit! Why aren't you wearing it?"

"I don't see how that's any of your business," the mole replied, acting annoyed, "but if you must know, I'm heading to the gym after this. Then I'll have lunch before getting back to work. Any more questions?"

Mr Milton made a face and muttered something the mole couldn't decipher before storming up the stairs without another word.

\* \* \*

Axel's story was a remarkable one. With great detail, he recounted every game he'd played at the ball, and every player he'd fooled. It pained Professor Jackson to admit it, but he was impressed. Even if it was all a lie, the lie itself deserved some respect. Some of the ways the man claimed to have deceived people were nothing less than ingenious.

Once in a while, someone on the panel would interrupt with a question or two, but there was no hesitation in Axel's answers.

He had just described how he'd beaten one of the top players, when Principal Cunningham raised a hand and silenced him. "Thank you, Mr Hallman. I think we'll pause here for now. Why don't you head down to the restaurant and have yourself some lunch? We'll call on you when we desire your presence again."

Axel looked confused. In all honesty, so did many of the panel members. Nevertheless, the young man nodded and left without word.

"Well then," the principal continued and looked at the others. "What do you say?"

The question sucked Professor Jackson back to the dull reality of the here and now. He had to admit he'd been very captivated by Axel's story. Picking up his pencil, he started turning it between his fingers. "This is an extraordinary tale," he said, "but how do we know if it's true?"

"If he's lying, then he's the best damn liar I've ever seen," Professor Evans said, leaning back in her chair with a wide grin on her face. "My God. I told you he was good, didn't I?"

"You never said he was *that* good," said Professor Williams, teacher in global and business economy. He took off his rimless glasses and rubbed both eyes with the palm of his hands. "Is it possible that we've underestimated the man?"

"I'm finding this a bit much to swallow." Professor Plouffe turned to the principal. "Sir. You were there. Is this possible?"

"I never saw Mr Hallman play his games," Principal Cunningham admitted, "but I *can* confirm that he had a lot of diamonds on his chain at the end of the evening. You saw them. There were also rumours of a young guest defeating several experienced players. My only concern is that Ms Swan told me that one of the guests attacked them at the end of the party. The attacker claimed Mr Hallman had cheated, but I just can't see how that would've been possible."

Professor Jackson shook his head. This was incredible. He stopped spinning his pencil and pointed it at Dr Young. "You're the analyst. What's your opinion? Is Mr Hallman lying?"

"He might not be telling us everything, sir, but I don't think he's lying. My team and I will analyse the video recording of this meeting, but I'd be very surprised if we found anything odd."

"It just seems impossible," Professor Plouffe grumbled.

I agree, Professor Jackson thought.

"Well, I disagree," Professor Evans said. "Not only do I know

Mr Hallman is good at reading people, he's a wild-card and wild-cards are unpredictable. Unpredictable, but also very skilled. I find his story plausible."

A low murmur of agreements came from a few other members of the panel. As usual, the principal sat quiet. Listening. Analysing.

"We haven't been very lucky with our previous wild-cards," Professor Jackson noted.

Ms Evans shrugged. "True, but neither Mr Sano nor Ms Wangai failed due to lack of skills."

Damn that woman! Why was she arguing with him?

Principal Cunningham looked at his watch. "Let's stop here for now. We'll continue this discussion at three. Professor Jackson, will you be so kind and stay a moment? I have a few things I need to discuss."

"Aye, sir."

"And, Mr Nakata. We're done with the recordings in here. Turn off the cameras and the microphones please."

"Hai, sir." Mr Nakata bowed his head and left with the others.

When the door closed and they were all alone, the principal picked up his phone and dialled a number. "Hello, Mr Hallman. I'd like you back please. Yes, immediately."

"Mr Hallman," the principal said, watching Axel with his small beady eyes. "I want you to continue your account of yesterday's events. I need you to be as honest as you were before. As you can see, it will only be Professor Jackson and me. Depending on what we hear, we'll decide what can and cannot be shared."

There was no hint of surprise in Axel's eyes. Instead, he began to speak. He took his time, telling how the bull-masked player had refused to accept defeat. As his story unravelled, Professor Jackson sat amazed, his cup of coffee growing cold in front of him.

Once Axel reached the end of his account, Professor Jackson felt empty inside.

"I appreciate your honesty, Mr Hallman," the principal said, "although I'm a bit puzzled by your report."

Axel's eyes darkened. "I'm not lying."

"I didn't say you were. Nor did I imply it. What I meant is that I'm puzzled none of us foresaw this. No other student has been close to winning as many diamonds as you. To be frank, we didn't expect you to be the first."

"I see." Axel gave the principal such a defiant glare, it made Professor Jackson itch to lean over and smack him. "Have you ever thought about the fact that I'm the only student who thinks for myself?"

One of the principal's eyebrows rose. "I beg your pardon?"

"I'm being criticised for asking a lot of questions, for challenging the obvious. But here's the thing. I question because I want to learn, and I challenge in order to see if your arguments hold. The other students agree to anything you say as long as it'll get them one step closer to graduation. If you tell them to jump, they jump. If you tell them to shit, they'll shit. How's their behaviour any different from that of a follower?"

Professor Jackson felt his mouth drop. What the…? He turned to the principal, dying to see how this would unfold.

Principal Cunningham gave the kind of smile that seemed to be anything *but* a smile. "I'm afraid you've missed the point, young man. You're like a puppeteer who keeps asking why your marionettes have strings attached to them. Don't get me wrong. I applaud your determination to think for yourself, but I can't help but wonder why you feel a need to challenge your professors? Do you not trust us? Is our success not proof enough of our knowledge? Or is it the concept of leadership you have trouble accepting?"

In a split second, fury flashed across Axel's face. His grey eyes hardened and his jaws tensed. Then he blinked and cracked a smile, not unlike that of the principal's. "I have no trouble accepting your theories or arguments. What troubles me is your fear of me questioning them. It makes me wonder if perhaps there *is* reason to distrust you."

Amazed, Professor Jackson gaped at the young man, and for a heartbeat it seemed the principal was unsure how to proceed. How fascinating.

"What you're doing, Mr Hallman, is neither beneficial nor intelligent," the principal warned. "You're wasting your time, and ours. I expect you to change your behaviour from now on."

Axel did not reply.

"Now, before you leave there's another matter I want to raise," the principal continued. "With success comes envy. I've asked Ms Swan to inform the other students about your success at the ball, but I fear not everyone will be happy for you. Chances are, your fellow students will hate you for your achievements."

Axel shrugged. "I'm sure they will."

"Then I expect you to be prepared for it. As to your time with The Hostess, we're keeping that to ourselves. Believe me, it's for your own good. If you need to talk about it, come to Professor Jackson or me. Do we understand each other?"

"Yes, sir."

"Good. Then you can leave."

Axel and Professor Jackson exchanged a brief look. As they did, the young man gave a slight smile. Surprised, the professor cleared his throat and offered a tiny bow in return.

"He's telling the truth about the events at the ball," Principal Cunningham said when they were alone. "The Hostess confirmed it."

"I beg your pardon? You spoke to The Hostess?"

"I did. Or rather, she spoke to me. Gave us a warning."

"A…ahem…warning?"

"Indeed. She told me that if we ever hide a talent like Mr Hallman from The Seven again, she'll 'skin us alive'."

The blood drained from the professor's face. "We haven't been hiding him."

"Mr Hallman impressed The Hostess to such a degree, she feels

184 · C.C. MONÖ

she should've been informed about his 'exceptional talent', as she put it. She now demands that we give him our fullest attention until he graduates. In the meantime, she'll consider how to use him in the future."

"The future? Sir? We can't even promise he'll graduate."

Standing up, the principal took his cup of tea and walked over to the window. "She's part of The Seven. If she wants him to graduate, we make sure he graduates. Or, to be specific, *you* will make sure he graduates."

CHAPTER 39

The next few days were uneventful. While the Belgian capital baked in sunlight, Axel wandered about the premises, brooding. He had told Principal Cunningham as much as he could without mentioning Thor, the cheating, or Axel's own involvement in Mr Gallo's punishment. Still he worried what might come of it all.

To keep from thinking too much, he busied himself. He went into town, took long walks in Bois de la Cambre, read books, watched movies and hours in the Speechomat, practicing. One day he even rang up Mikael. For once, it was nice to hear about his friend's dull, monotonous life. Mikael blabbered on about things he found important, such as his studies, films he'd seen and parties he'd been to. It was strange to think that the two of them had been such good friends. Now they had nothing in common.

On Thursday morning, July fifth, Axel woke up to the chime of the doorbell. A group of servants stood in a half circle, with Mr Milton in the middle.

"Happy Birthday!" they yelled with feigned enthusiasm and filled the hall with a cacophony of blowout whistles. One of the servants pushed forth a trolley with a grand birthday cake on it, made in the shape of a proud eagle.

"Congratulations on your twenty-third birthday, sir," Mr Milton cheered, pushing back his spectacles as he spoke. "Not just a year older, but a year better. Your parents and Mr Mikael Andersson have left messages, congratulating you on your big day."

"Thanks. I'll call them."

"The principal also sends his regards. He's on his way to Japan for a large leadership conference but wishes you a joyful day."

"Japan? I thought he was here."

"I'm afraid not, sir, but Professor Jackson is, and he has a little surprise for you."

God no, Axel thought. "What kind of surprise?"

"To be honest I have no idea, sir, but he'll pick you up at eight-thirty tonight. You're to be dressed in your formal suit."

Fabulous. This was going to be a real stinker of a birthday.


At eight-thirty, on the dot, Professor Jackson knocked on his door. As always, he looked immaculate.

"Good evening, Mr Hallman," the professor said with a cheerful manner that made Axel wince. Whenever Professor Jackson looked happy, it usually meant someone else was in trouble. "You look good, young man. Let's go."

Axel stared at the man. Had the professor really given him a compliment? "Where are we going, sir?" he asked, closing the door behind him.

"As Aristotle put it, 'Patience is bitter, but its fruit is sweet'."

"In other words you won't tell me?"

"No."

They took the elevator to the garage, where a giant of a man awaited them. "Good evening, professor," he said, his graceful voice a strange contrast to his brutal size.

Professor Jackson gave the man a nod. "Good evening, Mr Thorn. Are we ready to leave?"

"Yes, sir." The huge man led them down a short flight of stairs to the concrete parking lot. Here, luxurious vehicles stood lined up as if on display. Three black BMWs had been prepared for their departure. Julien, the driver, held open the rear door of the middle one and Axel got in.

Mr Thorn squeezed himself into the front seat next to Julien. Professor Jackson entered last and pulled out his phone as he did. "Let's go," he ordered.

The three vehicles rolled out of the building onto a back street.

Streetlights cast their orange glow over the asphalt. Under the starlit sky, the city was quiet and still. As the procession made its way onto *Avenue Louise,* Axel felt his sting of fear. This wasn't right. The streets were deserted.

"Sir?" Axel shifted in his seat, scanning the emptiness around them. "I think something's wrong." His words pulled the professor from his phone. "The streets. They're…empty."

A quick glance outside, and the professor smiled. "Oh, that." He turned his attention back to his phone. "Nothing to worry about, Mr Hallman. I've had the streets cleared for us."

It took a moment before the professor's words sunk in, and when they did, Axel struggled to believe them. "You've cleared the streets?"

"Aye."

"But…is that even possible?"

"For us it is."

It was the most absurd feeling. Not a vehicle or pedestrian in sight. Not even a dog or rat. "Is this a joke?"

For a second, the professor's normal, sourpuss expression returned. "Do I look like a man with a sense of humour, Mr Hallman?"

Fair enough. Axel looked out of his window and furrowed his brows. "Why clear the streets, sir?"

The professor held out his hands in an amused gesture. "Because I can. And, because it's fun. Mr Thorn, why don't we show Mr Hallman why we do this?"

"As you wish, sir." The large man lowered his head and spoke to his collar. "Speed up, gentlemen."

Showing a perfect set of teeth, Professor Jackson grinned. "Prepare for a bit of fun, Mr Hallman."

The three cars let out a unified roar. A moment later, the procession thundered down the street. It happened so fast, Axel spent the first few seconds trying to realise what had happened. Outside, the world passed in a blur, and all too fast, they approached *Avenue Legrand*.

"Sir…!" Axel peered out of the front window. "Sir, we're coming in too fast. Julien! Slow down!"

With the utmost calm, the assistant principal removed a piece of hair from his trousers and settled back. "Do you know what some people call that thing?" he asked, pointing at the handle above Axel's door.

There was no time to answer. The procession entered the intersection at full speed. Julien turned. Wheels screeched, and the back of the vehicle slid along the pavement as if it'd been ice.

Axel clung to the door handle with all his might. The seatbelt bit down on his shoulder and for a moment, he thought they'd crash into the other cars.

"Holy shit!" he cried as the car finally found its grip.

"Ah-hah," the professor exclaimed. "Very good, Mr Hallman. That's exactly what they call it, a 'shit handle'." He turned back to his window and snickered. "And people think I lack a sense of humour."

* * *

Police cars blocked all connecting roads as the procession soared down the empty *Chaussée de Waterloo*. Having public streets emptied for his enjoyment, filled Professor Jackson with an immeasurable sense of satisfaction. He glanced at Axel who looked amused.

I believe he's growing on me, the professor thought, somewhat displeased with this realisation. He'd disliked the boy since day one and didn't feel comfortable changing his opinion. Doing so would suggest he'd been wrong to begin with.

A light drizzle started to fall, the first in almost two weeks. Professor Jackson glanced at his watch. "All right, Mr Thorn. Make us vanish."

The three cars slowed as one, and at the next intersection, they parted in different directions. Julien chose a narrow street lined with large villas. No more than two minutes later, a grey Bentley appeared at their rear. The car followed them until they reached a more secluded area near a little park. Here, where hedges and trees lined both sides of the street, and thick branches created a ceiling out above them, the two cars stopped.

Mr Thorn jumped out, far too light-footed for a man his size. He held open the right rear doors, while Julien attended to the other. Twenty-eight seconds later, they were all sitting in the Bentley, heading down the street again. These security measures were a bother, but until there was a technology that allowed one car to transform into another at the push of a button, this would have to do.

Axel had grown quiet and serious, staring out of his window. Professor Jackson watched him for a while, without being too obvious of course. Then he adjusted his tie and gave his left sleeve a light tug. It was time to give the man a little lesson.

"When I was about your age," he said, "I realised that the world isn't as complicated as many make it out to be. There are two kinds of people; those who lead, and those who follow. Although you can't have one without the other, there's no denying that rulers are more important than servants are. Look at Mr Thorn, for example. As my personal bodyguard, he'll die to protect me if needed. Why? Because he knows I'm more important than he is."

"Sounds a bit harsh," Axel replied, eying the large guard who hadn't reacted.

In the rear-view mirror, Professor Jackson could see Mr Thorn smile to himself. "Perhaps, but I'm being pragmatic, and so is Mr Thorn. All large-scale nuisances, from war and famine to economic collapse and pollution, are a result of bad leadership. People of power have no idea how to rule, which is why the world needs The EKA. We're saving mankind, by training talents like you. That makes us the most important people alive."

Axel made a face. "When you say 'us', you mean The Academy management, right? Not us students?"

"Life is a pyramid, Mr Hallman. Not everyone can be at the very top."

"What if that's what I'm aiming for? The top?"

Professor Jackson raised a brow. This young man was full of surprises, and not all of them were bad.

"Just because you did well at the Diamond Ball, doesn't mean you're fit to rule," he said. "First you must learn how to conform. Once you master that trait, I believe you can go far."

Axel regarded him with his cold, grey eyes. There was something unforgiving about them. Something unreachable. Like staring at the moon.

"Conform? You want me to be a puppet?"

"Don't be an idiot. I told you we're trying to make the world a better place, didn't I? Our former students are rulers and may do as they please. Yet, sometimes we require their services. For the greater good, if you know what I mean."

"Aha." Axel turned to his window. "Sounds like a puppet to me."

The arrogance was striking. Axel's body language, tonality, and words; everything was a challenge.

"You want to talk about puppets?" Professor Jackson snorted. "Then let me tell you this. Any fool can play with a marionette's strings and make it move, but a true puppeteer uses his dolls for a *purpose*. He follows a screenplay and makes his puppets dance accordingly. If you want to graduate, you have better accept one thing; you'll be a puppeteer, but *we* are the playwrights."

"How did you shut down the streets?" Axel asked in a calm voice, turning back from the window.

Professor Jackson smiled and paused long enough to pop a mint tablet into his mouth. A shift in topic, meant to distract him. It seemed the young man was learning the tricks of the trade.

"Easy," he replied. "All it took was a simple phone call to a former student. No questions asked."

"Interesting. Is that an example of 'greater good'? Shutting down a street so we can have some fun?"

Bastard! Professor Jackson crushed his mint tablet hard. It gave off a loud pop. "Look," he said, struggling to release tension from his jaw, "you impressed some powerful people at the Diamond Ball. Now that you've gained their attention, you'd do best to know your place among them. You are *not* their equal. You're not *my* equal, and like Mr Thorn, you are expendable. If you're to get anywhere in this business, you better well learn that."

\* \* \*

Professor Jackson appeared to have said what he wanted. Turning his attention back to his phone, he showed Axel no more interest than the air around him. Outside, the rain gained in strength.

As images from the Diamond Ball crawled into Axel's mind, he considered the professor's words. *'You're not their equal.'* Well, neither was the professor. The Seven owned him, same as they owned Principal Cunningham and the entire EKA. Professor Jackson was as much a puppet as Axel was.

"We're here," Mr Thorn declared.

The 'here' was a dirt road running through dark fields. Without the Bentley's headlights, it would've been impossible to see anything. Rain splattered hard against the windows. "Where are we?" Axel asked, staring into the darkness.

"At our destination," came Professor Jackson's taunting reply.

The road turned around a cluster of trees and Axel spotted the taillights of a parked car. Julien pulled the Bentley off the road and brought it to a stop next to a black Rolls Royce. Mr Thorn hurried out of the car to open Axel's door.

"Behave yourself," Professor Jackson muttered, refusing to look at his student.

"What's going on, sir?"

The car door opened and Professor Jackson made a shooing gesture. "You'll see. Now hurry up. You're letting in the wet and cold. I'll see you back at The Academy…I hope."

Mr Thorn held out an umbrella, keeping Axel somewhat dry as

he stepped out into the night. The driver of the other vehicle opened the rear door of the Rolls Royce with a polite bow.

In the back seat, someone moved. Axel approached with false confidence, staring at the shape in the soft light. As the contours took a more solid form, a prickling fear spread down his neck.

Oh no.

CHAPTER 40

FOUR YEARS EARLIER

Hayato woke to the sounds of birds, barking dogs and the distant noise of a hammer beating against metal. The air was oppressive, making it difficult to breathe, and his bed sheets were drenched in sweat. Despite this, he lay in the murky light for a few minutes, staring at the tin roof as it cracked and popped in the morning sun.

They were in a small shed, barely large enough for a queen-sized mattress and some worn garden tools. The privy was a hole in the ground outside, covered by walls of dry branches. No roof. No toilet paper. No running water. Hayato had exchanged all the luxury in the world for this, yet he felt no regret. He knew what he was getting in to. His assistant did not.

"Jerome?"

The man stirred. "Yes, sir," came a drowsy voice.

"You should return to Colombo."

There was long pause. "Why?"

"Because you have no idea what you've gotten yourself into."

Jerome sat up and ran a hand through his blond, messy hair. "Where you go; I go."

"Don't be an idiot."

"I will do my best, sir."

"Then go back to Colombo."

Groping in the dark for his glasses, Jerome coughed. "What you've done with Francis Security is remarkable, sir. You've now graduated from The Academy and signed two important business deals that will make you legendary. You can do or be anything you like. Therefore, I ask myself, why does he run?

"There are only two explanations as I see it. Either you're crashing on a psychological level, in which case you need my support. Or you've gotten yourself in the kind of trouble that even The Academy can't help you out of. If that's the case, then I'm in trouble too. You're my boss, remember? Whomever you're running from will have no one but me to face once you're gone. If they scare you that much, then *I* sure don't want to face them."

Jerome kicked off their shared blanket and got to his feet. "I'm not a brave man, Mr Sano. If you don't mind, I'd rather run with you than sit back and face the slaughter alone. Whatever it may be."

Jerome pulled on his dirty suit pants and began buttoning his now beige shirt.

"If you join me now," Hayato said, "then you can't go back. Ever. Do you understand? Your old life ends here."

For the first time, Jerome hesitated. "I understand."

"You won't be able to contact your friends or family again. To them, you'll be dead. Your apartment, cat, your things, all of it you leave behind. No more career, no more life in luxury. It's all over. The only thing left is a life in hiding. How can you make a choice like that without knowing who we're running from?"

"I take that to mean you won't tell me?"

"No."

Jerome shrugged.

"Then I'll just have to trust your judgement." He opened the door and stepped out.

Hayato moaned and got up. Once he was dressed, he stepped out and found Jerome standing with his hands on his hips, staring out at the endless rice fields that bordered the little shed. It was so green it looked unreal. Up above, an eagle rested upon warm winds.

"I won't ask you again, Jerome. This is your last chance to back out."

"It's a big decision," the assistant admitted, gazing up at a nearby palm tree. "I suppose the most logical thing would be to go back."

"Indeed, it would."

"Do I need to make this decision now?"

"I'll be picked up in about four hours. By then you must have made up your mind. Okay?"

A small nod. "Okay. Then we wait," Jerome said with a low voice.

They sat in the shade of a large tree, watching life go by in the fields around them. They shared the remainder of the biscuits and fruits from the night before, but spoke little. Hayato was preoccupied, going over the plan in his head, and Jerome sat like a statue, no doubt dwelling on his own future.

Around lunchtime, a red Toyota approached the shed. Hayato stood up, his ugly blue shoes stirring up a cloud of dust in the red soil. "It's time, Jerome. Shall we say our goodbyes?"

"Did I ever tell you I was married?"

Hayato smiled. "Uh-huh. I believe you called him 'an ungrateful dick'."

Jerome's laughter rang out over the paddy fields, and nearby, a startled stork took to flight. "Well, if anyone was a dick, it was I. I've put my career ahead of everything; my family, my friends, my husband. Now I've got nothing left." He dusted off his trousers the best he could. "A part of me has always dreamt of walking away from it all. To start over. To face new adventures." He looked out over the rice fields, then got to his feet. "All right. Where do we go from here?"

CHAPTER 41

PRESENT DAY

"It's nice to see you again, Mr Hallman."

The Hostess raised her glass in a cheer. Without the mask, she lacked some of her mysticism. It was a bit disappointing. As Thor would have put it, she looked cliché, like one of those rich Hollywood stars who had spent one too many sessions under a surgeon's knife. The skin was stretched over her face and when she spoke, her expressions came across as a little stiff. It was hard to tell her age; she was probably in her mid-sixties.

"The pleasure is all mine, My Lady."

"You recognise me?"

"I do." Axel undid the buttons of his suit jacket and settled back in the white leather seat. Some rational part of his mind told him he should be petrified, yet for reasons he could not explain, he felt more excited than anything else. "Your voice is familiar. Also, I remember that scar on your neck, as well as the small birthmark on your left hand. You tilt your head to the right when you speak, and you have a way of holding your wine glass by pinching its base with your thumb. According to our teacher in Leadership Etiquette, it's an acceptable but uncommon way of holding a glass."

Like turning off a switch, The Hostess' expression hardened. "Watch it, young man. I do not appreciate the word *acceptable*. I hold my glass with the utmost social etiquette. Unusual perhaps, but still with class."

Images of burnt faces flashed through Axel's mind. "I beg your pardon, My Lady," he said. "Poor choice of words on my side."

"Yes. Poor words indeed. You're lucky I'm not a sensitive person." Her face relaxed and she tittered as she pressed a button on her door. "Okay, Ray, let's go."

Axel stared at her. Jesus. Whatever went on in that head of hers, it frightened him.

As the Rolls Royce awoke with a low growl, Axel drew a deep breath and found the smile he'd lost. "I'm curious, My Lady. To what do I owe this honour?" he asked.

As the car started to move, The Hostess reached up and fiddled with one of her earrings, a pear-shaped diamond that glimmered in pink. "Business," she said.

"What kind of business?"

She handed him a large envelope. "Go on. Open it."

After a moment's hesitation, he obeyed. Inside was a set of photos that were among the most gruesome, most nauseating pictures he'd ever seen.

"Mr Gallo is now in my service," The Hostess explained. "That's what he looks like now, unrecognisable, but not blind. That's good. He's more useful that way. I will give him back to you after you've graduated. By then he'll be trained and everything."

Axel had no idea how he managed it, but somehow he kept his voice calm as he returned the photos. "Thank you."

"My pleasure, and now to more pressing matters." The woman flipped down a tray table. After placing her glass on it, she produced a thick folder from a portfolio at her feet. "We need to discuss what you want to do with Mr Gallo's fortune. The man has a net worth of twenty-three point four billion dollars. He owns a number of companies and holds seats on several boards. Most of his money comes from dealing with real estate. You can go through the details later. Right now, we need to deal with his nineteen-year-old son who'll be inheriting everything according to the will."

"I didn't know he had a son."

"Nor did I until we found the will. It doesn't surprise me,

though. Mr Gallo was a notorious playboy, although a bit intense in his love-making, I hear."

"That's sick."

With her typical tittering, The Hostess patted Axel's legs. He looked down at her hand and the oversized ring that rested upon her skeletal finger. It was shaped as a butterfly and covered in sparkling diamonds.

"Such an honourable man you are, Mr Hallman," she said, beckoning his eyes back towards her face. "Me, I don't judge people's sexual preferences. Whatever makes them happy. Anyhow, I can have the will destroyed by tomorrow if you like. Or we can take out the son."

"As in kill him?"

"Yes, but I wouldn't recommend it. Having both father and son vanish within a week might be a bit too obvious. There are a few other options we should consider…"

The whole thing was surreal. While the car made its way through dark side streets, The Hostess laid forth various possibilities for pilfering Mr Gallo's wealth. With her gentle voice, she spoke of dangerous and evil things, sounding no worse than a librarian giving suggestions on children's books.

"Now. What do you want to do?" she asked when she was done.

"You want *me* to decide?"

"Of course! Mr Gallo is yours. Anything that's his belongs to you." She paused. "No, that's not entirely true. I'll take forty-five percent of whatever you get. Consider it payment for the work I'm doing, and the risks I'm taking to help you."

Axel almost gaped at her. The woman was mad as a hatter.

"Fifty-five per cent of twenty-three point four billion dollars is a lot of money," he said. "If I have that kind of money, people will wonder where it comes from."

The woman brushed off his comment like lint on her shoulder. "Obviously it can't happen overnight, but I have some *very* smart people who will handle this for us." She smiled. "I'm not easy to impress, Mr Hallman, so when I find something that impresses me, I want it. Despite your young age, you have a remarkable talent for reading people. The Academy admitted you, meaning you're a person with great potential. Plus, you amuse me. Not many people do. Therefore, I've decided that I could use someone like you by my side."

Her smile broadened. "Once you've graduated, I want you to work for me, as one of my personal advisors. I'll pay you well and you'll have access to more power than you can dream of."

Axel's mouth went dry and as rough as sandpaper. His skin crawled, and the temperature inside the Rolls Royce seemed to drop several degrees.

The Hostess picked up her glass. "So? What do you say?"

"I…" Axel struggled to find the right words. He felt caught in a nightmare, and the way she stared at him, waiting for an answer, made it all the worse. "I'm overwhelmed as you can see," he said. "What an honour."

His words pleased her. She lit up and gave a toast. "Splendid! We'll have plenty of time to work out the details later. I know The Academy has plans for you, and for now we'll let them think nothing's changed. When the time is right, I'll tell them about our agreement."

Agreement. The word hung like a noose around Axel's neck. "You think they'll accept it?"

The woman leaned forward and placed a hand on his thigh. "I have more influence over The Academy than you can imagine," she giggled.

Axel tried not to wince, but he lowered his eyes and they fell upon the photos of Mr Gallo, tied to a hospital bed, his face burnt beyond recognition.

Oh God, what had he gotten himself into?

## CHAPTER 42

Mr Nakata spent a few minutes skimming through the document before making the call. As expected, Ms Brown answered at once.

"Yes, sir?"

"I read your report on Mikael Andersson's father; is this all you find?"

"I'm afraid so, sir. I was about to call you. One moment, please."

He heard her say something. A door closed and the background noise of murmuring people vanished.

"There's plenty of information about Mr Andersson senior, but the vast majority of it is related to his work. I'm referring to articles he's written and conferences he's participated in, that kind of thing. Nothing of interest, except for one thing. There's very little personal information dating back further than twenty-five years, about the same time he became professor at Uppsala University."

Mr Nakata scrolled through the document. "Department of Peace and Conflict Research?"

"Yes, and here is where it gets interesting. Any information prior to that is so meagre, yet well organised, I'm inclined to think that it's fabricated."

"Ah." Mr Nakata made a few notes. How interesting. "Keep searching," he said and hung up. Leaning back, he remembered an old proverb his father used to say; 'When the character of a man is not clear to you, look at his friends'.

Half an hour later, there was a hard knock on his door and Professor Jackson entered.

"Are you and your people ready?" he asked, his face grim and determined.

"Hai."

"Good. Mr Hallman should return soon. Let me know when it's done. In the meantime, I have to inform the principal about a little problem our dear Hostess has blessed us with."

Mr Nakata raised a brow. "Problem?"

\* \* \*

With a little sigh, the Rolls Royce came to a stop outside the main entrance. At night, spotlights lit up The Academy, turning the façade golden. The rain had subsided to a light drizzle.

"I'll set things in motion," The Hostess promised. "Everything will be in order by the time you start working for me. Meanwhile, my accountants will keep you updated on our progress."

"I'm speechless. You've been very kind." Axel was smiling. He told himself it was all for the show, but a tiny part of him was beginning to realise the consequences of what had been decided in their short time together. He was going to be a billionaire. A freaking *billionaire*!

They had discussed and agreed on a series of steps that would give him fifty-five percent of Mr Gallo's fortune. These steps included hostile takeovers, modifications of Mr Gallo's will, and a set of complex business strategies and money laundering that were nothing less than brilliant. The woman might be out of her mind, but the people working for her certainly weren't.

"I'm glad you're pleased," she said and patted his cheek. "I look forward to following your developments for the next two years."

"Thank you, My Lady. You won't be disappointed."

"I should hope not. I'm not very good with disappointments, but you will continue to impress me, I'm sure."

The wind caught Axel's suit jacket and threw it open as he stepped out of the car. *Avenue Louise* was once again full of traffic. A couple walking a small dog threw him a curious look but he ignored them.

"Mr Hallman. It's your birthday today, no?"

Axel turned back to The Hostess. "Yes, My Lady."

"Then happy birthday, young man. I've sent you a little gift. You can collect it at the reception."

"Wow, thanks. That's very kind of you."

"I know. Now, if you could close the door I'd appreciate it. I really must go. Toodle loo."

She waved her fingers at him, and a moment later, he watched the car disappear into the traffic. Once he became a billionaire, he'd buy one of those. A Rolls Royce.

An image of the burnt Mr Gallo flickered before his eyes, and shame blossomed upon his cheeks. Turning, he headed for the entrance.

Once he was through security, he made his way towards the elevators. As he approached the reception, Ms Davis looked up. "Sir," she exclaimed, her small fingers fidgeting with the edge of her gold scarf. "There's been a delivery for you."

* * *

The sun had yet to climb over the horizon. From the Presidential Suite at Park Hyatt Hotel, Principal Cunningham peered out over Tokyo. He stood barefoot by the grand piano, holding a cup of coffee.

"A car, you say?"

"Aye," Professor Jackson barked on the other end of the line. "A bloody Porsche 911! I've seen it. It's gold coloured. Stands in our garage looking like a feckin flamingo among penguins. There's no way we can hide this from the other students."

The principal shoved a hand into the pocket of his hotel robe. This was not a pleasant way to start a Friday. "What did Mr Hallman say about his meeting with The Hostess?"

"Nothing. He hasn't returned yet."

The two men shared a moment of silence, both considering the unfortunate events that had led them to this. Principal Cunningham drained his cup. "The woman's angry," he declared. "Part of this is her way of letting us know she can make things difficult for us."

"Aye, but does she know she's making it difficult for Mr Hallman as well?"

"Oh, I'm sure she does. My guess is that she wants to see how well he handles the pressure from the other students."

"Are…are you insinuating that she's got a plan of her own?"

Principal Cunningham watched the hint of orange in the sky. "Yes, I'm afraid so."

\* \* \*

The garage was empty except for Axel and Julien. Both stood next to one another, staring at the Porsche in disbelief.

"She's very nice," Julien said after a long silence.

"Yeah… Shall we take her for a test run?"

The driver shook his head, albeit with some reluctance. "Sorry, sir. Professor Jackson said we couldn't take her out. After today's ride, we need to lay low for a while."

"Mr Hallman."

Both Axel and Julien turned. An armed guard approached with quick strides. His eyes darted to the Porsche and back. "You are to come with me, sir. Mr Nakata wants to speak with you."

"I see." Axel gave Julien a grin. "Take care of her for me, will you?"

"Of course, sir," the man replied and gave a grave bow.

The guard took Axel to the fourteenth floor and led him through the grand corridor, past the pool area and gym. They entered a few smaller corridors and didn't stop until they reached a locked door at the very end of the building. Here the guard punched in a code and they walked into a circular stairwell that led to the roof.

A cool wind slammed against Axel as they stepped out onto a large helipad, engulfed in soft light. Mr Nakata stood some distance away, looking out over the Belgian capital, his hands on the railing. A sense of unease snaked its way into Axel's gut, and he stopped. Mr Nakata knew how much he hated heights. Why would he set up a meeting here?

The guard came up beside him. From the shadows on his left, another armed man materialised. "Sir," said the one who had led him up from the garage. "He's waiting for you."

It wasn't raining anymore but the clouds above looked dark and angry. Mr Nakata stood proud, his coat flapping in the wind.

"Good evening, Mr Hallman," he said, still gazing out over the city.

"Good evening, sir." Axel stopped some distance from the railing. His palms were already growing clammy. A sea of lights spread out below them, stretching as far as the eye could see. With the wind came the distorted sound of urban traffic; cars honking, a dog barking and the squeal of tram wheels against metal. "You wanted to see me?"

"Hai." The short man turned. "Where you learn about Sarah Wangai?"

The unexpected words came with a gust of wind that clouted Axel square in the face. For a brief moment, he did nothing but stare at the man. Then, as the words sunk in, he snapped out of his surprise, realising he was being studied. He needed to say something. Anything!

"Ms Wangai? The student who died?"

"Hai."

"Why do you ask?"

"Answer me."

Ignoring his thumping heart, Axel took a few seconds to scratch his chin, staring up at the black clouds. "Oh, I don't remember. I think I read about her in an online article."

"Where?"

Axel shook his head. "I don't know. Maybe at Stockholm University library." He was lying, of course. The Box had planted the article in his Speechomat only a few months ago. Before that he'd never heard of Sarah. Few had.

"University has no article," Mr Nakata said. "We have checked."

"Oh? Well…" Axel held out his hand and gave a sad smile. "Then I'm afraid I can't help you, sir. I just don't remember."

Mr Nakata looked at the two guards, and as one they both stepped forward, forcing Axel a little closer to the railing.

"Think again, Mr Hallman," Nakata said. "Think hard."

Dread snatched Axel by the throat, squeezing his windpipe in some kind of mental bear hug. He glanced down and saw the streetlights reflect in puddles of water. What had Thor said when they'd first met? The Academy had thrown Sarah off a roof?

"Maybe I read it on the web," he suggested.

"Or maybe you didn't read at all? Maybe someone *told* you?"

Axel tried to keep the panic out of his voice. "I doubt it, sir. I would've remembered."

"Your friend, Mikael Andersson, did he tell you?"

"Micke? God no!" Axel laughed, and then wished he hadn't. His nervousness rang out as clear as a knife's tap against crystal. Even *he* thought it sounded suspicious.

"Mikael's father, Walter Andersson, works at Stockholm University, no?"

"What has that got to do with anything?" Axel sensed the guards stir behind him. "Yeah, he still works there, I think."

"Did he tell you about Ms Wangai?"

"Are you kidding me?"

Mr Nakata looked at his men again and the two guards took another step forward, forcing Axel up to the wet railing. He could feel the dampness against his thighs and it took all his strength not to push back.

He glanced down. Far below, a young man entered a dark back street, looking no bigger than a Lego figure. Axel's stomach turned and for a frightful moment, he thought his knees would bend.

"Did Walter Andersson tell you?" Mr Nakata pressed.

Axel stood paralysed. The railing reached him below the waist. It wouldn't take much to throw him over.

"Last chance, Mr Hallman. Did Mikael's father tell you about Ms Wangai?"

With an exaggerated calmness, Axel gripped the railing. It was time to show The Academy that they couldn't push him around as they pleased. "Are you trying to frighten me, sir?" he asked with a little laugh.

With all his might, he threw himself back, forcing the guards to step back. Then, before they could react, he swung his left leg over the metal bar.

Both guards bolted forward to stop him, but Mr Nakata raised a hand and they froze. Summoning all his courage, Axel let his right leg follow the left. With his eyes locked on the railing, and his back against the drop, he paused, concentrating on his grip.

The metal was cold and unforgiving in his hands. His palms were already clammy again, and his knuckles white from the effort of holding on. The wind tugged at him, and all he could register was the emptiness beneath his heels.

With his heart thundering in his ears, Axel straightened his back as much as he dared. His gaze fell upon the shocked faces of the two guards. They stood hunched forward, ready to spring into action. Mr Nakata had his hands behind his back and said nothing.

Axel's left hand slipped a little. The wave of adrenaline was almost painful.

"Now then," he said, somehow managing a little smile. "Here I am, and as you can see, I'm scared shitless. Let's see if that helps my memory. What was it you wanted to ask me?"

Mr Nakata stared at him, his jaw tensed like a bowstring. He took a step forward, paused, before slowly leaning out over the railing. "Bravery impresses me," he said in a low voice. "Stupidity does not." Then with impressive speed, his hands shot out, grabbing Axel by the wrists. The impact was so strong, that with a cry, Axel's wet palms lost their grip and he fell backwards.

After that, time seemed to slow. Axel could feel his feet slip off the ledge as his weight pulled him down. There was a terrifying moment of falling, followed by a fierce jerk as Mr Nakata's powerful hands stopped him from plummeting to his death.

Pain shot through his shoulders and arms before he slammed against the wall. For a second he hung there, lost in a haze of shock.

"Who told you about Ms Wangai?" Mr Nakata hissed, his face hidden in shadows.

Hanging there, his life in the hands of another, Axel swallowed his pride. "Please," he wheezed and began to claw at the building with his feet, desperate to find something for support. "Help me!"

"Who told you?"

Behind Mr Nakata, the guards looked panic struck, but none of them moved. Axel heard the blood pressing through his veins. "No one, dammit!" he bellowed. "Pull me up!"

"Where did you learn about Sarah Wangai?"

"God!"

"Where?"

Axel's feet were now kicking frantically at the wall. "I read it! I don't remember where, I swear. Jesus! You're losing your grip! I can feel it."

With a mighty yank, the short man pulled Axel over the railing and onto the roof. He looked down at Axel sprawled on the wet concrete and snorted. "Either you lie, or someone lie to you," he said and turned to leave, the long coat billowing out around his legs. "There is no article on Ms Wangai!"

\* \* \*

In the warm glow of his desk lamp, Mr Nakata considered what he'd written. He sighed and closed the beautiful, leather-bound notebook. In it, he kept his personal reflections and observations, things he didn't want anyone else to see. After returning it to his inner pocket, he called Professor Jackson.

"Well?" the man answered without formality.

Strange how such an educated man could be so unpolished, Mr Nakata thought and rubbed his neck.

"Mr Hallman say he read article but can't remember where."

"You believe him?"

"I was very convincing."

"What the hell does that mean?"

Mr Nakata glanced at the two samurai swords hanging on his wall; the katana and the wakizashi. They had been in his family for generations, and one day, Mr Nakata would give them to his own son. "It means I believe him…for now."

CHAPTER 43

Paavo Nurmi sat in a cosy corner of the hotel bar, a beer in one hand and old man Andersson's latest bank transactions in the other. His mood was sour to say the least. It had been a shitty week. He'd been arrested for thievery, yelled at by his boss and had found no evidence suggesting the Anderssons were up to no good. Worst of all, a limp-dicked old fart had hit him in the head with a bottle. *A bottle!* The disgrace was unbearable. Paavo's reputation was crumbling and he needed to fix it.

The phone vibrated, saving him from further thoughts on the subject. When he answered, an automated voice requested his 'ID'. Paavo ended the call without a word, waited two minutes, then closed his laptop and hurried over to the stairs.

Back in the privacy of his own room, he dialled the Watcher's control centre. Once he'd passed the rigorous security checks, he was connected to the on-duty coordinator.

"Good evening, sir," she said with a calm voice. "Thank you for returning my call. Mr Nakata would like to speak to you. Is it safe to connect?"

Paavo closed his eyes for a moment. *Saatana perkele!* Until now, only Ms Brown had scolded him for his extraordinary slip-up. Although she hadn't mentioned any punishments, Paavo was far too experienced to assume The Academy had forgotten the matter.

With a deep breath, he stood up and braced himself. "Yes. Connect."

He had to wait almost a minute before Mr Nakata's voice penetrated his ear. "Mr Nurmi. How is weather in Stockholm?"

There was a pause, a very uncomfortable one. Paavo frowned,

then after a moment's hesitation, walked over to the window and pulled the curtains aside. "The weather is…good, sir. I mean, the sky's clear."

"Clear sky is good," Mr Nakata established. He sounded almost nice. "Any news on Anderssons?"

"No, sir. Not yet."

"Then I want your opinion. Terminate or continue investigation?"

Paavo's frown intensified. He was very confused. Was Mr Nakata asking for his opinion? Why wasn't he yelling at him? "If you ask me, sir, I want to continue. The Anderssons are up to something. I can feel it."

"Good. Then I have special task for you."

"A task?" Paavo couldn't hide his surprise.

"Hai. I want to know what Mikael Andersson's father did *before* working for Uppsala University. See what you can find and report only to me. Understand?"

"Of course!"

"Oh, and one more thing. Don't get arrested again."

* * *

Waiting for sleep, Axel stared at the hologram universe above his bed. Dark thoughts, memories and emotions hovered at the outskirts of his mind, but he kept them at bay with a simple breathing exercise. He'd been through a lot over the past few days and last night's events had been a challenge. Of course, it was nothing he couldn't handle. He had trained to deal with stressful situations.

Axel closed his eyes and tried to relax the muscles in his neck and back. He was proud of himself. Not only had he used his own fear to trick Mr Nakata into believing him, he'd proven that he couldn't be dominated by fear. That made him a difficult enemy to face.

He lay awake for a few hours, contemplating his situation until exhaustion grabbed him and he fell asleep. As he did, his mental walls crumbled and once again, nightmares entered his world, just as they had every night since the Diamond Ball.

Saturday came with the sun. Axel had his breakfast sent to the fourteenth floor terrace. It was a nice little oasis overlooking the city. He lounged in a wide cushioned chair, sipping his tea while the cool morning turned into a warm, sunny day. Reading the newspapers, he spotted a large photo of Mr Gallo, under the headline, *Billionaire Lost at Sea*.

It was a short article, describing how Mr Gallo had disappeared during a boat trip outside Venice. No one knew where he'd been going or what had happened to him. He'd simply disappeared.

"Hello, Mr Hallman."

The sweet voice embraced him from behind and his heart did a little somersault. Nicole stepped out on the terrace and gave him one of her alluring smiles. God, she was beautiful.

"Ms Swan," he said, fighting the urge to jump up and give her a hug.

They looked at each other. A warm wind caught a strand of her hair and gave it a tug. "I'm afraid I can't stay," she said. "I have a meeting in ten minutes, but I wanted to give you this, a belated birthday gift. I think you'll like page forty-three." She winked. "See you later, sir."

He watched her leave, following her contours through the large windows until his eyes slid across the windows facing the gym. That's when he saw her. Izabella. She stood with her arms crossed over her chest, a livid expression on her face. Before he could react, she had moved out of sight.

* * *

"You said it was urgent, Ms Martins."

Izabella sat down and met the principal's gaze head-on. The man had been her hero for as long as she could remember. She wanted people to respect her the way they respected him; to love her the way they loved him, and to speak of her with the same awe they spoke of him. That was why she held his gaze, for the principal feared no one, and neither would she.

"Yes, sir," she replied, leaning back and settling her arms upon the armrests. "It's about Axel…and to some degree Ms Swan, but mostly Axel."

She stopped and watched the principal as he folded his hands upon his desk. Behind the round spectacles, his small eyes studied her with analytical interest. "Go on," he said in his calm voice.

"Okay." Izabella looked down at her fingers as she ran her nails back and forth over the chair's soft leather. "I believe Axel is hiding something. I've actually suspected that for months, but haven't been able to prove anything. But on the first night in Italy, I was up late, studying, when I heard footsteps outside my door. It was around midnight, and I thought it was a little odd that someone was walking around the corridor at that hour. I looked out and saw Ms Swan entering Axel's room."

To Izabella's satisfaction, the principal furrowed his brow. "She entered his room?"

"Yes, sir. And she was there for…I don't know, maybe forty minutes."

Twenty minutes was more like it, but who would know?

The principal's eyes narrowed. "What do you think they were doing?"

"I wouldn't know, sir. At first I thought the two of them might have a relationship of some sort, but then I saw something else."

She told the principal everything; from Axel going to the secret garden, to his strange behaviour at the Diamond Ball. When she was done, Principal Cunningham shifted in his seat. He sat quiet for what seemed like forever, staring at a spot on his desk. "You know, Ms Martins," he said when the silence had grown so thick, she thought it'd suffocate her. "I must admit I find this information intriguing. Tell me everything again. From the beginning."

This time, as she spoke, the principal showered her with

questions. What had Axel said? How had he said it? Describe his body language when he'd said it? What colour had the envelope been? Had she heard Ms Peacock speak? At what time had Axel vanished from the Diamond Ball?

They spoke for two hours. Principal Cunningham cancelled three meetings. Afterwards he took off his spectacles and leaned back in his chair with a soft sigh. "You did well to come to me, Ms Martins. I need a day or two to consider it all. Have you told anyone else about what you've seen?"

"No, sir."

"Good. Let's keep it that way. I will call you to a new meeting soon. Until then, act as if you know nothing."

* * *

Nicole's gift was a book called *Wine for Dummies*. Axel laughed aloud when he read it, enjoying her clever sense of humour. On page forty-three he found a small envelope containing a note that read, *Meet me tonight. 16:30 at 69 Rue Paul Lauters. Second floor.* After that, Axel couldn't do anything but stare at his watch.

He got a short text from Thabo, wondering if he wanted to meet up at the pool for a swim. Axel declined, blaming a headache. He then spent the next few hours in his apartment.

At ten past four, he marched past the reception, informing Mr Milton that he was taking a long walk.

It was a nice afternoon. Warm winds swept over the city as Axel steered his steps towards *Rue Paul Lauters*. Pushing his nerves aside, he entered the small side street with its cobble-stoned sidewalks and charming townhouses. He caught his reflection in a window, and found he was smiling like a bloody idiot. Stop that, he told himself and conjured up a blank expression. You might be walking right into one of The Academy's tests. That thought dampened his mood, but only a bit.

Number sixty-nine was a red-bricked building, with a dark hallway that smelled of old wood and, for some reason, lemon. The polished staircase creaked and complained while he made his way up.

As he reached the second floor, one of two doors opened. Nicole stepped out, wearing a beautiful white summer dress. He froze and stared at her, paralysed by the sudden rush of uncontrolled desire.

"You came," she said, a hint of surprise in her voice.

"Nothing could have stopped me," he replied, still not moving.

The dimples in Nicole's smile deepened. She stepped closer and Axel slipped his hand around her waist. She leaned in and her lips found his.

CHAPTER 44

Nicole rolled onto her side and glanced at Axel where he lay panting beside her with a faint smile on his lips. She wanted to tell him how happy she was. How much she liked him and how she had liked him from the day they met. She wanted to tell him a million other things, but she didn't. Instead she leaned over and kissed his chest.

Axel let out a pleasurable moan. For a moment she thought he'd embrace her again, but he didn't. Instead he surprised her with a question.

"Who lives here?" he asked. His voice was easy-going, almost dreamy.

Nicole looked up. "I do. It isn't much but its mine, and I love it."

"Yours?" Axel heaved himself up on his elbows. "I thought you lived at the premises with everyone else."

"I have an apartment there, but sometimes I need a little distance from it all. Principal Cunningham is very understanding. He's been kind enough to allow me a place of my own."

Axel's eyes scanned the small apartment. It made her uncomfortable, as though he was scrutinising her personality. Without a word, he stepped out of bed. Dread filled her as he moved towards the other side of the room. There stood an easel with a partially blank canvas on it. He studied the simple sketch with interest. Then his gaze moved on and he began strolling around the room.

"Have you done these?" he asked and made a sweeping motion towards the many paintings on her walls.

She tried to read his face but got nothing. "Yes."

"Do you mind?" Axel turned on the ceiling lights. The brightness of it made him wince. Butt naked, he squinted as every corner of the apartment lit up with white light. "Ouch!"

"Sorry," she said, unable to stop a nervous laugh. "Daylight lamps. Can't paint without them."

"They're fantastic!" Axel moved from one painting to another. "Like a mix between Alfred Sisley's technique and Renoir's colours. Have you ever shown these to an art expert?"

For the first time in years, Nicole's cheeks blushed. "No."

"You must. You could sell these and make a fortune."

"No, I can't."

"I'm serious! They're amazing."

"You're exaggerating. Besides, each painting holds a memory that's dear to me. Like the one I'm working on, for example." She got up, careful not to reveal her back to him as she pulled on her thin robe. "Can you see where it's from?"

Moving back to the easel, he nodded. "Of course. It's the water gardens at La Villa Rossa. The bridge is a giveaway. You're really talented." He gave her a gentle kiss, surely not knowing how much it meant to her that he liked her work.

"I'm not sure how The Academy would react if they saw these paintings," she said. "Some of them are from inside the premises. I don't think they'd be pleased."

"Don't worry, I won't tell anyone." He grinned. "If I do, I'd have to admit to being here, and I can just imagine Professor Jackson's face if he found out."

\* \* \*

Whistling a little tune, Axel descended the dark stairwell, taking two steps at a time. The sweet scent of Nicole remained vivid, and the taste of her lingered on his lips. He was completely engrossed in romantic contentment when a man stepped out in front of him two steps from the ground floor.

Instinct threw Axel in reverse before he could think. He lost his balance, and with a large bang, he fell, striking his tailbone against the corner of the stairs.

For a brief moment, the pain stunned him. Then anger blossomed. "You!" he snarled and scrambled to his feet. "What the hell are you doing?"

Thor stared at him with a frosty expression. He wore his red cap pulled down low, and sunglasses despite the dark. His well-trimmed beard was once again blond. "You're a fool," he said. "How long do you think it takes before the two of you get caught?"

"You're following me?"

"The Academy is not the only one who sees you as an investment. We need to talk."

Axel took a step forward. He was getting really tired of people bossing him around. "We can talk later," he declared. "I need to get back to the Academy."

Thor didn't move.

"Will you be so kind and get out of my way," Axel demanded.

Thor still didn't move. Axel clenched his fists, feeling his blood steam. "Do I need to remind you that I'm an EKA student? You should show me some respect."

Thor's eyes narrowed. The scar cutting across his eyebrow crumpled. In one quick movement, he reached out and gave Axel's forehead a hard flick.

"What the hell?" Axel pulled back, rubbing the spot above his eye. "What's wrong with you?"

"A man who demands respect because of his title or position is a man who's lost himself," Thor observed calmly. "I don't mind being challenged on an intellectual level. I won't think less of you for having a different opinion. But the second you start acting like a spoiled little brat, I'll drag your arrogant ass back to earth with a monumental bump. There are too many people who believe themselves to be better than others. You will *not* become one of them. Understood?"

218 · C.C. MONÖ

Deep within, Axel felt his anger turn serious. "Piss off!" he barked and made a move to pass the man.

Thor lunged forward. One hand grasped Axel by his throat, and the other snatched his right arm.

Before he could react, Axel's legs had disappeared beneath him. He fell like a giant sequoia tree. The impact knocked the air out of him. A knee followed, striking him hard against the chest.

Unable to breathe, he buckled in panic, but Thor kept him pinned down with his own body. The grip around his throat hardened, and he had a gun pressed against Axel's forehead.

"You don't seem to understand," Thor whispered in an even voice. "We *need* to talk."

Axel stared at him. Thor's sunglasses had slipped down a little on his nose. It wasn't much, but it was enough for Axel to see the scar above Thor's right eye. It cut down into the man's eyebrow, nearly splitting it in half. Axel held his breath. Hadn't he seen that scar before?

A door opened somewhere above them. Thor froze, the gun still aimed at Axel's head.

"Hello?" Nicole's voice had a hint of concern in it. "Axel? Is that you?"

## CHAPTER 45

"Not a sound," Thor whispered.

The scar above his right eye itched. It always itched when he was under stress. Without thinking, he had released his hand around Axel's throat and was now pressing it hard over the young man's mouth.

Axel glared at him with unhidden hatred. Thor could feel his hot breath under his hand.

After a moment, Axel nodded. A few seconds passed. Thor stared at the ceiling, straining his ears. This was not the time, nor the place to face Nicole. If she came down those stairs, things would get difficult. The woman was a remarkable fighter.

As Thor listened, his attention on Axel lessened. That was a mistake. With a sudden "humph", the young man craned his back, hurling himself to the right. He was strong but lacked a fighter's skill.

Shifting his weight, Thor kept himself glued to the man.

"Is that you, Axel?" The stairway creaked as Nicole started to descend. Her steps were slow at first, and uncertain. Beneath him, Thor could feel the young man tense. Then something happened that made both of them flinch.

The tired hinges of the front door let out a sudden squeal. A whiff of fresh air and grey evening light fell into the cramped hallway as a man entered. He was tall and slim, his chin covered in thick, black stubble. When he saw the two men on the floor, he halted. Puzzlement grew in his face as the door closed behind him.

"Hello?" Nicole's voice grew louder and her steps more determined.

The man at the door looked up the stairway, then back at Thor. Axel let out another muffled cry and began to wriggle again.

"Axel?" Nicole's steps hastened.

Now the man at the door reacted. On quick feet, he moved over to the stairs and started ascending them at a light jog. *"Ah, bonsoir, mademoiselle,"* came his hoarse but merry voice a second later.

*"Bonsoir, monsieur."* Nicole sounded cautious.

"I am sorry, but I'm looking for a friend of mine…"

While a rapid conversation in French continued above them, Thor leaned forward, pressing his lower arm against Axel's throat. "Have you lost your freaking mind?" he asked in a faint whisper. "Do you think I'll let Nicole walk away if she sees me? You better cooperate now, or you'll be responsible for her death. My friend is vicious with his knives."

\* \* \*

"I thought you were smarter than this," Thor roared. "You're jeopardising everything, and you put people at risk. What the hell is wrong with you?"

They were rolling down *Rue Malibran* in an old Volkswagen while the setting sun coloured the sky purple. For security reasons, The Academy had a strict policy, forbidding students to be out on their own after dark. Another half hour and Mr Milton would react to Axel's absence.

"Are you kidnapping me?"

Thor gave Axel a puzzled look. "What? No! Why would we do that?"

"I don't know. You've forced me into a car at gunpoint. What do you expect me to think?"

"I told you. We need to talk."

The driver glanced at Axel through the rear-view mirror, and in the passenger seat, the man who had spoken to Nicole looked over his shoulder. Axel gave them both a passive aggressive smile. "All right. I'm here," he said. "What do you want to talk about?"

"There are rumours that you've met The Hostess a few days ago. After the Diamond Ball. Is that true?"

"Maybe. Maybe not."

Thor exhaled with obvious annoyance. "I advise you to take a moment and think this through. What do you think will happen if The Hostess figures out that you've been lying to her?"

She'll dip my face in acid, Axel thought and shifted in his seat. Thor held up his phone. "This is from Italy. Recognise it?"

The video had been filmed from a bird's eye perspective. It showed Thor handing Axel the list of potential guests coming to the Diamond Ball.

"I dare say The Hostess will be very disappointed if she saw this video," Thor mused as the audio recording of their conversation was replayed with perfect quality.

Axel struggled to appear indifferent. "Show her that and you'll expose yourself," he said.

"We're about to expose ourselves anyway," Thor countered. "Of course, we can do it with or without mentioning you. The choice is yours."

It would've been nice to see a glimmer of uncertainty in Thor's eyes. A hint of a lie, but no. As far as Axel could tell, the man meant every word he said.

"What do you want?" he asked, keeping a sudden sense of resignation from his voice.

Turning off the phone, Thor gave a little shrug. "For now, all I want is answers. For example; did you meet The Hostess after the Diamond Ball?"

"Yes."

"Did she give you a car?"

How the heck did he know about the car? "Yes."

Thor let out a low moan. "What did she want?"

"Nothing. She just wanted to talk."

"The Hostess won't say a word unless she wants something. What did you talk about?"

Axel drew a breath and gave himself a second to think. He couldn't say anything about Mr Gallo, the job offer or the riches heading his way.

"It appears I've impressed The Hostess," he replied. "She wanted to know more about me."

"That's it?"

"Yes. Look, you want me to destroy The Academy for you, right? Well, if I can nestle my way into the heart of The Seven, then wouldn't that give us a better chance of destroying it all; The Academy, The Seven, everything?"

"No! Jesus! You were supposed to gather enough diamonds to impress The Academy without gaining The Hostess' attention. I told you; no more than six."

"If you think six rocks would've impressed The Academy, then you don't know the people who work there." Axel kept his eyes on Thor as he spoke, but the man showed no reaction whatsoever. "To impress them," Axel continued, "it has to be big. Professor Jackson always says that 'Every great leader has to leave a mark on this world'."

"Which is why we live in a world full of scars," Thor replied. "Believe it or not, Axel, the biggest problem isn't The Academy or The Seven. It is people's acceptance of the leadership myth; the idea that we all need to be led."

"I beg your pardon?"

Thor waved a dismissive hand and turned to his window. "Did you know that by using Academy students, The Seven now control more than sixty-six percent of the world's most influential media?"

"No, I did not know that."

"Well, they do, just as they control the major social media pipes. This means they control the minds of the masses. Do you realise how powerful that makes them? As if that isn't enough, they're taking control of other fundamental areas, such as education, law enforcement, healthcare, environment, military; you name it. They're establishing themselves as rulers of the world, and people don't even know they exist."

Axel grimaced. "Professor Jackson says that people are slaves by their own ignorance. That's why they need leaders to guide them, or there will be chaos."

Thor pulled down his cap with fury, hiding that scar of his. "You know what? People *are* ignorant, but whose fault is that? Who determines the ignorance of a society? Who rules and regulates the education system? Who controls the media? It damn sure isn't the people. They're too busy trying to get by."

A sly expression flashed across his face. "Ever heard the song 'Working Class Hero' by John Lennon?"

"What?"

Still wearing his devious grin, Thor began to sing. "*Keep you doped with religion and sex and TV; and you think you're so clever and classless and free.*"

He stopped and his face grew serious once more. "The Academy says people need leaders to guide them. *We* say that those who call themselves leaders are manipulating people into submission and ignorance. They use religion, entertainments and dreams to keep us docile and manageable. And when that doesn't work, they use fear to control us.

"People are held prisoners without even knowing it, but together with you, we'll set them free."

CHAPTER 46

FOUR YEARS EARLIER

The train rocked and rattled as it crept forward over the hill. Hayato stared out of the open window, letting the warm wind nibble at him like a lovesick puppy. They'd been on the train for six hours and he was itching to get off.

It'd been a beautiful ride. The train had chugged on through jungle and eucalyptus forests, past waterfalls and small villages, through tea plantations and over high bridges. They'd been climbing ever since leaving Kandy, going through areas where the fog was so thick you could taste the water droplets on your tongue. Now they rode on top of a hill, the sky endless above them and the greenest valleys you could imagine below.

When they left Kandy, a few of the passengers had brought forth their instruments, and for two hours, the carriage had been alive with song and dance. During that time, Hayato and Jerome had stared out of the window with a sullen air around them, hoping to put off anyone who wanted to strike up a conversation.

A week had passed since they'd fled Colombo. They'd spent most of that time in a small villa, north of Dambulla, near the city of Anuradhapura. The owner of the house had provided them with all the basics; food, clothes, shoes, new phones, internet, even some English novels and playing cards. Hayato had paid for it all, of course. Then they'd settled back to wait until it was time to move on.

With their new phones, the two escapees got access to the news.

It was something they had longed for. What did the world say about the great Hayato's disappearance? It turned out they said nothing.

"I'm not surprised," Hayato had commented as they'd sat in their small room under the whooshing fan. "I guess The Academy is keeping it a secret, hoping to find us before there's a scandal."

"How can they keep it a secret? We had meetings scheduled the day after our disappearance. Why has no one reacted?"

Hayato had looked away at that point. "You don't know the breadth of The Academy's power, nor the depth of their determination."

That was all he'd said. What was the point of upsetting Jerome with the details? The EKA bribed, manipulated, tricked and killed to get what they wanted. If they could keep an entire school hidden, how difficult could it be to conceal the disappearance of Hayato for a few days?

It was a little different with The Box. They could expose the whole thing to the media if they wanted, but that would result in unwanted attention from The Academy. With Hayato gone, that was probably the last thing The Box wanted right now.

Three days after their conversation, Hayato and Jerome had been sitting in the kitchen eating dinner when their host had received a phone call. The old woman who'd helped Hayato in Wariyapola, had been found dead. "Her throat slit by robbers," the host had said, his eyes thick with tears. "She was my aunt."

Jerome had stood silent, his face ashen. Wrapped in shame and guilt, Hayato had bowed and expressed his greatest sorrow for the sudden loss. "I'm sure the police will find the guilty," he'd said in an attempt to comfort the distraught man.

That same evening, while they'd sat in their beds reading, Jerome had turned to his former boss. "Did The Academy do it?" he'd asked.

"I think so. Yes."

"Why?"

"Because The Academy never fails."

Outside, wild dogs had barked and howled as they'd moved around the neighbourhood in gang-like packs. Hayato had paid them little attention. His mind had been on Sarah Wangai; the student who never was. The twelfth student during the Year of Eleven. The first student to experience how far The Academy was willing to go to protect their image, to protect the leadership ideal.

Jerome had crossed his legs in front of him and furrowed his brow. "What does that mean; 'The Academy never fails'?"

"It means that my running away is a failure on their part. You figure out the rest."

As Hayato had picked up his book again, he'd felt such an immense sorrow. He was not angry or scared, just sad. Sad for mankind and its stupidity. Sad that some people had such a craving to control and dominate others. We're supposed to be better than this, he thought.

Later that night, when they'd turned off their lights and were lying in bed, listening to the clicking fan and the howling dogs outside, Jerome had rolled over in his bed. "Sir," he'd whispered. "What kind of institution *is* The Academy?"

Hayato had remained silent and pretended to sleep.

They had left the day after, unshaven and dressed like backpackers. This time they'd gone south by bus. In Kandy, they'd found a cheap homestay. Here they'd spent a miserable night on hard beds while the heavy traffic had thundered past their little room. In the early morning, they'd walked to the train station and bought third-class tickets to Ella.

The train jolted Hayato from his thoughts. He took a quick glance at the map and then the cheap watch on his arm. "We better get ready," he said in a low voice. "I think the next stop is ours."

CHAPTER 47

PRESENT DAY

The box was gold plated and looked very much like The Academy's official business card holders. Only this one was a fraction bigger, and a little heavier than the original.

"It's a communication device," Thor explained. He had pulled it out the breast pocket of his denim jacket. "Remember the business card you were given by the Swedish prime minister?"

Axel looked up. "You know about that?"

Thor showed his palms in a gesture that could mean anything. "The EKA has a complex security system that searches for technology used to record or transmit data. To minimise information breaches, they don't allow any foreign technology without rigorous tests."

"How do you know these things?" Axel asked with open scepticism.

"We do our homework. We know that nothing enters The Academy without being scanned for spy bugs and listening devices. But we've also learnt that there's a glitch in their system. The radio frequency scanners are positioned at entrances only. If someone manages to slip a non-Academy-adapted device past these scanners, then they can use it without detection.

"Do you remember what happened when you entered The Academy for the first time?"

"You mean the alarm went off?"

"Exactly, but the security team didn't care. Why? Because they *knew* it would happen. You had your private phone with you. What they didn't know was that you also had a very special card in your pocket."

"The business card?"

"Yes. Think of it as a tiny and simple computer." Thor tapped a finger against the lid of the little box. "This thing works as a projector. It contains no radio frequency and shouldn't be detected when you walk through the scanners."

"Wait a minute. What do you mean *shouldn't*?"

Thor gave a little grin. "Hey, it's not like The Academy has instruction manuals on the internet, but we've done our research. You should be fine."

These weren't very comforting words. Axel ran his tongue along the inside of his teeth while his mind worked. "Does this mean the prime minister is part of your network?"

"No."

"Then how did you get him to give me the card? Did you threaten him?"

"Don't be a dumbass. Of course we didn't threaten him. That would've caused all kinds of problems. No, there are other ways to make a man do what you want him to do. It's called manipulation." Thor scratched his neck, right below his Adam's apple. "You still have the card I hope?"

"Yes."

"Good. To activate the device, you place the card vertically against the lid and turn it forty-five degrees clockwise until it clicks into place." Thor flipped an invisible card over the box in Axel's hand, demonstrating what it would look like. "Then you hold your thumb against the word 'eagle' at bottom until your print has been scanned. That'll start it."

"How does it work?" Axel wondered, turning the device in his hands.

"It's a simple little thing. It can only send and receive text messages. There are a few important rules, however. As mentioned, the card will trigger the security system, so you can't leave the premises with it. Second, as far as we know, there are no security cameras inside the restrooms. Therefore, make sure you don't use it anywhere else but in there, okay?"

"All right."

"Also, always de-activate the device when you're done."

"How do I de-activate it?"

"Simple. Remove the card from the lid. You charge the device by placing it in direct sunlight or under a bright lamp. Be careful not to draw any attention to it, though."

"Fine."

Thor nodded as if pleased. "That's it. When you get back, send us a message. We need to know it works. I want you to activate the device at least twice a day. Once in the morning and once in the evening. We might send you instructions, and when we do, you follow them. I hate to threaten you, but we need your collaboration. If we don't get it, we'll be forced to send our video to The Hostess."

They dropped him off a few blocks from The Academy and he jogged back with the communication device bouncing in his pocket.

Without stopping, Axel marched right through the scanners, bracing himself for the alarm. It never came.

"Good evening, sir," said one of the guards and opened the doors to the foyer.

A hint of lilac and apple blossom hung in the air as Axel made his way towards the elevators.

"Sir, you came back," Mr Milton said with a little smirk. "I was getting worried."

"I'm sure you have better things to worry about," Axel muttered and walked past the short man without throwing him a glance. The man was a jerk.

Once back in his apartment, Axel got his wallet form the bedside table and walked into the main bathroom. Without hesitation, he activated the device. It worked exactly as Thor had claimed it would. The inside of the lid lit up like the screen on a cell phone. Below, on the gold surface, a digital keyboard appeared.

Trying it out, he wrote; *Activated. Now what?*

Two seconds later, the device vibrated. *Good. Now you wait until we give you further instructions.*

CHAPTER 48

Axel sauntered across the hard oak floor, following the waitress to his seat. The restaurant looked much like it had on his first day at The Academy. He scanned the magnificent hall for Nicole but couldn't see her in the dimmed lights. Instead, his eyes fell upon the marble statue of Hayato Sano. Ha! The man hadn't even been close to seventeen diamonds. Still he was a legend. Imagine what they'd say about him.

"You look handsome," Izabella observed, putting on a smile that didn't fit her cold eyes.

"You're not too bad yourself," he replied and turned to Thabo. "How are you doing?"

The young South African inclined his head. "I'm doing well. What about you?"

"Never been better."

Axel dropped into his chair. Peering up at the vaulted ceiling, he spent a couple of minutes watching the large hologram eagles. From the other tables came laughter and amused cries, but neither Izabella nor Thabo said a word.

A few minutes later, Paul arrived. He tipped his head back in a nonchalant greeting, his round cheeks flushing red. "There he is," he said and sat down. "Our new hero, huh?"

With a little smile, Axel shrugged. "I guess."

Paul took his napkin, folded like a lily flower, and flicked it open. "Heard you got a car," he continued, placing the napkin over his lap.

"It was a gift," Axel said and turned his attention to the hall.

"One hell of a gift," Paul growled.

"Yes. It's very nice."

It looked like Izabella was about to say something, but at that moment, the intro to AC/DC's *Thunderstruck* began to play.

\* \* \*

Principal Cunningham tugged at his sleeves. He wasn't nervous, just tired. The effects of jet lag grew worse with every passing year. Twenty-four hours had passed since he'd arrived back from Tokyo and he still felt as though he had a head full of cotton. Whether he wanted to accept it or not, age was becoming an issue.

"Twenty seconds left, ladies and gentlemen!" Mr Milton informed.

Behind the large doors, the music grew in strength. Professor Jackson straightened his back. One of the servants adjusted his pocket square, but the man himself stared straight ahead, eyes hard and his face blank as polished ice. Professor Jackson would never be a good headmaster, Principal Cunningham thought. There was too much anger in the man.

"Ten seconds!"

The teachers lined up, everyone fidgeting with something. Professor Evans checked her scarf, Mr Bell fiddled with his cufflinks and Professor Wilson was looking for his glasses.

"Five seconds!"

"They'll hate him for it," Professor Jackson said, eyes still on the door.

Principal Cunningham smiled. "They already do."

"Three... Two... One... Here we go!" Mr Milton clapped his hands twice and the doors opened to the sound of applause. One by one, the teachers stepped out. Principal Cunningham waited until everyone had taken their position at the teachers' table. Only then did he step out into the bright spotlight.

Three minutes later he led the pledge of allegiance to The Academy. Once the last words died out, he motioned everyone to sit. The bright spotlights blinded him, yet he scanned the Grand

Hall as though he could see every student and staff member.

"Tonight, is a very special evening," he began. "Not only does it mark the end of your first semester and the beginning of your second, but tonight you'll be assigned your mentors. This is an important step in your training. From now on, your schedules will be individualised, tailored by your mentors." He paused and turned to Professor Jackson. "What do you say, Assistant Principal Jackson? Shall we begin?"

The students let out a cheer. While Principal Cunningham sat down, Professor Jackson got to his feet. He looked out at the students, not with any warmth or encouragement, but with that stern glare that never seemed to leave his face.

"Good evening," he said as the wall behind the teachers lit up. A picture of Layla appeared. "Ms Layla Neferet! Your mentor will be Professor Evans."

The room exploded with applause and Layla beamed.

"Mr Federico Calvo, your mentor will be Professor Hess. Mr Edward Reed, your mentor will be…well, me."

More applause broke out, followed by laughter.

"Izabella Martins. Your mentor will be Professor de Mare…"

Principal Cunningham tapped his finger against his thigh in order to keep himself from losing focus. He listened as Dalilah got Edith Poma, professor of International Law. Paul got Professor Williams, and Thabo, Professor Plouffe.

One by one, the students got their mentors until finally it was just Axel left.

"Mr Axel Hallman. Your mentor will be…" Professor Jackson glanced at his papers and for a moment, he hesitated. "Principal Cunningham."

CHAPTER 49

At the Academy's security centre, a powerful strobe light began to flash, accompanied by an obnoxious, pulsating sound. In his private office, Mr Eli Peretz, Master of Guards, got to his feet the instant his watch started to vibrate. When the phone rang, he was already on his way.

"Status!" he demanded.

"Front entrance. Possible attack," the voice declared.

Mr Peretz cut off the line and marched into Eagle Eye with some appearance of self-control. It was buzzing with activity. "Well?" he barked.

His second in command stood ready by the monitors. "A driver on a motorcycle threw a package at the main entrance," he replied.

"Bomb?"

"If it was, it didn't go off. Yet."

"The driver?"

"Headed North on *Avenue Louise*. Ms Brown is sending two of her Watchers to follow."

Mr Peretz pursed his lips and glared at the monitor showing the small package by the door. "They're too late. They'll never catch up."

"Yes, sir. Ms Brown is aware of that but said it's her duty to try although their main focus will be on satellite imagery."

"What else?"

"We're doubling the guards at all entrances. Team Jaws is on their way up to the fourth floor."

"Good but keep them out of sight for now."

"Yes, sir. What do you want to do with the package?"

"Tell the guards at the main entrance to double check that the inner doors are locked. Evacuate the foyer and inform Mr Nakata and Principal Cunningham. Be discreet. No need to upset the students at this point." Mr Peretz paused, leaned forward and stared at the screen. "If that's a bomb, it's not a very big one."

* * *

The room fell silent. There was no applause or cheers, no comments or whispers. Just a long, painful silence.

Principal Cunningham watched his assistant principal. Bathing in bright lights, the man stood behind his chair, staring out over the great hall. "Well, that sums up the announcements," he said in a cold, contained voice. "Ms Jacobson, serve us dinner."

It took a couple of seconds before the maître d' seemed to realise she'd been spoken to. When she did, she clapped her hands. From somewhere in the dark, music began to play and lights faded in. Principal Cunningham kept his smile as he, with feigned disinterest, scanned the great hall.

Servants rushed about looking professional, carrying foods from the kitchen, and pouring wine into glasses, but their faces couldn't hide their amazement. As to the students, they didn't even try to hide their shock. He could see them whispering. It was, of course, understandable. Only one other student had received the principal as a mentor; Hayato Sano.

The principal's eyes found Axel. The young man was staring at him, looking a great deal like Professor Jackson with his blond hair, stern eyes and unreadable expression. I'll have to tread gently with that one, the principal thought as he held the young man's gaze. I fear he's evolving too fast, which means we risk losing control over him.

Axel's lips curved into a thin smile and he gave Principal Cunningham a tiny nod. The principal was about to return it when Mr Nakata leaned in over his shoulder. "Sir," he whispered. "There's been an incident. You and Professor Jackson should come with me."


Principal Cunningham looked around the crowded conference room. He was seldom down here at the Eagle Eye.

"There, sir." Mr Peretz pointed at one of the massive screens on the wall. It showed a petite woman straddled over a motorcycle, wearing black leather riding gear with a black helmet that concealed her face. "Twenty minutes ago, this driver approached the main entrance at high speed. Thirty metres from our door, she drove up onto the sidewalk. Camera SC4 shows her pulling out the package from a shoulder bag."

The image on the screen changed, showing the woman pulling a small box from a black bag.

"One of the guards saw this and pressed the panic button. Before the package struck the ground, we had all our entrances locked and secured. Nothing happened, but we've cleared the foyer and sent a team of guards to the fourth floor for your protection, sir."

"And the package?" Principal Cunningham asked.

"It's still out there."

"Do you think it's a bomb?"

"Hard to tell, sir."

"Well, we have to move it," Professor Jackson declared. "If it's a bomb and it goes off, then we'll draw all kinds of attention to us."

Principal Cunningham turned to Mr Nakata. "You're my security advisor. I believe this is a good time for you to advise me. What do you suggest we do?"

The Head of Security inclined his head in a slight bow. "We take package inside security checkpoint and scan it."

"What if it goes off?"

"Package is very small and entrance is reinforced to withstand smaller explosions."

The principal pushed up his glasses and thought for a moment. "Very well. Bring it in."

They watched as Mr Peretz gave the instructions to the two guards at the main entrance. Neither looked very happy about it, but they didn't question their order. One of them unbolted the front door and stepped out. Nodding at an elderly man passing the building, she squatted and picked up the package with both hands.

Once she had returned and the door had been locked behind her, the two guards set to work, scanning the package.

"It's not a bomb, sir," one of them announced a moment later. "It appears to be some sort of organic matter. We're transferring the images now."

Mr Nakata had several experts called into the conference room. After a quick consultation, a small fume hood was sent to the main entrance, along with two protective suits for the guards.

"I don't like this," Professor Jackson muttered as the guards donned their suits. "I don't like this at all."

"We're ready, sir," the male guard informed, placing the package under the fume hood. "Shall I open?"

All eyes turned to the principal. He gave a tiny nod. "Yes. Go ahead."

A tense silence fell over the conference room. The guard produced a small knife and began cutting through the tape with great care.

"What in the world is that?" the principal asked, wrinkling his nose at the screen.

The guard leaned over the box, hiding its content for a moment. "I don't know, sir," he replied. "It looks like a chunk of gel. Wait." He paused as he pulled out something from the box. "There's also an envelope here." The guard turned towards the camera and held it up. "I believe it's for you, Principal Cunningham."

Once the experts had scanned and tested the envelope for toxins, Principal Cunningham had it delivered to him. The small conference room was now empty save for himself, Professor Jackson and Mr Nakata. At the moment, the box and its remaining content was being analysed by an agent specialised in bioterrorism. On one of the large screens, the principal could see the agent poke at the jelly lump with crucible tongs as he performed various toxin tests.

"What do you think it is?" Principal Cunningham asked the others. They'd muted their microphone so that they could hear the agent, but he couldn't hear them.

A frown had settled over Professor Jackson's face, and by the looks of it, it was there to stay. He reached out to a smaller screen that displayed a 3D image of the box. Using his fingers, he manoeuvred the box until he could see its content from different angles.

"I'd say it's some kind of…jellyfish," he concluded after a while.

Mr Nakata stepped closer. "I see no tentacles."

"What's the name of the chap who cares for our animals? The vet?" Principal Cunningham asked.

"Don't know, sir," Professor Jackson answered, "but I'll get him and see if he can identify this thing."

"Good." The principal turned his focus to the small, soggy envelope on the table. *To Cunningham* it said in bold letters. With thin, latex gloves, he pulled out a damp note and unfolded it. With the others staring at him, he read it once, then again, and as his eyes grew harder, he read it a third time.

"Well? What does it say?" Professor Jackson asked.

Without a word, Principal Cunningham handed over the note. He drew one deep breath and turned to Mr Nakata. "I want you and your team to find the person who delivered this," he said in a low, growling voice.

The Head of Security inclined his head. "Hai." He accepted the note from Professor Jackson whose pale skin had turned ghostly.

"Tell Ms Brown that she can use *any* means necessary," the principal continued, "but she must keep the investigation discreet. Inform the rest of your people that this was an exercise designed to test their skills."

"Hai."

"Then speak with Ms Sokolova and give her the same story. Tell her that, as the Head of Staff, I expect her to brief the remaining personnel as soon as possible. I don't want to hear any rumours about us being attacked. Understood?"

"Hai, sir."

"As for you and I," Principal Cunningham turned to Professor Jackson, "we shall return to the dinner with the same, damn story to the other professors. Is that clear?"

"Aye."

Accepting the note back from Mr Nakata, Principal Cunningham read it one last time.

*A flea will make the Eagle itch,*
*A thousand, have it cry and twitch.*
*The Eagle thought itself a king,*
*Can't be killed by man or thing.*
*Pride comes before a fall they say,*
*The Eagle's end begins today.*

# CHAPTER 50

The following day, Mr Nakata entered the principal's office with his notebook clasped in one hand. Warm light fell through the large windows, bringing life to hovering dust particles. They swirled through the room like tiny gold flakes, filling the office with a sense of peace.

The principal looked up from the wide armchair he was occupying. "Good morning, Mr Nakata," he said, folding the newspaper he'd been reading. "Any news on yesterday's attack?"

"No, sir."

"Hm. Not the answer I was hoping for." The principal reached for his cup of coffee. "I must admit, I'm a bit confused. Someone has identified our location, yet there's nothing in the news. It seems the perpetrator has no interest in exposing us to the media. At the same time, I interpret the message itself as a threat. I'm not sure what to make of it." He brought the cup to his lips and took a small sip. "I assume you're investigating the people on our Judas List."

"Hai," Mr Nakata replied. "We find nothing yet."

The Judas List was a catalogue of individuals who for one reason or the other had officially criticised The Academy. There weren't many and most of them were either political or philosophical nutcases. The remaining morons were rejected applicants with a grudge. While Mr Nakata had ordered Ms Brown to follow up on the individuals on the Judas List, he doubted they'd find the perpetrator among them.

It had been a well-executed attack, suggesting someone had done a fair bit of planning. Another fact that worried Mr Nakata, was the timing of the attack. Students, teachers and most staff members had been up on the fourth floor. Also, the attack had occurred during the changing of guards, a ten-minute stretch at eight thirty. Could the attacker have chosen this moment on purpose? If so, that meant the perpetrator had inside information.

"I have a meeting with The Seven in five hours," the principal said. "Before then I want a security report, stating everything that is being done to find the attacker and protecting our students."

"Hai, sir." Mr Nakata bowed.

There was a light knock on the door and in came the principal's assistant and bodyguard, Mr Hennigan.

"Oh!" he said and looked startled. "My apologies, sir. I didn't know you were in a meeting."

"What is it, Mr Hennigan?"

"One of the students, Ms Martins, is here. She demands to see you."

The principal sighed and shook his head. "Bring her in."

* * *

With tight-pressed lips, Izabella marched over to one of the visitors' chairs and sat down, ignoring Principal Cunningham's scrutinising gaze. Although she was seething inside, a head-on collision was a bad idea. The man had too much power.

"You're angry with me," the principal observed.

No shit, Sherlock, she thought and caught herself grinding her teeth. With great effort, she relaxed her jaw, but found her legs tensing instead. Damn! She had a problem with her temper, and if she was ever to become a great leader, she must learn how to conceal it.

"*Why*, is a brilliant word," came the principal's calm voice. "It has saved me from embarrassment a great many times."

Snapped out of her thoughts, Izabella looked up and found the man watching her with a playful grin. "What I'm saying, Ms Martins, is that I suggest you ask me 'why' *before* you get angry."

The crease between Izabella's eyes deepened. "As you wish, sir.

After all I've told you about Axel, why have you chosen to mentor him? He's not worthy."

"I understand your concern, Ms Martins, but try to see things from my perspective. Your observations have troubled me a great deal. Far more than I think you understand. Something is amiss, but how can I find out what it is? I can't ask Mr Hallman, can I?"

Izabella sucked on her teeth and studied the principal for a moment. "You're mentoring Axel in order to uncover his secrets?"

"Indeed."

A warm sense of relief spread through Izabella's soul, followed by pride. The principal had not only listened to her, he had decided that her observations needed *personal* attention. She nodded and looked out of the window. "Makes sense," she said.

Principal Cunningham smiled. "I need you to help me ensure something."

"Of course, sir. Anything."

"We need the other students to believe I'm mentoring Mr Hallman because of his performance at the Diamond Ball. We can't have anyone suspecting the truth. Should anyone begin to divert from this assumption, I need you to inform me."

Sitting up a little straighter, Izabella nodded. "I will, sir."

"Very good. From now on, if you have a meeting booked by Mr Hennigan, it means you're meeting with me. No matter where the booking tells you to be, come to my office. Please make sure no one sees you. The last thing we want, are people asking questions."

* * *

"Right on time, Mr Hallman. Come in."

This was Axel's first session with the principal, and while Axel was excited about it, the principal himself looked like he was in desperate need of sleep. Dark circles surrounded his red eyes and he moved in a sluggish manner.

The office was big and cluttered. Most of it was filled with books. Hundreds, perhaps thousands of books in all colours and sizes. They covered three walls. On the fourth wall, made up of mostly windows, were a few framed photographs and a beautiful antique clock that was six minutes off.

Axel smiled as he turned on the soft carpet. "I take it you're not one for reading e-books, sir?" he said.

"Can't say I do. The way I see it, the enjoyment of a good book is one third reading the words, one third feeling the texture between your fingers, and one third breathing the scent of each page. Without all three, the story has no soul."

Axel laughed and glanced at the man's enormous mahogany desk. On it stood an elegant globe, lit from within. There was also a laptop and a few other office items squeezed in among piles of books.

"You've got a point," he said and walked over to one of the large windows. He peered out over the city. Two pigeons sat on a nearby rooftop, basking in the last rays of the evening sun. 'Flying rats', his father called them. Said they carried diseases. One year he'd bought his son an airgun and promised a nice reward for every crow or pigeon that Axel killed. Three months later, he'd backed away from that agreement, claiming it was becoming too expensive.

Principal Cunningham stepped up beside Axel and gazed out. "My late wife used to say that if you look out a window and think of nothing, then it's a sign of inner peace."

"How so?"

"I suppose a mind at rest will let you enjoy the scenery without disturbance. A nervous or worried mind is preoccupied with finding solutions to its problems." The principal gave a little laugh. "Well, what do I know? I've never looked out a window without pondering on a problem to solve. Tea?" He turned away and stepped towards a nearby table, holding a kettle and a few cups.

"Yes, please." Axel left the window and looked at the nearest photograph. It showed the principal with his arm around a smiling woman, several centimetres taller than he was.

"Why did you choose to mentor me?" Axel asked, studying the

photograph.

"Why wouldn't I?"

Axel didn't sigh, but it took quite an effort not to. He moved to the next photograph; a girl, five or six years old, dressed up as a bee. She was holding a Halloween pumpkin, looking happy.

"Don't get me wrong, sir. I'm honoured, but the other students seem to disapprove."

"Of course they do. Wouldn't you?"

"No. They're all idiots."

"The world is full of idiots, Mr Hallman. And as frustrating as it might be at times, they often make life interesting. What kind of tea would you like?"

"Kericho Gold with milk, please."

The principal opened a fine-looking wooden box and pulled out two teabags. "Yes, the world is full of idiots," he repeated, "and it might be that you and I are the worst of them. You for making such a spectacle at the Diamond Ball, and me for making it worse by choosing to mentor you. Our original plan was for Professor Evans to mentor you. I'm afraid I'm not as pretty as she is, but I do know a thing or two of value."

Axel grinned. "Pretty?"

The elderly man raised a brow in mock surprise. "Oh dear, you don't think she's pretty? Then what must you think of me?"

He gestured Axel to take a seat in one of the armchairs and placed a steaming cup in front of him. "There you go," he said before strolling over to one of the bookshelves and retrieving a large copper bowl. After filling it with water, the principal placed it on the mahogany coffee table and turned to his student. "What do you see?" he asked.

Axel leaned forward and eyed the object. All right, most likely, this was an assessment of his observational abilities. "Well, sir, I see a copper bowl filled with water. Its design and form are simple, narrow at the bottom and four times as wide at the top. The surface is smooth and the shape of it reminds me of a contact lens."

He stopped and looked up. To his annoyance, Principal Cunningham was focusing on Rupert. The fat and rugged cat sat on the man's armrest, glaring at the intruding student with apparent disgust. After a few seconds, it stepped onto the principal's lap with a scowl that seemed to say, 'Don't even think about it. He's mine'.

The principal looked up. "That's it?"

"No. The bowl is circular. You emptied an entire bottle of water into it, and I guess you'd need about…" Axel made a few quick calculations in his head. "I'd say you'd need about eleven more bottles in order to fill it to the rim."

Pausing again, Axel considered the man. "Shall I go on?"

"You know," said the principal, pausing to take a sip of his tea. "An ignorant man can be a nuisance, but an ignorant man with *power* is a disaster waiting to happen."

"Hmm…I couldn't agree more, sir."

"I'm glad you say that, Mr Hallman. Of course, the thing about ignorance is that it remains unknown to those who suffer from it. And if you don't know you're suffering from it, how will you know you're ignorant?"

With a sneaky feeling of being made a fool, Axel hesitated. "That's true, sir."

Principal Cunningham scratched Rupert behind the ear and the ugly thing started to purr. "To clarify, Mr Hallman; ignorance is not the same as stupidity, but both lead to foolish decisions." With a shrewd smile, he pulled out a gold ring from the depth of the cat's fur. "Like magic, wouldn't you say?"

Axel offered a small but polite laugh. "Very impressive, sir."

The man held out the ring between his thumb and index finger. "From your angle, the ring is now a perfect circle. If this was the only ring you'd ever seen, you'd think me senseless for claiming it is flat. Until I did this." The man flipped the ring between his pudgy fingers, showing it from the side. "From this perspective, it *is* flat."

He closed his hand around the ring and did a little movement with both hands. Genuine amusement sparkled in his eyes as he opened his fingers and showed Axel nothing but empty palms. Now that *was* impressive.

"You speak of that bowl as if it's a given thing, but it could just as well be a footbath or maybe a sculpture. It all comes down to how you look at it, or what it was intended to be. You assume it's a bowl of water. That affects your thinking. Soon it becomes the truth, and re-evaluating our truths is one of the most difficult challenges we face in life. It's easier for us to defend our flawed perspectives than change them.

"The world isn't black and white," the principal continued. "Or in this case, a bowl of water or nothing at all, but most people base their decisions on a single perspective. *Their* perspective. As such, they exclude all other options. They see a bowl of water and shut out the possibility that it could be something else. Their assumptions make them ignorant, and as we have concluded, ignorant leaders are dangerous."

Axel bit his lip, unsure whether or not the man had scolded him. "I have two questions," he said after a moment's silence.

"Go ahead."

"First, if I know that's a bowl of water, why waste time questioning it?"

"Ah. Tell me this; if you're wrong but think you're right, how will you ever know the truth? That thing was part of a costume I wore many years ago. My late wife and I attended a masquerade party in New York. I went as a satellite dish." Principal Cunningham let loose a warm and heartfelt laugh. "I keep it for sentimental reasons. It was a terrible costume, but my wife thought it was funny.

"To answer your question, the 'bowl' was never intended to be a bowl, but that doesn't mean it *can't be* a bowl. Like I said, it's a matter of perspective. What's your second question?"

Axel couldn't tell if the man was making fun of him or not, and it annoyed him. A lot!

"If lack of different perspectives makes us ignorant, why do some professors dislike it when I question their training?"

The principal shrugged. "Maybe they can't answer your questions. Or perhaps they don't want to. It could be that they find your questions irrelevant, or possibly stupid. Perhaps *they* are ignorant. Or maybe you are. Who knows? The possibilities are endless."

Axel stared at the amused face in front of him. "How am I to interpret your answer?"

"*That*, Mr Hallman, is a good question. When you find the answer to it, you'll have come a long way."

\* \* \*

The Academy's animal keeper and veterinarian was a lean chap in his thirties, with a quirky smile that never left his oval face. According to his file, the man came from Hawaii and had studied at some of the best universities around the world.

Principal Cunningham closed the dossier and leaned back in his office chair until it squeaked.

"Tell me, Mr Kealoha. What have we got here?"

"Sir. The specimen you gave me was a *Chironex fleckeri*, or sea wasp as most people call them."

"Never heard of it."

"It's a type of jellyfish found in the Indo-Pacific region. They're part of a venomous species called box jellyfish." The man produced his phone and shared a picture of the animal on the large screen in front of them. "It has a square-shaped bell that is almost transparent. From certain angles, it looks like a human skull. Look. You see?" He pointed at the image with excitement.

"It's venomous, you say?"

"Very. A single one can kill up to sixty people. The tentacles can grow to about three metres and they contain millions of cnidocytes—"

"What's that?" Professor Jackson interrupted.

"Think of it as an exploding cell, sir. A cell that fires a threadlike dart containing toxins. The tentacles have millions of them filled with powerful venom."

"What about the one you examined?"

"It had been dead for a couple of days, and someone had cut off its tentacles."

"I see." Principal Cunningham handed back the touch-pad and took off his glasses. "Thank you, Mr Kealoha. I believe you've been told to keep this to yourself."

"Yes, sir."

"Splendid. Then I shall have your boss give you a little bonus as appreciation for your help. You may now leave."

When the vet closed the door behind him, Principal Cunningham turned to Professor Jackson and Mr Nakata with a grim expression on his face. "Gentlemen. It seems The Academy has an enemy."

CHAPTER 51

Mr Nakata was not a spiritual man, and unlike his father, he was flexible when it came to the old traditions. Nonetheless, he was proud man, who valued his country's long and rich history. Although his office was more Western influenced than Eastern, he made sure to always have a degree of 'home' nearby.

On the edge of his clean desk stood a one-hundred-year-old bonsai tree, brought with him from Okinawa. At the moment, this magnificent tree was in the hands of Professor Jackson, who looked at it with bored scepticism.

"The Academy has been attacked," he said in a low, guttural voice. "I need that file."

"You think there's a connection?"

"Could be."

Mr Nakata clasped his hands in front of him. "What you expect to find?" he asked, hiding the concern in his voice.

"I'm not sure."

"I cannot enter archive without breaking rules."

Exhaling, Professor Jackson returned the small tree to its place on the desk. "All I want is to read the file. No one will have to know."

"I told you, professor. If I enter system, people can see. It will create problems."

Professor Jackson made a little noise of repulsion. "And haven't *I* told you; find a way to hide your tracks! You're in charge of the security, aren't you?" He got to his feet. "We've been attacked, and I want that file!"

\* \* \*

It might be his imagination, but Axel felt as though there had been a blanket of retained uneasiness smothering The Academy. Professor Jackson stormed around the premises like a hurricane in a bad mood. He was worse than usual, shouting and yelling at anyone who crossed his path. His lessons were getting unbearable.

Then there was Mr Nakata. He remained unseen for most of the time, but more guards were circulating the building than usual. As for Principal Cunningham, he grew more tired and distracted with every passing day.

Finally, Axel asked Nicole about it, but she hadn't heard anything and waved it off as nothing more than the typical autumn stress.

The summer vacation was now but a memory. Thor and his network kept their silence. Axel still hadn't figured out where he'd seen Thor before. He thought about it now and again, but life at The Academy had grown harsh and intense once more. Besides, Axel's initial excitement about working with the principal had begun to fade and that occupied his mind a fair bit.

Principal Cunningham's demanding schedule meant that he and Axel could only meet once a week. The other students met their mentors four or five times as often.

To compensate, the principal signed his student up for every subject offered at The Academy. While the other students focused on a few subjects, Axel had to do it all, from Global Environment and Coaching, to Followership Psychology and Leadership history. It sucked!

Another thorn in his arse was the other students. One late August night, as Axel was about to crawl into bed, Thabo knocked on his door. "We need to talk," he declared.

Axel ordered up a cheese tray from the restaurant and a bottle of wine for Thabo. Twenty minutes later, they sat in the living room, lit only by the dancing flames from the fireplace and the eerie blue of the massive aquarium that covered an entire wall.

"You're in trouble," Thabo declared, placing a thick slice of Brie on a cracker. "The others are turning against you, especially Izabella. Everyone's upset that Principal Cunningham chose to mentor you. They envy your car, and they hate the fact that you gathered seventeen diamonds. Now they're trying to figure out how you cheated and how to get you expelled."

Axel yawned. He reached up and pulled a leaf off the large potted tree, stretching its branches over the sofa. "I didn't cheat."

Thabo shook his head. "Don't you understand? It doesn't matter if you cheated or not. Right now, the others are angry students, but once they graduate, they'll be angry *leaders* with a great deal of power. You must be careful."

Axel stopped himself from laughing as he thought about The Hostess. "I'll be powerful too, remember? Perhaps more so than you think."

Thabo sat quiet for a while, sipping his wine and staring at Axel's shark as it slid through the clear blue water. "Even if you are right," he said at last, his voice restrained. "Even if you become more powerful than the rest of us, you'll never be more powerful than all of us together."

Softening his tone, Axel offered a little smile. "I know you're trying to help, but I'm not apologising for being better than they are, and that's final."

Two nights later, when having dinner with Nicole at her apartment, Axel surprised himself by telling her about Thabo's visit. He wasn't sure why he mentioned it, perhaps he felt some sort of guilt for how he'd treated his friend, or maybe he just needed someone to talk to.

"What are you going to do?" she asked.

"Nothing. The others don't frighten me."

"Well, they frighten me," Nicole admitted. "I don't want anything to happen to you. Perhaps you should speak with Principal Cunningham? He'll know what to do."

"Good idea." Axel smiled and leaned over to kiss her.

Of course, he couldn't speak to the principal. Not about this. First of all, it would make him look weak and passive. Second, the man had a nasty tendency to turn any discussion into a philosophical debate. If Axel asked about the secrets to group motivation, the principal would turn that into a question of his own. 'People see what they want to see. How does that affect society?' Or 'Everyone can be motivated into obedience, what motivates you?' It seemed the principal was determined to avoid answering any of his student's questions, and as the weeks passed, Axel's frustration grew.

\* \* \*

Several hundred kilometres away, in the Swedish capital, Mikael said goodbye to his friends and hurried over to the university library. He found the small study room he'd booked and dialled the Box's secret number. After entering his personal security code and passing the voice recognition test, he could join the meeting.

"…also, what are the chances Paavo will uncover the truth," came his father's voice over the speaker.

"The fact that he's turning his attention to you, suggest he's already found something," Thor replied. "At least something that has drawn his attention to your background."

"Mikael, I see you've joined us." As always, Pixie's voice was kind and attentive.

"Yes. Got stuck in class. What have I missed?"

"We've established that Mr Nurmi is becoming a serious problem. For some reason, he's turning his attention to your father, rather than to you. We're not sure why. As far as we know, his official orders are to monitor you, but if he uncovers your father's background, then things would become very, very complicated."

"So we need to draw his attention back to me? Is that what you're saying?"

There was a brief pause. "We haven't decided anything," Falcon said at last.

Mikael paced back and forth in the little room. "Cat and I need to complete our task, but we've been avoiding a physical meeting since Mr Nurmi entered the picture. Maybe it's time to change that?"

"What are you getting at?" Cat asked.

"Well, if I travel abroad, do you think Mr Nurmi will follow me?"

"I believe he has to," said Thor. "What are you thinking?"

CHAPTER 52

FOUR YEARS EARLIER

Little more than two months had passed since they'd arrived in Ella. Their safe house was a small bungalow, snuggled in on a green hill. From here, they had a breathtaking view of the valley below.

Hayato seldom ventured outside their door, choosing to bury himself in what he referred to as 'work'. What this entailed, he wouldn't say, but every morning, before the last star had faded from the sky, he left his bed and made a cup of tea. Then he sat down behind his desk, vanishing in a world of scribbling and pondering.

Left to his own devices, Jerome spent his days hiking. He strolled through tea plantations among the hills, watching the colours change on the distant mountains. It was a far cry from the hectic life he'd lived, but he tried his best to embrace it.

The daily walks had given him a nice tan. He shaved his head on a regular basis and wore a wild goatee that made him look ten years older.

On this particular evening, Hayato sat bent over his notebooks, scribbling in the light of a burning candle. Jerome lowered his phone and looked at the man. "Are you hungry, sir?"

"No." Hayato picked up his glass of wine and gazed out of the large window in front of him. There, in the pallid moonlight, Little Adam's Peak reached for the endless sky. Somewhere behind it was the small town of Ella. "I'm fine."

"You're not fine. You don't eat enough and drink far too much wine."

Hayato scratched the sad attempt of a beard he'd grown over the past few months. "Can I ask you something?"

"Of course."

"Why did you become an assistant?"

Surprised, Jerome put his phone down. "I guess I like helping people," he said, "and I enjoy having a lot to do."

"Ever dreamt of becoming a leader?"

Jerome had to laugh. "I wouldn't mind the power, sir, but no. I wasn't born to be a leader."

"Why do you say that?"

"I don't like telling people how to think. Doing so would require me to have all the answers; to know what is right and what is wrong. I don't." Jerome shook his head. "I really don't. The world is far too complicated for me to understand and judge."

Hayato looked over his shoulder, his gaunt face staring at Jerome with burning intensity. "My God, you're spot on! Rulers speak as if their subordinates only have two options; one that is good and one that is bad. Because people have neither the time nor the energy to do any critical thinking, they tend to accept that. They accept that they only have two options, and as easy as that, the ruler has turned his people into pawns." Hayato's eyes sparkled in the soft light and he let out a soft, almost sad laugh. "They were right."

"I'm sorry?" Not following the logic, Jerome frowned.

"They were right; people *are* manipulated. They are manipulated, tricked or sedated into submission. That's why nothing's happening. That's why we can do this forever, trying to teach people how to lead, and it still won't change a thing."

"Sorry, sir. I'm not following. Who are 'they'?"

Hayato wasn't listening anymore. His face had turned dark, and his eyes found their way back to the window again. "I think I've made a colossal mistake," he mumbled.

A week later, Jerome came home from a hike and found the

bungalow in a complete mess. There were toppled chairs, shattered wine bottles, and torn notebooks all over the floor. In the middle of the rubble sat Hayato, crying. The world-renowned leader was a mess. Jerome did his best to figure out what had happened, but the man wouldn't speak and refused to be touched.

In the end, as the sun rolled over the edge of the horizon and disappeared, Jerome gave up. He sat down on the floor beside the man he admired more than anyone, and felt an overwhelming sense of helplessness.

They sat together in silence, until the moon had risen behind the mountains. Only then did Hayato allow Jerome to help him to bed.

The following day, after having cleaned up the mess, Jerome sat on the terrace, leaning against the building. He was reading a book on his phone, letting the morning sun kiss his face. Then came the sound of shuffling feet, and Hayato stepped out, squinting in the bright light as he looked towards Little Adam's Peak.

"His name was Ashen Herath," he said with a thick voice threatening to break. Jerome decided that silence was the best answer. He watched as Hayato drew a long breath before sitting down. In the morning light, his skin looked grey and cold.

"My mother is half Dutch and half Indian," he continued. "My father is Japanese through and through. The two of them met in Tokyo. When I was four, we moved to Bangalore. Ashen and I went to the same school until I was seventeen. That's when I moved back to Tokyo. We lost contact, but then about a year and a half ago, I realised I was in a lot of trouble."

"May I ask what kind of trouble, sir?"

"Serious enough to make me realise, I had to run." Hayato leaned back, tilting his head towards the sun. "I knew it wouldn't be easy, so I contacted one of the brightest people I knew; Ashen. To cut a long story short, we used a secret communication platform that he'd developed several years ago. Together we began making our plans. His grandmother was from Sri Lanka, and he had relatives there. I came up with an idea of moving our headquarters to Mumbai. That way I could transfer money into India and have some of it end up in Ashen's hands. It was money I needed to fund a life on the run."

Jerome stared at Hayato, both impressed and horrified at the same time. "You laundered money?"

"Yes, but that part of the plan was easy. It's the running that's been difficult."

Jerome frowned. "I thought we'd done pretty well," he observed.

"No. The old woman who helped me on the first night, the one who was killed by robbers, she was Ashen's great aunt. Six months ago, his cousin, the one who hid us in his shed in Dambulla, died of a mysterious heart attack. Then three weeks ago, Ashen's uncle, the one who hid us in Anuradhapura, was found drowned in his neighbour's pool."

Jerome grew cold despite the sun. He needed a moment to digest it all. "How do you know this, sir?"

"From Ashen. He reached out via our communication system two weeks ago. The Academy is on their way."

"Are you certain?"

"Yes."

"What shall we do?"

"The original plan was for us to escape the country via a fishing boat from Pottuvil. Ashen had a relative there. Then a friend of a friend of his uncle was to pick us up in the Bay of Bengal and take us to Myanmar. We should've left a month ago."

"Why didn't we?"

"You need a passport. We can sneak into Myanmar, but to move on from there we need papers. My ID and passport were organised long ago, but I didn't expect *you* to come. I asked Ashen to get you the right documents, but a good passport is hard to find. He promised to have it done by end of this month. Now we'll have to come up with a different plan."

Jerome held his breath and Hayato closed his eyes. "I suspected something was wrong when Ashen stopped replying to my messages a few days ago. Then yesterday I found a small notice in The Indian Express. Ashen has been found floating on the Yamuna river in New Delhi. Shot in the head."

CHAPTER 53

# PRESENT DAY

Paavo stood by the window and stared out at Tallinn's Freedom Square. It was mid-October and a dense fog had settled over the city. Icy winds blew in from the sea, and above, the sky was turning black. He'd been to Estonia many times and liked the country. The first time he'd visited was with his family. He hadn't been more than seven or eight years old.

The phone rang, and his mind released the memory as if it was a dried leaf in a storm. He stepped away from the window and answered.

"We've spotted Mikael Andersson," said the coordinator. "He took a taxi from the airport thirty seconds ago."

"When will he be here?"

"As far as we can see, there's no traffic to speak of. He should arrive outside Hotel Palace in eight minutes."

"Copy that."

Nineteen minutes later, Paavo sat on his bed, headphones plugged into his ears, listening as Mikael entered room 314. Then followed a few long hours of eavesdropping while the young man took a shower and watched TV.

Paavo was flipping through a sports magazine when, at last, he heard Mikael open and close his door. Throwing the headphones and magazine aside, Paavo grabbed his jacket and darted out of his room.

He reached the foyer in time to see Mikael stroll out of the front door into the foggy night. Following, he found the young man crossing the Freedom Square. He then made his way through the medieval walls and into the lower part of the old town. Here the streets were narrow, lined with small shops and charming buildings dating back to the fourteenth century.

Few people were out and about on a night like this. Careful not to slip on the wet cobblestones, Paavo picked up his speed so not to lose sight of Mikael in the grey, soup-like fog. His target walked with his hands in his pockets, shoulders drawn up to his ears. Despite the cold, Mikael seemed at ease, never once turning back to see if he was being followed.

Then Mikael reached a set of wide double doors. He slipped through them, letting both light and music pour out into the cold, eerie street.

Keeping his pace, Paavo passed the entrance, noting the name of the restaurant as Art Priori. Through the windows he could see his target take off his jacket.

With a curse, the agent walked on to the nearest corner where he stepped into the shadows of a small tree. Unzipping the bottom of his blue Academy jacket, he pulled out some excess fabric, turning the jacket into a short coat. He shoved his hat and gloves into a pocket, ran a hand through his hair, and waited fifteen minutes before heading back to the restaurant.

It turned out Art Priori had several rooms. Mikael was nowhere to be seen. Paavo considered this and then asked for a table near the main entrance where he could see anyone coming or going. Having had no dinner, he ordered in wild boar ravioli and a glass of beer.

In this warm, cosy atmosphere, he began to relax. Sipping his beer, he listened to the low chatter of the nearby guests while waiting for his dinner. When it arrived, he was starving.

He had no more than taken a bite when Mikael appeared with his coat under his arm. With quick steps, he aimed for the entrance. There he stopped, turned to Paavo with a smug grin that made his silly moustache bend upwards. Then he was out of the door.

What the hell? Paavo scrambled to his feet. He fumbled with his wallet, pulled out a one hundred Euro bill, and threw it on the table. By the time he'd exited the building, Mikael was gone.

* * *

Mikael meandered his way through the old town, careful not to slip on the wet cobblestones. Cat was waiting for him in the shadows of a gated entryway in an empty alley.

"Hi," she whispered and gave him a brief kiss. "Got a call from Pixie. Her agent reports that Mr Nurmi has set off to find you. Let's go. The hotel is this way."

Cat took his hand and he followed her through a myriad of small streets. The fog seemed to swallow them whole. From the harbour came cold winds that nibbled at his skin, and he pulled the scarf tighter around his neck.

With a little tug at his arm, Cat changed direction. They turned another corner and almost collided with a large figure. Mikael's heart stopped. Mr Nurmi seemed just as startled as they were, and his eyes widened as he recognised Cat.

"What…" he said, eyes darting from Cat to Mikael and back. "What are *you* doing here?"

Cat took a step back. Mr Nurmi's jaw hardened. "Don't," he warned. "You two have a lot of explaining to do."

Mikael stared at the large man when something behind Mr Nurmi caught his eye. Out of the fog came a small figure. It was a short woman, moving with utmost care. Mr Nurmi didn't hear her until it was too late. He didn't have time to turn. The woman leapt forward, plunging a needle into his neck.

Mr Nurmi's eyes bulged with surprise and pain. Spinning around, he let out a growl, hands pulling two long knives from inside his coat.

The short woman stepped back and crouched in a fighting stance. Mr Nurmi attacked. At first, he was fast with his knives, slicing and stabbing as he forced the woman back, but after a few seconds, he stumbled to the side and a moan escaped his lips. He did a few more lunges, then without warning, dropped his knives and pressed his hands against his chest.

Pixie's agent looked up at Cat and Mikael. "You better leave now," she whispered. "I'll deal with the body."

CHAPTER 54

Thor looked at his watch, finished his espresso and stood. Although it was still early in the afternoon, the Jat Café was bustling with life. The smell of coffee and pastries hung heavy in the colourful interior, mingling with a dissonance of cheerful voices.

He slipped out into the cold and set off down *Rue de Namur*. It had been raining for days. While the nights grew colder and darker, the trees in the city discarded their green coats, replacing them with colours of red, yellow and orange.

A slender man with a vicious vulture's neck, stood waiting for him in the corner of *Rue Théréssienne,* outside the pharmacy.

"You're on time," Thor said, taking off his glove and shaking the man's hand.

The mole nodded. "I need to get back in a few minutes."

"I understand. So do I. Come, let's walk."

The narrow side street of *Rue Théréssienne* was deserted. The mole kept peering over his shoulder.

"You've got to stop doing that." Thor smiled and stopped, letting the man read his lips. "Makes you look nervous."

"I *am* nervous," the mole muttered.

"Nothing attracts as much attention as a nervous man. Tell me, how's the script coming?"

"Huh?"

Thor repeated his question, articulating better without raising his voice. The mole rubbed his nose, glancing over his shoulder again. "I'm done."

"Good, can you run it this afternoon?"

The mole's eyes darted from Thor to the buildings around them. He leaned in. "I thought we were doing it in two weeks."

"That was the plan, but we had some issues. Now we need to divert The Academy's attention away from both Axel *and* the killing of one their agents."

"Oh God!" The mole slapped both his hands over his forehead. "You killed a Watcher?"

"We had no other choice." Thor gave the nervous man a reassuring pat on the arm. "It'll be fine, but we need you to run the script today. Can you do it?"

The mole closed his eyes and let out a deep groan. "Yes. I can do it."

\* \* \*

Axel was in a bad mood. From an objective perspective, his future was crap. The Academy expected him to be their little pet, as did The Hostess. The Box on the other hand, wanted him to become some sort of weapon. Either way, all of them wanted to control him, which meant that sooner or later, things were bound to blow up in his face. He needed a plan.

To make matters worse, the other students were now travelling around the world, doing brief internships or fieldwork as part of their training. They even met with prime ministers and presidents. All the while, Axel remained confined to The EKA premises. He still upheld a cheerful front whenever he entered the principal's office, but deep inside, his resentment grew. Why wasn't he learning anything relevant?

On a positive note, he had Nicole. Whenever their schedules allowed for it, she'd invite him over to *Rue Paul Lauters*.

They spent most of their time in bed, enwrapped in a blissful haze as they explored each other's body. Sometimes they had dinner together or sat in front of a fire and just talked about anything from art and film to what it was like to live and work at The Academy.

The fact that their meetings contained more than only sex, made their relationship feel real somehow; more conventional.

It was an illusion of course. Once their time was up, it was back to The Academy. Back to hard work and Axel proving himself. Back to playing the game.

It was three o'clock when Axel entered Room C. Here the walls, floor and concave ceiling functioned as screens. On this particular day, the room portrayed a small paradise island in the middle of an endless, turquoise ocean.

Axel was the first to arrive, followed by Federico, Ava, Cordelia and Julie. They greeted him with icy nods before heading over to the back of the room.

Soon thereafter, the door flung opened and their teacher in Followership Psychology, Professor Wilson, stepped in. His massive moustache hung like a dead ferret under his nose. With the support of his cane, he shuffled over to the teacher's desk and sat down with a moan.

"Morning," he muttered and coughed. "Let's see…" His wrinkled hands pulled out a pair of glasses from his breast pocket. Once they rested on his crooked nose, he turned his attention to his briefcase and withdrew a set of papers. "Harry S. Truman once said that 'Leadership is the ability to get men to do what they don't want to do and like it'," he said before pausing. With a grumble, he nodded towards Ava who held her hand up. "Yes?"

"Sorry, sir, but we haven't pledged our allegiance…"

"Ah, bugger the Allegiance," Professor Wilson snapped.

Everyone sat stock-still.

"You ought to know it by heart by now. Don't you?"

"Of course, sir."

"And the rest of you?"

"We know it, sir," said Julie.

"Well then." Professor Wilson wiggled his nose, making his moustache dance. "If you all know it, what's the bloody point of going through it again? You're here to learn, not repeat what you already know."

No one replied and Professor Wilson looked pleased. Somehow, so did his moustache. "Seeing as this is our first lesson together, I'll ignore your lack of judgement, Ms Taylor. If I skip something, it's because I want to, not because I forget. I'm old, not senile. Now if you don't mind, I'd like to continue." He wiggled his nose again, then gave it a good rub. "Let's see. Oh, yes. Leaders and followers depend on…" The screens in Room C flickered and died. Professor Wilson let out a low growl. "Now what?"

They sat in complete darkness, except for a tiny, pale light that appeared on the wall behind the professor. It grew in size, as if heading for the students from a distance. The movement was irregular; a sudden jolt forward. Pause. Another jolt forward, growing bigger with each movement.

Professor Wilson's silhouette emerged as the light grew. Axel leaned forward. A jellyfish?

The animal was near transparent with a box-like bell and long tentacles that swayed behind it. Hypnotised by its movement, Axel stared at it, until without a sound, it blasted through the screen, turning into a hologram. It came to a dead stop at the centre of the room, the tentacles still moving behind it.

"What's this nonsense?" Professor Wilson coughed.

At that moment, the hologram shattered. It exploded with a deep sound. Axel could feel the vibration through his body. Light filled the room. Tiny hologram particles flew in all directions.

The screens flickered, then all of a sudden, the students were sat in the middle of a medieval battlefield. Around them swords clashed to the sounds of metal against metal. Men crying out in pain. Hologram horses thundered past them.

Then just like that, the scene changed. This time they sat in the mud of no man's land while World War I raged around them. Stumps of trees were all that was left of once green fields. Men dying around them, blown to pieces. A hologram soldier fell over Axel as his chest exploded from an angry bullet.

Snap! Another scene. World War II. They were in the middle of a concentration camp. Then the scene changed again. Vietnam. More bombs and dead people. Women and children fleeing their villages.

Axel found himself grasping the edge of his table as scene after scene, and war after war passed around them.

Then it all stopped and a penetrating voice echoed through the room. *"Billions of people have died in the struggle for power or dominance."* A new scene appeared. This time they sat among people scavenging on a mountain of garbage. *"Leaders put a man on the moon in 1969, but to this day, they can't ensure that children are fed, educated or protected from war."*

A new scene. This time they were in a great hall full of luxury. Around them strode some of the most prominent leaders of the world. *"Leaders don't solve our problems. They ARE our problem!"*

CHAPTER 55

Ms Brown dropped into her sofa with a bag of chips and her laptop. She was exhausted. Never before had The Academy experienced a security breach, and for obvious reasons, Mr Nakata had taken it as a personal insult. He was, after all, Head of Security.

They'd held an endless number of meetings with every security expert The Academy had to offer. After hours of discussions, they'd concluded that the perpetrator had triggered the video from inside the premises. This resulted in Mr Nakata ordering further investigations, which in turn meant more jobs for the Watchers.

Having worked more than eighteen hours straight, Ms Brown longed to crawl into her soft bed. Yet, no matter how tired she was, it was her duty to go through the day's reports from her Watchers around the world.

She popped a chip in her mouth and started with the first report on her list. Twelve reports later, she frowned and began skimming through the lists of remaining reports. Then she called the on-duty coordinator.

"Good evening, ma'am," said the woman on the other end of the line.

"Have we not received a report from Paavo Nurmi today?" Ms Brown asked.

"One moment," came the coordinator's voice. There was a sound of quick fingers dancing over a keyboard. "No, ma'am. Not yet."

"Is he still in Estonia?"

"According to our notes, yes. We were in touch with him yesterday at five o'clock, Central European Time. He was awaiting the arrival of a Mikael Andersson."

"Hm." Ms Brown pursed her lips. "Inform me as soon as he contacts you."

"Yes, ma'am."

\* \* \*

The incident in Room C was on everyone's lips. Theories and speculations flowed among the walls of The Academy. Some thought it was a prank, but most were worried. Axel could see the tension in the eyes of the staff while they pampered him, as well as in the way the guards at the entrance clutched their weapons. Teachers appeared distracted and for a while, the other students treated Axel as if he was no longer an issue.

Axel worried too, but for different reasons than everyone else. His greatest fear was that somehow, The Academy would connect him to the attack. He'd been in touch with Thor via the communication device, demanding to know what the hell they were doing.

*Harmony begins with chaos,* Thor had replied.

*What's that supposed to mean?*

*It means this is all part of the plan. Just focus on your studies and everything will be all right.*

At the moment, Axel lay snuggled up with Nicole in her bed. She was lying with her head on his chest, letting him run his fingers through her thick hair. He was careful not to go below her neck, for by now he knew that if he came too close to her back, she'd pull away.

They both stared into the fireplace, listening to the sizzling and popping of burning firewood. "If I tell you something," Nicole said, gazing up at him, "will you promise me you won't tell anyone?"

"Of course."

Nicole sat up, covering her back with the sheet. "The video in Room C was triggered from *inside* The Academy. Mr Nakata says it's impossible to find out who did it, but it had to be someone with access to the system."

Axel thought about Thor. Could the man be part of The Academy somehow? A servant maybe?

"The problem," Nicole continued, "is that *all* staff members have access to Room C's system. You see, it's part of the employee intranet. Therefore, all employees are suspects, even me."

"Not the students?"

Nicole smiled. "No. You're safe, but the rest of us… It's very unpleasant. Mr Nakata's people are questioning us as if we're criminals. Dr Vella is upset. She claims some of the interrogation techniques are bordering on psychological torture. She's informed Principal Cunningham but he's determined to find out who did this. He's not pulling back. I understand his motives, but…"

She shook her head. Axel leaned over and kissed her forehead. "Uncovering a rotten employee may sometimes require extreme means."

"Perhaps," she replied. "I know I'm merely an assistant, but it seems wrong to treat *everyone* like a rotten employee, when ninety-nine percent are not. The employees have great respect for the principal, but this treatment is testing that respect."

* * *

Axel stepped through the security checkpoint. He saw Mr Milton behind the reception desk, flipping through a file. Axel strolled across the large open space, pretending not to pay the man any attention.

"Ah. Good evening, sir," Mr Milton said with an oily smile. "Back from another walk in the park?"

"Yup," Axel replied without slowing.

In the corner of his eye, Axel saw how Mr Milton lowered the file he was holding and glanced down at Axel's shoes.

That's it, Axel thought and stopped. He spun on his heels and gave the surprised man a half-smile. "May I offer you some advice,

Mr Milton?" he asked, keeping his tone friendly.

"Eh…of course, sir…I'd be honoured."

"I doubt it, but I'm giving it anyway. If you're going to spy on me, do it with style."

Mr Milton's face lost all colour. "Sir?" he squeaked and his lower lip trembled a little.

Axel pointed at the file. "For the past few weeks, every time I return to The Academy after a walk, you've been standing there, reading *that* particular file. I know this, because part of the logo is worn off at the back. Also, the left corner has been bent."

Mr Milton stood paralysed for a second before he flipped the black dossier and looked down at the abraded gold logo, worn by years of use. "But it's—"

Axel raised his hand. "I'm going to spare you the embarrassment of lying to me."

"Sir! I wasn't going to—"

"Enough!" Axel barked. He'd had enough of this man. "Last week I asked Ms Davis to show me that dossier. Did you know it contains a bunch of old schedules from twelve years back? The Head of Staff, Ms Sokolova, has asked you to get them copied into her system, which by the way, Ms Davis did eight months ago. Since then, the file has been lying there, waiting for someone to decide what to do with it."

Mr Milton opened and closed his mouth, and then the pale face turned red as blood rushed to his cheeks.

Axel stepped forward, eyes locked on the man. "You know," he said, leaning over the counter, "this is a bad time to be caught spying on people. Everyone's a bit edgy after the Room C incident. It's easy to be taken for a traitor. If I were you, I'd mind my own business."

* * *

It was half-past eleven. Professor Jackson and Mr Nakata sat in a soundproof room within the Eagle Eye.

Professor Jackson grounded his teeth. "We have a traitor," he fumed.

*Traitor.* The word burnt like acid in his mouth. It made him want to spit, growl and bite. It made him want to kill. Literally.

"Hai." Mr Nakata snatched the bottle of sake he was drinking. As he poured himself another glass, he spilled a little on the polished surface of the table. Both men stared as the liquid formed a small puddle around the crystal glass.

"It explain many things," Mr Nakata said with a thoughtful tone. "It explain how Mr Hallman was locked inside Chamber last semester. It explain how attacker know when to throw jellyfish—"

"Jellyfish," Professor Jackson interrupted with a low grunt. "We're being mocked, dammit. You know that, don't you? Whoever's doing this, is playing with us. Or rather, they're playing with *you*. You're the goddamned Head of Security."

The short man stiffened. He didn't say anything. Instead he picked up his glass and began to spin it between his fingers. Only God knew what he was thinking.

"We must attack this from all angles," Professor Jackson continued. "This is why I want that file."

Mr Nakata shook his head. "I can't."

"Don't be a fool. Your career is on the line—"

A sharp knock interrupted him. Professor Jackson turned and saw Ms Brown standing behind the glass door. Mr Nakata beckoned her in.

"I'm sorry to interrupt," she said, adjusting the thick braid of her long, snow-white hair, "but we've found Paavo Nurmi."

"Where is he?" Mr Nakata asked.

"At the moment in a morgue. According to the police, they found his body in the small town of Türi, south of Tallinn. The local coroner says he died of a heart attack."

Professor Jackson rubbed his chin. "Wasn't Mr Nurmi the one who kept an eye on Mikael Andersson?"

"Yes, sir." Ms Brown paused. "If you don't mind me saying so, sir, there have been many strange happenings as of late. I know heart attacks can happen to the best of us, but according to Dr Vella's medical records, Mr Nurmi was as fit as a thirty-year-old."

Professor Jackson turned to Mr Nakata, hoping the man could read his expression. I need that file.

* * *

"What's the status, Ms Martins?"

Izabella looked up from her cognac and met the principal's gaze. After two months of regular meetings, she had come to relax around the man. Her respect for him grew day by day, and the feeling seemed mutual.

"More or less the same," she said, raising her glass and breathing in the tickling, alcoholic fumes.

"I understand." The principal loosened his tie. "Has Axel mentioned any of his friends in Stockholm at all?"

Izabella laughed. "Excuse my French, sir, but Axel's an arrogant shit. I doubt he has any friends. Besides, he's not talking to me. Or any of the others for that matter. After the Diamond Ball, he seems to think he's too good for us."

"Is it that bad?"

"Yes, sir. We've reached a point where some of the other students are considering ways to teach him a lesson."

"I see." If her words had surprised the principal, he didn't show it. Instead, he took off his spectacles and gave them a good rub with a handkerchief. "What are your thoughts on the matter?"

Izabella swung her left leg over the right and leaned against the armrest. "I want him to know that we're not idiots, that he's nothing more than a wannabe. And, I want to know how he cheated."

"Hmm." The principal held up his glasses towards the light, inspecting his work. "Have an idea, do you?"

"Yes, sir. As a matter of fact I do, but we would need some help from you."

## CHAPTER 56

October passed as though the calendar was ashamed of it. The Academy organised a large Halloween party, inviting both students and staff.

"Perhaps this party can help reduce some tension," Nicole said to Axel one evening. "Mr Nakata's people are still interrogating the employees, and their methods are getting rougher. I don't like where this is going."

Axel shared her concerns, but for very personal reasons. What would happen if The Academy found the mole? Would they expose him? Being that it was impossible to know, he tried not to think about it.

On the night of the party, Axel went as Death, his face elaborately painted by one of Madame Garon's staff members. Dressed in a black-hooded robe, he entered the restaurant at eight and found it decorated with the utmost detail. There were hundreds of burning candles, bone-chilling music, and terrifying hologram ghosts flying among the guests.

The on-duty staff members were dressed as mummies, shuffling about the tables, offering smoking drinks and vile looking hors d'oeuvres. With his hands in his pockets, Axel sauntered over to the bar and ordered a drink. He sat down on one of the high bar stools and scanned the great hall for Nicole or Thabo, the only two people he felt he could talk to. Neither had arrived yet.

"Do you have a moment?" Izabella stepped up beside him, dressed as a witch. It suited her in every sense of the word. Raising a finger, she got the attention of the bartender, a young fellow with a live snake around his neck. "A rum and coke," she ordered and turned back to Axel. "Look, I'm not one to beat around the bush, you know that. We have a problem, and we need to do something about it."

"What problem are you referring to?" Axel asked, spinning his glass between his fingers.

Izabella grimaced. "Some of the others feel you're ignoring us, as if you think you're better than we are."

Axel looked up at her and smiled. "I don't want to come across as rude or anything, but I have seventeen diamonds that prove I *am* better than you."

Izabella's jaw dropped.

"I don't mean to be disrespectful," Axel continued, "it's simply a fact. I did better than you. If you can accept that, then I see no reason why we can't be friends."

It was truly amusing to see Izabella lost for words. It didn't happen very often. He could see her struggling, but not a word came out of her. Instead her eyes shifted from him to the other students, and he followed her gaze.

They sat hunched together at a table near the dance floor, doing their utmost not to look at the bar.

"All right, I'll tell them," Izabella said at last, showing him a row of bleached teeth as she managed a stiff smile. "I hope we can bury the hatchet."

"So do I."

Izabella nodded. "Anyway, it was nice talking to you again."

"Likewise," Axel lied.

As he watched her walk away, he realised how much he'd changed since the Diamond Ball. Having met The Hostess, he understood something that Professor Jackson had been trying to say since day one. Gaining and maintaining followers was one thing, fighting your way to the top was another.

Sipping his drink, he scanned the great hall. Nicole was still not to be seen. He saw Professor Evans in a two-headed beast costume that was pure brilliance. A few minutes passed, and Axel began rubbing his eyes.

"Is something wrong?" Thabo appeared at his side, wearing a bizarre Frankenstein costume.

"No, I'm fine."

Grinning, Thabo took a seat next to his friend. "Are you sure? You look deathly pale, my friend." He laughed.

"Very funny, tin-head." Axel closed his eyes and pinched the bridge of his nose. "How…was Paris?"

"Good." Thabo waved at the bartender and ordered a beer. "It's interesting to see how politics work behind the scene." Thabo quieted and looked at Axel. "Seriously, what's wrong?"

"I don't know. Maybe I'm coming down with something. My head's spinning."

Thabo leaned back. "If you're not feeling well, you should go. I don't want to get sick."

Pressing his fingers against his temples, Axel nodded. "Yeah. I think…I think I'd better call it a night."

By the time he reached his own floor, he was staggering. With a trembling hand, he leaned against the wall as he stumbled towards the door, but before he could unlock it, his legs buckled and he fell.

* * *

"Hurry up."

They got Axel into his bathroom and tied him to a kitchen chair using silver tape.

"What are you doing?" he slurred.

Julie fidgeted with her plastic sword. She dressed as Wonder Woman, a role that didn't fit her weak personality. "Have we got clearance to do this?"

"How many times are you going to ask me?" Izabella scoffed. "If you don't trust me, then get lost."

"No, Julie," Federico countered. "You're not leaving. We all want to know how he did it, so we all stay."

"Thabo's not here," Julie objected.

"Yeah, but he's unpredictable in this case."

Edward squatted next to Axel and poked him in the face. "This can be unpleasant if you don't cooperate," he said with a cheerful tone.

"Let's get this over and done with." Paul came up and stood next to Izabella. She knew he had a thing for her, and some day it might come in handy. For this reason, and this reason only, she placed her hand on his arm and spoke kindly to him. "Can you film this please?"

He nodded and pulled out his phone. Men were so easy to fool. She looked down at Axel. "We know you cheated at the Diamond Ball. If you tell us how, we don't have to go through the hassle of shoving your head down the toilet. Understand?"

\* \* \*

Axel awoke shivering in darkness. With a moan he sat up and stretched the stiffness out of his neck. For a moment, he sat quiet, listening. Then he got to his feet and groped the air around him until his fingers found the light switch.

Furious bright light sprang upon him like an assailant. The costume from the night before lay shredded on the floor, along with the t-shirt he'd worn underneath it. On the mirror, someone had written; *Cheaters do not belong here,* in capital letters. Through the reflection, he saw the same sentence on his naked chest. With his anger rising, he turned where he stood and read the same sentence on the walls, floor, and even the ceiling. *Cheaters do not belong here!*

It took a long and hot shower to clear the text from his chest. Once he was done, he pulled on a warm robe and reached for the communication device behind the towels in his bathroom cabinet.

*Thanks for the warning,* he wrote.

The reply came in a matter of seconds. *Did they attack?*

*Yes. Yesterday. At the Halloween party.*

*Status?*

*As you suspected, they tried to slip something into my drink.*

*What did you do?*

*I swapped glasses and let them think they'd drugged me. I ended up spending a cold night in the bathroom.*

The device buzzed with a reply. *Well done! Now lay low.*

Axel looked at the scribbles on the wall. The hell he would!

CHAPTER 57

The black van stopped in front of the thick gate. Behind it, the automatic garage doors closed. Two armed men stepped out from a side door. Papers were shown and phone calls made. After that, the van and its content were examined with great detail. When everything proved to be in order, the gate slid open and the van entered The EKA.

* * *

Dalilah sat at her desk, working on a *Case Cracker*, a business case sent in by one of The Academy's sponsors in need of help. It was a quarter before midnight and she would need another hour to complete her task.

She reached for one of her books, but froze. For a split second, she sensed someone behind her. Before she could react, she was yanked back with brutal force. Her head struck the floor hard. Three masked men in black uniforms appeared in her vision, machine guns aimed at her head.

One of them bent down, and she noted the small golden scorpion embroidered on his chest as he heaved her towards him. Then the world grew black as someone pulled a hood over her pounding head. She went slack, allowing the men to drag her out of her apartment. This was another test, she reminded herself, and the best way to deal with it was to go with the flow.

Soon she was in one of the elevators and felt it descend. After a gentle stop, the men dragged her through carpeted corridors, until they entered a room, where they forced her onto a hard chair. As they taped her arms and legs to the cold wood, she remained calm.

It was just a test.

Somewhere behind her, a door closed and she heard it lock. Her awareness shifted. She realised she could hear the sound of a slow, beating, heart. Thump-thump, thump-thump. Simple as it was, it made the hairs on the back of her neck stand to attention.

Under the hood, her breathing quickened. She sensed a faint pressure on her right shoulder, and whatever it was, it moved.

At last, someone pulled the hood from her face. Gulping fresh air, she turned to the movement on her shoulder, and came eye-to-eye with the curved tail of a large scorpion. For once, words failed Dalilah.

She was inside the Chamber. In the faint light she saw nine other students. Like her, they were taped to chairs, and positioned in a large circle.

In the middle of it all stood Axel, dressed to perfection in his formal, black suit. He clasped his hands behind his back, reminding her of Professor Jackson.

Her eyes found his, and when they did, she felt her skin prickle. He was staring at her with a calm, calculated expression on his face. At that moment, Dalilah realised the magnitude of their mistake.

Axel was neither weak-minded nor insecure. On the contrary, he was a *very* dangerous man.

\* \* \*

Axel stared at the terrified faces around him and for a moment his confidence wavered. Had he gone too far?

No, he told himself. This wasn't his fault. He had never wanted to play these kind of games. The others had challenged him, and if he hadn't reacted, things would have escalated. He was protecting himself, just as he had at the Diamond Ball. This was self-defence.

They were all there, everyone but Thabo who had always treated Axel with respect. There was no need to involve him in this.

Axel cleared his throat. "I apologise for dragging you out of bed like this," he said, his voice echoing in the empty chamber. "But you see, we need to set a few things straight."

He started walking around the circle of students, staring each one in the eye. "First of all, I did not cheat at the Diamond Ball. I'm sorry if that hurts your ego. I can appreciate that it must be difficult to accept the fact that I'm better than you. You've underestimated me for a long time."

"Screw you," Edward snarled, but his words cracked with uncertainty.

Axel felt his anger rise. "I'm going to make myself very clear. You can continue to underestimate me; I really don't care, but *don't* provoke me. I mean it. You have no idea what I'm capable of. This"—he made a sweeping motion towards them all—"is nothing compared to what I'll do to you if you attack me again."

Axel returned to the centre of the circle. He stood there, letting the silence grow intrusive.

"If you don't believe me," he said after a while, "consider this. We're inside The Academy. You're tied to chairs. There are video cameras everywhere, and yet no one's here to help you."

A few of the students glanced at one another. "In fact, I've got a team of men holding you at gunpoint." From the shadows, armed men appeared, black masks over their faces. "See?"

"Get it off me," Ava whispered. Her scorpion had climbed up her neck and was making its way under her hair. "Please! Get the damn thing off me."

Axel stepped up to the woman. "Who initiated the attack on me?"

Ava clamped her lips shut.

"No?" Axel watched as the inquisitive scorpion disappeared under Ava's hair. He nodded towards one of the soldiers. The man lowered his weapon before picking up a bucket. From it, he took another scorpion and placed it on Ava's head.

"Whose idea was it?" Axel demanded.

The soldier picked up a third scorpion and placed it on Ava's arm.

"I'll tell you," said Dalilah in a clear, composed voice. "It was Izabella, Layla, and Edward."

"Bitch!" Layla howled.

"Yeah? You guys said he wouldn't remember anything. It was a stupid idea to begin with!"

"Shut up!" Edward shouted.

Julie moved her head away from her scorpion and turned to Izabella. "You said The Academy wouldn't punish us? What the hell do you call this?"

Turning to Dalilah, Axel smiled. "Thank you. I appreciate your help." He nodded and a soldier removed the scorpion that had crawled down her back. He cut her loose from the chair and she stood up, massaging her wrists.

"To be honest," she said with a glare, "I don't like or trust you, but I have faith in The Academy. If they believe in you, then I shall respect that."

Axel had to admire Dalilah. She used her loyalty towards The Academy as an excuse to give in to her fear and offer Axel what he wanted. That way she could protect herself and still save face.

He watched her walk out the Chamber with a proud sway of her wide hips.

"I don't care what you think about me," Axel said, turning to the others, "but from now on, I would appreciate it if you mind your own business."

No one answered him. He hadn't expected them to. It would've been the same as admitting they were wrong. Therefore, he let them all go, all but Izabella, Edward, and Layla.

"Spend a few hours being angry if you must," he said to the three remaining students, "but when the sun rises in the east, you better come to the conclusion that I'm not to be tampered with."

CHAPTER 58

"You have to admit," The Hostess said, her face glowing with delight, "the young man's got style." She spun the conference chair away from the screen so she could face Principal Cunningham and Professor Jackson. "He'll be a great leader one day, *if* he's given the right kind of training." In an instant, her joyful face turned cold. "Therefore, gentlemen, I wanted you to explain yourselves."

"My Lady," the principal began, his face relaxed and reassuring. "Ms Martins approached me a few weeks ago. As far as she was concerned, Mr Hallman had been arrogant and self-centred since his performance at the Diamond Ball."

"Seventeen diamonds gives him that right," said The Hostess looking at her watch.

"Perhaps, but we've worked hard to get our pupils to realise that the only test worth facing is the one that defines their power. Ms Martins asked for permission to teach Axel a lesson, as she put it."

"And you gave her your consent?"

"Of course. They would've punished him one way or the other. At least this way I could keep track of what they were up to."

Professor Jackson looked at the principal and had to admit the man's aura of confidence impressed him. The Hostess, on the other hand, gave both men the impassive glare of a true aristocrat. "Naturally, it's not Mr Hallman's safety I'm worried about," the principal continued. "It's those around him. You may not have realised it yet, but the man has a sixth sense when it comes to the game of power. If you don't guide him right, we may end up with more trouble than we can handle."

She scowled. "With all due respect, Mr Cunningham, I'm

beginning to wonder if you're losing your grip. These attacks on the school and you failing to see a genius student when he's right under your large nose…it makes me worried."

"I'm sorry to hear that, My Lady."

"Don't be sorry! Be proactive. If things don't improve, The Seven will have to intervene."

With that, The Hostess marched out of the conference room. Professor Jackson looked down at his hands. His face was blank, but deep inside he smirked. Maybe at last, The Academy was ready for a new principal.

* * *

Once back in his apartment, Axel took a few seconds to calm his nerves. He'd done well. After kicking off his shoes, he headed for the living room.

A woman stood in front of the aquarium, dressed in a marine blue suit, tracing her hand over the glass. "Hello, Mr Hallman."

"My Lady? What a surprise."

The Hostess turned to look at him, her face glimmering with amusement. "If you *were* surprised, I'd be disappointed."

Axel returned the smile and stepped up to kiss her cheeks in a friendly greeting. Of course he wasn't surprised to see her. It was *her* men he'd used in his little scheme.

He had taken a huge risk, asking her for help. Having no way to contact her directly, he'd asked the woman's accountant to pass on a little message.

The Hostess had called him later the same day. Once he'd presented his plan, she'd given him her consent on the spot. It had even been her idea to use the scorpions as additional pressure.

Her lack of objection and quick approval of his plan suggested to Axel that his plot had somehow fitted well with the woman's own agenda, whatever it might be.

"Revenge can be a costly thing, Mr Hallman," The Hostess said, shifting her hazel eyes back to the aquarium. "You do realise that your fellow students will also be at the top of the hierarchy one day?"

"Yes, My Lady, but I didn't do this only for revenge."

"Oh?"

"No. The others have made it very clear that they'll never respect me as an equal. If I can't get their respect, then they must fear me. How else can I position myself at the top?"

A tight-skinned smile flashed across The Hostess' face. She snapped her fingers and a servant appeared from the shadows by the inner door. Axel almost flinched. He hadn't seen the man.

"I couldn't have said it better myself, Mr Hallman," The Hostess said as her servant helped her on with a blue coat. "Respect or fear. That's how you gain power. But remember, controlling others by fear is an art. Push too little and you'll get no effect. Push too hard, and the target will feel as though they have nothing to lose if they challenge you. It's a tricky balance, and it takes years to perfect it. Believe me." She adjusted her coat, then took Axel's head between her long, cold fingers and gave him a dry kiss on the lips. "You did well," she whispered. "I'm proud of you."

* * *

Principal Cunningham rolled up the sleeves of his white shirt and settled back in his armchair with a glass of whiskey in his hand.

"I am at a loss here," he said, feeling the muscles in his lower back begin to relax. "Have we failed with Mr Hallman or are we seeing the first signs of a tremendous leader?"

Professor Jackson stood by the tinted windows, staring out into the night. "The Hostess is impressed by him."

Which worries me, the principal thought looking into his glass. Axel's little display had revealed a darker side of his personality, the kind of darkness The Hostess was attracted to.

"What shall we do with the three students sitting in the Chamber?" Professor Jackson asked, before letting out a slow breath. He left the window and strolled over to one of the empty armchairs.

"Let them be. Learning that failure has consequences is an important part of growing as a leader."

The two men sat in silence for a while, each with his own thoughts to ponder. "I must ask," Professor Jackson said at last. "These attacks on us, the death of Paavo Nurmi, Mr Hallman's peculiar behaviour and The Hostess' interest in the man; it can't all be a coincidence, can it?"

Principal Cunningham shook his head. "Funny you should say that, I was thinking that it feels as though our attention is being deliberately pulled in different directions. As if someone is trying to keep us from focusing on whatever it is we ought to be focusing on."

\* \* \*

The morning sun hid behind a carpet of grey clouds. Izabella stood in front of the principal's desk, arms folded over her chest. She came from a long line of proud women, women who didn't take nonsense from *anyone*. "You promised," she fumed. "You said we wouldn't be punished! Why turn against me when all I've done is try to help you?"

Principal Cunningham sighed, his face dark and weary. The round spectacles sat on the very tip of his nose, threatening to drop off at any second. "You took it too far," he said. "I agreed you could question Mr Hallman, not hurt or taunt him."

Izabella felt her cheeks tingle as her fury gave them colour. "He wouldn't speak, sir. We gave him the damn drug, and still he said nothing. What else were we supposed to do?"

The principal shook his head. "Ms Martins, you've stirred up more trouble than you can possibly understand." Clearly seeing her confusion, the principal's expression softened. "I'm sorry if I disappointed you, but believe it or not, there are certain things that are beyond my control."

Beyond his control?

An image flashed through Izabella's mind. She stared at the man in front of her and all of a sudden she understood.

"The soldiers who helped Axel," she said. "They had a gold scorpion embroidered on their chests."

The principal leaned forward. "Listen to me, Ms Martins. It's time for you to let this go."

"They were not Academy guards, were they?"

"Let it go."

"Is someone else helping Axel?"

"Ms Martins…"

"No. Tell me! What's going on?"

"That's enough."

"No!"

Principal Cunningham stood up and walked around his desk. "I appreciate everything you've done," he said, "but from now on, I'll deal with Mr Hallman myself."

"But who would want to help *him*?"

Without warning, the principal snatched Izabella by her collar. He pulled her close. She could feel the heat of his breath against her skin.

"Dammit, Ms Martins. For your own good; stay away from Mr Hallman. Do *not* provoke him."

"But—"

"No. I'm telling you to forget and move on. If you don't, I'll have you expelled."

Izabella opened her mouth to object, but for once, her words seemed stuck in her throat. What terrified her were not the words he used, nor the manner in which he told them. What scared her senseless was the fear she saw in the old man's eyes.

CHAPTER 59

December came with icy winds, carried to the Belgian capital from the north. Inside The Academy, Chief Interior Designer, Madame Jacques, set her team working on the Christmas decorations. Soon they had filled the premises with Christmas trees, mistletoe and snowmen. On one occasion, when Axel returned from the gym, a hologram Santa and his reindeers ran him over. The damn thing came whooshing through the air in the middle of the long hallway, scaring Axel half to death. A nearby guard cracked a smile but Axel gave him a thunderous scolding. He was in a murderous mood and had no patience whatsoever.

While the other students continued to travel abroad, meeting and working with former Academy students, Axel remained in Brussels. He still spent no more than an hour a week with his mentor. Even that might have been acceptable, if the sessions hadn't been so damn tedious and inadequate.

What Axel wanted, no *needed*, was practical advice on how to gather and rule followers, yet the principal's sessions were nothing more than philosophical debates that lacked essential meaning. It was absurd. As the weeks passed, Axel began to suspect that his mentor was holding him back on purpose. The question was, why?

He considered sharing his thoughts with Nicole but decided against it. She always spoke of the principal with great affection and was quick to defend him if Axel made the slightest hint of disapproval. Besides, he'd rather not waste his limited time with Nicole discussing things she couldn't do anything about.

One afternoon, when they were half naked on the floor in front of the fireplace, Nicole's phone started to vibrate. Axel pulled his lips from her neck and sat up with sigh. He turned his back against the warm, crackling fire and watched her as she reached for her phone.

"I'm sorry," she said and kissed him on his cheek before answering. "Good evening, Mr Milton. What can I do for you?"

"Hello, Ms Swan."

The silver-tongued voice slithered out of the speaker, loud enough for Axel to hear. He frowned and made a vomiting gesture. Nicole gave him a push and covered her mouth to keep from laughing. "Where are you?"

"I'm in town, doing an errand for Professor Evans. Listen, we're in a bit of a sticky situation. The Danish prime minister is arriving in an hour for tomorrow's session with the students. Could you meet him at the airport?"

Nicole's smile vanished. "I thought Mr Hennigan was picking him up."

"I know. I'm sorry, Ms Swan. We've had a lot happen the past couple of days. It slipped my mind."

"What did?"

"Mr Hennigan is in a meeting until seven-thirty tonight. Could you go? There's no one else."

Letting out a deep breath of disappointment, Nicole glanced at Axel. "Of course. Tell Julien to wait for me by the main entrance in twenty minutes."

\* \* \*

The winter evening was growing darker. A few lonesome snowflakes settled on Mr Milton's coat as he pocketed his phone. It was ten past five. Somewhere in the distance, sirens blared, but on this particular street, everything was still.

He rubbed some heat into his fingers and pulled up his scarf over his mouth and nose. The latter was more to hide his face than to shield himself from the cold. Shoving his hands into the pocket of his long coat, he stood back to wait. Damn, he longed for a cigarette.

It took seven minutes before the door opened. Mr Milton moved back under the small overhang, trying his best to become one with the shadows. He saw Nicole step out, open an umbrella before hurrying off towards The Academy. Pushing back his glasses, he waited.

It took five more minutes until the door opened again and a tall figure stepped out.

Got ya!

* * *

"Sir, do you have a minute?"

For crying out loud! Professor Jackson looked up from his newspaper, ready to kill. He'd just taken a seat in a massage chair by the pond in the foyer. In this tranquil part of The Academy, hidden among greenery, the professor had planned to enjoy a peaceful moment with his first cup of coffee and the morning papers.

Moments like these were rare indeed, thus his first impulse was to strangle the idiot who had disturbed him. "What do you want?"

Mr Milton approached with tentative steps, wringing his hands as he did. "I'm sorry to bother you, sir, but I need a minute of your time. I was hoping to speak with Principal Cunningham but Mr Hennigan says he's booked all evening. He suggested I'd talk to…"

"Spit it out, man. What do you what?"

"It's about Mr Hallman. He's been…uh…out for plenty of walks the past few months, and…well, sir, I've noticed a few things." Mr Milton paused, and seemed to gain a little confidence. "First of all, sir, whenever Mr Hallman comes back after a walk in the park, his shoes are spotless. I don't see how that's possible. My shoes are always in need of a good polish when I get back from a walk in Bois de la Cambre. It's the same with the other students. I've checked."

Professor Jackson folded his newspaper and threw it on a nearby coffee table. This could be interesting. "Get to the point, Mr

Milton."

"Yes, sir. You see, it's not only the shoes. It's how his walks correspond to Ms Swan's schedule. It seems he's always taking a walk when Nicole has an 'external meeting' booked in her calendar."

"Really?"

"Yes, sir." Mr Milton looked pleased. "And that's not all. There's more. Much more."

\* \* \*

In the restaurant on the fourth floor, near the elevators, stood a gold statue. It was of a large eagle, wings spread wide, pressing a snake into the ground with its feet. The serpent coiled itself in agony, mouth open in panic and fury. It was an impressive thing, under which was a sign stating: *'Our Future; Our Hope.'*

Someone had put a small Santa Claus hat on the eagle. How undignified, Izabella thought as she pressed the elevator button. "Are you looking forward to going home for Christmas?" she asked the others.

"I am," Julie confessed. "I miss my sister."

Aseem stifled a yawn. "I've decided to stay here."

"Me too," Federico said. "I spoke to Professor Wolf the other day, and she said The EKA Christmas parties tend to be awesome."

"I don't like Professor Wolf," Edward declared. "She's too cheerful. Makes me wonder what she's hiding."

A soft 'ding' brought all heads towards the elevator. The wing-shaped doors began to open, their beautiful gold feathers unlocking. "Well, I'm going ho…" Izabella found the rest of her sentence evaporating in her throat.

"What is it?" Ava asked, stepping up beside her. A second later, they all stared down at the body.

"Oh God!" someone whispered. "That's Ms Davis!"

Before anyone could respond, a hologram appeared.

CHAPTER 60

The room was dark and silent. Every manager and teacher within The Academy were there, staring at the hologram jellyfish, hovering mid-air. It had a skull encapsulated in the bell, and the whole thing was large, almost the size of a full-grown man.

*"This is a warning,"* a dark voice declared. *"The world is about to change, and the people will be liberated. We'll give them a choice, for with choice comes freedom.*

*"The EKA represents everything that is wrong in this world. But each of you has a choice. You can change your path; choose good instead of evil; collaboration instead of oppression. As you can see, we're powerful. We've entered the heart of your fortress. A place you thought impenetrable. You can't stop us, but you can join us. When the time comes, if you publicly support us, we'll consider you a friend. Those who remain silent or oppose us, we shall treat as enemies.*

*"We are The Box. We will make this world a better place."*

The hologram died, but only for a few seconds. Then it started up again with *"This is a warning…"*

Mr Nakata reached out and turned off the portable projector. A long and edgy silence followed. Everyone turned to Principal Cunningham.

He leaned forward, resting his weight on his elbows. "There's a traitor among us," he said with a low, rumbling voice. "I give you twenty-four hours to bring me that person. I'll reward whoever succeeds. If twenty-four hours pass without anyone finding the guilty, I'll punish one of you. I don't know who or how, but by God, one of you will suffer." He paused, letting each word eat itself into their minds.

"After that, I give you another twelve hours to find the guilty. If you still fail me, I'll punish a second person. Twelve hours after that; a third and so on. This is an attack, not only on The Academy but also on our way of life. The world needs our students, we must defend them!"

* * *

Professor Jackson and Dr Vella said nothing. Mr Nakata looked down. He had dishonoured his name and shamed his family. For a second time, he'd failed his employer, and the fury in Principal Cunningham's eyes burned like hell itself.

Three hours had passed since the students had found Ms Davis, the junior receptionist. Mr Nakata had every available Watcher and guard working the case. If they didn't find the traitor within twenty-four hours, his career would be over.

"What do we know?" the principal asked.

With his head still lowered in a bow of shame, Mr Nakata turned on his touch-pad. "Mr Hennigan called reception at eleven-fifty-two. The main printer on Administration floor had no ink. Ms Davis promised to fix problem.

"Eleven-fifty-nine: Mr Poska from Back Office arrive to relieve Ms Davis for lunch. Twelve-o-two: Ms Davis enter south elevator and press button to thirteen floor to get ink. Three seconds later, someone override surveillance system."

"What do you mean 'override'?" Principal Cunningham interrupted.

"Someone…" Mr Nakata took a second to brace himself. "Someone hacked our system and froze all cameras in elevator and on thirteenth floor."

"Hell roast me," Professor Jackson moaned. "How could your team miss that?"

"We have 3,464 cameras, sir. Elevators and thirteenth floor are low-risk areas, and—"

Principal Cunningham bit off his reply. "We'll discuss your

failures later. For the time being, I want information, not excuses."

Mr Nakata lowered his head a little further, overwhelmed by embarrassment. "Hai, sir," he replied in a quiet voice. "Twelve-seventeen: Mr Hennigan call reception, wondering where Ms Davis is. Mr Poska say he doesn't know."

"Where was Mr Milton at this time?" Professor Jackson asked.

"In meeting with Ms Sokolova."

"Has this been confirmed?"

"Hai." Mr Nakata waited. When there were no more questions, he continued, "Mr Poska and Mr Henning call Ms Davis several times. She never answer. Twelve-thirty-four: Izabella Martins call me. Ms Davis had been found on fourth floor."

"What did you do then?" the principal demanded to know.

"We started lock-down of main entrances and initiated protection procedure number six."

"We need to review that feckin' procedure," Professor Jackson said. "I was dragged out of my office by two armed gorillas. I was still holding my teaspoon when we arrived in the bunker. My cup remained on the desk."

"Do we know if Ms Davis reached the thirteenth floor?" Principal Cunningham asked, giving Professor Jackson a sideways glare.

"Hai. Our tracking system show her getting out of elevator and entering storage room nineteen."

"Excuse me," Dr Vella interrupted, her brows knitted in a suspicious frown. "What 'tracking system' are you talking about?"

Mr Nakata glanced at Principal Cunningham. Since a few years back, The Academy had tagged all their students and personnel, except of course himself, the principal and Professor Jackson, with a special DNA mark. It was an invisible, irremovable, and odourless liquid, secretly dabbed on personal items such as clothes, shoes, watches and jewellery. Each staff member had his or her own unique code. When they passed through a door inside The Academy, a small detector scanned the code, sending information to a server. If needed, and if permitted by the principal, Mr Nakata could track the whereabouts of personnel or students inside the premises.

"We traced her phone," Mr Nakata lied.

"What about this?" Professor Jackson wondered, grabbing the small black box that was sitting on edge of the principal's desk.

"That's an EP-450. It is one of our older hologram projectors. According to IT, all 450 modules were discarded a year ago."

The principal's face darkened. "Are you telling me that whoever did this, stole that projector a *year* ago?"

With his head still bent, Mr Nakata managed a little bow. "Hai. That what we assume, sir."

"Tell me, Mr Nakata," Principal Cunningham said. "As Head of Security, do you have *anything* to go on? Any lead at all?"

"We are exploring every—"

The principal held up his hand, cutting him off. "I take that as a no." He turned his attention to Dr Vella. "What about Ms Davis?"

"She's doing well, sir," the psychiatrist replied. "Considering the circumstances, that is. I believe the attackers used some kind of dissociative anaesthetic. Perhaps ketamine. I've taken some blood samples and we should know the result in a few days."

"Is she hurt in any way?"

"Physically she has a few cuts and bruises. On a psychological level…" The woman shrugged. "Only time will tell. She's a nervous wreck at the moment."

"We must talk to her," Mr Nakata said, desperate to regain a sense of control. "Soon."

He could almost hear Dr Vella shake her head. "You'll have to wait, sir. She's sleeping at the moment. Maybe in a few hours."

"No. Wake her up now," Principal Cunningham commanded. "We have wasted enough time on this nonsense. I'm about to inform The Seven of our situation, and I need to have some answers. Now."

CHAPTER 61

Axel was furious. Mr Nakata had locked the students in a safe room for hours while military-armed guards secured the premises. The room itself had been comfortable and the other students hadn't bothered him too much, except with their mere presence.

Professor Jackson had come by in an attempt to assure the students that The Academy had everything under control. Bloody moron. The Box had attacked The EKA at its very heart. It was pretty damn clear that The Academy wasn't in control.

From now on, there would be more guards on duty, the professor had declared. Most students appreciated it. Axel thought it was a waste of resources. He doubted more guards would stop The Box, considering they'd pulled this off.

Then came the real blow. From now on, the management wouldn't allow students to leave the premises on their own. At all. Axel felt his blood boil just thinking about it. How could he be with Nicole if he couldn't leave The Academy?

It was after ten when Axel finally got back at his apartment. Two armed guards stood to attention outside the elevators. They saluted him as he thundered by, but he didn't acknowledge them.

Once inside, he lit a fire, made a cup of tea and threw himself on the sofa to study. He suspected that Mr Nakata's people were watching the students with great care today, so he took his time. When half an hour had passed, he walked over to the bedroom, hung up his suit jacket before going to the main bathroom. There, in his only room of privacy, he activated the communication device.

A new message was waiting for him. *Are you all right?*

*Who's the traitor?* he wrote back.

The answer came four minutes later. *Who says there's a traitor?*

"Very funny," Axel muttered to himself, his fingers snapping over the tiny keyboard. *What's the point of this attack? To show your muscles? To prove that you have access to The Academy?*

*A bit of both.*

*Do you really think students will join you?*

*No.*

No? Axel sat down on the edge of the bathtub and stared at the text. His mind struggled. If The Box didn't think the students would join them, why go through all the trouble of... He stiffened. Oh. Of course!

*You're not interested in the students,* he wrote. *You're targeting the staff!*

*Yes.*

*But why?*

*This revolution must be led by the people, not those you consider leaders.*

*That doesn't answer my question,* Axel typed. *Why target The EKA staff? Why not the general public?*

This time it took a while before Thor answered.

*Two reasons. First, if we can attract defectors, it'll show the rest of the world that The Academy isn't as great as it claims to be. Second, we're not ready to approach the general public yet. The only reason we're provoking The Academy at this time, is to shift their focus from you.*

Axel took his eyes off the little device and considered what Thor had written. He had to admit The Box was far more organised than he had first anticipated, but he still had no idea what they were planning. How would they go about 'changing the world', as Thor had put it?

Then another thought struck him. Turning back to the device, he wrote, *If rulers can't lead this revolution, what do you need me for?*

The small screen flickered. *You will be our trigger.*

* * *

Most of The Academy slept. Hell, most of Belgium did. It was two in the morning, and Professor Jackson walked down the wide, empty corridor with his bodyguard trailing behind him like a massive shadow. A cheerful Christmas song was playing at low volume, but the professor had too much on his weary mind to be annoyed.

Their situation was grave, not to mention incomprehensible. Why would anyone want to attack The Academy, the greatest and most appreciated institute in the world? And who could be so flat-out crazy to question the importance of leadership, but still be smart enough to enter the heart of the E.K.A? For the first time in The Academy's history, the management lacked control.

Professor Jackson tasted the two words in his mouth. *Lacked control.* It was true that Mr Nakata was to blame for the failed security, but in the end, it was the principal who bore the sole responsibility for The Academy. Including its failures. How long would it take before The Seven had had enough? Their patience was notoriously short.

Despite everything, a surge of unashamed excitement filled him. *Principal* Jackson, now that had a good ring to it.

He reached the guarded door of Principal Cunningham's office and gave it a firm knock. "Wait here," he ordered his bodyguard before entering.

Mr Nakata was already there. He stood in front of the principal, looking miserable. Not that the principal looked any better. The old man sat hunched in his chair, glaring at Professor Jackson as he entered.

"Let us begin," he said, turning his angry eyes to Mr Nakata. "Twelve hours have passed. What news do you have?"

The short man looked down at the gold touch-pad in his hand. "I talked to Ms Davis," he began, swaying ever so little on his heels. "She very upset. Say attack happened after she left storage room. Thinks there were two or three attackers."

Principal Cunningham sat up with a start. "I beg your pardon!"

Mr Nakata swallowed and inclined his head. Was it a sign of shame or merely a confirmation? "She say someone hold her legs, another sit on her back," he said, his English growing worse by the minute. "She don't remember being injected with anything, but next she wake up in Dr Vella's office."

Professor Jackson was not a man who feared conflicts, but the compressed silence that hovered around the principal worried him. It took a lot to infuriate the man, but once he got enraged, Principal Cunningham would turn on you with all his might.

All of a sudden, Professor Jackson felt he needed to step in and defuse the tension. Why he wanted to help Mr Nakata, he had no idea. Nevertheless, he cleared his throat and got the principal's attention.

"If I'm not mistaken, sir, Ms Davis' father is a friend of yours?"

"Mr Davis is a well-respected businessman, and yes I know him. What's your point?"

"Could this be personal?" Professor Jackson turned to Mr Nakata. "Do you think Ms Davis was the intended target, or could it have been anyone?"

"We think anyone," Mr Nakata replied. "There are no more than six visits to storage every day. Any staff can enter. We are now looking over movements of students and staff before and during attack."

Principal Cunningham shook his head. "I am not impressed, Mr Nakata. Nor are The Seven. You have twelve more hours. Then you will tell me who did this."

CHAPTER 62

FOUR YEARS EARLIER

Hayato was awakened by a brusque hand shaking his shoulder. When he saw Jerome's haunted face and heard the wild dogs barking, he knew. They had been found.

In three seconds he was on his feet, pulling on a pair of shorts while navigating into the security system on his phone. He flipped through the various infrared cameras. Then he saw them; four figures moving towards the bungalow at a slow jog.

"It's them," he whispered, feeling his heart walloping inside his chest. It seemed to make an awful lot of noise. He pulled his escape pack from under the bed and flipped to the camera views of the back of the house.

"All right. They're coming in from the front. We'll go with plan B. Remember?"

"Yes." Jerome already had his rucksack on his back and was putting on his shoes.

"Good! If I'm not at the car in fifteen minutes, you leave. Agreed?"

"Agreed."

"And use the blanket."

Jerome nodded, then hunched over and ran towards the terrace door. There he stopped and knelt on one knee.

Hayato pulled the bottle of lamp oil and matchbox from under his bed. He poured some of the oil over the mattress, lit a match. "Ready?" he whispered to the dark.

"Yes," came Jerome's tense reply.

The flames rose towards the ceiling with a self-assured 'whoosh'. Hayato stumbled back, feeling the heat against his face. Black smoke rose and swirled like anguished demons pulling themselves free from the fire. In an instant, the smoke was in his lungs.

With his rucksack on his back and a t-shirt clamped over his mouth and nose, Hayato ran to his desk. He poured the remaining oil over his notebooks and had another burning match kiss the drenched surface.

From the bedroom, the flames crackled and hissed. As Hayato ran for the terrace door, he saw the bedroom curtains engulfed in fire. He couldn't breathe. The smoke had sucked the air out of the bungalow.

On his way out, he snatched a blanket by the door. Surviving a direct attack by The Academy, or The Box for that matter, was near impossible. It meant escaping their infrared cameras, night-vision goggles and drones.

The fire had two purposes. First, to draw attention away from the back of the bungalow, giving Jerome and Hayato time to leave the house. Second, the fire would attract attention from neighbours and passers-by. That meant the Watchers had to work fast or someone would catch them at the scene.

With one giant leap, Hayato cleared the building and threw himself over the railing. He fell about two metres and landed with a soft thud in a flowerbed constructed for this purpose. The mounds of soft soil absorbed some of the impact, but it still hurt.

Stretching his arms forward and up, he gripped the blanket from underneath like a shield. Then he ran.

His feet drummed against the black soil. The blanket fluttered behind him. It got tangled up in trees and shrubs, yanking his arms back and slowing him down. Still he held on. According to some research, a wool blanket could hide an individual from a drone-carried infrared camera. At least for a little while.

It was a fool's game, but what else could they do?

Behind him, the fire roared. Someone yelled and there was a loud crash. Hayato didn't turn. He didn't stop. He didn't think. He just ran.

The slope was steep. All of a sudden he lost his balance and almost tumbled over. Regaining his balance, he took a few more steps, then tripped over a root. With cry, he fell forward and struck the side of his face against the ground. Thick grass, tall as a man, cut his hands and arms as he scrambled to his feet. Leaving the blanket, he ran.

The night was black as ink. With no moon to guide him, luck was his best hope. Then his feet found the narrow dirt road. Jerome was not there. Hayato turned around and glimpsed the burning bungalow before he fell on all fours and vomited. His body had had enough.

When he was done, he wiped his mouth with the back of his hand. That's when the world seemed to explode in light. Powerful beams struck him from left and right. Blinded, he threw an arm over his eyes. He heard car doors open and footsteps approach.

"I must admit I'm a bit disappointed, Mr Sano. You stepped right into our trap."

CHAPTER 63

PRESENT DAY

Professor Jackson stood by the windows and looked out as wet snow fell over Brussels. It came tumbling down as if uncertain whether to be snow or rain. Behind him, the principal sat at his desk, writing something on his laptop.

There was a confident knock on the large, wooden door. Professor Jackson turned from the grey sky and went to open it. Mr Nakata gave him a pale glance then stepped in. "Hello, sir. I—"

"Who did it?" Principal Cunningham asked, looking up from his computer.

"We have track all staff on day of attack," Mr Nakata replied. "We have used video and DNA tracking. No one was on thirteenth floor when Ms Davis was attacked."

"No one?"

"No, sir."

"All the staff members have been accounted for?"

"Hai."

"And all the students?"

"Hai."

Without warning, Principal Cunningham slammed his pudgy fist into the polished surface of his desk. "Then how the hell did Ms Davis end up attacked in *my academy*?" he bellowed.

Mr Nakata lowered his head into a submissive bow but didn't answer.

"Could Ms Davis have done this to herself?" Professor Jackson asked.

"Not likely," Mr Nakata retorted. "Her blood had trace of new anaesthetic, Ketam X. It is modification of Ketamine, not available on market yet. The drug is in phase three of clinical research—"

"Wait a minute," Professor Jackson interrupted. "If the drug isn't available yet, how in God's name did it end up here?"

"It was stolen from laboratory in Canada. How, is unclear."

Principal Cunningham let out a low, rumbling moan and shifted in his chair. "Let me see if I've understood you correctly," he said with a dangerous glint in his eyes. "Ms Davis was sedated with a *stolen* drug, a drug she couldn't have had access to. She says that two or more individuals attacked her, yet we *know* there were no staff members on the thirteenth floor when it happened. Correct?"

"Hai."

"Nor do we have any evidence of anyone entering the premises unlawfully, but *someone* hacked into our security system?"

Mr Nakata winced. "Hai."

A silence fell over the three men. From the large hearth came the gentle sound of a crackling fire. Professor Jackson glanced back out of the window. The snow fell with more confidence now, plummeting down over the Belgian city without any form of elegance.

"One thing is certain," he said after a while. "This is bigger than a cranky employee wanting attention."

Principal Cunningham ignored him, his eyes remained fixed on Mr Nakata. "Do you know who attacked Ms Davis?"

Mr Nakata met the man's glare and squared his shoulders. "No, sir. Not yet."

Facing the window, Professor Jackson closed his eyes. Damn, he thought.

\* \* \*

The days following the attack on Ms Davis had been turbulent. There were guards everywhere, extra security at the entrances, and snipers on the roof. An automatic, personal drone followed each student when they moved around the premises. The damn thing sent live video images to Eagle Eye, and although they kept out of apartments, classrooms and restrooms, they were still a bloody nuisance.

Everyone was edgy. Students and teachers avoided moving around the premises on their own, afraid to end up like Ms Davis. Or worse.

Of course, Axel wasn't afraid. He was angry. All he wanted was to spend time with Nicole, and now, because of The Box, the two of them couldn't meet.

He'd passed her a few times in the corridors, and she always smiled at him with that alluring look that made his hormones go haywire. It took a fair bit of self-control not to scoop her up and kiss her. There were times when he feared his feelings were too obvious, but he needn't have worried. Everyone was too busy discussing Mr Nakata to notice anything else.

Principal Cunningham had demoted the man for failing to do his job. Interim Head of Security would be Ms Tanya Brown, Master of Watchers. She would also take over Mr Nakata's lessons.

The news had come as a shock and only two days later, Axel had seen Mr Nakata standing guard outside one of their classrooms. The man looked like shit, which was quite understandable. Not only had he been demoted to the bottom of the hierarchy, he was now forced to stand where his former students could see and mock him.

At that moment, Axel was making his way through the dim corridor on the eleventh floor. It was the week before the End of Year Exams. After that, they'd all enjoy a two-week holiday.

Hologram snowflakes fell from the wooden ceiling, creating an illusion of true winter. With everything that had happened, The Academy did their best to boost the general morale. The staff walked around with phoney smiles and a constant "Merry Christmas" on their lips. Still, Axel could smell the fear behind their chirpy facades and wondered what went on behind the scenes. Were Watchers still interrogating them?

When he reached the principal's office, three armed guards saluted him. Ignoring them, Axel raised his hand to knock. Before he could, the door flung open, and Professor Jackson stormed out. When he saw Axel, he flinched and wrenched on some kind of smile.

"Good afternoon, Mr Hallman," he mumbled and hurried off down the corridor, followed by one of the guards.

Axel's drone attached itself to some kind of charging device above the principal's door.

"Come on in, Mr Hallman," the principal said. He was sitting in one of the large armchairs, Rupert in his lap and a cup of steaming tea in his hand. Weariness had painted the skin around his eyes dark. His lips were dry and his face pallid.

"This will be our last session together this year, I'm afraid," he continued as Axel took a seat opposite him. "The mess we're in requires me to go to Singapore tonight. I won't be back until Christmas Eve."

He looked down at the ugly cat, nestling his left hand into the thickness of the animal's fur. "I've organised so you'll be celebrating Christmas with your family at a lovely cottage on the island of Gotland. It's secluded, fully functional and everything is compliments of The Academy. There will be plenty of Watchers to protect you. You'll be safe."

"Thank you, sir." Axel smiled. "I appreciate it." That was not entirely true. He'd much rather have stayed in Brussels with Nicole. He needed to see her. To be with her.

"Ms Swan will get back to you with tickets and itinerary," the principal continued. "You'll leave after the exams. Then on January the second, you'll begin your Challenge. From Sweden you'll head straight to Mombasa in Kenya."

Axel straightened. "Africa?"

"Indeed. Your Challenge is to turn a rundown hotel into a

profitable business in twelve months."

"A rundown hotel?"

"Yes. It's situated on the south end of Galu beach, not too far from the Tanzanian border. You'll get the rules of the Challenge, as well as your instructions, on the day of your arrival. We'll organise your flight from Sweden to Kenya but after that, everything is up to you."

Axel stared at the man. Two thoughts occupied his mind. First, he would have to spend twelve months without seeing Nicole. Second…

"You want me to run a shabby hotel?"

The principal's calm expression hardened at the outburst. "Excuse me?"

"I got seventeen diamonds. Seventeen!"

"Calm down, Mr Hallman."

"I am not calming down," Axel yelled. "Why are you doing this to me?"

"I said, *calm down.*"

"The others are travelling the world, doing internships and shit, but you keep me here, giving me bullshit lessons."

"I'm warning you, Mr Hallman."

"I heard Izabella's Challenge will be to lead a small marketing company in Madrid. Cordelia is setting up an NGO in Bangladesh. Thabo said—"

Principal Cunningham let out a hard, scornful laugh and stood up with such an abruptness, Rupert fell from his lap. The ugly cat hissed and vanished under the chair.

"If you don't know the complexity of a Challenge, how can you judge it?" the old man exclaimed. "If you want to graduate, you better pass the exams next week. You'll do the Challenge I've chosen and you'll do it with a smile on your face. If you refuse, or give me any reason to doubt your sincerest efforts, I'll have you expelled, regardless of your relationship with The Hostess! Now, if you excuse me, I have things to do. Enjoy your holidays, Mr

Hallman. We shall talk again after Christmas."

* * *

Principal Cunningham watched as Axel thundered out of his office, slamming the door behind him with such force, the windows rattled. For a few seconds he stood motionless, listening to the silence. Then a smile spread across his lips.

CHAPTER 64

It was late and Nicole was exhausted. All she wanted to do was go home, still she stopped by the reception to welcome Ms Davis back to work. The poor girl stood small and pale behind the large counter. It looked as if the entire structure was about to swallow her whole. How could Mr Milton leave her alone on her first day back?

Ms Davis kept her head down, watching her right-hand massage the fingers of her left. With an angel's patience, Nicole took her time. She led their conversation to Christmas and Madame Jacques' amusing decorations. They spoke of the students and their nervousness about the upcoming exams. They talked about everything and anything that wasn't connected to the attack. It took a while, close to forty minutes, but as sure as winter turns to spring, the young woman began to smile again.

When Nicole felt confident that Ms Davis would be fine for the evening, she started buttoning her long coat. Tonight she was sleeping at *Rue Paul Lauters*. She wished Axel could've visited her, but he wasn't permitted to leave the premises. Next year he would face his Challenge, and it would be harder for the two of them to meet. She hoped he would end up somewhere in Europe, for then she was certain she could find ways to visit him.

"It's my fault," Ms Davis whispered, her eyes tearing up.

Nicole dropped her thoughts. "I beg your pardon?"

"Mr Nakata. He lost his job because of me."

"No, Ms Davis. We can blame a lot of people for what happened, but you're not one of them."

"It happened so fast. I never heard them coming. It was as if they dropped down from the ceiling."

Nicole frowned, then realised that Ms Davis was staring at her with large, frightened eyes. "Oh, I can't imagine what you've gone through, but one thing is certain. This wasn't your fault."

On her way out, Nicole found Mr Nakata standing guard at the entrance. He stood there with one of his former subordinates. The awkwardness was plain to see. "Good evening," she said to them both, wondering if there was any way she could spare the former security chief's feelings.

He looked at her with empty, dead eyes. Unlike the other guard, he didn't reply.

Heading back to her apartment, Nicole called Ms Brown and told her about the conversation with Ms Davis.

"Of course we've checked the damn ceiling," the interim Head of Security said. "It was one of the first things we did." Then, after a pause, she sighed. "I wish people would stop meddling with this investigation. The principal fired Mr Nakata for failing to protect us. Now all of a sudden, everyone checks on me to ensure I do what *he* did. It's idiotic."

The line went dead as Ms Brown hung up.

Nicole liked Ms Brown. It couldn't be easy taking over after Mr Nakata. The man had been very good at what he did.

Principal Cunningham meant the world to Nicole, but sometimes even the greatest people made mistakes. Ms Brown was good, but she was no Mr Nakata. Demoting the man *had* been a mistake. Professor Jackson was furious about it. There were now whispers of a brewing conflict between him and Principal Cunningham.

Nicole sighed as she entered *Rue Paul Lauters*. She couldn't help but feel that there were dark times ahead of them. Dark and dangerous times.

Once she made her way up the old stairs towards her apartment, weariness began to set in. It had been a long day. As always, the lock objected as she tried to turn the key. A light bump and a shoulder against door helped convince it to obey. With a quiet moan, the door swung open.

Nicole froze. Cold, flickering light from her television mingled with a warm orange glow. Eerie shadows danced across the walls, and an acrid smell slapped her in the face.

A thought ran through her mind. Should she call the police? No. A thief would steal the TV, not watch it, and an aggressor would not warn their victim about their presence. Nonetheless, memories of Ms Davis' attack remained vivid.

In one swift motion, Nicole dropped her coat to the floor. It was easier to fight without it. Then she kicked off her shoes and stepped in. That's when her heart shattered.

There was no one in her apartment, but the walls were barren. Someone had lit a fire in the hearth, using her paintings as wood. She let out a sound, something between a gasp and faint cry. Her paintings. Her memories. Her soul!

Running forward, she pulled out a burning frame and slapped it with her bare hands. Most of the canvas was long gone. One corner was still intact and she recognised the painting. It had portrayed the foyer on the day she'd brought Axel to The Academy. A good memory.

A few broken frames still burned. Pieces of canvas smouldered, stinking of scorching paint. Now it was all gone. Nicole's breath quivered as she tried to draw a breath. Sitting on her knees, holding the ruined painting in her hands, she became aware of a faint but familiar sound. Very slowly, she turned.

First, she saw the envelope placed on top of the television. Then she saw the video.

\* \* \*

Lise Davis watched Nicole leave. She liked the woman. Unlike many people inside The Academy, Nicole was kind without expecting anything in return.

The young receptionist turned off the computer and began

organising the papers spread out on the desk.

"Closing for the night, Ms Davis?"

The calm voice startled her and she spun around. When she saw who it was, she relaxed. "Oh, Mr Hennigan. You frightened me."

"I apologise, miss," the man replied, uttering the words with a calm kindness that seemed heartfelt. "I should have visited you earlier, but there's been a lot to do since…you know."

Mr Hennigan was something of an enigma. Some of the staff called him 'Mr Shadow' because he was seldom seen at the premises. He functioned as the principal's personal assistant, bodyguard, and pilot, which meant he was always working.

"How are you doing?" the man asked, taking a step closer.

Ms Davis looked around the gigantic foyer, counting the guards as she did. Fourteen, and those were the ones she saw. How many more were out of sight, covered by greenery or observing her on monitors.

"I'm all right, sir," she said. "Ms Brown has increased the number of guards down here. I feel safe."

"I'm glad to hear it." Mr Hennigan fished out a letter from his pocket. "Listen, Principal Cunningham and I are leaving for Singapore tonight. I need to get this letter posted first thing in the morning. Do you think you could do that for me?"

"Of course, sir." Her hand trembled as she reached out for the envelope. As she was about to take it, Mr Hennigan pulled the letter away from her.

"It's very important that you don't lose it," he warned. "Therefore, I would prefer if you didn't leave it here unattended until the morning."

Ms Davis hesitated. "Perhaps, if you don't mind, I could bring it with me to my apartment. I'll post it first thing in the morning."

Mr Hennigan smiled and handed her the envelope. "Thank you. That would be kind of you." He turned for the elevators. "Your contribution is much appreciated."

Ms Davis watched him leave, then gathered her things,

including Mr Hennigan's letter. She waved goodnight to the nearby guards and made her way back to her small apartment on the first floor.

As soon as she went in, she locked the door behind her and turned on the lights. To be on the safe side, she opened her wardrobe and looked under her bed. There was no one there. With a visible sigh, she got up and placed her things on the kitchen table.

A glass of water and an aspirin later, she shuffled over to her small washroom where she knew there were no cameras. There, with the lights dimmed, she pulled out Mr Hennigan's letter and ripped it open.

*Well Lise*, it began, *we pulled it off. I'm sorry we haven't been able to talk sooner, but I hope we'll celebrate our success soon. I'm off with the principal to Singapore. Professor Jackson will confront Axel tonight, and depending on the outcome, I might not return. Stay low for a while. As you can see, I'm giving you Hayato Sano's old card. Do you remember how to use it? Just attach it to your Com device. We'll stay in touch that way. All the best. T.*

Ms Davis picked up the thick business card and gold holder from the envelope. She grinned with excitement. After tearing the letter to pieces and flushing it down the toilet, she hid the business card and the holder on top of the wall-mounted bathroom cabinet, well out of sight.

Yeah, she'd done well.

On the day of their third attack, Mr Hennigan had called her as expected. God she'd been nervous. She had to wait exactly ten minutes before stepping into the south elevator. It had been the longest ten minutes of her life.

Mr Hennigan had told her there was another mole within the Academy, and whoever it was, the person had turned off the security cameras.

Lise wished she knew who the other mole was. She wanted to tell him, or her, how impressed she was. Shutting down the security system had to be next to impossible.

Once on the thirteenth floor, Lise's training had kicked in. She'd spent two years in Zimbabwe, training with four other Box agents. As she stepped out of the elevator, her nerves vanished and she had become completely focused on her task.

She had hurried over to storage room nineteen. There she'd found the hologram projector, hidden in the air ventilation system as Mr Hennigan had instructed. She'd taken it with her, along with an ink cartridge.

Halfway back to the elevators, she placed the cartridge on the floor, as if she had dropped it there. Then came the part she was truly proud of.

In her hair she had hidden a sharpened hairpin. Using it, she had cut her neck. The challenge was cutting deep enough to make it look serious, but not so deep it would be dangerous. It hadn't hurt as bad as she had expected, probably because she was full of adrenaline by then.

With the blood dripping down her neck, Lise had begun pounding her arms and thighs until the first signs of bruises began to appear. She had then wiped the pin clean and hidden it in her hair again.

Next, she'd swallowed the pill that Mr Hennigan had given her weeks before, and by the time she'd returned to the elevator, she had already been drowsy.

After that, she didn't remember anything until she woke up in Dr Vella's hospital bed.

CHAPTER 65

FOUR YEARS EARLIER

They had shackled him like a dog. The cold chain around his neck reeked of grease, dirt and metal. The bucket by his side stank from his own excrement. Grey light forced itself into the cell from a barred opening, three metres up. Hayato shifted on the concrete floor, stretching his legs, letting the blood back into his feet.

The sounds of the jungle slipped into his cell. How many days had he been here? Four? Six? Eight?

His fingers found the padlock pressing against his Adam's apple. He lifted it away from his skin. For a few seconds he felt the relief as the pressure vanished. Never had he realised how sharp the edges of a lock could be.

When he heard steps echoing through the corridor, he dropped the lock and braced himself. Two men stepped into the cell, dressed in black suits and ties, polished shoes, dragging Jerome's limp body between them. Hayato's eyes met one of them, a large man with an ugly grin. He'd seen the fellow a few times at The Academy. Never liked the look of him. In the back of his mind, the name Nurmi appeared. Paavo Nurmi

"I told you," Hayato spat. "He doesn't know anything."

The men disregarded him and pulled Jerome to the opposite corner. One held up Jerome's face while the other looped a chain around his neck. Then came the padlock. The big, sharp padlock. It gave such an insignificant 'click', and yet, the sound rang of dehumanisation.

Once the men had left, Hayato looked down at Jerome. He was wet and bruised. It had been two days since he'd stopped speaking. Why did they come for him every day? It was Hayato they were after.

Without the moon, the cell was black as a tomb. Jerome moaned as he rolled over on his side. Thunder roared in the distance. Cold drops started to fall through the open ceiling, soft at first then harder and harder until it poured down in torrents.

"I'm sorry," Hayato whispered, shivering in his wet clothes.

Jerome didn't reply. An hour passed, perhaps two. Then he moved again.

"I'm sorry," Hayato repeated.

Still no reply. The third time he said, "I'm sorry," his friend moaned, the kind that asks you shut up.

In the morning, when the clouds had moved on west, the Watchers came for Jerome again. They kept their distance from Hayato's feet; still he yelled, spat and kicked at them. He wanted them to know how much he hated them. How much he wanted to kill them. So he kept going until the door closed. At that point, he rolled up into a ball, covered his ears and wept.

That night, Hayato began to speak. He wasn't sure why. Perhaps he wanted to save Jerome. If he told his friend everything, and Jerome told The Academy, then maybe they'd let him be. Or perhaps it was the guilt, the idea that his friend would die without knowing why they were here. Or maybe it was plain old selfishness again, the need to occupy his mind with something. Anything.

Whatever it was, Hayato decided it was time to share his secrets.

Jerome was lying in the foetal position, close to the centre of the cell. After a moment's hesitation, Hayato left his corner and crept over until the chain around his neck stopped him. Reaching out, he got hold of Jerome's arm. Careful not to hurt him, he pulled his friend close. Then he lay down beside him, breathing his next words into the man's ear.

"I'm going to tell you everything," he whispered with a voice so soft, the words barely left his lips before they vanished. "First, you must know this; to be well-informed is not the same as to be wise. You can read all the papers in the world, but if you don't think for yourself, you're a puppet on a string. Believe me, I thought I knew everything, yet I knew nothing at all.

"A month after I entered The Academy, they contacted me. They told me about a former student. Her name was Sarah Wangai. You've never heard of her, but she was a wild-card, just like me…"

As the night progressed, Hayato lay on the damp floor, whispering his tale into his friend's ear. He spoke of Sarah Wangai, and of The Academy, built on clichés and myths. He described The Seven and the power they had. He told of The Box and the revolution they prepared, how they'd chosen him to trigger the intellectual uprising, and how, in the end, he had refused.

With Jerome lying quiet and unmoving, Hayato spilled it all. He described the fear he'd felt, the plan he'd made, and the regrets that filled his soul. By the time he was done, his mouth was dry and his throat ached despite the whispering. Outside the sky was now a bluish black, the first sign of morning.

"I could've changed the world," he ended. "Now I'll die, and for what purpose? What have I achieved?"

His words disintegrated in the pre-dawn darkness. The concrete beneath him was cold. Mosquitos buzzed in his ears, and something howled above them. He was drifting to sleep, when Jerome's tired, crackling voice rose from the dark.

"What right do you have to expect such grandness of yourself?" he asked, uttering each word as if they pained him. "How can one individual change the world, when we all shape our future?"

No one came for Jerome that morning. The night withdrew and it started to rain again. Hayato pulled back and pressed against the wall, trying to escape the thick drops. Jerome didn't move.

It was still raining when the door swung open. Hayato snarled and was about to launch, when in strode a man with a familiar face.

"Well, well, well, Mr Sano," he said with a grin. "Long time no see."

Hayato stared at the man. "Mr Hennigan?" he croaked back.

CHAPTER 66

PRESENT DAY

"Sorry to bother you, sir," Mr Milton said after a stiff bow, "but I was asked to deliver a personal message." He held out a small envelope and stood shifting his weight from one foot to the other, as if desperate to leave.

Axel snatched the envelope from his hand, glared at the two guards standing to attention by the elevators, then slammed the door shut.

He'd been studying for his exams and was in no mood to be disturbed. With quick fingers, he pulled out a note. *Meet me by the pool at 22:30, Nicole.*

Axel's heart lit up, and twenty-five minutes later, with a wide grin, he stepped out on the fourteenth floor. The guard closest to the elevators turned. "Good evening, sir," he said with a monotonous tone and saluted.

Being in a good mood, Axel gave the man and his submachine gun a little nod and walked on. He even laughed when halfway down the corridor, a hologram Santa and his reindeers ploughed through him with a hoarse, "Ho, Ho, HO!"

As he stepped into the pool area, he could hear his drone connect with one of the chargers above the door.

At this hour, the pool area was dark. Axel drew a deep and humid breath. Then he set off towards the pool. Low lights lit up in sequence in front of his feet as he trod down a small path. Among the trees, birds shifted in their cages, made nervous by his movements.

He strode with confidence and found Nicole waiting for him by the edge of the blue pool. She was beautiful as always, but as he stepped closer, he realised something was wrong. Her smile was gone.

"Good evening, Ms Swan," he offered with a tentative glance at the darkness around them. "This is an odd place to meet."

"Did you tell Professor Jackson about us?" she asked, her face stern.

Baffled by her question, he stared at her. "What?"

"You must have. How else would he have known?"

"What are you talking about?"

"He knows about us. Everything." She clamped her mouth shut and averted her eyes from his gaze. Reading her posture, he saw anger, sorrow, and something he couldn't quite interpret. Maybe shame. "They've got us on film. When we're…in bed…together."

"I don't understand," Axel said, shaking his head. "I haven't told anyone. Why would I? I love you."

Nicole closed her eyes the way one does when it's all over. A single tear tumbled down her cheek, and at that point, Axel realised his mistake. It was a trap.

"My, my, Mr Hallman. Aren't you a sneaky little bastard?" From the shadows, Professor Jackson came, hands in his pockets and a grin on his perfect face. Behind him followed two black-suited guards. "Screwing the secretary, are you? For Christ's sake. Have you forgotten how many leaders have ruined their careers because they couldn't keep their pecker in their pants? Huh?"

Axel didn't move. He had only one thing on his mind. Who had betrayed them?

Nicole remained standing with her eyes closed. Without thinking, he reached out and took her hand. She gave it a gentle squeeze before letting it go.

"Ahh. Aren't you a sweet couple," the professor jeered.

Axel didn't reply. His mind was tumbling, until all of a sudden, he knew. He knew without a doubt, who'd betrayed them.

"Mr Milton," he hissed.

"Now, now, Mr Hallman. Calm down. Our Concierge Manager is just doing his job. It's not his fault you're breaking the rules." The professor stepped forward and his grin vanished. "You bloody fool! I could have you suspended for this."

Straightening his back, Axel met the professor's anger head-on. "Go ahead," he spat.

The slap came fast and hard, catching Axel right over the ear. God it stung. More surprised than anything else, Axel stumbled back. Professor Jackson raised his finger. "You're letting your emotions rule you," he growled.

"Unlike you, you mean," Axel said with a grin, letting his fingers touch the side of his face.

"I'm warning you."

"What are you going to do? Hit me again?"

That was exactly what the professor did. A hard blow that spun Axel's head ninety degrees to his right. "That's enough, Mr Hallman."

"You can't dictate who I date."

Another powerful blow, this time, forcing Axel to sidestep. "What have I told you about conforming? You will obey us, no matter what! Besides," he turned and glared at Nicole, "I sure as hell dictate who *she* dates."

Axel knew the man was right, but he refused to accept it. Some things in life are worth fighting for, and Nicole was one of them. But as he opened his mouth to object, she reached out and placed her hand on his arm. "It's over Axel," she said with a voice soft as a feather and a smile so sad it broke his heart. "It was never meant to be."

* * *

Nicole could see the hurt in him, as if her words had been daggers. She wanted to embrace him, to apologise, to take his hand and run.

It was a childish thought, sprung up from a deep desire to love and be loved.

"Your disloyalty is sickening," the professor barked, his face growing red in anger. "After all we've done for you. You're a simple assistant, and yet you earn more money than a brain surgeon. Why would you go behind our backs like that?"

Nicole looked up at the ceiling to prevent her eyes from tearing up again. She couldn't answer. Her voice wouldn't allow it.

"You have jeopardised Mr Hallman's entire training," the professor bellowed.

"Sir," Axel objected, but Professor Jackson ignored him.

"God knows why, but the principal wants to give you a second chance, Ms Swan."

"Thank you, sir."

"There are a few conditions, however. First, stay away from Mr Hallman. Don't talk to him, don't write to him, don't even look at him. If you see him coming your way, you turn and walk away. Understand?"

Nicole managed a strained bow.

"Second, you're to give up your private apartment. You have twenty-four hours to get that settled. Third, you'll report to me if you want leave the premises. I'll decide whether or not to allow it. Forth, no more painting."

"Sir!" This time Axel stepped forward.

As one, both guards raised their guns and aimed at him. He stopped and glared at them. Then he turned to the professor. "Come on. Let her paint," he said with a pleading voice. "What harm will it do?"

That almost broke her. His kindness. She looked away.

"No," was all Professor Jackson said, still staring at her. "Finally, we'll downgrade your security clearance. We'll begin monitoring all your phone calls and internet usage. I don't care how much Principal Cunningham likes you. If I find any reason to doubt your loyalty again, any at all, I'll make it look like you were never born. Have I made myself clear?"

She nodded, afraid of what might happen if she spoke.

"Good, then leave. The guards will accompany you to your apartment. Sort out what rubbish you want to keep. You have twenty-four hours, remember that."

CHAPTER 67

In two days, he would have to hand over his office to Ms Brown. Soon after, she would be moving in to his apartment. As a regular guard, Mr Nakata had to settle for a small room inside the guards' quarters.

He looked down at his letter. For the first time in days, he felt at peace. There was only one more thing he needed to do. Turning to the computer, he logged on to the locked employee archive.

He worked fast, shutting down the security tracker and entered the archive via a secret profile he'd created hours before Ms Brown had stripped him of his broad security access. Within two minutes, he had downloaded the file Professor Jackson wanted. Now all he needed to do was to print it.

\* \* \*

Axel watched Nicole and the two guards leave through the trees, heading for the exit. Professor Jackson stood quiet for a very long time. He appeared to be lost in time.

"I was young once," he said, his voice almost kind. "I've felt the temptation of a woman's embrace, but you have to stand above it. People will depend on you. They must know that no matter what, you will do what's right, even if it hurts you. Great leaders have to make great sacrifices. Of all the things you must learn, that is the most important."

"I know you think she's just an assistant," Axel countered, "but she's smart, funny, beautiful…"

"She's still an assistant, a simple servant who interfered with your training. That means she's jeopardised your future. You understand that, don't you?"

With the waterfall murmuring behind them, Axel thought about Nicole and her smile. He thought about the way she'd run her fingers over his chest, the sound of her laughter, and the way she always urged him to be careful. He remembered their first kiss, their conversations in Italy, and the risks she'd taken to help him.

Yes, Nicole had interfered, but only because she cared for him; only because she wanted him to graduate. For that, he loved her.

Professor Jackson stood silent, watching and waiting until almost as a reflex, Axel nodded.

"Good," he said. "I know it doesn't feel that way, but we're trying to help. It's a brutal world out there. It's our job to make sure you're prepared."

A memory of Mr Gallo's burnt face flashed through Axel's mind. "Yes, sir," he replied.

"Then let's go, young man."

Side by side, they made their way back to the elevators. When they stepped out into the main corridor, a hologram Santa and his reindeers came thundering through them with a joyful, "Ho, Ho, HO."

"I need to have a serious talk with Madame Jacques," Professor Jackson growled. "Her obsession with Christmas is unacceptable."

Axel didn't respond. His world had crumbled and nothing would ever be right again. Nicole was gone. The only person he trusted. As the drone hovered behind him, Axel felt his legs grow uncooperative. Professor Jackson's presence irked him, and all he wanted was to be alone.

"How are you feeling about the exams next week?" the assistant principal asked as they reached the elevators. His tone was cold and formal, back to its usual self.

"I'm confident," Axel mumbled, struggling to keep his emotions out of his voice.

"Good. I'm sure you'll do better this time. The other professors are pleased with your progress."

"Thank you."

After what seemed to be forever, the elevator arrived, and as the winged doors opened, a man stepped out with two suitcases.

"Mr Hennigan," Professor Jackson said surprised, and eyed the man with a hint of contempt. "I haven't seen you in a long time."

"I've been busy helping the principal, sir."

"Hm. I thought you and Principal Cunningham had left already."

Mr Hennigan glanced at Axel who gaped back. "We got a little delayed, sir."

"Well, enjoy your flight."

"Thank you, sir." Mr Hennigan bowed and turned to Axel. "Have a nice holiday, Mr Hallman. Hope you get a lot of rest. I hear you've got a real challenge ahead of you."

The scar across Mr Hennigan's eyebrow made a condescending twitch. The beard was gone and the nose was smaller and straighter. Without the sunglasses, Axel could see that the man's eyes bore an almost violet colour. The man looked so different from the Thor Axel had come to know.

Holy shit!

Staring at the man, Axel realised that not once since entering the Academy had he seen or spoken to Mr Hennigan. He'd heard of him. He might even have seen him on TV with Principal Cunningham. That would explain why Axel had felt there was something familiar about the man, but as Mr Hennigan, Thor had kept out of Axel's way. Axel hadn't even given the man a second thought. Why would he? Mr Hennigan was an *assistant*. Students didn't care about assistants.

"Goodbye then," Thor said with a smile and turned.

Axel said nothing.

"I've never liked that man," Professor Jackson whispered as they watched Thor walked away with long, assertive strides. "He says he's always busy, but I never see him around. And he's got an attitude."

Axel felt his head spin. The Box had gained access to the very heart of The EKA. Their threat of destroying The Academy was real.

CHAPTER 68

FOUR YEARS EARLIER

Thor looked down at the two prisoners. "Jesus. They stink!" he said to the guards. "And what's wrong with this one?" He poked at Jerome with his polished shoes.

The Watcher grinned. "We've been teaching him to swim, sir."

"Damn it. On whose authority?"

A veil of hesitation fell over Mr Nurmi's ugly face. "On Mr Nakata's, sir."

Thor raised a finger. "Principal Cunningham will not be pleased. I'm here to speak with the two of them. You better hope that one is still talkative."

Mr Nurmi's grin returned. "Shouldn't be a problem, sir. He talks all right. With a little help."

"So this is what a traitor looks like," Thor growled, ignoring Mr Nurmi.

The man on the floor didn't look away. Nor did he answer. Thor sighed and without another word, he left.

Steering his steps towards the stairs, he heard the cell door slam shut and lock behind him.

"Sir?" came Mr Nurmi's voice before the man himself caught up. "I thought we were—"

"I can't work in that smell," Thor snapped, wrinkling his nose. "Send someone to wash the stench off them while I have lunch. Then get me a chair in there."

"Yes, Mr Hennigan."

"Also, I want the video and audio of your sessions with Mr Sano's assistant."

"Yes, sir."

"Has anyone else seen them?"

"Everything has been sent to Mr Nakata, sir."

Thor clamped his jaw shut and marched out into the sun. They were somewhere at the border of the Knuckles Forest Reserve, outside a remote Sri Lankan village called Meemure. Thor had long since stopped wondering how Ms Brown and her team found the properties they used, but this was a dreadful place. Getting here had been a pain. For obvious reasons, Ms Brown didn't allow any helicopters or decent cars. It would draw too much attention. Instead they'd used a second-hand minivan to bring him in last night.

"What about last night's video from the cell?" Thor asked, as the two men trudged back to the shabby bungalow.

"I had a meeting with Ms Brown earlier this morning, sir. The traitor spoke to his assistant for several hours, but we can only decipher a few words. None of them of value. The traitor's assistant, on the other hand, says something about how all people contribute to mankind. It sounds as if he's scolding the traitor. Would you like to see it?"

"Yes."

They walked on along the dirt path in the kind of silence that grows between two people who don't like each other. "My orders are clear," Thor said as they reached a burn barrel outside the bungalow. "We've wasted enough money and time on Hayato Sano. I'm giving it two hours tops, then we're leaving. In other words. Start packing up."

"Yes, sir."

"Do you realise what you've cost us?" Thor asked as he sat down on the chair by the door. Water covered the black concrete floor. Outside the cell door, the hose lay coiled up together with the prisoner's clothes. Hayato and Jerome sat naked in their respective corners, hugging themselves, shivering. "Principal Cunningham wants to know why. *I* want to know why."

Thor used his hour to the max, questioning the two prisoners, but Hayato didn't say a word about The Box. Maybe he thought they'd punish him if he did. He answered all questions with more or less the same answer: "I don't want to be a leader anymore. I want a normal life. That's why I ran."

Thor pushed and threatened, but Hayato kept to his story. "I want a normal life."

When it was over, Thor breathed out a mental sigh of relief. Neither the interrogations, nor video surveillance from the cell, contained anything that could expose The Box. That said, Hayato had set them back several years, and the anti-climax was indescribable. They had expected a revolution, but had got nothing but a few valuable lessons. It was time to end this chapter so they could start anew.

"Okay," Thor said and looked over his shoulder at the Watcher who'd been standing quiet by door. "You can remove the equipment. I'm done."

"Yes, sir. May I use the chair?" On quick feet, she removed several cameras around the small cell. The prisoners stared at her without much surprise. While the Watcher worked, Thor stood in a corner and fidgeted with his phone.

"That's it," the Watcher declared after a couple of minutes and jumped off the chair.

"Excellent." Thor nodded towards the door and she walked out, tiny cameras and microphones in her hands. He followed her. At the door, he stopped and looked at the prisoners. "If I were you, I'd say my prayers, traitor."

Thor stepped into the bungalow where the Watchers resided. Mr Nurmi and his team were in the process of packing up.

"How are we doing?" Thor asked.

Mr Nurmi looked up, still rolling a cable around his hand. "We'll be ready in ten. Shall I send someone to finish the job?"

"No. I'll do it myself. Where's the gasoline?"

"By the door, sir." Mr Nurmi nodded towards two gasoline containers. "Need any help?"

"No." Thor's phone began to ring, and when he saw who it was, he answered at once. "Hello, sir."

"Hello, Mr Hennigan." Principal Cunningham's voice was calm but to the point. "We want a report."

Thor stepped out on the shabby terrace and looked out in the general direction of the prisoners. "We're packing up, sir."

"Has it been done?"

"No. I was just about to."

"Any new developments?" It was Professor Jackson who asked the question, and he sounded impatient.

"Negative, sir. Mr Sano claims he ran because he wanted a 'normal' life."

"Normal?" the professor yelled. "Why the hell would anyone want to give up a life as an Academy leader, for an insignificant, fecking life?"

"Beats me, sir."

"I want the man to suffer," Principal Cunningham declared. "You hear me? The Academy never fails!"

"He'll burn, sir," Thor swore. "I'll make sure of it."

Five minutes later, he marched over to the barred opening in the ground where the prisoners were held. As he drew closer, he set down the containers and withdrew his gun. I have no choice, he reminded himself. I *have* to do it.

He stepped up and looked down. I have no choice.

The shots echoed over the small garden as he fired into the cell. Then he poured gasoline over the bodies.

* * *

Three days later, in a nice residential area outside Yala National

Park, two men sat under a tree, passing their time with a game of cards. They played in silence until the sound of an engine made them raise their eyes. A small white car was making its way up the driveway towards the house. It came to a stop near the two men.

Jerome began fidgeting with his cards, pressing them together into a stack, then unfolding them before pressing them together again. Hayato kept his hands still.

They watched as a stout woman stepped out from the driver's seat with a big smile on her face. She paused, looked around the garden and nodded towards one of the women guarding the premises. Then she turned back to Hayato and Jerome.

"Gentlemen," she said and threw her arms out wide as if wanting to embrace them. "Nice to meet you."

Her apparent thrill to see them made Hayato a little uneasy. He and Jerome exchanged a glace as the woman approached them.

"May I?" she asked, her East African accent weaving itself into her words. Before they could answer, she'd taken a seat. "My name is Pixie. You haven't heard of me, but I work for an organisation called The Box. I know you've heard of us," she added and gave Hayato a shrewd smile.

"Everything has gone according to plan," the woman continued. She waved off a fly that had settled on her thick arm. "Mr Hennigan, or Thor as we call him, phoned me yesterday. The Academy thinks you've moved on to better pastures, if you know what I mean."

Hayato turned his head in the direction of the villa. He saw one of the armed women standing guard in the shade of a tree. If she was there to protect them or keep them prisoners, he didn't know.

It was still hard to take in everything that had happened. In fact, Hayato's memory of the day they were saved was a bit muddled. He remembered the door to the cell opening, thinking his time had come; that he would be executed.

A serious looking woman had entered. "If you want to live, get changed now," she'd said and thrown him and Jerome a pair of camouflaged suits, similar to what she was wearing.

Hayato had not asked her who she was. At the time there had been only one thought in his mind; escape!

Once Hayato and Jerome had changed, the woman had hurried them out of the cell. On their way out they'd passed four other women carrying two dead men between them.

Six hours later, having escaped through the jungle and sitting in a car heading for Yala, Hayato had asked the woman about the bodies.

"Did you kill those men?" he wondered, fearing the answer.

"No. We stole them from a graveyard," the woman replied with a business-like tone. "One of them had died of an overdose, the other in a drowning accident. It's not something we're proud of, but The Academy has to see that someone burnt in your cell, or they will know you have escaped."

Escaped. Hayato shook his head and snapped back to present time. He had escaped The Academy, but not The Box.

A warm wind swept over the garden. Jerome's fidgeting worsened. "What do you intend to do with us?" he asked.

Pixie's smile faded. "We haven't decided yet. You let us down, Mr Sano. You destroyed years of work in a matter of minutes. Now we're forced to start all over again, with a new student."

Hayato looked down at his hands. "All I can say is that I'm sorry."

"Sorry is a nice word, but it doesn't change the fact that you can't be trusted."

"I made a mistake. Standing on that podium…I panicked. I'm sorry. All I needed was time to think; time to wrap my head around it all."

Digging her elbows into the table, Pixie leaned forward. "Let me tell you a little secret, Mr Sano. The essence of leadership is simple. So simple in fact, that most people have no idea what it is. And those who find out tend to grow disappointed."

For the first time in weeks, a smile settled on Hayato's lips.

"Yes, I think I've figured that out," he said, dropping his words on the table for everyone to see.

Pixie leaned back and crossed her arms over her chest. "Are you kidding me?"

"No, ma'am. I must say I'm amazed I didn't figure it out earlier."

After a second's silence, Pixie began to laugh. She had a warm, bubbly laugh that made everything seem a little brighter. "You've figured it out, you say."

"I think so. After all, you guys provided me with a lot of information."

"Well then, Mr Sano. Why don't you tell me what you've figured out, and we shall see what your future may hold."

CHAPTER 69

# PRESENT DAY

How can emotions, which are nothing more than a state of mind, create such agonising, physical pain? Axel felt as though he was being gutted. It wasn't only the thought of losing Nicole. It was his life. It was a nightmare.

The gold faucet, shaped like an elephant's head, spewed cold water into his hands. He splashed it onto his face, but it didn't stop the anger. He was nothing more than a marionette, controlled by the Academy.

Looking up, he met his own, pathetic reflection in the bathroom mirror. He stared into the sad grey eyes, and to his horror, he saw that he was crying.

That's when something snapped. With a primal cry, he slammed his fist into the mirror. Shattered pieces fell to the floor.

Axel watched and felt as though he was seeing his old life fall apart. Despite the blood dripping from his knuckles, he felt no pain. He stood there, staring at the mess while a new, horrifying emptiness filled him.

His life was a mess.

He stood there for what seemed like forever, shaping his thoughts. Then he drew a slow, deep breath and hardened his heart. It was time he took control of his life.

With determination, Axel turned on the communication device and found there were no new messages.

*All right*, he typed. *You have my attention. What is it you want me to do?*

Seeing as Thor was on his way to Singapore, Axel hadn't expected an answer so soon, but the reply came at once.

*Hi Axel.*

Hi Axel? That didn't sound like Thor.

*Who are you?* he wrote.

*I'm a member of The Box. I'll be your contact from now on.*

Axel didn't care. *Okay. Tell Thor I'm ready. Tell him I'll change the world as he requested.*

*We don't want you to change the world, Axel. A single brick will not build a house. You will not change the world. We will. Together.*

Axel glared at the small device. *All right, where do we begin?*

*You know that already. By ruining The Academy.*

*I mean, how do we do that?*

*By making sure you graduate.*

\* \* \*

Nicole stood alone in the dim light, staring at the remains of her burnt paintings. The two guards were waiting for her in the car with Julien the driver. She had declined their offer to help her. Nicole couldn't stand having them around. Not now.

The bag on the kitchen table contained a few books, some clothes, jewellery and a cup that Axel always used when he had visited her. Her paintings were gone. The rest they could burn for all she cared.

As she stood there, it washed over her. The pain of knowing she'd never be good enough for someone like Axel. She was an assistant, a servant. Nothing more.

With her head held high, she walked over to her bathroom. Once she'd closed the door behind her, she slid onto the floor and wept for the first time in many years.

It was hard to tell how long she sat there, but eventually the tears dried. When they did, she got to her feet, washed her face and reapplied her make-up. After a few deep breaths, she walked out and grabbed her bag. Then she paused, bit her lip before walking back to the small desk by the window.

From a drawer she retrieved her colour pens and two sketchbooks. Professor Jackson had forbidden her to paint, but the bastard hadn't said anything about sketching.

* * *

Professor Jackson stepped into his apartment and took off his suit jacket. The first thing he did was pour himself a large scotch. With his eyes closed, he stood by the cabinet, sipping the burning liquor as he tried to relieve some of his stress. When he'd emptied his glass, he re-filled it and walked over to his closet.

Behind the dark wooden doors, bolted to the floor, was a safe. Inside the safe was a small, battered photo album. It was one of the most precious things he owned.

Once he got a fire burning in the hearth, he dropped into an armchair with a sigh and opened the album. First, there were a few photos from when he was a child, among them a picture of him sitting in his father's lap. He liked that photo. It was one of his favourites, together with the one of his sister outside their home in Dublin. There were days when he wondered how she was doing. They hadn't spoken to each other in many years.

Some nights Professor Jackson would look at his childhood photos for hours, thinking about his past. Tonight, however, he flipped through these pages to a yellowing photo in the middle of the album. It was a photo of a cute young woman, with long, thin legs that disappeared behind a deep-green dress. Tilly had been her name. Her curly hair stood out in the wind. Freckles and glasses sat comfortably on her small nose. It was easy to see her joyful soul through that frozen smile of hers.

Professor Jackson leaned forward, and like many times before, he focused on her eyes. Yes. He could still see it, the stubbornness. The damn, pig-headed woman had refused to leave Dublin and her friends and family. How different life would've been if she'd joined him. Or if he had stayed. Maybe they would've been married. Perhaps even had children.

His phone vibrated as he received a text message. Professor Jackson let out a sigh and closed the album with a faint sense of loss. There had been a time when he'd felt a deep, uncontrollable sorrow for what he'd given up. Now it was just a memory. That's how he knew Axel would be all right. Pain faded.

The fire popped and hissed as the professor picked up his phone. He read the message from Mr Nakata twice before the implications of it struck him.

*I've left a small gift for you on bed. Tell my son I died an honourable death.*

\* \* \*

Dr Vella got the call minutes after having crawled into bed. Professor Jackson had ordered her to Mr Nakata's apartment at once. If it took more than five minutes, he'd have her fired! When she asked what had happened, he hung up.

She found the assistant principal sitting on a chair, staring at Mr Nakata. The room stank of blood, excrements and spirits. The minute she stepped through the door, she knew it was over. Mr Nakata had performed a Seppuku, an ancient Japanese ritual where a short knife was plunged into the abdomen and then sliced to the side. If done correctly, it was a painful but quick death.

"He's gone." She looked up at Professor Jackson and met his stern face.

"I know he's gone," the professor replied. "Do you think I'm blind?"

They both looked at Mr Nakata. He was on his side, in a type of foetal position, knife still in his gut.

"Has Principal Cunningham been informed?" Dr Vella asked.

Professor Jackson appeared not to hear her, so she repeated her words.

"You know," he said, still staring down at the man, "Mr Nakata once gave me some advice. He said, 'Tell your enemy what you value and he will know what to steal'. That's what the principal did. He stole the only thing that mattered to the man; his pride."

Without another word, Professor Jackson left, holding a thick, brown folder in his hand.

# EPILOGUE

Hayato Sano stared out of the window at the lead-grey sky. It had started to rain again. The heavy raindrops struck the weatherworn roof. Inside, a thick smell of coffee and spirits filled the tiny living room. "Are you sure he saw you?" he asked.

"Oh yes," came Thor's voice over the phone. "You should have seen his face. Very funny."

Hayato smiled. Thor was a remarkable man. He had nestled himself into The Academy, yet few paid him much attention. The man was, in many ways, a chameleon, and a damn good one at it. It had been Thor who gave Hayato the alias 'Falcon', claiming the animal symbolised vision. "Now that you're part of The Box, you must never forget what we fight for," he'd said with a sly grin.

Hayato's thoughts returned to the topic at hand. "Do you think Axel will tell anyone?" he asked.

"About me? I doubt it," Thor replied. "We have his balls in a tight grip, much tighter than we did on you. Should he utter a single word to anyone, we'll send The Hostess our video. It'll be the end of him. Also, Ms Davis got a message from Axel soon after he saw me. I'll pass it on to all of you after the meeting, but my interpretation is that he's coming around."

"That's great news," Mikael declared

The others agreed. With both hands around his steaming cup, Hayato listened as the conversation turned to the preparations of Axel's Challenge. They had been over it a million times, reviewing the risks and discussing various mitigations. They were about to enter the third phase. There was a sense of careful optimism in the air, and somehow that frightened him.

Hayato turned and looked at Jerome as the man took notes. They had been through a lot together. After escaping The Academy, they had spent a few months with different members of The Box, learning about the leadership myth and its effect on people. Jerome had grasped the new way of thinking with surprising ease.

"Do you know what frightens me?" he'd asked one evening, only a week after they'd arrived in Borneo. "Most people believe in leadership the way priests believe in God. They see it as our salvation, yet, like with God, people can't agree on what a leader is. As Friedrich Nietzsche once said, 'There are no facts, only interpretations'."

Hayato smiled where he sat. They were heading for uncertainty, he knew that, but whatever happened, he couldn't imagine a better friend by his side than Jerome.

\* \* \*

A week after Mr Nakata's death, Axel stood on the deserted helipad, looking out over a city at sleep. The cold wind tugged at his black coat, making it dance around his legs.

The news about the former Head of Security had come as a shock. Cardiac arrest. It seemed improper somehow. Mr Nakata should have died in a battle or something, not of a failing heart.

Ms Brown would continue as Head of Security on a permanent basis. The management would have to find a replacement for her role as Master of Watchers. It started to dawn on Axel that without Nicole, he couldn't get any inside information at all. She'd been very restricted with what she'd told him when they were dating, but she'd always told him something.

It began to snow. Axel looked up and closed his eyes. He missed Nicole. He missed her so bad it hurt. She was always on his mind; the way she smiled, the taste of her lips, the sun upon her skin, even the warmth of her embrace. It was all there, together with wonderful memories he now wished he could forget. He didn't want it to hurt anymore.

Axel opened his eyes again. In time, his wounds would heal. At least that's what Professor Jackson said. The man had invited Axel up to his office a few times, just for a chat. Strange as it was, these meetings had been…nice. They'd talked about many things, from what it meant to be a leader, to the death of Mr Nakata. Both of them were clearly on their guard, careful not to say anything that could provoke the other. Still, it was nice to have someone to talk to, even if it was the stone-faced Professor Jackson.

A tiny sigh escaped Axel's lips. In a few hours, he would board a private plane for Sweden. The exams were over. He knew he'd done well, even if the results weren't out yet. This time he hadn't thought outside the box, but rather repeated what he knew the teachers wanted to hear.

He stood motionless by the railing, staring at the lights stretching out around him. One year had passed since he first arrived. Inexperienced and naïve, he'd had no idea what awaited him. Now he felt as though the fate of the world rested upon his shoulders. Was The Academy a blessing or a curse? Was Thor right, or Professor Jackson? At some point, Axel would have to choose one or the other; between The Box or The Academy. And when he did, all hell would break loose.

He drew a deep breath. He would have to make up his mind. Soon.

## ACKNOWLEDGEMENTS

Cindy – you're fantastic! Thanks for your love and endless support, for listening and coming up with great ideas, and for reading my first drafts and returning them with honest feedback. I love you and I'm not sure what I would've done without you.

Zoey and Emmy – you mean the world to me and to the rest of my family and friends who've cheered me on throughout this project, thank you. I'm lucky to have you in my life.

I'd like to give a special thanks to a few individuals who've been particularly involved in this book. First of all my fabulous content editor, Shelly Stinchcomb, who challenges, supports and cheers like no other. Sarah Smeaton, my copy editor, who did a marvellous job refining the manuscript. Claire Rushbrook, who proofread and polished the text. Linda Curzola, for helping out with the Italian phrases used in this book. Jeremy Langley, for taking his time and explaining certain technological questions I had. Linn Järte and Anton Larsen for their invaluable help related to medical facts and medicines. Anna-Liza Stojkovska, Deborah Dobrin and Helen Boyce for reading the earlier drafts of this book, and returning them with great feedback. The book is better because of you.

I would also like to take the opportunity to thank Tracy Fenton and all the members of THE Book Club (TBC). They may not know it, but their encouragements and kind remarks regarding the first book in this series, The Academy, made the process of writing this book so much easier.

From the bottom of my heart - thank you all!